INKED IN ASHES

INKBOUND
SERIES BOOK ONE

NEW YORK TIMES BESTSELLING AUTHOR

SHANNON MAYER

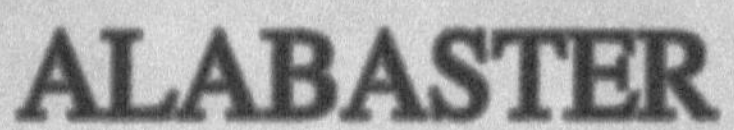

ALABASTER

Legend

1 Mew
2 Amphitheater
3 Grapple point
4 The Shroud
5 & 6 - Tunnels
7 Druzilla's
8 Harmony's
9 Cabin
10 Hoof & Saddle

5
6
7
8
2
Little
Alabaster
The Hollow
The Cradle
The Great Wall

ABOUT

Escape the page, or die trying…

I've spent twenty-five years in the Hollow, poor as dirt, cursed with a stepmother who hates me, and dreaming about a faraway land that I don't understand. Only two things that make life worth living are my falcon, Fetch, and my best friend, Molly.

But when Moll's plot to land a royal husband at the palace ball goes horribly wrong, I find myself staring at a king with a glass stiletto buried in his chest and a blood-covered Molly standing over him. We've got to move…and fast, or we'll both wind up swinging from the hangman's noose.

Worse? The palace sorcerer is using everything he can to find the culprit including raising the dead.

More complicated? Duncan…brother to the King, whose eye I've unintentionally caught, a man whose secrets might be deadlier than the undead soldiers breathing down our necks, is making me second-guess everything I've ever known.

With revolution brewing and a mysterious man calling to me from my dreams, I have no choice but to embrace my fate…

But what if my fate is beyond anything I could ever imagine? What if the only land I've ever known isn't home at all?

What if I'm trapped inside a fairytale, and the only way out…is through?

For all the readers who ever wanted to literally dive into the pages.

PROLOGUE

Freya looked around at the thin, dirty faces staring up at her and forced a smile through the despair that churned in her belly. Only six children left to care for in the orphanage—the world was a harsh place, and tonight it felt even darker.

There was no meat for the two older children's thin broth tonight. She'd given the last of it to the four young ones who were still growing and needed it most. Essie and Logan would go to bed with empty bellies.

Again.

Essie's dark eyes seemed over-large in her wan face. Logan looked more like his father every day—bless his taken soul. The only thing Freya could do was distract them for a time, perhaps even give them something to hope for. She shifted her weight in the old rocking chair, running her hands over her swollen knuckles. But was it fair to give them that hope?

"Tomorrow we'll go scrounge the heaps," Logan said with a weary sigh. "Get to the market early, look for scraps."

Essie's long dark lashes fluttered against her cheeks. "Maybe we will find a few apple cores. Bless us let it be."

Apple cores. That was the most they could wish for?

Freya stopped her rocking. If a different kind of hope was all she could give them, so be it. She would do all she could to fill them up with it.

"Logan, Essie, get closer to the fire, you two and keep warm while I tell you a story I've been waiting a very long time to share with you, hmm?"

They nodded, huddling closer as they hung on her words. Logan draped an arm over his sister's shoulders.

Treason was not a thing to commit lightly. And yet this story…hovered on the edges of it. Freya lowered her voice until it was barely above a whisper.

"Once upon a time, before Almira the witch became our ruler, C'an Saas was different. A place filled with sunshine, and joy. The tree branches were heavy with fruit in the early spring of the year, the fields teemed with pigs, cows, and sheep. Families worked hard to tend the land, and the land provided. We were blessed with a good king." She lowered her voice further, a shiver running through her as she spoke the forbidden name. "Alistair MacInnes. He lived in the palace with his true love, Queen Marin, and the two of them ruled with kindness for decades. But they had no heir. They waited, year after year, with no news of a child. Their people laid blessings at the gods' shrines on their behalf all those years. And, after decades of trying, a baby daughter was finally born. They named her Harmony. Fitting, as she did indeed bring music to the land. The people rejoiced, feasted, danced, and sang in her honor. For four years after she was born, C'an Saas continued to flourish. Until one day, a childhood friend-turned enemy of King Alistair's returned from the darkness. Her name was Almira, and she came for revenge…"

Logan and Essie's eyes were locked on hers, and Freya dove headlong into a story that held all the hope of the land within it, and all the fear that the hope would never come to fruition.

Twenty-five years before…

Alistair MacInnes, King of C'an Saas, closed his eyes and sucked in a deep breath. The screams grew closer now, even as the acrid smell of smoke filled his nostrils. It was utter carnage beyond the walls of the keep. Entire villages were razed by the tornado she rode in on.

Almira had returned with a literal vengeance.

The blood of soldiers flowing like the mighty River

Claren. People—*his* people— incinerated in their homes.

And despite being the most powerful man in all his kingdom, there wasn't a blessed thing he could do about it but hope that his outmatched forces somehow managed to prevail. Such were the ways of magic. A fickle bit of chaos that could be as miraculous as it was terrible, depending on who was wielding it. The woman who wielded it at this very moment?

Was hellbent on destruction.

He forced his eyes open and shot a glance at the arched doorway just over his shoulder before turning his attention to the hourglass clutched in his hand on the armrest beside him. The granules of sand seemed to have been moving in slow motion since he'd last checked, and his stomach sank like a stone.

If he failed, all would be lost.

The sound of boots on stone caught his attention and he looked up to find General John Wallace striding into the room, his armor catching the sun's rays.

"Your Majesty, they're cutting through our forces like soft cheese. The witch's consorts are scaling the walls. I fear we only have moments until she breaches the gates."

Alistair nodded, a grim smile tugging at his lips. "She's a formidable enemy to be sure."

There was no fear in the eyes of the trusted General as he continued across the floor of the great hall, moving to stand directly before his king.

"I'm sorry for this, John. If I could go back and do it differently, I would. Keeping Harmony close was selfish beyond measure."

"Respectfully, Your Majesty, that's bollocks," John shot back, his craggy face twisted into a scowl. "She's a child. She'd have never made it this long if we hadn't. And watching her grow up, even from a distance…even for a short while, was the greatest of gifts. I know my sister would agree."

Alistair had done his best not to think of her in this moment, but Marin filled his thoughts most every day, and his efforts were in vain. He spared a glance at her portrait, hung on the east wall. Glorious, dark curls exploded in a riot around her shoulders. An easy, mischievous smile perched on her lips, color in her cheeks, a bright light in her honey-colored eyes.

Damn it to hell, I'm so sorry it's come to this, my love.

A loud crash followed by a fresh chorus of screams echoed through the great hall, and he tore his gaze from the portrait. He'd be seeing her soon enough. His only hope was that he could face her in the afterlife without shame.

Those thoughts were derailed by the wail of a battle horn, a final cry to charge the enemy.

"That'll be Hamish, Your Majesty."

Hamish.

The last remaining guard positioned at the entrance to the main keep itself. A living alarm, blaring the final warning. The end was near.

The steady note ended in a sharp squeal, followed by an eerie silence. No more screams. No more cries for mercy.

No more time.

Alistair lifted the still trickling hourglass before him and shook his head slowly, a wave of nausea rolling over him. He'd already asked so much of his men, this one—his brother by marriage and best friend—far more than most.

And yet…

He met the other man's unflinching gaze. "John, Gayelette needs more time to complete the spell. For Harmony to be sent to safety. I—"

"Say no more, brother. More time you shall have, then."

John laid a gloved hand on the falcon crest etched over his heart as he stared at the hourglass, his face filled with steely resolve.

"So long as your sorceress does her part, know that I shall do mine. Whatever it takes to ensure the music lives on. That Harmony is safe."

As fierce a warrior as John was, their enemy was tenfold in numbers and magic. Neither of them expected to survive this battle.

So long as the last grain of sand fell before they did.

Alistair rose from his throne for what he knew would be the last time and reached for the bear of a man before him, gripping one broad shoulder with his free hand. "We've had a good run, haven't we?"

John nodded and let out a snort. "Better than most."

"See you on the other side?"

"I pledge it. But mark me," John replied, eyes narrowing as he stepped back and unsheathed his broadsword. "I'll be taking a pound of the bitch's flesh and as many of her consorts as I can with me on my way out."

With that, he wheeled around and cut a swift path to the main doors, disappearing into the shadows beyond them. Alistair waved a hand, his magic curling around the open doors and closing them. He laid a simple locking spell across it. His magic was not that of a sorceress, but every moment he could gain, he would take.

The next few minutes passed in a haze of memories, regrets and grief.

The sounds of a vicious fight just beyond the entrance of the great room reached Alistair's ears, but he shut them out with a ruthlessness he'd rarely shown as king. Attempting to help his friend now would do nothing but ensure that John and the others killed already had given their lives for naught.

"John," he muttered under his breath. "Hold out a little longer, my friend. For Harmony."

But when the halls again went dead silent, he could still hear it. That damnable sand, trickling to the bottom of the glass.

A maniacal laugh rang out a moment before the door flew off its hinges and into the wall just inches from where he stood. Darkness seemed to spill through the opening, like storm clouds gathering before the tempest unleashed.

"Alistair, you pathetic bastard. Is this where you've tucked yourself, then?" a shrill voice called seconds before a slight female figure drifted into the room. She wore not armor, but a trailing dress of deepest gray. Flecks littered her skirts. Blood of his men. John's blood. Her smile was as wicked as ever. "I'm disappointed. I was rather looking forward to a game of hide and seek, like when we were children. I do so miss those days."

Those early days, with the four of them running wild along the moors like a pack of wolves were long gone, as was the girl Almira had been. Her reminiscing might help him stall though, so he indulged her.

"We were close, the four of us. Do not do this, for whatever love you once had for Marin."

Her laughter was soft and low. "Love abandoned me when those I loved abandoned *me*. I am no longer the child you knew, come to take my dues as the queen I should always have been."

He gripped his sword hilt. "It took me far too long to see it, but you were never a child, Almira. Not really. You've always been a demon's spawn in disguise, waiting to come into your own. And now, here you are, in all your vile glory."

He set the hourglass on the throne behind him and turned to face his enemy once again. It was only when the hood slipped from her head that he realized she was covered in blood and her once eternally youthful face was in ruins. One cheekbone was caved in like it had met with a large fist, and a bloodied, empty socket sat where her left eye used to be. She glared at him through its crystal-blue mate, defiant. Furious.

The state of her face elicited a true belly laugh from him despite the dire circumstances.

"Oh ho, Almira-girl! That had to hurt, more than your bones, yeah? I don't know if even you could fix the ruins of your face. Was it John, then?" he asked.

Fury rippled from her in waves. Her beauty had always been a tool, and now it was broken. "It was, John, yes." She cocked her head, full lips twisting into a sneer. "He took my eye only seconds before I disemboweled him. In fact, he's just at the bottom of the steps, writhing in agony as he tries to stuff his entrails back into his belly. I'll bring you to die by his side if you tell me what I want to know."

Alistair paused to absorb the words, keeping his expression blank as he heaved a sigh. "As much as there are worse places to die than at John's side, you know I can't do that."

"Yours is a lost cause. I'm far more dangerous than the girl I used to be, and you certainly aren't the boy I remember. You look beat down, dog-fuckingly old, and weak as hell," she murmured as she swept closer, her emerald cloak flowing behind her. "Shame. Had you picked me instead of Marin, I could've kept you virile…

kept you strong. We could've ruled this world for an eternity."

His only thought was to keep her talking. Gayelette needed time. "I'd rather have died in the belly of the desert dragon, burning for a thousand years than be tethered to you for a day. And as for this old goat, we've been alive the same number of years. Difference is, I've lived every one of those years topside, in a world marred by hardship. It takes a toll."

She slowed to a stop a few yards away and the thin veneer of calm crackled.

"Hardship?" she hissed, her remaining eye suddenly wild with fury. "You imprison me in the Dreadkeep, powerless and alone for nearly a century, and you *dare* speak to me of hardship?"

He'd hit the nerve he'd been aiming for. Anything to keep her talking and the sands of time in motion. But his needling would come with a price—and he knew it would hurt.

A price Almira collected a moment later as she lifted her thumb and forefinger in the air and pinched them closed with a whisper.

His left eye exploded like an overripe grape and the pain had him stumbling back and swaying, barely able to keep his feet. He gripped the arm of his throne for purchase as blackness threatened to swallow him whole.

"There. That's better. Let us be on even ground, yes?" she said with a grin that disappeared as quickly as it had come. "Now, stop being tedious, Alistair. It's been a long day, what with all the murder, mayhem, and reclaiming of *my* kingdom. Give me the girl, and you have my word that her death will be painless. Of course, I can't say the same for you. Too much water under the bridge for that, I'm afraid. You understand…"

He swiped at the blood and warm, clear liquid running down his cheek and then lifted a hand to his crown. The second he touched it, the space between them shimmered and grew hazy.

For a second, she just gaped at him. Then she tossed her head back and laughed.

"Ah, well fuck me. Is that what your little witch gave you for protection? Pathetic." She let out a snort and shrugged. "Maybe I was better off in the Dreadkeep after all. Plenty of time to hone my skills."

She flicked her wrist, sending a bolt of power straight at his head, but it bounced away, leaving his shield and crown intact. Her one good eyebrow snapped down, fury ripping across her face.

Alistair waggled his brow. "Not too shabby for a *little witch*, aye?"

His old friend squared off with him, even as he steeled himself for the onslaught.

She shot forward in a blur, three blades flying from her belt. Each one stabbed and slashed at him from a different angle, moving as if wielded by three separate master swordsmen. The king staggered back, narrowly sidestepping a thrust at his neck while batting aside the other two blades with his shield.

Almira hung back, directing the blades like some kind of twisted conductor leading a deadly orchestra. Agony pierced his side as one of the swords plunged deep in his side, and he rolled under a follow-up slash only to see a massive ball of fire shooting directly at his chest.

He staggered backward, barely blocking the fire with his shield, going to one knee—even so, without the protection of his crown absorbing most of the heat, he'd have been a cooked goose. Almira let out a cackle, advancing on him in a blinding flash.

It was now or never.

Alistair sprang toward her, his crown hot and glowing red from the fireball it had absorbed. His blade shot toward her neck, and her eyes widened in shock. For the briefest of moments, he allowed himself to hope. He was already planning his next move when she dissipated into smoke a split second before he would've made contact. He stumbled forward, and she reappeared before he'd even registered what'd happened, slamming her fist into his side with a sickening crunch, her magic making her blows ten times stronger than she truly was.

"You really thought you'd catch me with a silly trick like that?" she asked, scowling as she stood over his prone form. "You were right to let John try his luck first. His plan was much better."

Alistair's vision blurred as he glanced at the hourglass, but not so much that he couldn't see the teeny, tiny mound of sand remaining at the top. He cursed, sucking in a sticky, wheezing breath as he pushed himself to his feet.

He was running out of ways to keep her busy.

"Release," he whispered, and the fire magic his crown had absorbed pulsed to the surface, consuming him in flames. His vision went crimson, and energy surged through him as he parried a flurry of attacks with his flame-wreathed blade.

Almira's swords withered and melted beneath the heat, no match for this attack, but it wouldn't last. Once the crown ran out of the energy it had taken in, it was over for him.

Think, man.

But there was no time. Stone cracked and rumbled beneath his feet, and Almira sprang forward as he struggled for balance.

A blizzard's worth of frost and snow, condensed to the size of a man, washed over him, and he barely got his shield up in time to block another of her animated blades. His crown's magic was gone, cut even shorter by her ice spell, and the chill sank into his bones, but he advanced, nonetheless. His eye flitted toward the hourglass.

If he could just hold out for thirty seconds more…

He let out a primal roar and moved forward, each step a herculean feat of will, each parry more excruciating than the last. Raw magical energy spiked toward him from the side, and he hefted his shield just in time to block, but the cold had sapped the last of his strength. A moment later, his arm began to tremble with the effort of wielding the shield's weight. The witch smiled, no doubt seeing his end.

"Too bad we couldn't make this last longer," she said, snicking her tongue in disappointment. "I can't believe there was a time you were actually able to best me."

She thrust hard, and her blade slid through his belly, slow and sure. He felt every inch of it, but joy won out over agony as he watched the last grain of sand slip away.

A sudden flash blew the door in the corner of the room open even as the hourglass shimmered and exploded into a cloud of iridescent green dust. He turned, desperate for one last look at his daughter. Her dark curls bounced, her eyes going wide as she levitated in the air, a small book clutched in her hands. To Fetch's credit, the falcon perched on her shoulder held tight as the two of them were sucked into a much larger book on the floor, disappearing without a trace.

It was done.

Thank the gods, it was done.

He slipped to the cool stone floor, his body limp, turning his head toward the now-open room. Almira howled, no longer concerned with him as she released her sword and bounded toward the door where Harmony had been.

As she passed through, he caught sight of his royal sorceress seated cross-legged on the floor on the other side of the book. She was slumped over, chest heaving, clearly spent. But not so spent that she couldn't lift her head to meet Almira's gaze.

"Almira."

"Hello, Gayelette." The witch turned her remaining eye to the massive, leather-bound tome lay on its side between them, the page edges gilded in gold.

Fairytales of the Ages.

"Where is she?" Almira whispered as she shook her head and let out a snarl. "What have you done with her, you simpering bitch?"

Alistair watched as her expression twisted into one of fury. But as his vision went dark, the very last face he saw was that of his beloved wife Marin waiting for him on the other side.

And she was smiling.

"AND THAT *WAS* THE END…UNTIL now," Freya said, lifting her head to find the two children staring at her, eyes wide. Tears filled Essie's eyes. The tale was if nothing else, bittersweet. A father's love for his daughter, and for his people.

"Is Princess Harmony still inside the book?" Logan asked.

"She is."

"But will she actually come to save us?" Essie whispered.

"Legend has it that she will. She's stayed safely tucked within the pages for the past twenty-five years, growing wise, brave, and strong enough to defeat Almira. We must keep our heads up a little bit longer until she finds her way home."

But she'd better hurry, Freya thought, hoping her worry didn't show on her face. Because as Almira's fury grew, so did the darkness.

And now they were all running out of time…

CHAPTER 1

From within the pages...

"WELL, looks like I'm not going to the ball after all. Prince Heinrich will be crowned king tonight, every eligible bachelor left in Little Alabaster will be there, and I'm going to miss it."

Molly came crawling out of the closet a moment later, red-faced, sweaty auburn curls plastered to her cheeks.

"I'll have to accept the fact that I'm going to die a lonely, shriveled up, impoverished virgin."

The first three of those maybe, but we both knew the ship had long sailed on that last. Moll was in her feelings right now, so I let her get away with it. But the muttering had been going on for the past hour, and it clearly wasn't going to stop until I gave her the attention she was looking for.

I set the jeweler's loupe—a small magnifying glass the size of a large coin—next to the mound of gleaming stones I'd been studying and spun my chair around.

"What's the problem?"

She let out a snort. "The *problem* is that I have nothing to wear, and no matter how deep I dig into the closet there is no magical tree within growing gowns that would be suitable."

"What about in your cedar chest?"

"I sold all those for oats and cabbage." Molly ran a hand over her riot of curls. I peered past her to see what was left hanging. Only four dresses left that I could see. Things were tight, and we were both doing our best to keep our heads above water.

"How about the green one?"

Her cornflower eyes went wide as she pushed herself to stand.

"You're kidding right? It's so out of fashion right now, I'd be arrested for assault of the senses. The shape of it makes me look like a bloody pine tree anyway. I planned to sell it next week at the market." She sighed heavily. "This is the *Winter Jubilee*, Harm." She pressed her knuckles to her lips and shook her head. "If I show up looking anything less than perfect, they're going to spot me as an outsider. I need them to believe I'm one of them if this is to work."

I wanted to argue...call her vain or silly. But, while

she could be a bit of both at times, she was also sort of right. She was attending the party with a forged invitation, courtesy of yours truly. Calling attention to herself would be bad. If she got caught in Little Alabaster on a normal day, she'd be beaten. If she got caught in the palace crashing a royal ball while impersonating a noble?

She would be hanged. A chance she was willing to take, despite how much I tried to talk her out of it.

My only question was, why were we talking about this now? The party was only a few hours away.

"I know what you're going to say, but I did have a plan," Moll said in a rush. "Stefan was supposed to take me to the shops yesterday, and I'd hoped to get him to buy me some ribbons and notions. Apparently, a hog needed butchering, though, so he canceled. I was going to fix up the purple gown, add some lace and such, but..."

But, we were dirt-ass poor, so we couldn't afford lace *or* such, no matter how many dresses she sold over the last few months. Hell, there were weeks we barely scraped together enough to eat. Frippery was far off the menu, unless Moll's sometimes boyfriend, current friend Stefan was buying. But her dreams hinged on always looking her best. In the twenty-plus years we'd known each other, she'd plotted her course like a decorated general strategizing for battle. She attended every event in Little Alabaster that she could, legality be damned, and eventually, she hoped to make one of those rich men fall madly in love with her. That was her plan.

So madly would said man fall, that he would take her—correction, *us*—away from all this.

"All this" being the two-room hovel we shared at the heart of The Hollow.

The Hollow was a shanty-town full of have-nots, where the largest part of Alabaster's population lived, worked, and barely managed to eke out an existence. As pretty as Moll was with her striking coloring, people from Little Alabaster almost never married people from The Hollow.

Regardless of the odds against her, for the past ten years, Moll had used her amazing talents with makeup, clothes, and hair to disguise herself before worming her way into every fete, festival, gala, and ball she could in hopes her "prince" would come and sweep her off her feet.

First, it was Lady Ashlynn Coddington, on a visit all the way from Bryngarde. A porcelain-skinned beauty with straight, waist-length black hair and an intriguing mole above her lip.

Then, it was Lady Letitia Meriwhether. With her honey-colored locks and heart-shaped face, she'd been so convincing, even I was fooled.

Miss Caroline Theobold had been a personal favorite. A golden blonde with a waist corseted so tightly, two hands could've spanned it, I'd even managed to create a pair of eye lenses that had changed the color of Moll's irises from blue to green. Alas, poor Miss Caroline wound up fainting in the powder room from lack of oxygen and had to leave that particular gala early before anyone could see them.

But despite creating a line of beauties, each more charming than the last, Moll had come home at the end of each party the same as she'd left.

Single and broke as a church mouse.

She'd done everything right, gotten the proper accent down pat, knew to nibble on the hors d'oeuvres but not truly eat them, regardless of her growling stomach. She knew how to charm and cajole and tease. But so far, all she'd managed to get were a few rushed, sloppy kisses followed by a slew of broken promises. And now, at the ripe old age of twenty-nine, I could see her fraying at the edges.

I glanced at my friend's tear-stained cheeks and swallowed back the acid that had risen to burn my throat. Just because I didn't agree with her strategy to escape our lot didn't mean I wouldn't help her. She was the only person I truly trusted in this world, and there was nothing I wouldn't do for her.

Even if it made me want to puke for fear of her being caught.

I met Moll's teary gaze, bit back my irritation, and forced a smile. "Alright, so let's get into problem-solving mode here, shall we?"

"Yeah." She sniffled and nodded, her eyes lighting with hope. "Yeah, alright."

"You drag out that one red dress—it's your best and most current, even if you think the purple is— and get a needle and thread ready." I shot one last wistful glance at the faux gemstones and swept them into my hand. "Add some sparkle with these."

I'd managed to create the little beauties using a gadget I'd invented that tumbled mundane stones over and over against even harder materials until they glittered like diamonds of every shade. Then, I'd painstakingly faceted each one. It had taken nearly two months to complete the process from start to finish. And now I had to give my first batch away.

"Are you sure? They are so beautiful!" Moll gushed as she rushed forward to accept the stones.

I wanted to say no. I wanted to tell her to forget her plans and remind her of the danger. But she'd point out that she hadn't been caught yet in all these years. Even I couldn't argue with that track record.

"I'm sure, Moll."

She ran a hand over the stones, spreading them across the table, watching how they caught the light. "I'll sew them on tight. As soon as the party is over, I'll give them right back!"

She wrapped her arms around my neck from behind and squeezed so hard, she nearly crushed my windpipe.

"I love you like a sister, Harmony Marie Fallowell," she whispered.

"Still not my middle name," I reminded her for the

thousandth time. I knew my first, and I'd taken my foster family's last, but if I had a middle name, I didn't remember it. Yet another little perk of being a foundling with amnesia left to be found in a forest.

Huzzah.

"Oh, no."

I untangled myself from Moll's chokehold and stepped back to see her stricken face. "What now?"

"I have no shoes to match. You're right about the red dress—it's the only one that suits— but it's cut shorter at the front and will show off my shoes." She covered her face with her hands, bowing her head. A sob rippled from her.

Damn it. I hated to see her cry.

But maybe there was still something else I could do.

I made my way over to a basket in the corner of the room and dropped to a squat. It took a minute to sort through the broken crap that I hadn't gotten around to fixing, but then I found it. The brown box I'd tucked away for a rainy day, and today, it was raining like all the be-damned summer monsoons. Moll's tears didn't usually bother me too much. She'd be the first to admit she was melodramatic. Which made them even more pathetic than usual. Because today, she'd figured out what I'd known for a while now.

Her hopes of a rich Prince Charming coming to rescue us were fading fast. Men like that married very beautiful, very *young* women, from families like their own. It had already been an uphill battle coming from

The Hollow. The second a servant dropped a glass and Moll bent to pick it up, or someone made a ribald joke, and she let out her deep belly laugh, she marked herself as new money at best. Now, in addition to her own upbringing, she had to deal with Mother Nature. Despite good bones that would serve her well until she was six feet under, her once-smooth skin was marred by just a few laugh lines around the eyes. She had a premature hint of silver gilding the burnished copper of her hair. Life in The Hollow was hard, and it took a toll on all who lived here. Moll was getting older, and there was nothing she could do to stop it. In her view, every new, subtle sign that appeared was like a death knell. The sound of her dreams dying. She wasn't ready to let that happen yet, and I wasn't ready to pick up those pieces once she finally broke.

Shoving aside the last of my reservations, I picked up the box, realizing there was a four-inch hole in one corner that looked like it had been chewed through. Moths? Mice?

No.

As I bent closer, I realized it didn't even look like a regular hole. It was more like a tiny chasm of inky black…like if I stuck my finger into it, it would disappear into the ether of the Shadow Abyss…

"That imagination of yours is going to get you carted off to the asylum!"

My stepmother's warning rang in my head, and I blew out a long breath. I didn't often agree with the woman, but lately, stress had me thinking the strangest thoughts. I couldn't shake the sense that something big was coming.

"What's that?" Moll demanded, eyeing the box as the flow of tears halted.

With one last glance at the hole, I turned my attention to Moll. "Xavier convinced me to give him a nice, fat squirrel for these silly things two weeks ago, and I agreed because I was thinking I might be able to sell them at the next market."

I held out the box and Moll's eyes went wide as she took it. "For me?"

"For you."

She lifted the top off and instantly let out a squeal. "Are you kidding?" Her eyes shot to mine, tears replaced by astonishment. "Harm, these are *fabulous*!"

I was no shoe aficionado, but even I knew when I'd first laid eyes on them that the glass shoes were special. No surprise from Xavier, one of the artists in The Hollow. Even the poorest of people still managed to find a way to make music and art. Maybe because we needed it more. That didn't make the shoes any less ridiculous, though. They served no practical purpose at all, really. I'd only bought them because of a story about a girl with a dress made by mice and wore glass slippers in my childhood fairytale book.

I winced at the bolt of fury that still shot through me every time I thought of it. The one thing, besides Fetch, that I had from my real parents, and my piece of shit stepbrothers had destroyed it before I was old enough to even read the thing on my own. That alone would've been reason enough to hate them, but they managed to give me plenty of those over the years.

"If I add the gems to the red dress, and maybe a silver ribbon as a sash pulled from that white dress, with these shoes…it would work. It will work!" She set the box down, eyes shiny with tears all over again, and threw her arms around me. "You're my hero!"

I hugged her back and then pulled away before she started blubbering and got snot all over my old wool sweater.

"I'm nobody's hero, Moll. But I am your best friend which means when it comes to you, I'd face the Shadow Abyss itself to help you find your happy ending."

Her smile wobbled. "Me too. For you, I'd do the same."

Despite whatever vain streak she had, I knew she was being honest. We looked out for each other. That's what friends who'd become chosen family did.

I cleared my throat. "Well, you'd better get started on hair and makeup if you're going to be on time. Who are we tonight, anyway?"

She lifted her chin and wiped the last of her tears away. "Me."

My heart stuttered as I stared at her in shock. "What the hell are you talking about?"

She flapped her hand and let out a chuckle. "Not *me*,

me. I'm going to use a fake name, of course. But I have the strangest feeling. Like tonight might be my last shot." She looked away from me for a second and then met my gaze again. "All this time I've been trying to find the man of my dreams and future father of my children using everything I'm *not* to attract him. If I've only got one more go at it, I'm going to bet on myself. Red hair, blue eyes, no corset. Who knows?" She popped off a wink. "I might even skip the lipstick."

If I wasn't chilled to the bone by her previous words, I'd have laughed out loud at the thought.

"Moll…are you sure that's a good idea? What if someone from The Hollow recognizes you?"

"If someone from The Hollow is at that party, they're where they shouldn't be, same as me. Who are they going to tell?"

"That's fine for the guests, but what about the servants? It seems like a foolish gamble."

She frowned. "More like a calculated risk. I've never seen anyone I recognized at any of the other events. You know as well as I do that the palace gets all their staff from The Smudge, and it's nearly impossible to climb more than one rung up the ladder. You're being a worry wart."

She had a point. Unlike the two other kingdoms that lay between Alabaster and the Shadow Abyss far far away, we lived in a caste system that didn't even pretend to be anything else. And Alabaster was constructed in the confines of a series of three walls, each smaller than the last, like a target with the bullseye in the middle.

Within the confines of the outermost Great Wall that protected all of Alabaster including The Hollow, there stood the second wall. Known as The Cradle, it loomed high in the sky, enveloping Little Alabaster and separating it from us losers in The Hollow.

Citizens there, most of the merchant class or better, feasted and politicked, free to turn a blind eye to the squalor we peasants had been left with. As far as the crown was concerned, people like Moll and I were the lowest of the low. It was a rare thing to even *see* someone from Little Alabaster in these parts, barring some random guards roaming the streets every so often in search of beggars to beat or shopkeeps to harass.

Wedged in a narrow band right between us and our betters, there was another group we called Smudgers. Even though they were mostly craftsmen like many in The Hollow, they were a step above us in the hierarchy. The royals, nobles, and wealthy merchants needed servants and people to do the jobs they didn't want to do themselves. So, while they were kept on a tight leash, Smudgers were permitted to live in a band between the Cradle and the Hollow, shoved into their own district in the northernmost part of Little Alabaster. Even though life wasn't exactly easy there either, Hollowers leapt at any opportunity for a "promotion" to the Smudge. That privilege was only given to a handful of people each year, but it did wonders for keeping the masses in line in hopes of being one of the chosen few.

Then, last but not least, to the south, stood Alabaster Palace. Where rules were made to be broken, and laws didn't apply. The royals enjoyed ultimate, unchecked power, and weren't afraid to use it.

"See, you're doing that thing again," Molly muttered, interrupting my thoughts. "You're imagining every possible bad thing that could happen, and that's not the energy I need right now!"

"I'm not! I'm just…thinking."

"Yeah. You always are. But this isn't up for debate, Harm. I'm going, as me, and I need you to be okay with that."

I was gearing up to continue the fight, but then I caught sight of Moll's solemn face and snapped my mouth shut. Gone was my funny, silly, and sometimes vain friend. In her place was a desperate yet resigned woman, very aware of her circumstances.

"I want to have children so badly, but I refuse to bring them into this—" she broke off and let out a snort of disgust, "life, if that's what you want to call it. I need to find a way out. I'm *going* to find a way out. For both of us. For our future."

I worried at the hangnail on my thumb, wracking my brain for some way to change her mind.

"Stop doing that. You're going to make it bleed again." She blew out a soft sigh and then shrugged.

"Fine. I don't want you in a panic all night, so how about a compromise. Red hair stays, but I'll wear the stupid green lenses and do some contouring. On the off chance I get recognized by the help, it'll at least make them question themselves enough to keep mum for fear of being wrong and accusing a proper lady of fraud."

I mulled it over and finally nodded. "And this will be the last time?"

The thought was enough to make me giddy. If we'd had a proper rug in this shithole, I'd have worn it bare pacing those nights she'd been off husband-hunting in enemy territory.

She dipped her head. "Pinky swear. If it doesn't happen tonight, I'll find another way."

Relief nearly swallowed me whole. I'd worry about those "other ways" another day. The very idea of her finally letting go of this fantasy that some man was going to save us from our fates was cause for cele-bration.

We locked little fingers and wiggled them before parting.

"Okay, then. You go get ready. I've got to head out. Past two evenings I saw a family of rabbits in the clearing by the woods grazing the last of the green grasses. Hoping to catch them while Fetch is with me so we can have some meat to go with the potatoes and cabbage we have left. We'll have a midnight supper of stew and ale while you fill me in on the party."

The hunting trip would also help keep me from worrying my head off about the possibility of Moll losing *hers* if she got caught crashing the Winter Jubilee.

"Perfect. And if I can sneak some daintique puffs into my bag when no one's looking, we can have dessert too! Maybe the ones with the berry filling, like last time."

Of course, we both knew, despite the mountains of food they'd be serving at the ball, Moll would eat none of it. Even without a corset squeezing her guts out, the bullshit rules of high society dictating that women should eat like sparrows meant she'd be all look, no touch. Then, when she got home, we'd sit in the dark, and she'd spend a solid hour describing the offerings across the tables in torturous detail.

Guinea fowl stuffed with lemon, rosemary, and thyme paired with duck fat fried potatoes.

Asparagus tips wrapped in bacon perched on top of a pearly white, flaky cod filet.

A pastel array of crisp on the outside, chewy on the inside macarons sandwiched around a dollop of tart, raspberry jam. Then there were the daintique desserts, bite sized morsels that tasted as if magic itself had been molded into the pastry.

My stomach grumbled as I made for the door, pausing to shoulder a worn bag and my bow and quiver.

"Wish me luck!" she called.

"Be safe, Moll. More than luck, be safe," I said, tossing a wave her way and then headed out into the brisk winter night.

How many times over the days that followed would I wish I'd never left…That I'd convinced her to skip the Jubilee and stay home?

A thousand.

Because life would never be that simple again.

CHAPTER 2

I let out a sharp whistle as I hit the muddy, cobbled street and Sir Fetchington Von Buren came soaring my way. Even after all these years, I still marveled at his grace. His speckled feathers looked as fresh as a falcon half his age and gleamed in the fading light of the day as he settled on my extended forearm. The weight felt good. Right.

"Fetch, my feathered friend. How are you this evening?" He bobbed his head, and I grinned. "Sometimes, I really do feel like you can understand what I'm saying. Then again, I might not be completely sane, so there's that to consider…"

Always making things up, things that aren't real. My stepmother's voice regularly reminded me of one of my many faults. I pushed her away and focused on what I was headed out to do—getting some food.

Fetch and I made our way into the town proper, but I'd barely stepped a foot onto the street full of shops when a familiar voice called to me.

"Did you read the news?"

I squeezed my eyes shut and tried to keep the irritation from my voice as I turned to face Preacher Pete. "If you mean the flyers the palace littered our streets with in the middle of the night, no, I didn't read it. Because that's not news. It's nothing more than a bunch of lies made up to keep us quiet."

The neighborhood nut spent every day from morning until night standing on the corner atop a makeshift podium telling anyone who would listen how lucky we were to have such a benevolent monarch. He'd been at it for so long, he never even got pelted with rotten fruit anymore. Then again, the past five years or so had been so bad in The Hollow, people would've eaten the fruit, rotten or not.

"One day, you will all see the truth about the crown. One day, you'll apologize to me for—"

"Yup, sounds good. I've got to get going now, though!" I hurried off with a rushed wave, but I'd only made it another block before I heard someone else call my name.

"Harmony!"

I turned to see Cissy Petway leaning on a nearby lamppost, grinning a gap-toothed smile. She was dwarfed by a coat three sizes too big, her signature white-blonde hair covered by the hood, only her freckled face visible. She hadn't celebrated her ninth birthday yet, but she was already the head of her own little gang of scoundrels. They milled around, chattering amongst themselves as she pushed off the post and came my way.

"Where's Moll tonight? Is she coming into town later, ya think?"

Much as I wished Moll was here instead of headed to the ball… "Not tonight."

The little girl's face fell for a second, but I didn't elaborate.

"Well, can Fetch come play with us, maybe?"

We both knew that "play" meant "steal from local merchants", and I shook my head with a snort.

"Nope. No can do. I got an earful from Mrs. Benson last week, and she threatened to make Fetch part of her dinner menu if she caught him snatching her figs again."

I leaned in so Cissy could pat the falcon's head, and he chortled happily when she obliged.

"She's got like a million of 'em," the little girl grumbled. "How many figs does one person need, for crying out loud?"

Shrugging, I looked past her to where the infamous fig tree lived, behind the high rock fence surrounding Mrs. Benson's tiny home. "Enough to sell and use that money to buy something different to eat, I would imagine. She's probably sick of figs."

"Exactly." She ruffled Fetch's feathers one last time

and stepped back. "Which was why I was trying to take them off her hands. It's a public service, when you really think about it."

I bit back a smile. Had to hand it to the kid, she was sharp as a blade. Maybe if the palace hadn't cut funding to the only school in The Hollow, she could've had a shot of getting out of this godforsaken place.

Then again, probably not. Just the application to legally breach the Great Wall was more than most of us earned in a year, not to mention the cost of hiring a hot air balloon pilot to make the trek to Bryngarde or Valencourt. Assuming, of course, that your application was even approved.

And let us not forget the murderous flying mantises…

"Do you think Moll will be at the barn tomorrow, maybe?" Cissy asked, interrupting my thoughts.

Over the past year, Moll had taken to rounding up the kids who were interested on Sunday mornings to at least help them with their letters and basic math. An empty, dilapidated barn on the outskirts of town had worked well enough in the milder months. Once the truly frigid weather came, though, she hadn't been able to find a place big enough to fit them all with any reliable source of heat. I wasn't sure who missed those sessions more, Moll or her students.

"It's still way too cold, kiddo. Probably not until Spring."

The hope in her eyes died, and I dropped a hand on the top of her head with a sigh.

"How about this? If Fetch and I get anything good to eat tonight, I'll come by the house and drop you and your mom off a little something?"

She swiped a dirty hand across her nose and nodded, brightening. "Deal!" With that, she turned and ran off to rejoin her crew.

"We're going to have to try for two rabbits tonight, my friend," I murmured to Fetch, the pressure of the hunt mounting with every step. I needed to hurry—

"Harmony!"

"Damn it." I grumbled, fixing a smile to my lips as I turned. "Hey, Xavier."

It only took one glance and a sniff of the air around him to know that he'd already been to the pub. His dark eyes were glassy, and he weaved on his feet with each word he spoke.

"Did you ever wind up wearing those shoes we traded for?"

I pointed to my mud-covered boots. "Can't say that I've had a cause to, no." He looked so disappointed that I found myself trying to soften the blow. "They're more of a showpiece in any case, don't you think? Like art."

"So, you're saying you're never going to wear them?"

"No, I'm just—" I broke off and tossed up my hands. "Okay, fine. Yes. I'm saying I'll never wear them. Even if I had a place to go—which I don't—they're not really my style. Do you see me in ball gowns?" He shook his head, and I plowed on. "They're gorgeous, but I traded for them because you needed a meal, and I figured I could sell them." He looked totally crestfallen.

Double damn. I hated seeing him so low. I took a breath and tried again. "I'm sure Moll will wear them, though."

He perked up even as I realized I probably should've kept that tidbit to myself. "Excellent. Where to?"

"Just around the house, probably. You know how she likes to play dress up and such."

He nodded, a little less enthusiastic than before. "Well, yes. But art is made to be seen, she should be out here, showing off her shoes and the legs attached to them!"

I winced. His unrequited affection for Moll on full display was uncomfortable, but I used it to my advantage. "Well. believe me, she'll be looking at them every day. She's in love—with the shoes that is. I swear. I've got to get a move on, though. Fetch and I have an appointment with a family of rabbits."

"Rabbits! Ahhh, it's been a long time since I've had rabbit..."

I wanted to bite off my own tongue. Hell, maybe I should and just eat that, since I was so hellbent on giving away all the dinner I hadn't even caught yet.

I swallowed a sigh. "If we have a good hunt, I'll bring some by your place if you're home."

"Oh, I'll be home! And I'll make sure I've got the fire

crackling and ready." He rubbed his hands together in anticipation of a meal I had yet to provide. He toddled away as I strode off again, sending up a silent prayer that there would be no more interruptions. I needed to make it to the edge of the woods, downwind before the rabbits came out.

Still cursing myself for running my stupid mouth and offering food to half the freaking Hollow, Fetch and I made it to the edge of the woods a few minutes later. The temperature had been steadily dipping as the sun lowered. It didn't help my mood that the only clear patch of ground I could sprawl on was still coated in frost from the night before, hidden in the trees and kept from the light and warmth of the day.

"Fuck glass slippers. Next trade I make is for a new coat," I whispered, dropping low and stretching out on the icy grass with a wince as the cold bit through my worn clothes. Fetch fluttered down beside me, nestling into my neck. "Thanks, buddy."

Twenty minutes later, my woolen sweater was soaked through, and my stomach was so cold it felt hot and prickly. I was just about to stand and jog in place to get the blood flowing when Fetch pulled away from me and cocked his head. I squinted, searching the landscape in front of me, but saw no movement.

"What do you hear, buddy?" I whispered. And then, he was gone, springing into the air and spreading his glorious wings. My heart pounded as he gained altitude ten feet, twenty, then thirty, before dropping from the sky like a stone.

"Come on, you beautiful bird. Mama needs a warm meal." And so did more than a few others.

The shriek that pierced the night sent a hot rush of adrenaline through me. It could only mean one thing—he'd snagged something. I heard the whoosh of wings before I saw him and turned my head just as Fetch glided toward me, something clutched in his talons.

Something small.

I had to shove back the stab of disappointment as he dropped his catch on the ground in front of me.

A squirrel.

Not that there was anything wrong with squirrel. It mostly tasted like chicken, but it wouldn't go far. Especially not with all the people I'd promised to feed tonight.

"What a noble, fine hunter you are, Fetch," I cooed as he preened, nudging at his feathers with his razor-sharp beak. I pushed myself to stand, snagging my bow and the still-warm squirrel by the tail. Our cover was blown. If there were rabbits nearby, they'd already run in the opposite direction of whatever had just taken out their furry friend.

Which meant plan B: Scrounging around in the woods for edible fungus, starchy roots, and any winter berries the sparrows hadn't already gotten to before the light faded completely. If I was lucky, maybe I'd find a meaty hen of the woods mushroom to add to our sad little stew.

A second shriek sounded in the distance, but this one had me freezing in place.

Far louder than the triumphant cry of a falcon, it sent a hot bolt of terror from the ends of my hair to the tips of my toes.

Mantis.

CHAPTER 3

etch hunkered down more tightly, his body almost becoming one with mine as I held a finger to my lips as if he knew what I was saying.

Silence, my friend. Not a sound.

I closed my eyes and tried to hear through the pulse suddenly pounding in my head. The people out on the street had clearly heard it too, because the silence was absolute. Everyone knew the best way to avoid getting eaten was to stay still and quiet.

And pray.

I had just started on the latter when a scream pierced the silence.

My eyes shot wide, and I reached for my bow as I let out a low hiss. "Cissy!" I lurched into motion, the nocking of my arrow made near impossible by the trembling of my cold, clammy hands.

"Cissy!" I called, this time in full voice as I sprinted through the icy grass back toward the cobblestones.

The town center came into view at the same time Cissy Petway did, and I skidded to a stop in horror. She was ten feet in the air, suspended by the insectoid creature who had her by the too-large coat, locked between its mandibles. Cissy kicked her feet wildly as she hollered, desperately trying to free herself. Luckily, the mantis was not yet an adult, which meant its movements were hampered by the extra weight it was carrying.

I raised my bow and blew out a breath. If I could get off a clean shot, maybe I'd at least stun the insect into dropping her. It would be a hard landing but given the choice between that or the thing dragging her back to its nest, slicing into her stomach with its blade-like limbs, and slurping her guts out, it would have to do.

I was just about to fire when Fetch pecked my cheek in a stern warning.

The mantis had only taken two flaps to lift it and its captive a dozen feet higher. Despite its youth, its wings still seemed massive, at least ten feet from tip to tip.

Maybe the play wasn't to go for a vulnerable bit at all. Maybe I should shoot for a wing, and hope the hole I left behind made it—

"Hellllp!"

Moll was right. I spent too much time thinking. It was time to act, before it was too late.

I lined up my shot, steadied myself, and let loose.

My aim was true. The arrow sailed toward the mantis with pinpoint precision…until the thing lifted its mighty wing and batted it out of the air like it was a toy.

"Damn it!" I brushed Fetch from my shoulder with a stern warning. "Stay back. You'll be of no help." Then, I ran into the middle of the street, waving my arms like a lunatic as I chased the mantis. Cissy was slowing it down, but we were only a few hundred yards from the Great Wall. If it got to the other side, it was game over.

"Hey! Ho! Here, you big dumb fucker!" I howled.

The mantis swung my way in a jerky motion.

"Yeah, look at me. She's barely a morsel, and I'm a whole meal!" I dropped the squirrel I'd been holding and lifted my woolen sweater to bare my belly.

The mantis's pupils narrowed, like it was considering my offer.

"Come on," I urged, wriggling my hips and pushing out my lean stomach as far as I could manage. "You know you want me. My spleen is super juicy, or so I've been told."

"Let me go, you bastard!" Cissy flailed hard, her legs wheeling violently as she flung her arms with wild abandon. She managed to connect the toe of her boot with the creature's chest, and it let out a screech, dipping lower in the night sky. It was then that I noticed the top few buttons of her coat had come undone.

"Cissy, listen to me!" I called. "Try to wriggle free of your coat!"

The mantis picked that moment to make up its mind, going with the bird in the hand over me in the bush, and wheeled back around, heading straight for the wall.

Bile bubbled in my throat as I broke into a sprint after them, legs churning as fast as I could make them.

"Do it now! Right now, Cissy." Panic clawed at my chest as the creature steadied itself and increased pace, hitting its stride. Thirty seconds to the wall at this rate. Maybe less. "You're not so far from the ground now! You can—"

A sudden streak of orange flashed through the darkness and my breath stilled. What the hell?

A loud, animalistic scream echoed through the night as the flame slammed into one of the mantises' legs, severing it in a shower of sparks.

My thighs burned as Cissy dropped from the sky and I poured it on to reach her before she landed, to no avail. She hit a patch of frozen earth a short distance from the Great Wall with a grunt and a cry of pain.

"Cissy!" I bent low and gently rolled her onto her back so I could see her face. "Are you all right?"

"She's fine, thanks to the skill and bravery of the king's guard!"

I turned to see Preacher Pete dragging his pulpit from the street to the grassy area and climbing on top with a beaming smile as a palace guard stalked past

Cissy and I toward the mantis, writhing and screeching about ten yards away.

It made sense now. The orange streak had been a flaming arrow. Hollowers weren't allowed to have them, despite being closest to the wall that separated us from the mantises. But the palace guards and the wealthy people on the other side of the Cradle? That was a whole other story.

There was one last, weak cry, and then silence.

The grim-looking guard came our way, looking over Cissy with a cursory glance before meeting my gaze. "I've got to get back to report this. According to the heatseeking wards around the perimeter, there are no other threats in the area. Apparently, there was one, small weak spot that needs to be reinforced. Total fluke the thing found its way in but should be fixed by morning. We'll send a palace falcon to patrol the area in the meantime, just as a secondary precaution."

With that, he turned on his heel and headed toward the horse he'd apparently rode in on.

"Witness the greatness of our monarchy here in Alabaster," Preacher Pete crowed, clapping his hands in glee. "Tis truly like no other! Their love and benevolence have again shone upon us and saved this child."

"Give it a rest, would you," I muttered, "A little girl was nearly killed tonight." I gathered Cissy closer, inspecting her scrunched face. "Talk to me, kiddo."

"Well, for starters, I'm not a little girl," she managed, her voice barely above a whisper. "And secondly, I'm pretty sure if you guys gave me a little more time, I might've been able to take the bastard."

Her words got the smile she'd been aiming for, and she smiled back, but given her chalk-white cheeks and wide eyes, there was no doubt she was shaken to the core. Who wouldn't be?

But life in The Hollow meant being resilient. You bounced back quick and kept on going. There was no other choice.

"Don't tell my ma. It'll only worry her," she added as she sat up with a grimace.

I nodded, not bothering to point out that her ma was going to hear it from one of the dozen or so people watching from the alleyways or through their windows.

"Cissy? You okay?"

Cissy's gang had come out of hiding, looking shamefaced and worried, but she kept up the same brave front with them as she pushed my helping hands away and stood gingerly.

"Yeah." She flexed both hands and stretched. "Yeah, I think I'm good. I was telling Harm that I was just about to kick that thing's ass when that guard showed up. You guys all right?"

They exchanged looks and nodded.

"Yup. We were trying to come up with a plan to come help, only…"

"Harm had it under control," Cissy said with a brave grin. "We're pretty tough."

I ruffled her hair and let out a sigh. "I'm glad no one was hurt, but I think it's probably time to head home. There's been enough excitement for the night, and we need to give the palace time to fix whatever went wrong."

I half wondered if she might argue with me, but instead, Cissy nodded and gestured to her friends.

"Come on, guys. Let's call it a night."

I took a few minutes to retrieve the squirrel I'd abandoned and walk each of them home. But it wasn't until the last had closed their door behind them and locked it that I let myself slump at the waist and feel the feelings.

Hot tears flooded my eyes as the image of Cissy in that thing's grip flickered through my mind. That had been way too close for comfort. We'd lost people in the past, but it was getting more and more rare, and I could hardly remember the last time one had snatched a child.

I was no fan of the crown, but Preacher Pete had it right for once. That guard had saved Cissy's life. And he'd saved me from having to go to sleep at night, watching her death on a continuous loop for all eternity after having failed her.

"Fucking hell."

I straightened and Fetch returned to his perch on my shoulder, nestling his face into my neck.

"I know it's freezing out here, but I'm afraid to say, our day isn't done."

As much as I wanted to go home to recover from the shock and horror of what just happened over a hot mug of tea, I still only had a single squirrel and a lot of mouths to feed.

Cissy would sleep a whole lot better with some hot food in her belly, and so would Fetch and I.

I headed back toward my original hunting spot, bone-tired now that the shock and adrenaline had worn off. Instantly, my thoughts went to Moll. She'd be at the jubilee by now. I hoped word of the mantis attack wouldn't reach her. She needed to stay focused and worried about her own skin, not wondering what was happening back at home.

"What do you think, Fetch my boy? That mantis probably scared all those rabbits away anyhow. Maybe we're better off foraging after all…"

A loud rustle directly behind me had both Fetch and I wheeling around in surprise. I dropped my bag and nocked an arrow in one motion. Whatever had made that sound was a lot bigger than a squirrel. If it was another mantis or a bear, I'd be on the wrong side of that fight even with my bow. Lucky for me, it turned out to be neither.

I blinked in total shock as a four-foot-tall wild turkey scuttled into view, its bright red waddle wobbling as it gobbled.

Sweet Mother, he was a big bastard. Thirty pounds if he was an ounce.

I sucked a breath in through my nose and held it,

closing one eye as I aimed. I knew as soon as I released the bow string that it was a good, clean head shot. The bird dropped to the grass without a sound or a struggle.

I muttered my thanks to the animal, both elated and a little sad as I rushed toward it. Killing for our meals wasn't something I enjoyed. If it could've been avoided, I'd have done so. But we lived in the worst part of a cruel world, and that was a fact. Death came to us all in The Hollow, usually sooner rather than later, but I was doing my best to stave off his visit to me and Moll.

I couldn't stem the rush of tears that sprang to my eyes as I laid a hand on the turkey's downy chest. This would feed us all—even those I promised meat too—tonight and tomorrow, including Fetch, who was decidedly pro-cannibalism.

"Even better than a rabbit," I whispered, filled with gratitude.

I tugged the knife from the belt around my hips and began the tedious work of dressing the animal. When I was done, Fetch napped in a tree with a belly full of offal, and my hands were numb and aching from the cold. It didn't dampen my mood, though, because I had two sacks filled with meat and one of feathers for pillow-making. Moll was going to positively lose her mind when she saw the haul. I had to hope it would be enough to pick her up after what was sure to be the final, failed turkey hunt of her own.

I let out a whistle and Fetch left his perch to settle on my shoulder as I started the walk back to town.

"We'll stop off at Druzilla's and give them one of the legs," I said to Fetch, turning my focus to the positives. "Then, we'll stop by Cissy's and Xavier's with supper for them."

The walk to my stepmother's house was not far, and I used every second of the time daydreaming about turkey stew. I was sure we had a bit of flour left, which meant dumplings were a must, just floating in that savory, rich broth...And if Moll came through with some pilfered daintiques from the jubilee?

It would have gone from a wretched day to a great one.

I slowed to a stop as my childhood home came into view. Or, at least, the part of my childhood I remembered. Black smoke puffed from the chimney of the squat little house, and a sense of relief mingled with the dread that always came from visits home. At least I could get warm and dry.

"You head on back to our place and I'll meet you there when I'm done," I said to Fetch, who seemed to nod in agreement before flitting off without a moment's hesitation.

Who could blame him? If I wasn't bound by family duty, I'd have avoided Druzilla and her dumb-dumb sons at all costs. But you didn't always get to choose your family.

Correction.

I didn't, at least. They had gotten to, though. Or at least my father had. Druzilla and her sons Wayne and Spalding—who I privately referred to as Pain and Suffering—had all voted *no* on adopting me. But dear old dad, Willliam Fallowell, had decided that the day he found me hiding in a hollowed-out tree in the woods, curled around my little book, Fetch guarding the entrance. That was the one day he put his foot down with his shrew of a wife and the jackasses he called sons. He'd made the decision to keep me all on his own.

At four years old—give or take—there was no way I would have been able to survive on my own, even with Fetch on my shoulder, so his choice had kept me from starving to death or being eaten by a predator. On the flip side, it had also caused him a load of grief. Constant badgering about already tight finances, and "one more mouth to feed" were regularly thrown at both me and him. Indignant scoffs and shots about blood being thicker than water and real men putting *their* children first. It had been tough on my father, but he never complained.

Not that it was all peaches and cream for me, either. I grew up not knowing who I was or even where I'd come from. Because the book in my arms was made with a type of leather my father had never seen, and the stories within were unknown to him, he theorized that I was from one of the other kingdoms. Although, why my birth parents would've sent me here, to the undisputed worst of the three Kingdoms, I couldn't imagine. Maybe they were bad people who didn't really care what happened to me. Despite vague memories of a beautiful woman with dark hair and tawny eyes like my own, and a man with a beard and a soothing, deep voice, I didn't remember them at all, so I'd never know.

It was a fact that haunted me.

Eventually, Druzilla had grudgingly accepted the title of stepmother, but even at that, had insisted I call her by her first name except when in public. We had to keep up appearances, after all. Behind closed doors, it was worse. Always the blame fell to me, never given credit. I got slapped far more often than I got hugged, and waited on Druzilla, Pain, and Suffering like I was the hired help. But as meager and shitty as they were, I got three meals most days and a cot to sleep in. More than if I'd been left in the forest.

And, for twelve years, I had my dad.

William T. Fallowell. Willy to his friends, and "Sir" to me when Druzilla was around. But when we were alone, I called him Pawpaw, and he called me Cinderella just like the girl in one of the stories in my book. A fly on the wall might've thought that was because I was always covered in ash from cleaning the fireplace, but they'd have thought wrong. I earned that nickname fair and square when I was taking my first crack at making explosives that would help me, the earliest version of what I now called "bang 'em ups."

They could break up boulders into smaller, usable stones for building a wall. Back then, I wasn't as cautious, and my invention worked *too* well. The next thing I knew, my test bomb exploded in my face. The black soot clung to me for two days. It could've been a real tragedy, but it only cost me my eyelashes for a couple years, my best jumper, and a few layers of skin off my back when Druzilla tanned my hide over the jumper.

Worth it, in my opinion. Me and Pawpaw had secret nicknames, and they didn't.

At least none they *knew* about.

As I made my way to the front door, my hands broke out in a clammy sweat. Druzilla couldn't hurt me, physically or emotionally. Not anymore. Still, I felt a little nauseous every time I stepped inside. Moll spit on the ground whenever we walked past and had been insisting for more than a decade that I stop giving them the time of day. But that wasn't what Pawpaw would've wanted. For reasons I would probably never truly understand, he loved them.

So here I was, for the promised weekly visit he'd secured via a deathbed request, with a food haul for them to complain about—and yes, they would complain, I had no doubts on that front.

"Just think about the dumplings, Harm. Get through this, and straight home to make dumplings and stew," I muttered under my breath as I lifted a fist and rapped on the door.

"Who is it?" a raspy male voice shouted from inside.

"It's Harmony. Open up, it's freezing out here."

The sound of locks tumbling open, then the door swung wide to frame my youngest "brother", Wayne.

"Well get inside before you let all the hot air out, then," he grumbled, stepping to the side and waving.

"Tell her not to bring that winged rat in here with her. I'm pretty sure that's where my precious Minuet caught those fleas from!" My stepmother's voice rose high and demanding. Again, as per usual.

I forced a tight smile and slipped past Wayne, sighing as the warm air enveloped me. The room opened straight from the entry hall into a sitting area, a roaring fire dominating the center of the far wall. "Fetch isn't with me, but birds don't get those kinds of fleas anyway."

Druzilla's once blonde hair was shot with more silver now, but she still had it done up in the most current fashion of a braid ringing around her head, like a crown. It suited her really; she'd always been queen of the house. She was wearing a deep blue gown—well-worn and older in fashion with the heavy velvet—that brought out the sharp blue in her eyes and accentuated her pale skin. She'd been a beauty once, but her sharp tongue made it hard for me to see.

She shot me a quelling look and shifted in her over-stuffed chair. "Thinks she knows everything, this one," she muttered to Spalding, who sat across from her on a sofa that had seen better days. Spalding was the shorter of the two boys—dirty blond hair with a receding hair-line, blue eyes too, but all washed out, like a poor copy of his mother's coloring. Wayne favored father. Deep brown hair, like the color of tilled soil, and blue-green eyes. Even his frame was like Pawpaw's—strong and heavily muscled, like an ox.

Spalding snorted and cracked his knuckles. "Yeah, she's a real smarty-pants, this one. So smart that she didn't even bother to wear a coat outside. Use your head, Harm. If you catch your death of the cold, who's gotta come up with the coin to bury you?" He poked a beefy thumb at his own chest. "It's me, that's who."

There was no point in reminding him that he didn't have a job, and that I wanted to be cremated anyway, which was free.

The name of the game with these visits was speed. Get in, drop off the food, and get out. Duty done, safe for a week from their pointed jabs.

I held the largest bag high. "Turkey. A big one, at that."

Druzilla wet her lips as her greedy eyes narrowed on the bag. "Hmmm. I prefer pheasant..."

"Oh, okay then," I replied, shrugging. "I'll just keep the whole thing for myself and make a pot pie for the rest of the week."

"N-no, no!" she leapt to her feet and patted down a stray gold and silver curl. "At least it's not squirrel again as the last four weeks have been. Give it over." She wiggled her fingers at me, and I handed over the sack containing the turkey leg, which she promptly dropped into Spalding's lap. "Get that into a pot and heat some water for tea." She shot me a look and then whispered, loudly, "Don't waste the sugar, though."

Gods above, she was insufferable. I held my hands up, stopping Spalding. "Oh, no tea for me. I'm going to warm my hands by the hearth for a minute and head back home. I've got loads of work to do."

"Of course you do," Wayne said with a bright smile. "Who else is going to break stuff and catch themselves on fire if you're not out there doing it, am I right?"

I smiled sweetly and aimed for the low hanging fruit. "Still pissing the bed, Wayne, or did you finally grow out of that? Hard to get a wife when you can't hold your water."

Spalding let out a guffaw and Wayne popped him hard in the diaphragm, sending him into a coughing fit, gasping to catch his breath. I fought not to wince—I'd been on the receiving end of Wayne's fist and catching your air after was a chore.

Wayne's eyes narrowed. "Shut up, Harmony. It wasn't piss. I spilled some water, I told you that a million times."

I tipped my head. "You know I had to wash the sheets that week? Water doesn't stain yellow, Wayne. Oh, that rhymes. Wayne the Stain."

Spalding managed a breath and used it to pile on. "Wayne the Stain! Oh, that's good!"

Wayne spun on his brother, both fists curled. He

lunged at him, and they tripped over the low coffee table, dragging it across the floor with a screech.

"Enough!" Druzilla's voice cracked through the room like a whip as she stood, and the three of us froze as if we were children still. "All of you, stop! I've got a headache to start, and you're only making it worse with your arguing!" Druzilla pointed a finger at Spalding, then directed him toward the tiny kitchen. "Tea. Now."

Spalding scuttled off, and she turned to me and Wayne. He glared at me, and I smiled oh so sweetly back.

"You may as well sit and chat a minute while you wait for your tea," she said, retaking her seat with a sniff. I padded toward the fireplace and knelt low, letting the heat seep into my icy skin. Despite my protests, I was going to have to stay for the tea now.

I had zero interest in chatting, but I also knew this was part of the ritual. Like me, Druzilla felt some warped sense of obligation to my father. Hers didn't extend to helping me in any way, shape or form, but when I showed up, she made sure to spend ten minutes asking me stupid questions and feigning interest in my life.

"So...how are things?" she asked, her tone stilted by the effort of exchanging pleasantries with someone she could not have cared less for.

I should probably mention the whole mantis attack

thing, but I still wasn't fully recovered, and if I had to watch Pain and Suffering gleefully reenact the event, I was liable to start swinging. Besides, we both knew Druzilla had no interest in my problems. Instead, I mentally thumbed through the approved script and smiled. "Really good. Great, actually. Everything is just great."

Her head bobbed. "Good to hear it."

"And you?" I asked dutifully, already prepping to tune out the coming list of complaints.

Druzilla didn't disappoint.

"My gout has been acting up, and I think I have that rash on my back again. Do you want to see?"

I certainly do not, ma'am. "That's okay. Seen one rash, you've seen 'em all, right?"

She narrowed her eyes at me but then her face cleared. "Oooh, did you hear, it's the Winter Jubilee at the palace tonight, oh, how lovely it will be! Every ten years they host it, the last I was at was before…" she trailed off, then leaned back and laid a hand on her sagging bosom. "Imagine how glorious it must be. The costumes. The decor. The food!"

Druzilla knew all about the balls and jubilees. Better than anyone else in The Hollow, at least. She'd been born in Little Alabaster, after all, and spent the first sixteen years of her life there living in splendor and excess. Until she ran away to marry a boy from The Hollow.

The story went that she and Willy Fallowell had met at a merchant bazaar, one of those rare times in the past when folks from The Hollow were allowed through the single gate in the Cradle that was usually locked tighter than a mantis's jaws on a meal. For a few, blessed hours, they rubbed elbows with the wealthy folks over silks and spices only the latter could afford while feasting on ham hocks and ale that the crown provided as a rare, strategic show of its so-called benevolence.

The attraction between Willy and Druzilla had been instantaneous.

She was a handsome woman at the time, but unmarried long enough to hear the whispers of "spinster" due to her sharp tongue, despite her young age. Willy was funny and sweet, but more than that, he was off limits. To a spoiled rich girl who had been spurned by her own, what could be more attractive than forbidden fruit?

It had taken six months of wedded bliss for the bloom to rot off that rose, but by that time she was very pregnant, and there was no going back. She'd made the mistake of giving up a life of leisure and material wealth for life in The Hollow—her parents had declared her dead to them, and she'd be stuck here until she truly died.

From that day forward, she'd made it her whole personality to ensure that Willy paid for the loss of luxury.

As for his part, he took whatever she dished out. Because, despite being a great provider by Hollow standards as a blacksmith, he accepted the blame for his wife's change in circumstances down to his very bones.

"I'm sure it's a nice party, but I hear it's not all roses on the other side of the Cradle," Wayne said with a sneer, drawing my attention from the past back to the conversation at hand. "Apparently, the Prince Regent has been a real handful since he's been back. Developed an eye for the ladies in his travels and has a habit of taking them whether they want to be taken or not, if you catch my meaning." He waggled his brows like he was talking about a steal of a deal at the butcher shop as opposed to rape.

"Where did you hear that?" I demanded, frowning. "From Bigsby down at the pub? You know you can't believe anything that tree stump has to say. He once told me he swallowed an apple seed and shat a whole-ass apple a few weeks later."

Wayne cracked his knuckles and shook his head mulishly. "Not Bigsby. For your information, I have it on good authority. You know Tilda from the bakery? Well, her cousin is a maid at the palace. She said she found a woman naked and bloodied, wandering the halls at night, babbling about the prince hurting her and needing help. They helped her, alright. Nobody's seen or heard from her since, and it's been two weeks. Her family was told she was so ashamed of her immoral behavior, she exiled herself to The Hollow. If she's here, I sure haven't heard tell of it, have you?"

Bloody hell, that was horrifying. Tilda was a straight arrow and, while we weren't exactly friends, I'd never known her to be an idle gossip.

"Best tell Moll not to be nosing around on the other side of the Cradle either," Wayne continued, inspecting his dirty fingernails. "Apparently, he has a real taste for redheads in particular. Curls too."

I let the words sink in, swallowing back a rush of nausea as I straightened.

"You're making the last bit up," I managed, my tongue feeling thick and clumsy in my mouth.

Nope. Not now. Please, God, not now.

I squeezed my eyes closed, sucking long breaths in through my nose and out through my mouth. Lights flickered behind my lids as my head began to throb with a pulse of its own.

Surely, Moll was alright.

Surely even if Prince Heinrich noticed her, he would never risk hurting her in the midst of a palace filled with people? It only made sense that she was safe.

But my experience with wealthy, powerful men told me different. And so did my gut.

Damn it, Moll.

I could hear Wayne talking, but he sounded a million miles away. "Why would I make that up, Harm? Moll's alright, even if she does hang 'round you. I wouldn't be opposed to courting her myself, if not for you."

"Good gods, she's doing the *thing* again," Druzilla muttered as I grabbed onto the mantel for purchase. "You're almost thirty years old, broke as a church mouse, and a spinster to boot. Surely you've grown out of these weird spells by now."

The vice on my skull tightened. I could not afford to go under when Moll needed me!

Shit, shit, shit.

Thwack!

I don't know what jarred me back from the brink, the clash of teeth as my head snapped back, or the sharp sting in my cheek that redirected my attention. Whatever the case though, suddenly, the headache was gone. My eyes shot wide, and I found Druzilla staring at me, her expression flat.

"All right then? You need to get control of yourself, Harmony."

I nodded, rubbing my cheek absently as I stuffed the other bags into her hands.

"Yes. Thank you. Have one of the boys bring Cissy's mom and Xavier some turkey. If they don't, I'll hear about it," I added with a warning glare. "I've got to go...run an important errand."

"What the hell are you on about, missy? We don't work for you, you know—"

But the rest of her words were lost as I bolted for the door, brain already ten steps ahead of my body.

There was no time to forge myself an invite. Even if I had more supplies to do it, it had taken nearly eight hours to get Moll's just right. No, I would have to get over the Cradle and into the palace the hard way.

Step one?

Find a dress for the Winter fucking Jubilee.

CHAPTER 4

 few hours later, I was standing in front of the massive door of the palace church, wearing one of Moll's blonde wigs and a black dress that was more than a decade old and a full size too small.

The dress I'd worn to my father's funeral, only I'd hastily hacked the high neck into a deep vee in an attempt to make it look more stylish. I should've tried it on first, because as it stood right now, my cups were one deep breath away from running over.

"It's going to be fine," I muttered under my breath.

I'd already managed to get over the Cradle and into Little Alabaster with my grappling hook. I'd even managed to bypass the guard gate onto the palace grounds thanks to the maze of temporary scaffolding that had been built to allow laborers working on the new moat to transport supplies. After that, it was smooth sailing as most of the night guards were busy at the main entrance of the palace monitoring those coming in and out of the party.

Now I just had to break into the church that I was *fairly* certain had a second entrance from inside the palace and I was *in*.

I bent low to examine the door lock and then let out a happy sigh. She was as straightforward as they came. I plunged a hand into my bag and tugged out my easy lockpick. Then, I slipped the device into the hole and closed my eyes. A couple of turns and two twists—

Click.

Security was lax as it had been decades since the last uprising, and the masses were too busy staving off starvation to bother with yet another doomed revolution. The only true threat to anyone in Alabaster were the flying mantises. And if any more of those creatures found their way past the magical wards that reinforced the high walls of The Great Wall around the Hollow like tonight, the rich here in Little Alabaster would have plenty of time to prepare because they had a massive village full of Cissy Petways to act as a buffer.

Or buffet, was more like it.

It wasn't until I got inside the church and ambled along the wall to the door on the opposite side of the room that I realized I'd been a bit hasty in my judgment. This lock wasn't as straightforward. In fact, I'd never seen its equal. Instead of having three or four cuts made to fit a typical key, this was much more complex, like a little maze. Reason I hadn't seen its kind in The Hollow? The mechanism itself was probably worth more than anything anyone in my neighborhood had worth stealing. I spied silver, and what looked like platinum. Damn.

I made a mental note, already updating the blueprint of the easy lockpick in my mind for the future as I looked around the room for another way in. There, in the corner, a gorgeous, stained-glass window.

I reached back into my bag for the glass cutter I'd brought along just in case.

"This is crazy. Absolutely insane. You should just turn around and go home."

But even as I whispered the words, I soldiered on, pressing the suctioned end of my glass cutter to the windowpane. I'd never forgive myself if something happened to Moll while I was just hanging around The Hollow waiting for her to come home, knowing what I knew. Best case scenario, everything was fine, I watched until she left on her own, then slipped back out myself with Moll none the wiser. Worst case? Well worst case I'd deal with when it happened.

If it happened.

It wasn't my first time using the glass cutting tool, and it wasn't long before a circular chunk of the pane gave way. I reached a hand through the hole, unlatched the window, and swung it open. Then I hiked up my skirts and climbed inside.

The chapel was an annex, added onto the palace about five years before, once the king found out he was terminally ill. Religion hadn't cured him and, judging by the damp, musty smell and all the cobwebs, he'd given up on salvation long before he died a few weeks ago.

I lowered myself gingerly onto the marble floor and took a quick look around.

Empty, and utterly silent.

I let out a breath and bent at the waist, sucking in a few steadying breaths.

"She's fine," I murmured. "I'm going to get in, find Moll, and get out. We'll be home laughing about this tomorrow while we gorge ourselves on turkey stew and dumplings."

I hurried to the door that looked as though it led to the main palace, based on the layout. My instincts were right and a short while later, I stood at the end of a long hallway listening to the music playing in the distance. I followed the sound, on high alert, until I caught sight of a powder room. I slipped inside and tried not to notice the marble tiles, the brilliant gold fixtures, cushioned chairs and innumerable pots of make-up ready to be used.

Grabbing a comb—ivory and gold—I worked it through the wig, taming the worst of the mess.

Once I fixed my hair, refreshed the lipstick I'd stolen from Moll's vanity, and stowed my bag deep in the trash bin, I was as ready as I was going to get. They wouldn't be checking invitations on the way *out* of the palace, after all.

I exited the powder room and hung a left, the music almost on top of me now. Massive, double doors were swung wide to reveal a ballroom the size of fifty houses in The Hollow. And despite that, the place still managed to feel crowded. There had to be a thousand people in attendance.

Talk about finding a needle in a haystack. Maybe that was a good thing, though. If I couldn't get a bead on Moll, maybe the Prince Regent wouldn't either. Hope flared in my chest that I was overreacting. I'd take a scolding from Moll all day long as long as she was okay.

A pair of young women passed me, heads pressed close together as they giggled and made their way toward the powder room I'd just left. They barely spared me a glance, which was exactly how I wanted it.

I shook off the worst of my nerves and stepped up to the doors. No one stood guard or tried to stop me. In fact, there was a long, purple carpet laid out, beckoning me in.

"Don't mind if I do," I whispered.

I ambled down the runner, keeping my back as straight and elegant-like as possible in case anyone was watching me. They weren't, though. They were far too busy enjoying what had to be the most amazing party ever.

It took everything inside me not to stop and gape at the fancy stuff around me. The ceiling was at least a hundred feet high, and from it hung countless fairy lights suspended by whispers of magic, as I could see no lines holding them aloft. They twinkled merrily, like snowflakes, only it wasn't cold because crackling fires dotted the walls of the room every dozen yards or so, flanked by twenty-foot spruce trees decked out in ribbons and bows. The musician-less orchestra played on its own, facing a dancefloor brimming with party-goers. A rainbow of streamers whipped through the air, wafting to and fro on a magical breeze.

It was awe-inspiring and infuriating all at once. We had precious few Whispers—those who had magic in their blood—in The Hollow, and even at that, they knew better than to flaunt what little magic they had. Here, though, behind the Cradle, wealthy Whispers were permitted to show off their party tricks without fear of persecution.

Must be nice.

Anger-fueled adrenaline coursed through me but drained away in a rush as I sniffed the air and turned. I realized with a start that, perched above every one of those crackling fires, hung some sort of game, roasting on a spit. Juices sizzled as they bubbled and dripped, giving off an aroma that nearly had me drooling. Using every ounce of discipline I had, I turned and walked away without even plucking a morsel off the tender-loin closest to me.

"You're a fucking champion," I muttered under my breath as I slipped into the crowd. I'd infiltrated the enemy. Now to find Moll and get the hell out of here before someone realized two of these things didn't belong and they decided to end the night with a double hanging.

When minutes turned to an hour, though, I started getting desperate. Not only hadn't I caught sight of my friend, but the prince was also nowhere to be found. Weird, since the party was being thrown in his honor. Or maybe not so weird, if he was taking advantage of someone.

My lips started to go numb as I rounded the corner and saw a smaller room just off the west side of the ballroom. A group of men sat around an oval card table groaning as a blond man wearing a gem-encrusted crown stood and leaned forward, sweeping more gold coins than I'd ever seen in my life into a pile in front of him. Then, he retook his seat, stacking them into neat rows.

I glanced around quickly and caught sight of a server adding flutes of champagne to a tower.

"Excuse me…Is that, Prince Heinrich?"

He followed the direction of my finger and nodded.

"He was crowned a couple of hours ago, so it's King now, but yes, ma'am."

"Thank you."

Relief flowed through me, and I slumped, any concerns about proper posture out the window. Wherever Moll was hiding, Heinrich the Molester wasn't with her.

Another server balancing a tray of canapes passed

by, and I reached out to snatch a few in celebration. Shrimp puffs, by the looks of them. My mouth watered as I popped one in, whole. The puff pastry crackled and then melted to mingle with the succulent shrimp and fresh dill.

I pondered my options as I chewed, the best I'd felt since Wayne had opened his trap back at the house earlier that evening. Heinrich might be as evil as Wayne said he was. For the moment, though, he was in plain sight, seemingly content to gamble, which was a huge load off my mind. Now, I just had to find Moll and figure out how to get her to leave without giving me too much grief.

I tossed another puff in my mouth and let out a groan of pleasure as I chewed.

"Excuse me, miss."

I turned to find a handsome stranger dressed in black sidling up next to me. His dark brown hair was flecked with gold and his broad shoulders seemed to be straining against the confines of his perfectly cut waist-coat. Fully aware that my cheeks looked like I was storing nuts for the winter, I chewed faster, not sure whether it would be ruder to talk with my mouth full or just ignore him altogether.

"Yesh?"

He frowned and leaned in to study me more closely.

Please don't ask me for my invitation.

Things had been going so well...my cover was

about to be fucking blown because of a few shrimp puffs.

"I hope I'm not overstepping, but you have a little —" he gestured with his index finger, a few inches from my chin.

I swallowed hard, the giant wad of shrimp and crust getting caught somewhere in the middle of my chest.

"Oh. Thank you!" I said, swiping my hand over my lips and downward, only to realize I didn't have a *little* of anything on my face. I was basically sporting a beard made of pastry crumbs.

Lovely.

"I saw you from across the room, and thought to myself, 'That woman doesn't belong here.'"

I must've looked as horrified as I felt, because he rushed to continue.

"Sorry. That came out wrong. I mean it in a good way. I just…I don't think I've ever seen anyone look so thoroughly enamored with a canape before."

My cheeks burned.

"Yes, well, I didn't have any lunch and, to be fair, it was an exceptional canape." I looked down and realized I was still storing some of it in my cleavage. You could take the girl out of The Hollow but there was no taking The Hollow out of this girl.

"Duncan Westerly." He stuck out a hand and cocked his head. "And you are?"

My brain skittered to a stop, freezing on the name.

Duncan Westerly. Second Prince of Alabaster, more

precisely. Half-brother to Heinrich, although word about town was that there was no love lost between the two. Like Heinrich, who had traveled and wound up staying in Brynegarde until their father's death, Duncan had spent much of his life far from Alabaster, in Valencourt. He'd come back a few years ago, but I'd only seen him once as an adult when the royal family had visited The Hollow to spread some sort of propaganda or another, and even that was from afar.

This time he was closer.

Really close. Close enough to see the exact shade of his smoky gray eyes.

Fucking hell.

"And you are?" he repeated, a glimmer of a smile activating the most amazing dimple I'd ever seen. I was still staring at it, and how it transformed his whole face into this open, sexy, invitation, when I finally found my voice again.

"Harmon-" I broke off, realizing my error, and coughed loudly to buy myself a second to think. "Ica. Harmonica."

Double fucking hell. What the hell kind of name was Harmonica? He'd never believe it.

But his smile never wavered.

"Well, Harmonica, I was actually coming over to see if you would like to dance with me."

I stared down at his still-extended hand, about to refuse. Then I looked up, right into the face of the server restocking the caviar station. And this face?

Was one I knew.

Genevieve Salim. Sister of Guy Salim, who ran a farm-stand down the street from my stepmother's house. I hadn't seen Genevieve in years. How the hell had she managed to work her way into the palace? She'd been one of the few plucked from The Hollow to work for a rich family in Little Alabaster around the age of twenty. She'd traded poverty and freedom for slightly less poverty, tucked away in The Smudge, with a side of indentured servitude.

Six helpings of one kind of manure, half-dozen of another, in my view. But I was in the midst of a shit-storm of my own, and Genevieve's job satisfaction was the least of my concerns right now.

Her recognizing me would be disastrous. She could out me to her employers, gain a hefty, little reward for pointing me out. I didn't know her well enough to know if she would care that I would hang for the offense.

I turned my head as fast as I could, took the prince's hand, and worked up a smile.

"I'd love to dance, thank you."

It was a two-fer. I could get some distance between me and Genevieve and use his royal highness to lend me some legitimacy as I looked for Moll. Surely, no one would dare ask me what I was doing there while in the arms of a prince?

The "band" had just started a lively new tune as he led me to the dance floor. I'd have been outed immediately if Moll hadn't forced me to play the role of Dashing Suitor for the past fifteen years. I was thanking the gods the whole way now for every agonizing practice session.

Yep, under the threat of violence, I'd learned every reel, waltz, and cotillion ever created. New dances, old ones, didn't matter. I was pretty much a master. Which made it super annoying when Duncan and I glided onto the floor and the whole affair felt more like a barroom brawl than a dance. We folded into the mix easy enough, taking our place in the crowd of couples moving clockwise as a unit. But as I tried to pull off a spin so I could get a full 360 of the dancers around us in hopes of catching a glimpse of Moll, we bumped knees.

Hard.

"Oh!" I muttered, flashing him an apologetic smile before quickly resuming my search for a certain redhead. "Pardon me! I can be so clumsy at times."

"Not a problem. But I must know...What or who are you so intent on finding? A better dance partner, maybe?"

Damn. I hadn't even considered that I was being rude, which was far less forgivable than my ill-fitting dress or sloppy eating habits when it came to pretending I belonged.

"Not at all! I'm just, uh, taking in all the gorgeous gowns. Did you see that gold brocade number over there? She looks like a living goddess."

He spared the dress a glance before turning his full attention back to me as we rounded the next corner. His full attention was...a lot. The thick, wavy hair brushing his collar. The jawline that looked like it had been chiseled out of marble. The piercing gray eyes studying me with such curiosity. But it really was the solitary dimple that took it over the top.

This man might be a proper gentleman on the face of it, but something told me he was a rogue at heart—I didn't know if it was his intensity, or the strength in his arms as he spun me around that tipped me off that I needed to be careful.

Or maybe it's just that damn dimple.

My pulse stuttered and I went for the spin move again, promptly stomping on his foot.

"Damn it to hell," I hissed under my breath. "I am so, so sorry. Really..."

"Don't worry about it," he said, a grin tugging at his firm lips, "But it might go a bit easier for us both if you let me lead."

I could feel the heat working its way up my neck as I realized he was right. In every fake ball or fete scenario with Moll, *I'd* been Prince Charming. I had no clue how to cede control.

"Don't think. Just feel. Ready?" He must've sensed my hesitation, because suddenly, he tightened his grip, and that dimple flashed. "Here we go!"

He didn't wait for a response. A second later, we were skittering across the floor like a pair of skaters on ice. At first, I tried to fight it, but then I let go. Relaxing my muscles, I let the rhythm of the music flow through me, felt the subtle pressure of Duncan's fingers on my hips, urging me this way and that. It didn't take long before I was completely swept up, like a leaf on the winds of a wild, giddy storm. The music reached a crescendo and I realized with a stab of disappointment that the dance was almost over.

He twirled me left, then right, before bending me back into a low dip and staying there. Holding me steady, he stared down at me, eyes gleaming, his smile an echo of mine.

"That's more like it."

I was about to reply when I caught a flash of deep, red curls in my periphery, and I remembered myself.

Moll.

What the hell was I doing?

I tightened my grip on his forearm and tugged his sleeve, struggling to catch my breath.

"Excuse me, but I'm feeling a bit dizzy. Can you—"

He instantly righted me to stand, concern knitting his brow. "Sorry about that. Should we get some air?"

"No. No thank you. I think I'll get a glass of punch and have a sit down for a few minutes."

But he insisted on navigating me through the swarm of dancers—none of whom were Moll—and walked me to the punch bowl.

"He's a very lucky man."

"What? Who?" I asked, sparing him a quick glance before resuming my search.

"Whoever it is that you've been looking for all night." He reached down and took my hand, his thumb grazing the inside of my wrist in a way that sent a hot bolt of lust straight to my belly. "If you don't wind up finding him, come find me. I'll make it easy. I'll be by the buffet table until the clock strikes midnight. I don't know what he's got that I don't, but if you'd give me ten more minutes, I'd make you forget all about him..."

His eyes were full of promise as he held my gaze and backed away, melting into the crowd.

"Holy hell," I muttered, swallowing hard. I'd never in a million years imagined I could be attracted to a noble. How could a woman respect a man who'd never known a day of hard work in his life? But I'd been here in Little Alabaster less than two hours, and here I was drooling after a prince with firm hands and a devilish dimple.

Pathetic.

I ran a shaky hand over my upswept wig and threw my shoulders back. I was here on a mission, and it was time to get back to that—I had to get Moll out of here. Then, I could go back where I belonged and forget all about this place and the people in it.

I did another round of the room, sticking close to the perimeter in hopes of not missing anything, but there were no more Molly sightings. I was starting to wonder if maybe she'd decided to cut out early and head home. One more walk through, and if I didn't find her, I'd do the same. Now that I'd witnessed the sheer size of this place, it seemed very possible that Moll and Heinrich hadn't even crossed paths. Besides, it was nearing midnight. The ball would be ending soon. Thank the gods.

I made my way toward the card room again, pausing to peek in. The King's bounty of gold was still piled high, but his seat was empty. Pressing myself against the wall and out of sight, I focused in on the chatter of the other men at the table.

"Robbie is right. We might as well call it. He won't be giving us a chance to win back our money. Not tonight, at least."

"I knew as soon as he caught sight of the chippy with the red hair and those glorious tits, he'd be a goner."

Red hair. Glorious tits.

Molly.

My stomach churned as I closed my eyes and strained to hear over the noise of the music behind me. What were they saying?

Maybe...something something...the gardens...something something...followed behind like a man possessed.

I jerked upright and made a beeline for the powder room to dig my bag out of the trash. Then, I headed for the open double doors I'd passed a dozen times by now.

Cold, fresh air curled through the opening. Just

outside was a long pathway to the palace gardens. I hadn't seen anyone brave enough to venture out with the chill in the air, but apparently, King Heinrich did what he damn well pleased.

"She's okay. I would know. I would feel it if she wasn't okay."

Mind you, I'd felt *something*, or I wouldn't be here in the first place. Even so, I kept the low litany of positive affirmations going as I took a quick glance around to make sure no one was watching. Then, I slipped out the doors onto the garden path. I kept my eyes glued to the ground in front of me, trying not to think about how there were two sets of prints pressed into the frost. One big, one small and very obviously a set of heels with the shape of the imprint. I just kept moving, one foot in front of the other. And soon enough, a woman's frame was silhouetted in the distance.

I wanted to call out, but that would be foolhardy. Instead, I walked as fast as I could, hands icy with dread. The rest unfolded like a bad dream.

"Moll?" I called softly, my voice so hoarse it was almost unrecognizable.

The figure didn't budge. Was it a statue maybe?

I moved closer, but I didn't have a chance to repeat her name. My attention shifted to the man lying on the ground a few feet away. The low shriek that escaped my lips was camouflaged by the peeling of the bells as the clock in the chapel tower struck midnight.

The man's face was pale and lifeless, body limp.

Blood, so red and thick it looked black, spread over his bright white waistcoat, the stain growing bigger and bigger even as I watched. And protruding from the center of it, one, very familiar looking, crystalline slipper, its stiletto heel buried to the hilt.

Worse than that?

If there was any doubt that it was King Heinrich, the crown still jammed on his head over his blond hair left no doubt.

And he was dead as a fucking doornail.

"H-harm?" She whispered my name.

I turned back to Molly, who stood a few yards away, trembling from head to toe. Her dress was torn to the waist, one of her breasts exposed and bleeding from what looked like scratch marks. Her eyes were all pupil and out of focus as she blinked up at me, her face almost as white as the full moon shining above us.

"I-I think I did something bad."

Her voice was reedy and thin as she swayed toward me. My palms were clammy, and my head began to throb. I found myself wishing Druzilla was here to slap me. Instead, I focused on my friend and crammed the sensation back to the darkest recesses of my mind.

Don't look at it. Don't think about it. Focus on the task at hand, and only the task at hand. This is an extraction mission now, so get to it.

"Nope. It's okay, Moll. You didn't do anything wrong," I murmured, already scoping the surrounding area and formulating a plan. "We're going to fix it, okay? Me and you. You just do what I tell you, and we're going to be fine. Got it?"

She clenched her chattering teeth and nodded. "G-got it."

"Did you tell him your name at any point?"

"No. He thinks I'm a noblewoman named Francesca visiting from Bryngarde. The Gris Isles."

"Did you see anyone you knew? Genevieve Salim?"

She shook her head. "I saw her near the food when I first got here and made sure to avoid her. She never saw me."

I hoped she was right. "Okay, that's good. We're going to exit the gardens from the back way and cross the moat to get off palace grounds. No one will come looking for the two of you for a while. It will be like we were never here. We'll be back in The Hollow before you know it."

But first…

"Turn around for a second, okay, love? Cover yourself while I…tidy up."

She hesitated and then nodded, giving me her back. "Okay."

The breath sawed in and out of my lungs as I approached Heinrich's body.

It's just a dummy, made of straw, I told myself. *This is all fake. A test to see if you pass.*

I stepped over the body, one foot on either side of his hips for leverage and then took hold of the shoe and yanked with all my might. Other than the blood running even faster, it didn't seem to budge. I tried again, this time putting my back into it. For a second it seemed to give, but then stuck again, catching on his sternum maybe? Hell, I lifted his body with the force of my pull, before he hit the ground again with a thump when I released my grip.

"Son of a—" I was interrupted by a sharp, familiar cry overhead, and I recognized Fetch's call. He'd followed me? More than that though, his cry cut through me.

A warning.

Not a moment later, the sounds of horns, and a voice called out, deep and resonant.

"King Heinrich, it's time for your speech!"

My stomach dropped as distant footsteps grew closer. We were out of time. There was no way I was getting this fucking shoe out. Damn Xavier and his fucking craftsmanship.

"Harm?"

"Yup. All set, let's get going," I whispered, reluctantly releasing my hold on the shoe and rushing back to Molly's side. "Give me your other shoe," I demanded.

She handed it over without question. I did my best to help her cover her bare skin even as I dragged her with me, toward the south side of the palace. Luckily, I was right about one thing. There was an exit at the back of the gardens, and we hurried through it. Once we reached the moat surrounding the palace grounds, I scooped up a heavy stone, wrapped my wig around it and the slipper, tying the loose long ends of the hair around the weighted bundle and hurled them into the water without slowing down.

Please sink. Please, gods, let that bundle sink.

We'd almost reached the scaffolding to cross the moat when screams cut through the night air, and lights flooded the space behind us.

"It's the new king! Gods above! He's been attacked!"

CHAPTER 5

I heard the crashing waves before I saw them. The beach was near enough I should have been able to reach out and touch the water.

But how?

The sea was at the western edge of the earth, hundreds of miles away, and the only deep body of water I'd ever seen aside from those in a ratty old picture book was the murky moat sludge outside Alabaster Palace. But as I ran harder toward that magical sound, the ocean came into view. And, gods, was it grand. Deep blue crests bent like blown glass and then scattered into white froth across the sugary sand.

I took a quick glance up and down the beach and reached for the hem of my nightdress.

"If you go, I'll go."

I turned to see a raven-haired man in his thirties a few yards behind me dressed in all black, a scabbard hanging from his lean hips. His face was all sharp angles and onyx

86

eyes—scars faint but there, whispered across the bare skin I could see.

Danger, this was one danger incarnate. Like a predator and he was looking at me like I was...prey.

His eyes roved my body, crown to toe, as if he were drinking me in. Desire lit his features, a slow grin building across his lips that did not ease my concerns that he saw me as something to conquer.

I should've been afraid, but somehow, I wasn't. "Do I know you?" I asked, unsure if he heard me over the whipping winds.

He nodded. "In a manner of speaking. But the better question is, do you know you?"

I frowned. "Are you a ghost or something?" They were notorious for cryptic double-talk, after all.

Before he could answer, a bolt of lightning split the sky as black clouds rushed in. The dark stranger looked up and let out a low sigh. "As much as it pains me to admit, there's no time for swimming today. You need to open your eyes now, Harmony."

I followed his gaze to the ominous clouds. "Or I could just sleep some more."

"I wish you could." His face was filled with a longing that made my heart ache. "But you can't finish this part of your story until you turn the page. Go on, now...Molly needs you."

"Stop! No, I said stop!"

Moll's shrill cries penetrated the haze of sleep that clung to me, and my lids popped open.

"Get your bloody hands off me!"

I rubbed the grit from my eyes and then reached down to pat Moll's forehead.

"You're alright, Moll. It's just me. You're safe. No one's going to hurt you."

She quieted instantly and burrowed her head into my lap with a sigh. She'd been out cold for at least a few hours, which was a relief. I wasn't sure she'd be able to fall asleep after all she'd been through. Hell, I wasn't sure I would either, but apparently, we'd both managed, which was good. I'd need my wits…every bit of them if we had any chance of getting out of this mess alive.

Which made it even more annoying that I'd dreamt of *him* again. The dark stranger who spoke in riddles, and made my belly ache with a strange pressure that—

Focus, Harmony!

The last thing I needed to be thinking about was a stupid dream when we were knee-deep in a fucking nightmare.

Once I'd realized there was no way we were getting out of Little Alabaster the night before, we'd circled back, taking another path to get a little more distance between us and the palace. Fetch led us to the forest as I did my best to cover our tracks on the frozen ground, all while trying to keep one step ahead of the shouting guards. By the time we'd come across a tiny hunting shack made of tightly crossed-hatched logs deep in the woods, we were exhausted and shivering.

The sudden and intense freezing rain that fell was a

blessing and a curse. It would help cover our scents and maybe muck up the scene of the murder, but it left the hut even colder than it would have been.

We'd huddled together under a horse blanket, Fetch perched on the arm of a rickety chair.

Now, seeing the space for the first time lit by the early morning sun, I breathed a small sigh of relief. Hunting gear hung on hooks along the back wall along with a heavy flannel shirt, and some riding jodhpurs. Beneath the clothes sat a pair of massive, muddy boots that were too large to be of any use unless I was looking to trip and break my neck.

The plan that I'd begun to form last night looked weak in the light of day, but the clothes left behind by some hunter would help. I'd be able to get out of this too-small dress and head into Little Alabaster for some supplies for said plan without calling too much atten-tion to myself. I'd need the stones we'd sewn onto her dress; they had some value and right at the moment, were the only thing I had for bartering.

First order of business, though? Making sure Moll looked nothing like Moll the next time anyone in this town saw her. Which meant a drastic make-under that she was going to hate with the fire of a thousand suns. I'd have to cut and dye her scarlet locks at the very least. Hopefully, she'd forgive me once we were on the other side of this and she'd had a chance to realize I was doing it to save her life, not ruin it.

Knowing her as I did, the trauma she suffered

would be shoved down deep, and she'd focus on the fact that she was out of the running for any lord's hand in marriage.

I still didn't know the whole story of what happened in the gardens, but the fact that both of them still had their clothes on when I found them gave me some hope that she'd stiletto'd him before he'd actually raped—

"Harm?"

"Yeah, love?"

"I'm going to wind up swinging by the neck for this, aren't I?"

Okay, so maybe this thing was too big to tamp down this time.

I'd looked at our problem from every angle before sleep had claimed me. I put the odds of us surviving this at less than twenty percent, and even that was generous. Any hope we had at all relied on us both keeping calm and quiet…

"Definitely not. You're going to be fine."

"I'm so, so sorry. I didn't mean to kill him. He just wouldn't stop, and—" She let out a little hiccup and I had to take a second to rein in my rage.

"Not your fault. He was an animal, Moll. You saved countless other women from having to live that nightmare. That makes you a hero in my book."

That part was true. Every word of it. Now we just had to make sure our Moll didn't go from "hero" to "martyr".

"What are we going to do?"

I patted her and scuttled away so I could face her as she sat up.

"I have a plan, but you're not going to like it."

She blinked her bloodshot blue eyes at me and swallowed hard. "Does it involve you leaving me here alone? Because I'm feeling like it does, and that's literally the only thing I don't think I could handle right now."

Panic had seeped into her voice as she leaned in and squeezed my hand hard enough to make me wince.

"We do better when we stick together," she continued in a rush. "In fact, that's exactly what you tried to tell me when I was planning to go to that stupid ball all week. You said, 'Moll, you don't need to do this. I know you want to get us out of this shithole, but if we stick together, we'll figure it out eventually.' And you were right, I was a fool to believe in happily ever afters, to believe a prince was a better deal," she whispered urgently, her gaze pleading. "None of this would've happened if I'd listened to you."

I couldn't let her lingering terror from the night before sway me from the plan I had in mind. "But it happened. You did what you felt you had to do. You went to the ball because you wanted to take care of us." I had to look away, my eyes tingling with unshed tears. "So now you have to let *me* try to take care of us, okay?"

"Right." Tears leaked down her face. "I make the mess, and you clean it up…"

"No. No!" I tugged her chin up until we locked eyes. "*Heinrich* made the mess. Never forget that, Moll. This wasn't your fault. But people of his ilk don't see it that way, so they're going to be looking for someone else to blame. My guess is that Little Alabaster will stay on lockdown as they search—we can't get back to The Hollow. Not yet. We've got to hide you in plain sight until we can figure out how to get over the Cradle. And the only way to do that is by making sure you look nothing like the woman who left the ball with Heinrich. I've got to go into town without you to get some supplies, which means you have to be brave and stay here. I'll be as quick as I can."

Dead broke and with very little knowledge of the surrounding area, it'd be a miracle if I got back before sundown, but I wasn't about to tell her that.

A soft chortling sound caught my attention, and I automatically stuck my arm out for Fetch to land. He lighted on my forearm and worked his way up to my shoulder.

"Hey there, buddy. Did you sleep alright?"

The bird craned his neck to nuzzle my face.

"I'll leave him here with you. That way you aren't alone."

"No," Molly cut in, shaking her head. "You need to take him. We've no money, and he can maybe snag you a rabbit or nick something from a street vendor. He needs to stay with you. I'll be alright."

She stiffened her chin, but it wobbled anyway, and my heart broke and I reached for her.

"Moll—"

"Stop!" She drew back and held up a hand. "Don't hug me or get mushy right now. I'm barely keeping it together as is. Probably best if you go anyway. That way I can have a proper come apart alone. Then, by the time you get back, I'll be the old Moll. Ready for whatever comes our way."

She cracked her knuckles and pinched one eye closed in the saddest little wink I'd ever seen. It didn't stop her face from crumpling under the weight of her fear.

"Just...swear you'll come back, Harm. Promise."

I pushed myself to stand and reached out my free hand to help her up.

There was only one thing that could keep me from her, and in that case, I'd be too dead to feel guilty for breaking my promise anyway. So, I crossed two fingers over my chest.

"I swear."

She studied my face for far too long, as if she was trying to memorize it.

I gave her hands a shake. "Cut that out. I'm going to be fine. I'll be back before you know it. In the meantime, do *not* leave the shack for any reason—if someone comes close, just hide under the blanket in the corner. And don't make any noise." I reached down and hefted the lopping shears and rusty knife from the table and handed them to her. "If someone should come, and try to hurt you, or take you—"

She nodded grimly. "Make sure I take a piece of them with me. Got it. What about you, though?"

I lifted the hem of my dress and gestured to the hilt of the dagger tucked inside my boot. "I'm all set. Can you pull the stones off your dress?"

With that, I made quick work of changing from my gown into the oversized hunting gear. It was large but once I'd tied the shirt at the back and tucked the jodhpurs into my shitkickers, I was off to the races.

"Good idea, you can maybe trade them for stuff, you think?" Moll reached down to yank the baubles off her dress, careful to pull all the threads away until all that was left was a mound of faux gemstones sparkling in her palm.

I took them with a nod. That was a good start. More than enough to get a pair of practical shoes for her and some clothes at the very least. I wasn't sure what the value of goods were like outside The Hollow. I could only hope my stones were enough to get what we needed.

"Come on," Moll said, waving a hand for me to turn around. She took my mass of curls down from what was left of the bun I'd fashioned to tuck under my wig and then pulled it into a ponytail. Her nose wrinkled as she plopped a dusty hat on my head for good measure, then stepped back to admire her handiwork. "There we go. You look totally different with dark hair and in that outfit, you easily pass for a stable girl or farmworker."

I didn't want to say goodbye. It felt too final. Instead, I popped off a salute and tried to keep my tone light. "Back in a flash with supplies. The rain barrel outside is full, so at least you'll have water until I bring some food."

With that, I headed out into the brisk cold, Fetch firmly latched onto my shoulder. I stopped to take my own fill of the icy rainwater. Then, I slunk away from the shack, straining to hear even the slightest rustle of leaves in the forest around me. As I navigated my way through the dense woods, Fetch lifted off and flew alongside me. I ran through the checklist in my mind.

First on the list, I'd need to get dye for her hair. As it stood, with her ripped dress and scarlet tresses, we were as good as dead if they found her like this—her for killing the king, me for aiding her. My plan was to find the seedier part of town to make a deal for some clothes as well as some less common items I needed. On the way back, I'd send Fetch ahead to hopefully score us a rabbit or something. If I managed all that, we might have a shot at surviving long enough to get us out of Little Alabaster with our heads still attached.

Relieved to have a plan—albeit a sketchy one—in place, I broke into a jog. If I had it right in my mind, the merchant center of town was just a couple miles north. When I got through the first mile without issue, I let out a long, shuddering breath. I'd half expected to get pounced on by a pack of slavering dogs right off the jump. For the first time since I'd seen Moll's silhouette in the garden, an ember of hope flickered to life in my chest, thawing the hunk of fear wrapped around my heart.

Maybe we actually had a chance...

Time was not on my side, though. I hurried, sprinting until the smell of wood smoke tickled my nose. Slowing, I let out a whistle which sent Fetch circling back to perch on my hand.

"I think the shops and such are right past that copse of trees," I murmured, stroking the bird's head gently. "It's all about confidence, Fetch. We stroll out there like we belong, find the entrance to The Smudge, and call it good. Right?"

Right.

The falcon didn't look any more convinced than I felt, and it took me another ten minutes to work up the nerve.

"Ready, steady..." I huffed out a breath. "For real now. One, two, three..." I paused and cracked my knuckles one at a time. "On your marks, get set...ah, fuck it."

I grit my teeth and march toward the center of Little Alabaster, wondering if the twitch in my eye was visible to others, or just one of those inside jobs where only I could feel it.

You've got this. You belong here.

I most certainly did not, but I had to fake it just long enough.

The sound of low chatter in the near distance almost made me turn around, but I forced myself to keep going. Once I broke through the tree line, I didn't allow my steps to falter. I just made a beeline straight onto the cobbled streets and into a small crowd of people gathered in front of a pub. Only then did I slow, the blood rushing in my ears receding enough to hear but kept my eyes on my feet.

"I heard his chest was in ruins. Just a mess of blood and gore," one man said. "The girl stabbed him a dozen times or more. Bloodthirsty little thing, seems like...I guess that's how women from Bryngarde behave."

The observation was just that. No censure or sadness in his voice. He was just stating the facts—or fictions, in this case—as he'd heard them.

"Yeah? I heard from the castle cook that she bit his ear off as well. And if the talk is right," the woman speaking dropped her voice low, "he deserved it."

Interesting.

I lifted my gaze from the street long enough to take stock of the people around me. Some looked like nobility, but there were also a fair number of merchants, traders, and other working folks. Well-dressed by Hollow standards but not dripping in wealth like so many at the ball last night. Judging by the expressions on their faces, not a one was a fan of the new king.

That was good.

Better than good. It meant that, even if the Crown was hellbent on finding Heinrich's killer, there was a solid faction of people in Little Alabaster that didn't care one way or another. And maybe even some who felt he'd gotten his due.

In short? Moll and I weren't *completely* surrounded by enemies looking to see us hanged, which was a small relief.

I backed away and was about to start scanning the shops when one of the women, dressed in a smart, gray servant's uniform, spoke up. The crest on her shirt marked her as a servant of some nobility.

"I'd better get going. Milady gave me exactly one hour to visit my dying mother this morning, and if I'm late getting back, she'll dock my pay."

With that, she turned on her heel and walked toward what appeared to be an ivy-covered wall on the other side of the street. Fascinated, I watched as she didn't veer off or slow down. She just strode straight into...and then through it. It shimmered and fuzzed, reforming a heartbeat later, none the worse for wear.

I jerked back, glancing around to see if anyone had seen what I'd just seen. Apparently either they hadn't, or weren't impressed in the least, because they'd already gone back to gossiping about the dead king. I cast my memory back to all the crazy rumors I'd heard about life in Little Alabaster in an effort to make sense of what I'd just seen, ticking them off in my mind.

1. Noble women here only wore a dress once, and then abandoned it to her closets, never to be worn again.
2. Homes were so large, they had as many bathrooms as they did bedrooms, and each had a soaking tub that could be filled with steaming hot water on a whim.
3. The men would go on hunts and sometimes just leave the kill for scavenging animals because they couldn't be bothered to collect their spoils.

And the one that pissed me off more than any other?

1. Food was so abundant, there was *actually* a place behind the palace where the king and his nobles tossed what they hadn't eaten so that it could be used to fertilize the soil later on. We did this in The Hollow too, except only with the inedible parts of foods, like eggshells, seeds, and rinds. But according to gossip, the one behind the palace contained finer food than most Hollow dinner tables. Sending it our way would make us feel entitled and serve as an annoying reminder to the wealthy that some people were starving out there, so they dumped it into The Rot instead.

Bastards.

But I hadn't heard of a magical wall.

I took one more glance around, sucked in a deep breath, and then headed straight for—and then through—the fake wall with only a minor gasp on my part. Other than just a bit of resistance that felt like no more than a stiff wind, I felt nothing of the magic.

I took in my new surroundings with a frown. It wasn't as bad as The Hollow, but nowhere near as nice as the rest of Little Alabaster. Muddy streets. Stores with crooked, worn signs. The familiar, if faint, whiff of sewage.

The Smudge.

Like most of the chatter about life here, I hadn't thought about it much, you know, in the midst of surviving. It was just another place I never thought I'd see. The 'wall' I'd gone through was a magical projection of some sort to hide the eyesore on the other side of it. An illusion so that the betters weren't forced to see how the other half lived. A place for their servants to be out of sight, out of mind.

I let out a snort, which Fetch seemed to mimic. "Fucking hell. Those in power really are ghouls, aren't they?"

People in The Smudge bustled more quickly, not so much time for idle chatter here, their heads down as they hurried to wherever they had to go. I dove into the fray and made my way down the street. I kept my head down too, peeking up every so often to glance at the shops lining the street.

Harrod's Meat.

Sewing Sundry.

Mabel's Bathhouse.

Part of me wished I could afford to go inside that last one. I took a surreptitious sniff of my underarm and winced at the sour smell of fear mixed with moldy straw and a rank twang of old man sweat from the hunting shirt.

"Flowers, trinkets for a loved one…information…" a low female voice called. "Flowers, trinkets, information…"

Surely, it couldn't be as easy as that?

I followed the women's call and found a forty-something brunette seated on a rickety stool next to a flower cart. It was painted bright orange, the color of an autumn squash, and emblazoned with the words, *Gayelette's Ha'penny Boteek, OPEN Sundays 8-10 AM* on the side painted in green. The cart itself held only a silver tray filled with cheap baubles and jewelry and three wooden barrels filled with blooms, but they were mostly deadheads or withered and brown.

"Hiya," she said, flashing me a row of stained, brown teeth. She turned her head to one side, let out a stream of tobacco spit and then faced me again. "Posey for your Prince, lass?"

I drew back at the question, an image of Duncan

Westerly flitting through my mind. It took a second to realize it was just a turn of phrase.

"No thank you! I was hoping for some…information, you said?"

"That's one of my wares, yes." She studied me so intently; I had to resist the urge to cover my face. "And I believe I can help you find what you seek. Ha'penny for one question."

She held out a grubby hand and wriggled her fingers.

"I don't have any coin. Are you willing to trade?"

She spit out another stream of tobacco juice and scratched at her sagging boob. "Depends. What have you got?"

"Semi-precious gemstones. Faceted and perfect for crafting fine jewelry."

"Show me."

I reached into the pocket of my dirty jodhpurs and fingered the stones, being careful to only take out three. Then I shook them into my palm and held it out for her inspection.

One brow rose high on her forehead, but other than that, she gave nothing away.

"Alright, then. One stone, one question."

"Only one question for each stone?" I said with a wince.

"Yep." She reached out and snagged the yellow citrine from my hand before I could close it. "That's question one. Looks like you've got enough for two more, so think carefully before you speak this time."

Fuck me, she was canny. I wanted to pry her hand open and take back what was mine, but the longer I spent here, the longer Moll was at the shack, alone, vulnerable, and terrified.

I was still contemplating my second question when Gayelette spoke, her expression softer than it had been a moment ago.

"I can see you're in a bad way, and I'm not heartless. Just give me the squarish purple one you're hiding, and you can keep the rest. I'll tell you exactly what you need to know."

I stared at her, mouth wide. How had she known about that one in my pocket?

She waved a hand at my face. "Be careful with that mouth open. The black flies around these parts are a whole lot worse than your usual type and you don't want them thinking it's an invitation."

I snapped my mouth shut and replaced the stones in my hand for the cushion-cut amethyst nestled in my pocket. She plucked it from my fingers with a satisfied hum and stuffed it into her own pocket.

Before I could form my first question, she started talking. "You can purchase some cheap threads and shoes at Ginny's cross the street. The blacksmith you're needing is Smitty, four doors down from Ginny. As for the other...you'll be wanting The O'Donnellys. They spend most of their time over at The Hoof and Saddle tavern on the corner at the very end of the road. They're closed on Sundays but come back tomorrow and bring something of great value or find you some cash. When you get there, rap on the door three times, then two, then three again." She held up both hands. "Be forewarned. What you seek won't come cheap. Tell 'em Gayelette sent you, that'll get you through the door."

Well, shit. She was a Whisper; she had to be. And a strong one at that. Far more powerful than any I'd ever encountered in The Hollow. That was the only way she could've known the questions I had without me saying them out loud. What really had my stomach churning, though…

What else did she know about me?

Her knowing eyes held mine, softening a little. "Don't fear. I've got secrets of my own, dearie. Besides, I'm not in the market of sharing my customers' private lives. Bad for business."

"Thank you." Her words settled my nerves some, but as I walked away, I knew the exchange would join the pile of worries weighing heavy on my mind.

"It won't be easy, dearie," she called after me, causing me to wheel around. "Just know this; You're exactly where you're meant to be, and you have every-thing you need to succeed. Stop fighting every step of the way and open yourself to what the universe is telling you." Her voice dropped to a whisper, and I could not help myself. I moved closer, pulse pounding in my throat.

"Open your eyes and you will see who to trust." She held out a wilted red rose. "Open your mind to the possibilities of the gifts *you* possess. Open your ears and you will hear those who speak. Only then can you fulfill your destiny. And remember, pressure makes diamonds…but you already knew that, didn't you?"

She shot me a wink as I accepted the flower in my numb hand.

"That there is on the house. Now go on with you."

CHAPTER 6

I grabbed the easy stuff first, knowing that I would need as much time as I could get for the last bit. In any case, the local blacksmith, an old fellow who went by Smitty Smithy, wouldn't rent me space until after ten am.

In the meantime, I found myself wandering through The Smudge, taking in as much as I could with my hat pulled low and head down. I had assumed it would be miles better than The Hollow but...if there was a betterment, it was only by the edge of a cat's whiskers. People were still struggling. There was still sickness, and scrawny kids without enough meat on their bones running rampant.

The biggest difference was the people in the streets openly using their abilities as Whispers. Nothing fancy, but magic was magic, and I could see how helpful it would be to have a skill even as simple as being able to light a fire without a match or see in the dark.

When the sun was a bit higher in the sky, I worked my way back to the forge and sat on the bench outside. Fetch rested on the rooftop closest to me, his eyes searching all around us for prey or a bauble to snag.

I shook my head. *Not here, Fetch. I have a feeling we'd be caught.*

As I waited, the sound of the bellows inside, the whoosh of the flames, it all lulled me, taking me back to a time that Pawpaw had been alive, and things… things had been simpler. Maybe still hard, but there had been bright spots.

"You're a real natural there, Cinderella!" Pawpaw clapped me on the shoulder as I held the tongs in hand and lifted my creation from the oil barrel. "But what is it?"

"I took a couple of horseshoes, and I wove them together with that round bar you had over there." I gingerly touched the metal, then gripped it tight. The warm steel felt good in my tired hands. At twelve, the tongs and hammer exhausted me.

He chuckled and took it from me. "But what is it? You made it quick enough."

"I could see it in my head." I shrugged and looked at my feet. "It's a puzzle."

He tucked a calloused finger under my chin, lifting my eyes to meet his. Kindness, only kindness, shone back at me. "What's the goal?"

"To get the ring off." The two horseshoes were connected from each heel to a bit of chain, which connected to the other horseshoe's heel. Around the chain was a solid ring.

Pawpaw squinted one eye and shook the metal a few times. "Well...I don't know, but I think you might have made it impossible to solve."

I grinned and wiggled my hands. He handed over the shoes, chain and ring and I turned away from him. In a quick series of motions, I twisted the rings and gave them a flip. When the ring slid right off into my palm, I spun back and showed him. "See? Like magic!"

His jaw dropped.

"Put it back on now."

I turned away again, not wanting to give away my secret, but he stopped me, a bit of fear in his eyes though he tried to smile.

"No, show me, child. Show me the trick so I can see."

It was only years later that I realized he'd been worried I might be a Whisper. Afraid that I might be dragged from our home for practicing magic, which was forbidden in The Hollow. Turned out I was nothing more than a clever kid with a big imagination and a knack for metal. Not much had changed on that front.

A knock on the wooden wall above my head startled me out of my memories.

Smitty Smithy stuck his head through the doorway, his hair capped under a tight bandana, his skin coated in coal dust which made his amber-hued eyes even more intense.

"Huh. You came back, wasn't sure you would. You got two hours for me first. Then, two hours for you."

I nodded and stood. "As we agreed."

Putting my sack of goods in the corner, I took a quick look at the forge and set up.

Better even than Pawpaw's. The anvil edge was crisp and sharp, the tongs didn't squeak and the handle of the two-pound hammer was smooth, not a single splinter was going to find me today.

I rolled the hammer handle and gave the anvil an experimental tap. The ringing cleared away any doubts.

"A knife you said? You got a style in mind?" I turned to where Smitty slumped into a short backed wooden chair.

"Partially finished. Need its shape and edge, then a handle. Make it nice enough to sell, whatever style you like."

Two hours was not a lot, especially when I saw the lump of steel that was his idea of 'partially finished'. He was testing me for sure. Not that it mattered, I didn't need him to hire me, I just needed the blade to be good enough that he honored his time commitment to me.

Using the tongs, I picked up the vaguely knife-shaped hunk of raw material and shoved it into the coal.

Wiggling it in under the first layer of coal, I reached for the crank handle of the air blower with my left hand—the piping went right into the base of the fire in the forge.

Hard not to be impressed, it was a far better setup than I was used to.

I needed the steel hot enough to manipulate it easily if I wanted to get this job done in time, so I worked the crank handle hard for a few minutes, the flames in the coal flickering brighter and brighter.

I settled into a steady pattern of steel in, crank the handle, steel out, hammer out the shape. Over and over, I worked until I had a beautiful blade that already I was loath to give up. The cutting edge was curved, like Fetch's belly, rising to the deadly point at the end. The spine of the blade I drew down to a gentle rising point, then dropped it away to where the tang began. Happy with it, I set about to tempering the steel.

Sweat dripped down my face and into my eyes, but I didn't slow. I could see exactly where each blow needed to land. Could see exactly how to finish the knife so that it would stand out in the crowd.

But that would come at the end. I went to the work bench where the handle materials were set—wood, bone, leather and some stone though that would be a right bitch. "What do you want for the handle?"

"Surprise me."

Fucking hell, if I thought it wasn't a test before, it sure as shit was now. I let my hands drift over a few things, stopping finally over a black piece of wood, charred on the outside. I scooped it up and got back to work.

It took me time, but once the handle was done, smooth and carved to be comfortable for a hand bigger than my own, the black of it was deep and glossy, like glass instead of wood.

Next was edging the blade.

"There's a pedal over there, pump it and the sanding paper runs on its own."

I blinked and saw what Smitty was referring to. Damn, a step up indeed.

"How…"

"Here, I'll pedal it, you sand."

The blacksmith joined me, using one foot to pump the machine to life. The sandpaper was on a vertical roll, and it began to spin, faster and faster. I pressed the knife to it, and grinned. "This is awesome."

The edge was unbelievably sharp in no time; it was ready for the last piece I could see in my mind.

"You got any wax?" I asked. Smitty dropped a lump of black goopy something in front of me. "What the hell is that?"

"Pine tar, a few other things." Smitty grunted as he flopped back into his chair. I had no idea how long I'd been working, but I had to finish this knife, finish my own project and get my ass back to Moll.

Pine tar and other things. It would have to do. I'd seen the acid etching barrel next to the oil, and I wanted him to be happy with what I was doing.

Taking pieces of the pine-tar-and-other-things, I rolled it in my hands, working it like sticky clay. Thinner and thinner I went until I had it where I wanted it. Then I laid it across the blade, avoiding the sharpened edge, spreading the pine-tar-and-other-things anywhere I didn't want the acid to etch.

I dunked the blade into the acid bath, counting down, and then pulling it out.

Satisfied, I used a chunk of wood from the floor, scraped off the pine-tar-and-other-things, and handed the blade to the Smitty.

He swiped it with his apron, his eyebrows shooting up as he studied the knife. "Where did you come up with this pattern?"

"An old book of fairytales I used to have. Had writing like that in it." It had been so long since I'd seen it, I couldn't remember the stories in detail, but the pictures inside along with the spiky letters and fancy scrollwork were still etched in my mind. "Seemed fitting for the blade. If you're happy with that—"

"Take as much time as you want in the forge. Tomorrow too, if you need it." Smitty stood. "Clean up before you go. You can use any of the scrap materials over there."

He thumbed to a pile of steel in the corner. Maybe he saw it as scrap, but I...I saw it as a fucking gold mine.

I tried not to let my emotions get the best of me as I shot him a shaky smile.

"You got it."

With a grunt he let himself out the door, and I all but dove into the pile of metal. No one was going to get the drop on us while we were stuck in Alabaster, not if I could help it. And I had a sweet little idea cooking up in my head, just for Moll.

A weapon that even she could use—a weapon no one would see coming until it was too late…

CHAPTER 7

Act like you belong, and no one will suspect a thing.

I mentally repeated the mantra as I hoisted the sack I carried higher over my shoulder. It had taken all morning and half of the afternoon, but I'd managed to get everything I needed, and then some. Now, all I had to do was get back to Moll without anyone noticing me and my sack of goods.

A guard strode out of the nearest alley, his helmet turning side to side, searching. I sucked in a breath as he locked his eyes on me but let it out when he wrinkled his nose in disgust rather than calling out to me.

To him, I must've looked like any other resident of The Smudge, certainly not of the ilk to be worthy of the King's attentions, never mind anyone capable of killing him. The guard's eyes registered disdain, not careful scrutiny. I tugged my hat lower over my eyes and started walking again until the sudden sound of frantic footsteps on stone behind me sent my pulse hammering.

Had that guard changed his mind and circled back with some of his friends?

I took a half step to start running, when a group of teen boys nearly bowled me over as they passed, one catching me in the shoulder and grabbing at my sack.

"Fuck off with you brats!" I let out a huff of air, heart pattering hard. I spared a quick glance toward the sky to make sure Fetch still circled. He tipped his head and gave a solid side-eye. I wiggled my fingers at him as I muttered under my breath. "I'm hurrying, I'm hurrying."

I didn't want to take the same path back to the hunting shack, so I took the long way, zigging and zagging to make sure I wasn't followed.

Along the way, Fetch snagged a couple of rabbits, and I found a bush of purple winterberries that filled up a small satchel. All and all, things were going even better than I could have hoped.

But by the time I got back bearing all the booty I'd managed to trade for the rabbits and berries, I was physically and mentally exhausted. Fetch's talons found my shoulder, and he settled his comforting weight there just as I nudged the door open with the toe of my boot.

"Moll?" I called softly. "You alright?"

The breath left me in a whoosh as something hit me center mass and I stumbled, grabbing at the door frame to keep us both upright. Fetch squawked and flew off to the rafters.

"Thank gods! Bloody hell, I had myself fully convinced you were in the town square being pelted with stones as they marched you about before they guillotined your head clean off." Her voice was pitched higher than usual, the panic clear.

Initially, I'd had to drop everything I'd been holding, but it was Moll's iron grip around my waist that kept me on my feet now. I slipped my arms around her and gave her a squeeze.

"Well, lucky for both of us my head is still attached. In fact, things went better than I expected."

"Really?" she croaked, stepped back and pulled me inside.

I did my best to keep my face neutral and pretended I didn't notice her reddened cheeks, still damp with tears. She'd been through something horrible the night before, and I hadn't been there to stop it. How many times had we promised to look out for each other? A hundred at least.

So, while I knew the feeling was irrational, it didn't break guilt's hold on me. She was like my sister. And the idea of her with that bastard pawing at her was more than I could bear right now.

In a feat of will, I pushed the dark thoughts aside.

One day she'd be ready to talk about what had happened. And when she was, I would be there to listen.

"What have you got? Some daintiques?" she asked, with a forced smile.

I turned the bag on its head, letting the fake leg, wooden crutch I'd fashioned out of a downed branch, and the pile of clothes drop to the floor.

She cocked her head, a frown dipping her eyebrows as she picked up the fake leg. "What's that for?"

"They're looking for the person who stabbed the king with their left shoe. They have the murder weapon in hand. They can't try it on someone with no leg, and it would be hard to suspect you because what would you be doing with a left-footed shoe anyway? It should fit easily over your leg. Might make walking a little awkward but shouldn't be too uncomfortable."

She let out a snort, her eyes showing a hint of life for the first time. "Only you would think of something like this, Harm."

Encouraged, I yanked the first of today's inventions from my pocket. I held the candle-sized rod out to her with a grin. The scrap metal at the blacksmith's had proved to be more than enough for my idea.

"And then there's this. I'm calling it 'The Incapacitator'. This is what took me so long. I had to work my time off in the forge."

She eyed the device suspiciously. "What is it?"

"A weapon. It's not perfect, but it's something. It's got a telescoping pole attached so if you need to use it on someone, they don't need to be super close. You press this button, it shoots out, and then you just flip the switch, here." I gestured toward the makeshift metal slider at the base of the handle.

Sparks danced through the air between two prongs as she turned it away from me and pressed it.

She let out a yelp and flinched as said sparks spit and bit like a caged animal.

"Whoa!"

"Exactly. It only has so many uses, and I'm not sure if I can recharge it, so only engage when necessary. Last resort sort of deal." I stomped at an ember that was spreading on a nearby bundle of hay.

She flipped it off, but she continued staring at the thing, entranced. "Is it… deadly?"

"Not deadly, but probably make a man shit himself, and stop a horse in its tracks."

Or a king.

I cursed myself for not giving her such a thing sooner. It'd taken only a couple hours to make, and it might've prevented all of this.

She turned to face me. "Thank you, Harm. This will help if ever—" she cut off abruptly, as her eyes filled with tears.

"It won't ever again, okay Moll? We'll make sure of it." I brought a hand to her shoulder and gave her an encouraging smile when she raised her head. She held the device reverently, giving it a final look before stuffing it into her bra.

I grabbed the bundle of clothes from the ground and tugged out a spotted orange dress.

"Then, we've got this. Great, right?"

She sputtered as she stared at the new-to-us dress, her face cycling through a dozen different emotions before landing solidly on horror. "Wh-What're we going to do with that?"

"It's for you. It's nothing like you'd normally wear."

"Oh my word. Yes, you're certainly right about that." She bit her lip and nodded, reaching out to grab the dress between her thumbs and forefingers as if it were covered in filth. "Ummm…Okay."

I pulled my own dress from the bag as well. "Maybe this'll make you feel better." She gawked as I held up a yellow dress with red and green berries, equally horrid as the other. "See, this one's mine."

Her lips twitched and she nearly smiled. "To be seen with you while you're wearing that is bad enough for both of us."

I laughed. "Agreed. Hopefully, anyone seeing us will be so distracted by my ugly dress, they won't look at you at all…But, in case they do…"

I held my breath as I bent to retrieve a small bottle of black dye and a pair of scissors that had been in the pile of steel. I'd sharpened them before I'd left the forge, knowing that this would be the worst part for Moll.

For a long moment, she looked perplexed, but then she drew back with a gasp, her hands going to her mouth.

"Harm, I can't!" She shook her head furiously and squeezed her eyes closed.

"Moll…"

"A wig, yes. But…My hair—"

I slice my hand through the air to stop her short. "Moll, we stabbed the fucking King. This transcends fashion. We have to survive now, whatever it takes! Your hair can and will grow back. Your head, and mine, won't."

Her gorgeous red mane was a point of pride for her and always had been. Something beautiful that even poverty couldn't take from her. Now I had to, and I fucking hated it.

I saw the moment she accepted her fate, and pride filled me.

She drew her shoulders back and opened her eyes, leveling me with a hard stare. "Okay. Okay, we'll cut and dye it. And once we're done with all this, we blend in. What then?"

Some of the tension left me as we got down to business. I motioned for her to sit in the rickety chair and set to cutting off her locks, swallowing hard as I made the first snip.

Molly flinched with each shush of the blades.

I cleared my throat and tried to make conversation to distract her. "If we keep a low profile, we should be alright for now. They're on a wild goose chase unless we give them something else to go off. I've run through everything that happened last night in my head a hundred times, and I can't think of anything else we might've missed." I shook my head slowly. "I don't see how they'd be able to tie this to us in any way—even with the glass slipper."

"What about getting back to The Hollow?" she asked, looking back at me, her brow wrinkling with concern. "We're not just on the run for stabbing the King, Harm. We aren't allowed to be in Little Alabaster in the first place."

"It's not going to be easy with them actually guarding the Cradle gate now, but I went to The Smudge today—that's where I got all the supplies—and I think we can blend in really easily there. I think we should head back there as soon as we're done here and find a place to stay for a couple of days so we can play it off like we're residents while I work the second half of my plan. I have a lead on some people who might be able to help us get back to The Hollow."

Moll's eyes lit with hope. "Really?"

I gently turned her head away so I could keep on snipping. "A family of smugglers, apparently. I'm hoping to meet up with them tomorrow."

I had hemmed and hawed the whole way back about whether or not to mention Gayelette and opted for the latter. I was shaken to the core by the woman's knowledge and more than a little confused by her advice. Until I figured out whether it was the rantings of a nut-job like Preacher Pete or some truly sage advice from a powerful Whisper, I was going to keep it to myself. We needed to stay focused on what was most important.

Keeping Moll incognito.

She cocked her head. "How was The Smudge, anyway?"

I paused in my snipping to scratch the tip of my nose. "Not much better than The Hollow, to be honest."

She snorted. "Hard to believe."

"Apparently, they've even taken to hiding it with some sort of magical shroud. It looks like a wall, but then you can just walk right through it."

"Seriously?" She let out a bark of laughter. "They don't want to make the fancy residents of Little Alabaster have to look at where the peasants live." She settled back, sighing once again as she glanced at the dress I'd gotten for her. "Speaking of eyesores…"

I touched her shortened curls and tried not to wince at the sheer amount of hair on the floor by my feet. "Time for the dye."

I squeezed in the dark liquid, a drop at a time, sending her deep red to a pitch black. "We're going to be okay, Moll. I know it," I said as I finished up the dye job. "Once we rinse out your hair, we can have a quick bite to eat. Then, we'll make our way to The Smudge. I think I know of a place we might be able to stay for the night. Then, tomorrow, I can try to find the people who can help us."

…And a way to pay them for their 'kindness'. I

gulped down my own doubts, keeping a brave face for her.

Molly nodded, though her eyes were locked on the red curls strewn about the floor. I bent and gathered them up and stuffed them under the mattress.

"There. Done."

Only it wasn't done.

This terrifying ordeal had only just begun, and I suspected we both knew it...

An hour later, with my hands cleaned of dye, and Moll's hair unrecognizable, I felt decidedly less confident as we meandered back toward The Smudge. Fetch flew ahead, circling back to us every few minutes.

"I still say we go with bear attack," Moll said. It was slow going with her on the prosthetic with crutches, and we didn't dare have her walk without them in case someone saw us. So long as we kept moving, we'd make it into The Smudge before dark.

Moll talked my ear off the whole time, trying to come up with a backstory for her prosthetic. And I was more than happy to let her, if it helped her get her mind off of things.

I shot her a quick side-eye and marveled again at the change. With the dark, shorter hair curled tight around her pale face, and her hideous, oversized dress, she wouldn't merit a glance from these people.

"I feel like word of a bear attack would've spread when it happened, though. Wouldn't people wonder why they hadn't heard of it?"

"It happened years ago," Moll reasoned. "When my mother and I were on a walk foraging for mushrooms, maybe."

"The more detailed you make the story, the harder it will be to remember," I reminded her gently.

"Well, what do *you* want me to tell them, then?"

"I'm not anticipating a whole ton of people demanding to know where your leg went, to be frank."

She rolled her eyes and continued on, "See, that's where you're wrong. Fancy people aren't as polite as they pretend to be. I want to make sure I'm ready when asked, is all."

Her problem was thinking that The Smudge was so much better than the Hollows that people would notice us. And after my trip into town, I was certain that was not going to be the case.

When we finally reached Little Alabaster's cobbled street, the late afternoon sun had started to set, and the crowd had begun to thin. We kept our heads down as I led the way toward the magical shroud that led to The Smudge.

We turned a final corner, and the wall of The Smudge came into view, straight across from us. I breathed a quiet sigh of relief. We'd made it, just a few more feet and we'd be able to dive into the masses that looked just like us. I held up my hand and Fetch dropped, landing on my arm.

"Let's go." I took a step and Moll limped along with me.

But fate was not done with us yet. A large caravan of guards rolled down the street, headed right toward us, their direction cutting off our entry-point if we didn't hurry. Residents of Little Alabaster were all around, and guards seemed to be posted on every corner. There was nowhere to hide. The only way out was through the shroud. We just had to hope our disguises held and keep moving.

"Eyes down," I muttered, putting a bit more confidence into my stride as I continued forward.

Dozens of guards marched in tight formation around a horse-drawn carriage, and we stepped off to the side of the street to give them a wide berth. I reached for Moll's hand, preparing to continue our move as the last set of guards approached.

We were nearly in the clear. Now, all that was left was to—

"Halt."

My blood ran cold, fight or flight instinct in full effect as I spun to face the source of the command. "Yes?"

The nearest guard had his eyes fixed directly on us, and he gestured for us to approach. "Smudgers," he muttered to his partner.

He stalked forward to meet us, and Moll shrank back as he hulked over us threateningly.

"What business brings you to this side of the shroud? On your way to work or on your way back home?"

"She...doesn't speak," I blurted, cutting in as Molly opened her mouth to reply. I cleared my throat. "She took a vow of silence several years back." Her fingernails dug even deeper into my hand, but I ignored it. "Doubt her voice would even work now if she tried."

He looked her up and down, then shrugged. "Then you do the speaking for her. What brings you here?"

"I'm a falconer," I said, gesturing to Fetch. "I was hoping to purchase a new leather glove as mine is tattered, but the prices were too high."

He glanced up at the darkening sky, gesturing toward it. "Cutting it pretty close to curfew, ain't ya?"

"We're on our way back home now."

He grunted, and his dark eyes drilled into me. "How long were you out of The Smudge?"

"Just a couple of hours." My sense of dread deepened as the caravan came to a sudden halt.

"Have you not heard the news?"

The door to the nearest carriage swung open, and I braced myself. Despite preparing for the worst, my knees nearly buckled when Prince Duncan stepped out onto the cobbled street. Memories of the jubilee flooded my mind even as blood rushed to my cheeks.

His strong hands at my waist. That damnable dimple flashing. His firm lips as he leaned in close, warm breath fanning my mouth...

Stop it.

How could I be thinking about any of that? We were in deep shit right now. Sure, I'd lost the blonde wig, and my dress was ugly as sin, but he'd know me the second our eyes met. And he'd know for sure that I hadn't belonged at that ball…

There would be no time for explanations or pleas. Either I was going to wait and die here on the streets like a lamb at the slaughter, or make a move, and go down fighting.

My free hand twitched toward the knife fastened to my thigh. Before I could complete the motion, Duncan's smoky eyes met mine. His nostrils flared, and his brows rose high on his forehead, but a second later, his face went oddly blank.

"Why have we stopped moving, Baldric?" he demanded, turning his attention back to the guard who had stopped us. "Night is nearly upon us, our party is weary, and we are done with the try-ons for the day."

Baldric's demeanor changed immediately, and he saluted as his prince approached. "Just interviewing these two, my liege. They haven't been checked for foot size yet." He reached into the satchel over his shoulder and pulled an all-too-familiar, crystalline shoe.

A puff of air escaped Moll's mouth as a squeak, and I gripped her hand like a vise.

Hold it together, my friend…

The shoe wouldn't fit me, but we couldn't have anyone taking too close a look at Moll's leg, either.

The prince circled us both, narrowing his eyes. My muscles stretched taut as his gaze caught on Moll's prosthetic. Fetch's talons pressed into my shoulder right through the pad, as if he sensed my stress. But the prince drew back after a moment, lips curled in disdain, so different from the easy charm he'd displayed at the ball.

"Don't bother with the shoe. It certainly isn't either of them. Heinrich would never…" He clapped Baldric on the arm. "Let's be on our way."

I swallowed hard as the blood rushed in my ears. Either he hadn't recognized me and was showing his true colors, or he was pretending because he wanted to help me.

But if so, why? His brother had just been killed. Red hair or no, surely, seeing a woman who had clearly snuck into the jubilee would at least make him want to double check that she hadn't been the murderer?

There was no time to ponder our good fortune. I should just be grateful that the universe hadn't seen fit to blow this up in my face like one of my bang 'em ups. Before he reached the carriage, though, a deep, gravelly voice cut through the air.

"I'd like a quick word with them, Prince Duncan."

A second man stepped from the carriage. His hair was fully gray, but there was something youthful about him nonetheless with his taut smooth skin, and his coal black eyes that seemed to stare into my soul. I'd never seen him up close, but his long, black robes speckled with gold stars gave him away.

Relyk, the palace sorcerer. I'd heard of his powers, which supposedly far surpassed any average Whisper.

While I dismissed much of the talk as idle gossip, it was true enough that his magic kept the mantises from flying into our cities and dragging citizens over the Great Wall in droves. Cissy had been the first near-victim this year, so he must've been doing something right.

I waited for him to speak but he just stood there, flicking a gaze between me and Fetch and then back again. It lasted so long that sweat broke out on my upper lip, and I had to swipe it away on the sly as I dropped into a shaky curtsy.

"What can we do for you, Sir?"

"The falcon on your shoulder seems well trained to sit quietly in all this commotion. Does he follow your commands?"

"He does." Anxiety prickled at my skin as I tried to piece together what he was getting at.

"We could use another falconer, my prince. Old Bertrand isn't getting any younger."

Duncan shrugged his broad shoulders and frowned. "Hardly seems like the time to be hiring staff with all that's going on…"

"And still, with a need for swift means of communication now more than ever, I think it necessary."

The prince tossed up a careless hand. "Do what you will. Just make it quick."

"You girl," he motioned at me with two fingers. "Go to your home and pack your things. Come to the palace tomorrow before noon." He turned to Duncan.

"We'll move her into one of the huts so Bertrand can train her. Hopefully, he'll have her up to speed in a few days' time."

I gnawed at the inside of my cheek, a dozen conflicting emotions rolling through me at once. Being on palace grounds was a dangerous game, but I couldn't very well refuse him. No true Smudger would dare. "M-my cousin here lives with me. Can she come?"

The sorcerer tipped his head. "Of course. Your names?"

I'd already given the prince something close to my real name, so I had to go with another. Like the name Pawpaw had given me, but shorter.

"Ella. And that's Molly," I added, realizing that my lie about the vow of silence meant that she couldn't answer for herself.

"The guards at the palace will be expecting you."

With that, Relyk turned on his heel and made his way back to the carriage, his cloak catching the wind, the gold stars glinting as if they were woven with real gold. And maybe they were. Duncan met my gaze with a long one of his own…followed by what I could've sworn was a stealthy wink. Only then did he climb into the carriage after the sorcerer.

What the hell?

Duncan seemed awfully unaffected for a man who'd just lost a brother. Although, that might be because he —like many around here, it seemed—knew that his brother was a truly terrible man and the world was better off without him. That, plus the fact that he would soon be king would certainly explain the lack of grief.

The caravan of guards and carriages moved on with a clatter of wheels, weapons and armor. Only then did we both breathe a sigh of relief.

Moll shook her head, dark curls bouncing. "That was way too close! I must say, though…I'm a bit surprised that Prince Duncan didn't recall seeing me at the ball, even in passing."

I stared at her, dumbfounded. "Is that *annoyance* I hear in your tone?"

She bristled. "Well, I mean, I suppose it's lucky that he didn't, but—"

"But what?" I let out a snort-laugh. "You'd rather hang from the gallows than accept that your tits are just not *that* memorable." I glanced at her chest, and how covered it was beneath the dress and the over-sized, knee length coat she wore.

A smile tugged at her lips. "Fine. I'm vain. And I suppose without the stunning hair and same dress, it *would* be difficult. But let's focus on what's important. Are we seriously considering moving onto the palace grounds? Enemy territory?" As she spoke, she dropped her voice to a quiet whisper that was filled with more than a little fear.

Hooking my arm with hers, I helped her balance as we made our way through the wall and into The

Smudge. "I don't think we have a choice. These people aren't used to being told no, and I've no doubt this is considered an honor, to be plucked from a crowd like that. It would only rouse suspicion if we don't show." With little choice in the matter, I focused on silver linings, my mind already racing ahead. This could actually work.

"And this time, Heinrich won't be there to hurt you. We go, and we hide in plain sight. You know the saying? 'Keep your friends close and your enemies closer.' We'll have food, shelter, some coin—I'm assuming they'll pay me. Most important, we'll have access to information about any moves they're making far earlier than the people here in The Smudge. I'll be assistant falconer by day and use the rest of my time to find someone to smuggle us out and back to The Hollow. And now we'll actually have money to pay them."

I steered her toward the blacksmith's shop, praying that my instincts about Smitty were right and he would allow us to crash there for the night. It would be warmer than the hut, at the very least.

She nodded, still looking dubious as we shuffled our way down the street. "If you think this is the right move, *Ella,* I'm in. I'll just have to do my best to keep my natural beauty in check, so Prince Duncan doesn't take a second look and realize I was the stunning redhead at the jubilee that night."

Duncan might not have recognized her, but after

that wink, I was pretty sure he'd recognized *me*...a secret I'd be taking to my grave.

A grave which I might be inhabiting sooner than planned if whatever amusement he was getting from this little charade faded. If I was right and he did know me, I'd just have to trust that he had his reasons to stay mum, and hope it continued.

Or Molly and I were both going to find ourselves on the wrong side of the noose.

CHAPTER 8

Smitty had let us sleep in the shop on the condition that I make him another knife, matching the one from the day before. A task which Molly amazingly slept through, despite the noise and how long it took me.

The second blade was more time-consuming than the first, because there had been no basic shape, and the hunk of steel was as raw as it could get. But all in all, I didn't mind. The repetitive nature of the task allowed my mind to plan, sifting through every possible pitfall and every potential benefit that came along with working alongside the royal falconer.

"Good job," Smitty said as he met us the next morning with a heel of bread and hunk of yellow cheese in hand.

"You haven't even seen it yet."

"I know your work. You did a good job, or you'd

still be at it." He strode to the anvil and picked up the blade that matched the first I'd made, down to the etched pattern. "You come on back if you want to apprentice."

I smiled, warmth suffusing me. This was a rare offer, with no ties, no strings. "I'm headed to train with Bertrand, at Relyk's…command."

His amber eyes whipped to mine. "Bertrand. The Falconer…he's a grumpy old bastard."

Ugh. I didn't need a grumpy bastard watching over me.

"But you don't want to cross Relyk, so you best be heading out."

I gave Smitty a nod. "Thanks. For everything."

He shrugged his wide shoulders and spared a quick wave Molly's way. "Get on with you then, but come back when you need."

Molly, Fetch and I left the warmth of the forge and headed back through the shroud to Little Alabaster, then made the trek over the palace grounds. We made it to the palace guard house just before noon.

While our plan made sense, adages about "keeping your enemies closer" or "hiding where they'd least expect" did little to convince my pounding heart that we were on the right track. The palace was danger, no matter how I looked at it. And it was clear, as Molly's already labored steps slowed even more, that she was feeling the same way.

I glanced at the beds of flowers and shrubs that

lined the palace walls, marveling. One of the most striking things about Little Alabaster was the vividness and color of it all, even in winter. Like they'd sucked the vibrancy right out of The Hollow and dropped it here... Just like they had with everything else worth having.

The row of guards came into view, and I turned to Moll. "Remember, quiet from here on." I shrugged as she shot me a look. "Sorry…again, but we just have to go with it at this point."

She dipped her head in a resigned nod, her lips pressed tight together.

I hefted our sack of meagre possessions higher on my shoulder as we approached the guard gate, doing my best to keep up the appearance of carrying something heavy. We'd been asked to bring our belongings, and it seemed strange to show up without anything, so we'd resorted to filling the sacks we had with sticks and stones and bringing those along.

The guard inside the gatehouse looked up as we approached.

"State your business."

His voice was formal, matching his crisp, unwrinkled uniform, but there was no trace of the disdain we'd gotten from guards previously.

"Hello," I said, trying and failing to keep the nerves from my voice. "We're here to—uh… Prince Duncan asked us to come here and move our things into a hut on palace grounds. Relyk said to—"

He glanced at the leather pad on my shoulder, nodding as the realization dawned. "The new falconer...Ella, right? Where's your bird?"

"Yes." I let out a quick whistle, and Fetch swooped down to me by the time the guard began his reply.

He pulled on some kind of lever, then gestured toward the gate. "This way. I'll take you over."

The ground rumbled beneath our feet, and I turned to see the massive gate rolling open. The dozens of carved figures and symbols stood out in the afternoon sun, with the large, pyramidal crest at the center sticking out most of all. Layers of increasingly vibrant colors filled the triangle, culminating in a gleaming, pearly white at the top.

The royal crest was a permanent reminder of the crown's supremacy, and of the inferiority of everything beneath it. Anger flashed through me as my eyes fixed on the putrid brown at the bottom, representing the Hollow, and I prayed it didn't show on my face.

The guard stepped out to meet us, halting in front of the half-opened gate. He eyed the bag. "Need any help with that?"

"We're fine," I answered, a little too fast. I winced at the light crunching sound that cut through the air as I made a show of hefting the bag further up my shoulder.

He raised an eyebrow at me, but shrugged, stepping toward the gate. "Follow me."

I strode through behind him, a wave of pure awe

washing over me as the palace itself came into view. The inside had been beautiful on the night of the jubilee, but seeing it from the outside in full daylight, and not creeping around the side to break in was a different thing entirely.

The opulence and glory of it all was like something…out of a storybook. A white pathway unfolded in front of us, lined with bushes of purple-and-blue flowers—impossible in this cold and yet there. And the palace itself was even more stunning. The bright white porcelain walls were broken up with glimmering, stained glass windows, and the three decorative, silvery spires that stretched into the clouds.

A kneeling servant worked a few feet away, polishing a single stone of the impractical white pathway, shivering in the cold, his hands chapped and red.

But that wasn't our direction. The guard turned from the main path immediately, following a narrower cobblestone walkway to the east of the palace. He jabbed his finger toward a group of houses in the distance. "Huts for essential staff are over there."

Was *that* what they considered a 'hut' on this side of The Cradle?

I shot Moll a glance, jaw gaping. They paled in comparison to the houses of nobles that ringed Little Alabaster, but they were luxurious by Hollow standards. Hell, they were luxurious by Smudge standards, as far as I could see. Each one easily had an acre of land between them.

"Which one are we in?" I asked as we neared the first of the homes.

"Third one from the—" He stopped abruptly, eyes flitting down to his uniform. He smoothed it and straightened his hat, then stood a little bit taller.

My heartbeat skipped a beat as I spun, glancing in the direction he'd been pointing. A figure stood with his back to us, as if he were inspecting our new home, his hand resting on a gold-hilted sword. Prince Duncan, looking gorgeous as ever, even from the back.

No, not gorgeous. Bad, Harmony, bad. Just average... yes, I would tell myself he was average at best.

I sucked in a breath, sparing a quick glance at Moll, our predicament slamming back into me. What the hell was he doing here? Had he remembered her, by chance? Had her tits in fact, outed us?

"Quite the honor to have him welcome you in person," the guard murmured, striding quickly as he approached the house, forcing us to hurry to follow. Duncan turned, noticing us, and the guard fell into a salute rather than a bow, "Your Highness."

A pointed glance from the guard sent Moll and me into curtseys of our own.

Prince Duncan rested his hand on his sword hilt and gestured us over. "Thank you, Crispin."

The guard dipped his head in acknowledgment. "Do you have further need of me, or shall I return to my post, Your Highness?"

Duncan flashed a crooked smile that nearly

knocked the breath out of me. "When are you going to stop with the formalities, my friend?" he chuckled.

"Appearances matter. Especially in times like these."

They shared a furtive glance that I didn't understand, and Duncan finally nodded, grin fading. "Fine. But I'll see you at tonight's event, and you better not be so polite. You can head back to the gate."

Crispin whipped off a second salute, then strode away.

"Welcome to your new home." The prince turned, his gaze fixing on me. "I thought I'd come show you around."

Again, I found myself wondering at how unbothered he seemed by his brother's death. If he was to be crowned king any time now, what was he doing here?

I'd think he'd be busy doing all the…kingly things needed of him.

He hadn't brought Heinrich's death up, so I wasn't about to, but it was definitely strange. Even if he and Heinrich hated one another, surely, he should be too busy preparing for his own coronation to see a servant to their quarters?

It didn't make sense.

Despite the niggling curiosity, my initial nerves at seeing him calmed some. He wasn't here with a warrant for my arrest or an ax-wielding executioner in tow, and that was good enough for now.

He pushed the door to the hut open, revealing a

cozy living room that would've been the envy of everyone I'd ever known. A fireplace sat in one corner, flames already going well, with a cushioned sofa and table in the other. We strode through the room, going to the kitchen next.

The prince gestured at a small, wicker basket full of onions and potatoes on the table in the middle of the room. A loaf of bread sat next to it, with a jar of purplish jam. "I had my people stock you up with some basics, so you shouldn't have to worry about that for a few days while you get your legs under you with Bertrand."

"This is perfect, thank you," I said, trying to keep the amazement from my voice. I reached for Moll's hand, gripping it tightly in mine as I caught sight of the second basket—this one full of fresh fruit—on the other side of the counter. Most of the people we'd grown up with would've killed for a meal like this. How long had it been since we'd had truly fresh fruit? Years…not since Pawpaw was still alive.

I cleared my throat, knowing that I needed to have some understanding of what was, and wasn't allowed— the last thing we needed was more trouble. "With regard to food going forward, is Fetch allowed to hunt nearby or should we go to market for meat?"

"By decree, the Northwest Forest and its game are reserved for royal outings and events," he said with a frown before gesturing to the back wall. "But he can hunt within the wooded area directly behind the huts for any small game. You can also purchase meat in town if you prefer."

We needed to save every coin we could get our hands on, so small game out back it would be.

Next, he led us into the bedroom, gesturing toward the two beds. Even at a distance, they were obviously well stuffed, with thick blankets and even thicker pillows. Moll shouldered her way past me to see, and I winced as her jaw dropped open, but thankfully no sound came out except a soft sigh.

"Feel free to get comfortable, if you like. I'm sure it's been a long day."

Moll took him up on it almost immediately, dropping her crutch and falling into the bed with a groan.

"These beds are so nice." I ran my hand over the top blanket, trying to draw his eyes from her as I caught sight of the harness that held her fake leg in place.

"Rather small for my liking, but they'll do the trick. Do you need assistance unpacking?" he asked, gesturing toward the bag I'd almost forgotten I was carrying.

"Er– no thanks. I'll just leave it here for now." I scurried quickly to the second bed, setting it down beside it, just out of sight. "I have a few more questions for you, if it's no trouble?"

He smiled, flashing that very average dimple. "Certainly."

Duncan led the way back into the living room,

stopping to stand beside the sofa as he looked down at me expectantly. Why did he have to be so…big? I resisted the urge to take a step back and then regretted it as his musky scent curled around me. He even smelled good? This was terrible.

He motioned and I sat on one end of the sofa, then he dropped himself onto the far side, his weight sending a shiver through the furniture. "You wanted to ask me something?" he prompted, his dimple flickering into view before disappearing again.

I shifted restlessly and cleared my throat. "Um, yes. Just about the job. What my duties will be and all."

"You won't need to start for a couple of days as we have some…things going on at the palace." A crease formed between his eyes.

Things I definitely didn't want him to associate with me, so I was happy to talk about the job at hand. "What should I do in the meantime?"

"You'll be training with our current falconer, Bertrand. You have some time to get acquainted with life on the palace grounds. You're also free to go to… the other side of town to visit family and whatever else you might choose to do."

Apparently, he couldn't deign to speak of The Smudge. The realization was a stark reminder that as handsome and easygoing as he seemed, we were *not* the same and he was *not* my friend.

I straightened and fixed a cool smile to my lips. "And as for wages…?"

If he was bothered by my change in energy, he didn't show it. "I don't know the exact amount, but it will take care of the two of you well enough—Falconers are valuable to the crown. Paid in coin, once weekly, after your first week is complete."

I made sure not to let the disappointment show on my face. We wouldn't be here in a week's time, gods willing, and asking for a loan against my wages day one would be bold to the point of rudeness. The last thing I needed was to stir up suspicion. I'd have to find another way to pay for us to get smuggled out of here, the sooner the better. Because as easy as it would be to fall into the fantasy that the soon-to-be-crowned King of Alabaster liked me, facts were facts; Birds of a feather stuck together. I was nothing but a curiosity to him that would fade as quickly as it had come, and we needed to be long gone before he realized something wasn't quite right with old "Harmonica" here and her one-legged cousin.

A silence stretched between us, and a warmth grew deep within me as his gaze drifted to my lips.

Not your friend, I reminded myself sternly. *And* certainly *nothing more. He can't even say "The Smudge" out loud, how do you think he'd like visiting you in The Hollow?*

His expression darkened some, and he turned away. "Also, there *is* an event tonight. They'll be ringing bells to announce it a few hours from now, and you can follow the other servants when you hear them. There will be a royal announcement at the amphitheater."

I'd heard of the place but still hadn't seen it despite all my sneaking around. "Is it close by?"

My heart skipped a beat as I realized how deeply "Hollow" the question probably sounded. If I truly was from this side of the Cradle, surely I'd already know the answer to that question...

If I outed myself though, his expression didn't show it, and the strange apprehension in his face faded as he nodded.

"Just behind the palace. In a more typical circumstance, done up for a celebration or holiday, it's quite a sight to behold."

His eyes shifted toward the fireplace. The silence lingered for a long moment, but his expression was unreadable when he looked back at me.

"In any case, I'd expect that there will still be some exhibitions and sparring after the announcement, but it shouldn't go much longer than an hour or two."

I got the sense that he was trying to reassure me, but his words only put me more on edge.

Exhibitions and sparring? When the king had just been killed?

Duncan hooked his fingers into his belt that held his sword. He didn't seem overly concerned with anything he'd spoken of—not like we were headed to a public execution. Right?

Right.

I nodded, unable to tamp down the niggling fear about the big "announcement." Had they found someone to pin the crime on? Or was this an attempt to gloss over the king's death and celebrate Duncan's coronation as quickly as possible, before some distant cousin or ambitious noble got any ideas about making a power play?

I'd have to wait until later to find out, but the suspense might just kill me.

"Looking forward to it," I said, forcing out the words.

The prince rose, glancing down at his pocket watch. "I should be going. I still have a lot to help prepare."

I scrambled to my feet and walked him to the door. He stepped out into the afternoon sun, then paused and turned back toward me. A slight frown worked into his expression, and he dipped his head in a good-bye. "I'll see you later. Ella."

I dipped into a curtsey so low that it didn't seem strange at all when I stumbled forward, bumping into him.

"Careful!" he murmured even as his hands clamped around my arms, steadying me as I stood back up, and away. I tamped down the rush that coursed through me at his touch even through the fabric of my coat.

"Apologies, Your Highness." I stepped back with a flustered smile. "I've still not gotten used to being in the presence of royalty. I'm certain it will wear off soon. Thank you again for showing us around."

His splayed fingers lingered a moment longer, but

then he released me and stepped back. "You're quite welcome…"

I closed the door behind him and leaned against it, my legs like jelly. "Fucking hell."

Moll crept back into the room and met my gaze, cocking her head in a silent question.

"It's fine, he's gone."

She let out a breath. "This vow of silence thing is going to be the death of me."

"I know. I wish I could take it back…" *sort of*, "But this will make you feel better."

I straightened and held out my open palm. Moll let out a gasp as she caught sight of what was nestled there.

"You stole his watch?" she hissed rushing to get a better look. "You sneaky little minx."

"It's surely made of solid gold, so I'm hoping it will pay for our safe passage back into The Hollow. I don't want to keep this ruse up longer than I have to."

A hot twinge of guilt poked at me as I pocketed the timepiece, but I shoved the feeling aside—this was survival after all, for me and Moll. Surely, the prince had plenty of other timepieces.

Instead of feeling bad, I made a beeline toward the crusty loaf of bread. I sliced it in half and slathered a healthy portion of the jam onto the top of it before carrying two plates over to where Moll stood. I chuckled, handing her a plate with half of the loaf of bread.

Excessive? Sure, but who knew when we'd get another meal like this?

If things went as planned, we'd be back in The Hollow in no time, safe, but starving just like we had been before we left.

"I'll admit, I was starting to worry you would explode trying to keep all the words inside."

Her mouth dropped open as she stared at the bread and jam. "If I'm going to explode, let it be from this." She tore into the food with a low groan.

I took a bite of my own, moaning along with her. The tart blackberry jam on the soft sourdough was nothing short of heaven, and I dropped to my soft featherbed with a contented sigh. I swallowed my first bite and paused. "I know we're fugitives and the entire city is looking for us, but this really does beat the hell out of being hungry, huh?"

Moll nodded eagerly, unable to speak around her mouthful of bread.

But a few minutes later, as I finished my last bit of jammy bread, I couldn't shake the guilt that rose inside me once again. Even though it was necessary, I felt awful stealing from him. He'd been nothing but kind, and helpful, and I'd taken advantage.

More unsettling than that, though…why hadn't he called me out yet for being at the ball? There were moments where he *seemed* to recognize me. Was he so taken with me that he'd decided not to turn me in?

Not likely.

My experience with men—especially wealthy ones—made it much more probable that he was keeping my secret because he wanted something in return. I just had to hope it was something I was willing to give freely. Or that I was long gone before he asked to cash in the favor.

Because saying no to royalty was a dangerous game, and me and Moll were running out of shoes…

CHAPTER 9

I slid the plate of diced potatoes down the counter to Moll before taking a whiff of the aromatic vegetables and spices cooking in the pan.

"Smells amazing."

After Duncan had left, and we'd stuffed ourselves full of bread and jam, we napped for a few hours. When I woke, I felt like a new woman. The feather beds were like clouds after sleeping in the blacksmith shop the night before.

Now, though we'd only just begun preparing it, I knew the stew would be delicious. So many vegetables, so many spices waiting to be used in the cupboards.

A soft cry echoed from outside.

"Oh, there's Fetch!" Moll dashed for the back door, going quiet as she swung it open.

The falcon dove right past her, his wingtips hardly an

inch away from brushing against her cheek, and his talons dropped into place on my leather shoulder pad. The rabbit he carried in his beak—the reason for his muffled cry—was plumper than the ones he caught in the Hollow.

Moll scurried over and snapped her fingers. "Fetch, drop!"

He met her with a dead-eyed stare.

"You know he's a one-woman guy. Fetch, drop." He let the rabbit fall to the counter before flying off to the makeshift perch I'd constructed for him at the front of our bedroom using one of the kitchen chairs.

"Stupid bird," Moll muttered.

No matter how much she tried to butter him up, he only ever released food for little kids, and me. He wasn't mean to her, precisely…no biting or scratching, but there was definitely a general aura of disdain aimed specifically at Molly that I could only credit to jealousy. They were the two closest friends I had. Family, really. And sometimes family was like that.

"This stupid bird just provided dinner, so be nice." I grabbed the kitchen knife, shooing Moll out of the room as I moved toward the rabbit.

She hated this part.

I skinned and prepared the rabbit for cooking as quickly as I ever had, laying the organ meat and other remains of the rabbit on a plate for Fetch.

Only then did Moll take back over prepping the stew and adding the meat as I worked on making a second incapacitator with some of the scrap Smitty had let me take before we left.

Moll finished up the stew, bringing me a taste. I pulled open one of the cabinets, grinning as I caught sight of a second loaf of bread. Exposed to luxury like this, how else could two Hollow girls be expected to act? We plowed through dinner as if it might be our last—again, a distinct possibility—and the pot was drained within minutes.

The sudden clanging of bells split the silence, followed by the crystal-clear sound of trumpets. A moment later, a sharp knock sounded at the door. I turned to Moll, putting a finger to my lips, then strode to the door.

A guard greeted me as I pulled it open, an annoyed expression already on his face. "Time to go. The event begins shortly."

"Yes, of course. We're coming." I called to Fetch, and he flew to my shoulder, landing lightly.

The guard dipped his head in assent, but waited for us to exit before moving on to the next hut a distance away.

"He seems fun," I murmured to Moll once he was out of earshot.

Despite my joke, I was worried. I'd tried to convince myself that this was just the formal announcement of the king's death and Duncan's ascension as his replacement, but part of me wondered if it wasn't just a big, fat setup. Were there a pair of nooses at the center of the amphitheater just waiting for me and Molly to walk into what would be our own public hanging?

I mean, it was the perfect way to get us not to run, to make it like they didn't know, and then at the last minute pull the plush rugs out from under our feet.

Didn't matter. There was no way out of it no matter how many scenarios I came up with in my head. Mandatory attendance meant everyone in Little Alabaster. Not going would only mark us for suspicion where there might be none.

"We'd better get a move on," I said to Moll, hoping my nerves didn't show. She tightened her hold on her crutches and followed me along the path.

At first, I wondered if we'd have trouble finding the place, but as we headed out into the cool evening air, I saw that Duncan was right. There were a lot of people —servants and even the lords and ladies of Little Alabaster, all walking in the same direction. The line stretched around the back of the palace, toward an ever-growing crowd.

"This way," I said to Moll, as if she couldn't see it for herself. She rolled her eyes and I smiled. "I guess I thought you were blind too for a minute there."

Her eye rolling only intensified at my poorly made joke. I couldn't help it, my nerves were getting to me.

As we folded ourselves into the fray, the tension was palpable. Despite some whispered wonderings of what was in store between a few servants, most walked in silence like they were as worried as us.

I just couldn't decide if that was good or bad for me and Moll.

Fetch tucked his beak behind my ear, and wiggled his head, soothing me. I lifted a hand to him, knowing that he picked up on my feelings. "I'm okay, buddy."

Once we rounded the palace toward the back, the massive amphitheater came into view.

I just stared at the size of it. Not as tall as the castle that stood in front of it, so it couldn't be seen from a distance, but huge, nonetheless. Four stories, and wide, squat like a giant frog sitting waiting to snag some oversized flies. But the sheer size of it wasn't nearly as shocking as the vibrant drawings that riddled its rough, brown exterior.

I blinked, staring. I had to be seeing things. Figments of my overactive imagination…

"Moll," I whispered, "Is that a dwarf with a pickaxe?"

Molly nodded.

"A-and a girl biting into an apple?"

An apple I *knew* to be poisoned…

Moll poked me with her elbow and held up both hands with a scowl.

Right. She couldn't reply. But she didn't need to, because the closer I got to the images, the more I knew they were real.

The first was a dead match to the illustration on the

cover of the fairytale book Wayne and Spalding had thrown in the creek nearly twenty years ago...

Fairytales that, according to my father and anyone I'd ever told about them, including Molly, were completely unknown in Alabaster.

Next to the cover image was one of a giant, orange pumpkin with wheels being drawn by a pair of white horses.

Cinderella.

My eyes flickered over the other two images, and the metallic taste of fear coated my tongue even as my eye began to twitch.

A pirate ship...a city made of emeralds...both exactly like the ones in my book. As a small child, I'd been too scared to listen to Pawpaw read those two particular stories, but there was no mistaking the skull and crossbones flag hoisted above the sails, and those ghoulish monkeys with wings.

What the fuck was happening here?

Dimly, I heard the murmurs of a trio of servants walking beside us.

"That last image appeared in the middle of the night. Same with the others on previous nights."

I spared a glance at the striking green palace and the monkeys swarming around it and realized she was right. The drawing was smeared at the bottom, like it had been partially erased, but I could just make out a hazy figure walking down a long, winding road in the foreground.

I tuned back into the conversation just as the girl continued.

"They still haven't caught the culprit. Clearly, it's some sort of Whisper trick, but the sorcerer thought somehow soap and water were going to fix it," one of them said with a snort of disgust. "I spent all day yesterday and most of today with eight other girls scrubbing them with lye and scalding water. They haven't lightened up even a bit."

"I heard Relyk himself was out here for hours trying to use magic to get rid of them, but all he managed to do was blur that tiny little section at the bottom. It would take him a month to get rid of them all at that rate," another chimed in.

What. The. Fuck.

I let my eyes drift shut to concentrate on the conversation better, leaning on Moll to lead the way.

"Want to bet it doesn't get mentioned tonight at all?" one of them whispered.

"I wouldn't take that bet," another replied. "They would never admit someone getting away with defacing the amphitheater right under the palace's nose. Especially not right after our king was attacked. It doesn't speak well of security around here, I'll tell you that much."

"How could they have had the time to do all that? The guards have been watching like hawks."

"Oooh, do you think whoever is responsible for the

murder is also making the drawings? Like as a symbol of some sort of rebellion?"

"But why these pictures, then? They don't seem all that rebellious. They look like they're from some sort of children's fables."

Exactly what I wanted to fucking know.

"Maybe the pumpkin carriage is a protest against the wealthy or about the people going hungry? And… and maybe the witch because so many in Alabaster aren't allowed to use magic?"

I opened my eyes and frowned. Not a bad guess, actually.

"I kind of hope whoever it is keeps it up," one of the servants whispered. "Seeing him nervous brings me joy."

"Shhh, someone might hear you!" another shot back.

Guards strode between us, cutting off any further attempts to listen as they ushered us into orderly lines, pushing us away from that section of the wall.

I'd been worried about the announcement, but now my heart raced for a whole new reason.

What I wouldn't give to get up close and have a really good look at those drawings…

Moll tugged on my arm, and I glanced at her. She frowned and lifted one shoulder in a silent question.

Of course she didn't understand why I was acting so weird.

I'd talked about the book before in passing, but it had been nothing more than a memory by the time I met Moll. And hearing about it and seeing the exact same pictures in real life were two different kettles of fish. This wasn't the time or place to try to explain, though. Especially when I didn't even understand what was happening myself.

"Fine, I'm fine." Maybe it was just a weird coincidence. Maybe whoever had painted them had come from the same kingdom as my real parents had. Maybe when we escaped, I'd travel and try to find their origins…and my parents.

For now, though, we were being moved in a way that felt eerily like cattle to the slaughter, and I needed to focus. Until we escaped Little Alabaster, I couldn't concern myself with anything but keeping the two of us alive.

I swallowed hard and continued forward on shaky legs as the nobles went in through the front entrance while the servants and lower class—us included of course—were brought in through a side door. A winding stairway went up several stories, and when we emerged, the massive interior of the amphitheater came into view for the first time.

Bare bone seats rose in at least a hundred rows, stacked tight on top of one another—the same color stone as the exterior. I wouldn't have thought there were enough people in Little Alabaster to fill it, and if I'd bet any money on it, I'd have lost it all. The ceiling was open to the sky above and the center of the massive building was a sand base by what I could see, round, with a few doors here and there that led to… gods knew where.

My eyes immediately latched onto Prince Duncan who sat across the way at ground level in a canopied section of seats. Relyk the sorcerer in his black and gold cloak stood behind a podium beside him with a small contingent of green-armored guards at his back.

Molly and I hurried to find seats. All told, it took nearly half an hour for the amphitheater to fill. Despite the fact that we were higher up, the grounds at the center were still quite visible.

Interesting though how quiet it was, there was hardly a single cough for all the people being brought in. It was…eerie.

"I wonder why the sorcerer is behind the podium instead of Duncan," I whispered to Moll. I pointed at a large box behind Relyk. "And what the hell is that?"

She shot me a sharp stare and shrugged, then tapped her lips.

Right, vow of silence and all that. Even if she could have replied she wouldn't have known I was just… speculating. Trying not to freak out.

Another round of trumpets split the eerily silent air, making both of us half leap out of our seats like a pair of skittish cats.

All around us the servants were still. Unmoving as if afraid to draw attention. Did they know something we didn't?

Relyk raised his arm, waving lazily in greeting. "The royal family welcomes you to the amphitheater on this day." His voice carried through the enormous chamber despite the thousands of occupants, as audible as if he was standing right next to me. "We are here today for a very special reason, and it is my honor and pleasure to announce the purpose for this evening's event."

His voice went solemn as he continued.

"The rumors you have heard are true. King Heinrich was attacked at the ball celebrating his coronation...stabbed in the heart by a female would-be assassin with red hair and a nefarious plot."

Moll let out a low snarl and I gripped her hand, squeezing her fingers.

Fetch ruffled his feathers, as if in agreement with her assessment.

"We have not yet found the person responsible, but it's only a matter of time." Relyk turned to the contingent of guards behind him and waved a hand as he continued. "Because we have someone who saw the entire thing."

A witness?

Black spots flickered before my eyes and blood rushed to my ears. Had we done enough to conceal our identities? Fuck, we were so fucked.

The sorcerer waved to the guards, and they moved to the covered box, pulling the curtain aside in a carefully practiced reveal. A hulking figure stepped into view, and my heart froze in my chest as I made out his features.

"He survived!" Relyk clapped his hands together.

Impossible.

Yet there he was. King Heinrich, his icy blue eyes alight in the setting sun. He looked far bigger and much more scary standing up than he had flat on his back. Moll's clammy hand trembled in mine, and it took all I had not to dive at the man and gouge his fucking eyes out.

Instead, I took a breath and dipped into a belated bow like the rest of the crowd as I tried to make sense of what I was seeing.

How could he have lived? The amount of blood… the location of the shoe, buried right where his heart should've been. I would have sworn on anything you'd asked of me that he was dead. There had been no breath in him, no beat of his heart. But was it possible that I'd missed it in the panic?

As some of the shock faded, I was struck by how… odd he looked. His pale skin was stretched taut across his face, and his movements were just a little too slow…too deliberate. Miraculous for a man who'd been stabbed directly in the heart, but *definitely* not like he'd looked at the ball.

The initial attack hadn't killed him, but maybe an ensuing infection would?

One could only hope. Because what if they brought us all up one by one? What if she'd told him something he remembered that led him to us? Even though he survived, it wouldn't matter. She'd attacked him. I'd helped her.

We were both dead.

It was only then that I realized Molly was shaking, gripping my hand so tight, it had gone numb. I spared her a glance and my stomach revolted when I saw the stark terror in her eyes.

I could do no more than pull her closer and murmur low words of comfort in her ear as Relyk continued on.

"And with that, I turn it over to His Majesty to give us our opening thoughts on the evening." The sorcerer fell into a bow as the king approached.

"We're going to be okay. I swear it, Moll," I whispered, leaning into her as Heinrich reached the podium.

A flicker of light passed from Relyk's fingertips to Heinrich's chest, and, when the king spoke, it came through with the same strength and volume that Relyk had managed.

Some kind of magic to amplify sound. Had the sorcerer's magic saved the king's life? That had to be it.

The king's eyes stared straight ahead. "A woman with red hair lured me into the gardens and then tried to kill me, but here I stand. Now, we need to work together as a people to find the traitors in our midst. Those who stand against the crown are a threat to *everything* this hierarchy was built to preserve. That way lies anarchy, chaos, and rebellion. Our enemies salivate at the thought of such things taking hold." He held up a fist. "We will increase our search in the coming days to root our enemies out, but tonight? Tonight we celebrate! For I survived, and their plot is foiled!"

A colorful display of fireworks erupted from the edges of the amphitheater, and the king strode back, taking a seat on the previously boxed-in chair without speaking another word. The gates on one side of the amphitheater slid open, and my jaw dropped as a familiar screech split the air. More than a few people shrunk back.

Flying mantis.

I winced as it came into view. This one's wings had been clipped, but there it was, in the flesh. It was a massive specimen, far larger than the one that had taken Cissy. A group of soldiers emerged from the other side of the amphitheater, but my attention was drawn to Duncan as he stood up. He strode over to the edge, slamming his gauntleted fist against his breast-plate, as if cheering them on.

The squad of three men stepped into the ring as the mantis let out another shrill screech, his arm-blades unfurling as it advanced, mandibles clicking. The gate guard I'd met earlier, Sir Crispin, was at the front, his shield held high as he circled the beast.

"Seems cruel," a servant whispered from just a few feet to my side.

Another servant let out a scoff. "Cruel? They're bloodthirsty monsters. The newborns eat their mother the moment they're born, and the injured are eaten the moment they can no longer fight."

I had to agree with him there. Despite high walls, before the protection wards had been put in place, the mantises had killed dozens of people every year. They were also the main reason there was so little trade between us and the other two kingdoms. The long journey to either was rife with mantis nesting ground. In truth, their existence was a core point in the crown's philosophy; how could humans hope to face off against such monsters, without the structure and centralization that a rigid hierarchy brought with it?

I bit at my lip as the thought occurred, cursing the royal family. So many bought into the philosophy without a thought that they might be being lied to. Even in The Hollow there were those who supported the crown buying into the propaganda and supporting their own oppression.

The beast flashed forward, closing the distance between them in the blink of an eye. A bladed arm smacked into the knight's shield, and he rolled sideways, absorbing the blow. The other two guards dashed forward in unison, punishing the monster with twin stabs to its torso.

Greenish blood spurted onto the dirt, but the monster looked unfazed as if it had not just suffered a massive blow. Its mandibles snapped at the closest guard as its arms swung toward the other, smashing into his helmet and sending him to the ground. Crispin surged back into action, appearing in between the beast and the last standing guard.

Those long-bladed arms struck his shield again, but this time he was ready. His legs threatened to buckle under the force, but his blade snaked forward, slamming right into the mantis's face.

The beast let out an agonized scream, like a hundred pigs being slaughtered, drowning out the cheering crowd. It moved forward despite the wound, lashing out, but the soldier batted it aside once again.

Duncan leapt toward the edge of the stage, his one hand on his sword hilt, the other fisted tight. He looked half a breath from charging in to help them. Crispin was tossed down again, and his shield flew across the ring. He rolled, but the mantis slashed across his leg before the other guard rejoined the fray, his blade finding the monster's flesh again. The Mantis exploded into a flurry of attacks, moving with a speed that went beyond anything I'd ever seen. It lunged at one guard, massive limb slamming into the shield with a rending sound that made every muscle in my body tense.

The shield dented and split, giving way to the beast, but the soldier never faltered, blocking the follow up blow with his sword. The monster kicked at him with razor sharp limbs, but he spun around it, letting the momentum carry him into a vicious slash to the beast's neck.

Green blood flowed like water out of the creature's neck as its head flew free of its previous attachments.

A sigh of relief slid out of me. Not that I'd thought the mantis would make it all the way to us but still…the monsters were hard to kill. If it had started climbing the stands….

The mantis dropped like a ton of bricks. Crispin limped over, lowering a hand to the wounded man, and helped him back to his feet as the crowd roared with shouts and applause.

My muscles finally unclenched. "Gods, that was crazy. Why would they risk their men like this?" I knew the answer even as I asked.

For the spectacle. To prove they could kill anything they wanted.

Risking lives for the viewing pleasure of the wealthy was just one more example of the grotesque lack of humanity here. Added into that, the show of power…it was a way to keep people from doing anything stupid. Like attacking a king.

My attention shifted back to the royal family. The king was clapping from where he sat, but he looked pale and groggy again, and it was Relyk the sorcerer who rose to speak once more.

"Well done. As you can see, our guards are as fine as ever, even in peacetime. Through careful, regimented training, the cream rises to the top, just as in the rest of our glorious society." He paused, waiting for the crowd's applause to slow. "But, if blood sports are not to your liking, we will continue with something a little lighter to our celebration. We welcome our falconer, Bertrand!"

That got my attention.

A wizened old tree of a man rose from the opposite side of the amphitheater, right behind the first row of nobles. He turned and kissed a stooped, elderly woman beside him on the forehead, then hobbled toward the stairs. The speckled pair of falcons on his shoulders sat perfectly still despite the noise of the crowd.

Fetch leaned forward and I put a hand on him, stilling him. I wasn't sure we'd ever seen another falconer this close.

Bertrand made his way to the center of the ring, ignoring the streaks of green blood that stained the ground as three men dragged the mantis' corpse away.

The old falconer moved with unexpected speed as he flipped a piece of jerky in either direction, and the birds shot into the sky in unison. They zipped off, catching their prizes and beginning to circle overhead. Bertrand let out a shrill whistle and they bolted upward even further, breaking into a series of tandem flips and twirls that had the crowd roaring.

He whistled again, deeper this time. They dropped their treats in unison, mid-flip, then fell into full-on dive bombs toward their falling strips of jerky. Each falcon went for the treat the other had dropped, and they smacked into them a couple yards above the ground, pulling out of their free fall to swoop back up and land back on Bertrand's shoulders.

Fetch fidgeted on my shoulder as the crowd roared with applause.

"Jealous?" I whispered.

He nudged at my ear with his beak, as if in response.

A series of other tricks followed, and with birds that well-trained, I found myself wondering why they needed to hire me at all…

The sorcerer Relyk strode back to the podium, raising an arm as the falconer dropped into a stiff bow.

"Old Bertrand has served us long and well, and we're thankful for all he has contributed to this great empire. But as we all age, new blood must be brought in. With that said, we have employed a second falconer, as apprentice to Bertrand." My blood chilled as he continued. "And now is her chance to show what she's capable of."

Fuck. Fuck. Fuck.

Moll's hand locked onto mine like a vise, but I forced myself to my feet. I should've thought ahead and expected something like this the second the old falconer had been called out, should have been planning what to do.

"Wish me luck." My vision darkened slightly as I walked mechanically toward the stairs, my heart thumping heavily in my chest. I gripped the railing firmly, eyes fixed on the king's feet as I walked. No point in making eye contact with someone I wish had died for real.

I was near the bottom by the time I even considered what trick Fetch and I would do. Given the circumstances, how well did I *want* to do? I would essentially act as Bertrand's apprentice for the time being, but more than that, we'd been planning to lay low. Now here I was in the center of the amphitheater, all eyes on me.

Anger spiked through me as I stepped into the ring.

"Bow to your king before you begin," Relyk instructed.

I would've expected to be more afraid, but in that moment, staring into Heinrich's cold blue eyes, all I felt was rage. I hoped it didn't show on my face. If it was possible, I would've leapt across the small barrier between us and jammed my dagger into his neck, finishing the job Moll started.

His thick, golden crown shimmered in the evening light, the Empire's insignia was printed on the center of his silken tunic. Starving gold miners died daily in The Hollow, beaten if they didn't reach their quota, hung if they dared to take so much as a flake of the stuff. How many had died just to make the things he was wearing?

The image of him standing over Moll replayed in my mind, and my hand ached as I squeezed it into a tight fist.

Could I really leave this place and go back to The

Hollow, while leaving this man in power to victimize others? But in truth…there was nothing I *could* do. I was no hero. I was no powerful Whisper. I was nothing but an orphan who was lucky to be on this side of the grave still.

He met my gaze for a long moment, his lips curling into a frown.

You need to bow. And you still haven't you idiot!

I dropped into as shallow of a bow as I felt safe giving—the only slight I could offer at this point. I didn't have time to figure it out now, but my previous plan had clearly been incomplete. Once I got Moll safely back to The Hollow and things calmed down again, maybe I *would* return to Little Alabaster.

Because this bastard did not deserve to rule. He was as monstrous as the mantis.

Heart pounding, knowing I was contemplating rebellion, the exact thing he'd warned against, I stayed in the bow, even lowering it a little.

Duncan would make a far better king. I could see that. But for Duncan to rule…Heinrich had to die.

For real this time.

CHAPTER 10

Rebellion was a terrible idea. Probably one of my worst to date. Moll would tell me so, and she'd be right.

Yet the word tumbled through me, over and over, as stupid as it was.

I tore my attention away from the king to focus on the task at hand.

Duncan met my gaze. "Good luck," he mouthed.

My heart skipped a beat as I turned and quickly scanned past Relyk, who raised his eyebrows, and across to the guards. Close up, the king's guards were far stranger than they had appeared from the stands. Easily a head taller than the average man, half again as wide, and each of them had a cloud of black flies that flitted in and out of their midnight-black armor giving them an effect as if shadows curled around them.

"Apprentice. Get to it," Bertrand barked, snapping me out of my thoughts.

I reached down shakily, tugging a dried chunk of rabbit jerky from my pocket. I'd have plenty of time to process the king's horrifying guards later. It was show-time. Fetch tensed on my shoulder as I strode out into the ring, and he shot from my arm like a bolt of light-ning when I finally tossed it into the air.

We ran through a series of basic tricks, and I did my best not to have him show up Bertrand's falcons. Getting a passing grade could be better than excelling, especially when you didn't want eyes on you.

I whistled him down at the end of our routine, but he shot up at the last moment instead, spinning through the air. He let the jerky fall from his beak, as if by accident, and I already knew what to expect when he snapped into a dive bomb a heartbeat later.

He plummeted toward the ground in a whirlwind of feathers and talons. The morsel hurtled closer and closer to the hard-packed earth below, with him just behind. His beak snapped it up only inches from the ground, and he whirled out of his dive, his wings blowing up a cloud of dirt as he whipped back into flight and onto my shoulder. The crowd erupted with applause, and he tossed the treat into the air a final time before gulping it down, letting out a final, triumphant screech.

Showoff.

I might be willing to take a backseat to Bertrand's

falcons, but apparently Fetch was not. Not that I blamed him—he was amazing.

My mood darkened as my attention shifted back to the royals, and the sorcerer cocked his head as I met his gaze. He shot me a thin smile, pulling his hands together for a single clap of his own.

"And here we have our palace's future falconer, *Ella*. We look forward to seeing what innovation she might bring in the coming years, should she apprentice well."

I bowed again, eyes fixing on Moll as I turned around and marched back up the wooden stairs. She was shrunk as small as she could be in her seat, leaning away from the king, trembling. Rage burned hot in my belly, setting my blood to boil.

For Moll, I would fight with all I had.

The sorcerer spoke again before I'd even finished sitting back down next to Moll.

"For our next exhibition...our very own Prince Duncan, along with Sir Crispin Locke. The strength of the royal family does not only lie in leadership and politics. The Prince has studied the blade since he was a young boy, and, as we all know, few can match him in skill. This exhibition will be yet another chance for him to *prove* that."

Duncan and Sir Crispin pulled on their helmets, leaving only their eyes and mouth visible, then strode over to the edge of the ring side by side. One of the black-armored guards moved to open the gate for them, but King Heinrich...

"Stop!" He made an unsteady march toward them.

"Your Majesty." Relyk stood and bowed his head.

What was happening? I couldn't see Duncan's face under the helmet.

After a quick exchange with Relyk that had the sorcerer backing away, Heinrich turned to address the crowd.

"I will take my brother's place in this bout to show the enemies of the crown just how strong their king is even after an attack!" His voice rang with emotion. At first I thought it was anger at his would-be assassin. But as he passed Duncan and shoulder-checked him without sparing him so much as a glance, I realized it was something else.

"Jealousy," I whispered, leaning close to Moll. "There's a sibling rivalry here at the very least."

Unless…did Heinrich think the attack on him had been orchestrated by Duncan? But that didn't make sense—Heinrich was aware of what he'd done that night, even if he would never admit it. He had to know that Molly acted in self-defense, nothing else.

It was a strange emotion to see from a man who ruled an entire kingdom and could have whatever his heart desired, yet there it was, plain to see.

He was jealous.

Thinking on it, Heinrich only decided to intervene when the sorcerer had started singing the younger brother's praises.

Interesting.

I tucked that bit of knowledge away. If anything, it made me believe that Duncan was the better choice as king more than ever.

Heinrich strode forward to the center of the ring to meet Crispin, who bowed low in respect before unsheathing his blunted blade. The limp from his previous fight with the mantis was obvious as they circled each other, but he advanced nonetheless.

The king stepped to meet him, his blade whipping forward with a testing strike. Crispin batted it aside and responded with an attack of his own, narrowly avoiding the king's armored chest.

Heinrich leapt sideways before lunging once again, his sword slicing past the man's face. Crispin stumbled as he dodged back, but recovered quickly, and the crowd roared as the tip of his blade clinked off the king's breastplate.

I held my breath as the king advanced in a wild flurry of strikes. His sword swung in and out, hammering at Crispin. The knight staggered backward as he blocked and dodged, unable to do anything but defend himself against the increasingly frantic onslaught. A dozen strikes in, Heinrich's blade slid just past his shoulder, smashing into the ground below with an audible *thunk*.

I leaned forward in my seat, unable to sit as I waited for what came next.

Would Crispin really risk striking the *king*?

It would be a death sentence.

Crispin spared the briefest of glances at the sword lodged into the dirt behind him, then thrust his blunted blade half-heartedly toward Heinrich. It bounced uselessly off the armor as it made contact, marking a second unanswered blow. I shot a quick glance at Duncan, who stood right up against the fence.

This was *not* going according to plan, of that much I was sure.

Just as Crispin moved to sheathe his weapon, the king let out a roar, yanked the blade from the dirt, and swung with all his might.

A killing blow, aimed to take the knight's head.

The knight ducked low, but his leg buckled in the sudden shift of weight, and the king's blade cut through the air where his head had been. But the king caught himself and settled for a backswing that landed hard against Crispin's shoulder. The arena was totally silent as Heinrich dove upon him, swinging his weapon into the wounded knight's chest plate and helmet over and over as Crispin covered his head with his bracer-clad arms. He couldn't fight back. Not really. If he did, he'd be killed.

But if he did nothing…I was sure we were about to see him lifeless.

One moment, it was just Heinrich brutalizing the defenseless guard. The next, it was as if someone had loosed a lion into the arena.

Prince Duncan leapt over the railing, and sprinted

toward them, his hand inching toward the hilt of his sword. "Enough! Enough, brother!"

Heinrich didn't seem to hear Duncan, his blows coming faster and harder on Crispin.

The air was thick with tension as the silent crowd sucked in a collective breath. Would Duncan actually hurt his own brother?

"Halt!" Relyk's voice boomed through the silent arena, stopping the king in mid-swing before the prince could reach them or fully draw his weapon.

Though the action was in the arena, it was the sorcerer I couldn't look away from.

Relyk's skin had paled to the point that it looked a sickly gray even from this distance. "As I say, halt. The fight is well met and done." He swayed on his feet as he lifted a hand. "A truly magnificent display of strength from our monarch. King Heinrich is the victor."

I turned my attention back to Heinrich to find him glaring at Relyk but still hunched over a fallen Crispin, who likely dared not move.

Would Heinrich finish the poor man off, just to make a point? After a few gut-wrenching moments, the king finally let his sword fall to the dirt. Then he stood and held up his fist in celebration. There was a beat of confused silence, followed by a half-hearted smattering of applause.

I let out a shaky breath and slumped back in my seat. That had been far too close of a call. The royals and those of Little Alabaster might look down on us people from The Hollow, but they were fucking animals. I was a thousand percent sure that if Relyk hadn't called the fight, Duncan's friend would be dead.

I'd never been more desperate to get back to my shithole of a home. I'd rather be poorer than dirt and struggling to survive than live right under the nose of a man who would rape, kill and do whatever the fuck he wanted, knowing there was no law that held him to a higher standard.

Duncan glared at his brother as he passed and then knelt to help Crispin stand. The man gripped his forearm and stood as Duncan's gaze snapped right back to the king.

"Brother, that was—" The prince's fingers closed over the hilt of his sword, but Crispin put a hand on Duncan's shoulder, halting him. Duncan stood stock-still with indecision for a long moment, body tight as a wire stretched. Finally, he took his hand from the hilt and just shook his head. "Well done, my king," he said with a curt bow.

The crowd breathed out in unison as the last of the tension faded. If it hadn't been for his knight's steadying hand, it was hard to say what would've happened. Had Duncan really been planning to charge the king by himself? A suicide mission, considering Heinrich's ominous armored squad of goons who no doubt would have stepped in. I had a feeling that, blood relative or not, Duncan would be shown no more mercy for attacking the king than anyone else.

Duncan and his knight exited the center of the arena a moment later and headed back toward their seats. It was easy to see that they had a friendship like Moll and I; they were connected in spirit instead of by blood. It was clearer now more than ever that the same was not the case between Duncan and his brother. A reason to trust the prince, or just a coincidence? Just because *he* wasn't a rapist, and knew his brother was a piece of shit didn't mean *he* was a good man.

He's still one of them, and you were just considering starting a rebellion you idiot, a little voice in my head reminded me. I couldn't let myself forget that, not for an instant.

The remaining events of the so-called celebration passed uneventfully, with exhibitions between guardsmen, some lighter entertainment featuring dancers and a pair of fire-eating Whispers. By the time things were coming to a close, the sun had long since set.

Relyk silenced the amphitheater with a clearing of his throat as he and the king stepped back up to the podium.

"I hope you've enjoyed this celebration as much as we have, but we must end on a less joyous note. A dark specter hangs over us this night. This woman—Francesca, she called herself—needs to be found and punished for her crimes. The palace guards have questioned every redhead in Little Alabaster, to no avail. That means she's likely altered her appearance, either by skill or by magic. An enemy of the kingdom lurks among us. An enemy that might well be hiding in plain sight, and every one of you has a *duty* to do all you can to bring this enemy to justice. If you suspect someone of being involved with this devious plot in any way, come forward and speak now. You will not be punished if you're wrong. In fact, you'll be lauded as a patriot trying to protect the crown."

Based on how the king had treated Sir Crispin Locke, a man whose job was to 'protect the crown,' I found myself questioning how much Relyk's promises were worth. And, even more concerning, how things would go for those accused. This could easily turn into some kind of insane witch hunt—especially if there was a tangible reward, or even a suspicion of one. But the crowd did not seem to share my worries as a hand shot up a few rows ahead of me.

The sorcerer glanced over, cocking his head and motioning for her to stand. "Yes?"

A flicker of light passed from Relyk to the servant. The woman's voice was hoarse and deep, and she labored over each word, but she was loud enough to hear every breath.

"Could be that it was Agnes Burrows. She's a Smudger who comes into town sometimes, and I can tell she doesn't like the rest of us...I caught her laughing about my purple bonnet behind my back a few weeks ago, she just seems like the type to try and hurt the king."

The sorcerer smiled benevolently at the woman.

"Any other…suspicious behaviors?"

The servant scratched at her chin and then shook her head. "Maybe, but not that I've seen with my own eyes."

Relyk laced his hands together, tight enough I could see the strain. "And how old is Agnes?"

The woman scrunched her face up and shrugged. "Sixty-odd."

"Our suspect is younger, and even a strong Whisper would struggle to create such a grand illusion for long, but I'll take it under advisement and inquire with my contacts in The Smudge."

A thirty-something year old man raised a hand, and Relyk gave him time to speak as well. "What about the young woman who breaks horses at the stables? I saw her talking with the king when she was riding earlier that morning. She was crying and cursing under her breath after he left."

The sorcerer *actually* seemed intrigued this time. "And what is her name?"

"Amelia."

A woman a distance away let out a low cry and shot to her feet. "It wasn't me! I was at the stable all night feeding and watering the guests' horses! I swear it!"

The girl couldn't have been more than nineteen, her brown hair shot with a hint of auburn. My blood ran cold as Relyk jerked his head at the fly-ridden henchman at his side. "I'm sure that's true, but we'll just have my guard confirm that with a few questions before you leave tonight."

He shot Heinrich a glance, but the king bobbed his head in confusion and then shrugged.

So much for an eyewitness. I was pretty sure Heinrich didn't remember fuck all about what happened in the gardens, what with having been nearly dead for a while there and all. Relyk had been trying to scare people into coming forward with that bit of fiction. If everyone calmed the fuck down and kept their mouths shut, eventually, they'd have to give up the hunt.

The guard marched toward Amelia, even as an older woman with the same hair color only speckled with gray leapt in front of her, arms splayed.

"No! Please, don't take her! She's my only living child. I can vouch for her." Her voice had taken on a note of hysteria and Molly's hand wrapped around mine in a bone-bruising grip. "I brought her a beef and bean pie late that night as she'd had such a long day. I saw her at the stables!"

"Keep your head down," I whispered to Moll, my arm shooting up more on sheer instinct than considered thought. "Excuse me? Sir?" I called loudly, causing every head to turn my way. "Why would a stable hand have a pair of expensive…what were they, glass shoes is what I heard? And how would she have been able to attend the Jubilee without an invite?"

Relyk shot Amelia's accuser a questioning glance. "Your thoughts?"

The man drew back, eyes wide. "Well...I couldn't say, could I? I—maybe she stole them. I don't know, I only told you what I knew and that's that."

"Where would she get them indeed?" Relyk muttered. "My focus was on healing the king, interviewing the invited attendees along with anyone who bore a resemblance to this criminal, but it's time to spread the search." He turned to the line of soldiers behind him. "First thing tomorrow you are to check all the shops in town and see if there is anything even remotely similar to those shoes."

Fuck, fuck fuck. What had I done?

I'd been so intent on drawing suspicion away from some innocent stable girl that I may have inadvertently helped them with their investigation. They'd start in Little Alabaster and The Smudge, but it'd only be a matter of time before they took their inquiries to The Hollow. Everyone there would know that only Xavier would create such a whimsical item. Hell, he was probably still bragging about those fucking shoes.

Sure, there were those of us who would never betray a Hollower to the crown, even if it meant death. But all it would take was a hint of financial reward and the handful of kiss-asses and turncoats would start singing like canaries.

I should've taken my own advice and shut the fuck up. Maybe it should've been me rather than Moll who had taken a 'vow of silence'...

Whispers and muttering rolled through the crowd

as both young Amelia and her crying mother were walked out of the arena, but the sorcerer pulled their attention back with a whistle.

"We will allow your annual Abundance Feasts to go on as scheduled and will be hosting a select group of guests at the palace that night as well. If our culprit is not found between now and then, it will be the last social event in Alabaster while we reassess our security protocols. This means no Year's End gala, or dinner parties in your homes, no fetes or balls hosted at the palace. None of it."

I was still trying to figure out how to help Amelia, but by the sound of the gasps that cut through the front rows, you would have thought that he had threatened castration instead of cancelling their stupid parties for a while.

But they weren't done yet. Heinrich stood to join Relyk, and something about his icy smile told me he'd saved the worst for last.

"And if, Gods forbid, we *still* don't find the person responsible by the time the frost melts? A team made up of your firstborn children will be selected by lottery to head out over the Great Wall and clear the mantis nests of any eggs."

There it was.

I could feel Molly flinch beside me, and I let my eyes drift shut.

Monsters. These people were fucking monsters.

"This is not meant to be a punishment, of course,"

Relyk chimed in. "There was an attack in The Hollow, and a little boy was nearly killed."

Girl. It was a little girl, you bastard.

I opened my eyes to see the sorcerer snick his tongue in fake concern as he continued with a shake of his head. "We just need to make sure that every family feels like they have some stake in keeping the people in this kingdom safe. You understand."

Judging by the dead silence, the masses definitely did not understand, but no one said a word.

"Now that's settled, you can all go home to your beds. Make sure to say a prayer of thanks for your beloved king's miraculous recovery."

King Heinrich's lips twisted in a cruel smile as he dismissed us all with a wave. We filed out of the amphitheater in orderly lines moments later. The mixture of fear and rage that consumed me was almost too much to bear and I had trouble taking it slow enough to let Moll keep up with me.

Would they truly let Amelia and her mother go once they checked her alibi? And if they didn't, was I as much to blame as the king himself for allowing her to be taken despite knowing she was innocent? Sure, I'd tried to help, but it had done nothing. Her status, pretty face, the color of her hair had damned her.

That and the fact that the king clearly didn't have a single fucking memory of the night he was stabbed. They were relying on descriptions from people who had seen Moll in passing. Good for us, not so good for every other woman.

We broke away from the rest of the servants on the way back to our hut, and not until we shut the door behind us did Moll let out a long, heavy breath.

"That was awful." She removed her prosthetic and absently rubbed at her knee. "I feel ill. I don't get it. How can he be alive? I keep seeing his *very dead* face in my nightmares…"

Fetch flew from my shoulder to an upper cabinet as I shook my head. "The sorcerer's magic must be stronger than anyone knows if he could bring him back from so close to dead that we all assumed he was."

But I got the sense the effort came at a cost. Relyk had looked more and more haggard as the night had progressed, and the king hadn't exactly been full of vim and vigor either. They were putting up a good front for the populace and the politics of the place.

Speaking of good fronts…

"What did you make of those drawings?"

"Well, whoever did them is an amazing artist, but I overheard those maids talking about them being some sort of protest against the crown, and I didn't really see it," she said with a shrug. "That one girl was right, though. The sorcerer definitely didn't mention it."

"They were a lot like," *Okay, exactly like,* "the pictures in that book of fairytales I told you about."

"Interesting. Maybe whoever drew them came from the same place as your real parents!"

I nodded, half-relieved that she'd come to the same —sane—conclusion as I had. Because the other possibility was that all this stress had jiggled something loose in my brain and I was on a straight path to madness.

What had Gayelette said again?

"Just know this; you're exactly where you're meant to be, and you have everything you need to succeed. Stop fighting every step of the way and open yourself to what the universe is telling you."

"Yeah well, the universe should be a lot more fucking clear, then," I mumbled, head suddenly pounding.

"What was that?" Moll asked, head tipped in question.

I cleared my throat and forced a smile despite the ache in my temples.

"Nothing, just thinking out loud. I don't want you to worry, Moll. We're going to get out of here soon. I swear it."

She nodded wordlessly, leaning her head into my shoulder. "I... Thank you. For coming for me when you knew I was in trouble. For staying and helping me, even though you don't have to. All of it."

"I know you'd do the same if the situation was reversed." I wrapped an arm around her waist and stood there, my resolve strengthening. I couldn't be wasting precious energy on fairytales and coincidences. I needed every cell in my brain for planning, revising, and planning some more.

Tomorrow, I'd still make contact with the O'Donnellys. But things had grown decidedly more complicated in the past couple of hours. Now, not only did I have to protect Moll until we made our escape. I also had to make sure Amelia and her mother didn't pay for our sins, and I had no idea where to start to help them.

This place had already been a fucking hell-scape of potential pitfalls and terror with just me and Moll to try and save.

Now that King Heinrich was *alive,* I had a sinking feeling that his reign of terror was just beginning.

CHAPTER 11

*E*arly the next morning, before I had to be at Bertrand's for my first day of falconer apprenticeship, I stood before The Hoof and Saddle.

Gayelette had told me this was where I could find the O'Donnellys, but instead of knocking as instructed, I stared at the front door frozen in place. And it wasn't due to the cold, though the wind was biting my nose and cheeks.

I'd spent the night tossing and turning, trying to decide if the ends justified the means, but I could see no other way around. There would be no escaping Little Alabaster and getting back to The Hollow without the help of locals who knew how to get us out. We needed them. But damned if I didn't feel exposed going to strangers who could as easily turn us in for a reward.

This would be the biggest risk I'd taken so far. I had

to trust that the flower-woman Whisper had been straight with me and that I could walk into this place to ask a group of total strangers to smuggle me and Moll out of here less than a week after an attempt had been made on the king's life…By a woman.

Surely that was a suspicious ask. What was to stop them from turning me in? Honor among thieves, perhaps?

Perhaps not.

A shared hatred for the crown and everything it stood for?

I was banking our lives on it.

I rapped on the door three times, then two, then three again as instructed. A minute or so later, a slat of wood slid to the side, and one brown eye stared out at me.

"I'm here for the O'Donnellys, please."

"Come on then," a raspy voice answered, muffled by the layer of thick wood between us. The door swung open, and I stepped inside. The place was empty but for the man standing at the door. He was short, barely five feet, and he scowled up at me. "You going to stand there and let out all the heat or are you coming in?"

"Sorry, are they even here?"

He let out a grumble and tugged me inside before slamming the door shut and locking it.

"In back."

I let my eyes adjust to the dim light before I carefully made my way in the direction he'd pointed. Once

I got closer to the open door in the back of the tavern, I could hear low, animated voices.

I peeked my head in the room to find four men gathered around a billiards table.

"The locks are too well-crafted. It's going to take a lot longer than you think just to get inside." A red-cheeked hulk of a man took a gulp from his pint, which looked like a child's cup in his ham-like hands.

A bald guy with a lean face and thick-framed glasses stepped forward, gripping his pool stick. "I say we–"

A crack rang through the room as the larger brother gave him a whack upside the head without spilling a single drop of his pint. "No one cares what you think, Jacob."

The smaller man—Jacob apparently—reeled, dropping his stick as his hand went to his face. He stared up, defiant as he fixed his now twisted glasses. "Remind me again, when did we vote on *you* being our de facto leader, Scotty?"

The third man let out a raucous laugh. A teenage boy stood at his side, silent, eyes wide at the interaction. "Like anyone would pick *that* chickenshit to lead." Closer in height to red-cheeks, the third man who'd spoken actually fit the bill of a proper smuggler—at least in looks. Dark curls with a hint of auburn hung just above emerald eyes, and he had a roguish smile that pulled it all together.

I cleared my throat and four sets of eyes snapped toward me in unison. "Are you the O'Donnellys, then?"

The largest one—Scotty—looked me up and down as he set his pint on the pool table.

"You're the chit trying to get back to The Hollow, yeah?" He leaned forward. "Gayelette mentioned you might be coming."

I swallowed hard, sparing a quick glance behind me. The lone bartender was still in the other room, keeping his nose out of our business. Just to be safe, I strode a bit closer before replying.

"Yeah," I kept my voice low in hopes they followed suit. "My friend and I need to get out of here and back to The Hollow as soon as possible."

The bespectacled Jacob rubbed at a wispy, flesh-colored beard I'd not seen at a distance, his eyes thoughtful. "Tough time for jobs like this... when do you need to be out by?"

"As soon as possible. I have family waiting on the other side. We just came here to—" I stopped short at a wave of the hand from big Scotty.

"Save it. We don't care about any of that. The less we know the better. Just tell us when the soonest you can leave is, and we'll tell you what it's going to cost you."

I blinked. "Um, we could leave as soon as tonight. As far as payment goes, I don't have cash, but I do have something of value." I paused briefly, pulling the prince's pocket watch from my pocket. It caught the light, and they all leaned forward a little, the gold beckoning them as surely as bees to honey.

Jacob narrowed his eyes, gesturing for me to approach. I did, staying alert as the smugglers eyed the gold watch with greedy, gold-lusting eyes.

What was to stop them from just taking it? Not much.

It wasn't a question I was new to asking. A few months in the Hollow would be enough for even a fool to pick up on the 'law of the coin'; you'd always be better off assuming others will do what nets them the most coin rather than to take them at their word. It was a simple enough premise, but it had served me well over the years, even if it left me more than a little jaded.

It'd be bad for word-of-mouth business if they just stole the watch from me, but that was assuming I made it out of this alive. With that said, they had no way of knowing whether I'd shared my whereabouts with others before coming here. Surely it wouldn't be worth the risk. I sucked in a breath and held it out, trusting my gut.

It wasn't like I had a lot of options.

Jacob flipped the watch over and his eyes widened as he inspected it more closely, smacking the largest smuggler's hand away disdainfully. Then, he glared at me. He pushed the timepiece back into my hand, shaking his as if trying to rid himself of its taint. "You would be so stupid as to bring this here?"

I tried to push the watch back toward him. "It's a valuable piece, pure gold, surely it's worth—"

"We don't want anything to do with jewelry stolen from the royals," he snapped.

I flinched, sparing a glance over my shoulder as I shushed him.

The handsome one chimed in. "Stealing from the royals, huh?" He flashed a crooked smile, and looked me up and down, as if taking my measure. "I like your moxie, but it's going to be a lot of trouble to get rid of something like that, especially at a time like this—you know, with all the trouble they're having right now."

"Don't sugar-coat it, Paddy," Jacob pushed up his glasses. "It'd be downright *insane* for us to buy it. No buyer in their right mind would even consider taking it off our hands."

"What if we filed the markings away?" Paddy grabbed the watch and flipped it over.

"As if someone wouldn't recognize the quality? Billy'd have us killed if we tried some shit like that, you idiot." Big Scotty reached out to cuff Paddy in the ear, but he dipped under it, leaping from his barstool to stand, still clutching his own pint.

He took a big swig, flashing me a wink as he stepped just out of reach of a follow up strike from the larger smuggler. He spun, chuckling. "Once a chicken, always a chicken, I suppose. If you're worried about being found out, how about we melt it down and sell it that way?"

Scotty grunted, scrunching up his face in thought for a long moment before shrugging. "As long as you're gonna be the one to get it melted then do as you please, but once you take the glass and all away, it's a small hunk of gold. Won't get her far. It's in the fancy workings of a Whisper made watch where the value is."

Whisper made. Fuck.

Jacob's eyes met mine as he cut in. "Scotty is right, for once. If I had to guess, it'll cover about half of one person's fare, assuming you have nothing else to offer us."

"Could I give you something on the other side?" I said, my hands beginning to feel clammy. This was going to be *way* more expensive than I thought, and I was running out of options. "I'm an inventor, I have plenty of stuff–"

Scotty waved me off. "We've been through that enough times to know it's more trouble than it's worth. You Hollowers are both broke and crafty and we aren't going to be chasing you down. We're smugglers, not debt collectors."

"What can you do for us *here*, if you're such a great inventor?" the teenage boy spoke finally, drawing my eyes to him. The smallest of the bunch, he shot Scotty a nervous glance. Judging by his appearance he couldn't have been older than thirteen.

I nodded to him, thinking fast. "Well…when I walked in you were saying something about struggling with some kind of lock." I paused, thinking out loud. "If you pay me some for the watch, I could use the money to build you a lockpick based on one that I invented. I have yet to meet the lock she couldn't break." The old one hadn't gotten me into the palace church, but the new version that I could already see in my head was going to be twice as good, so it wasn't a lie so much as a...promise of sorts. "What are you trying to open, anyway?"

Scotty raised a thick eyebrow. "And why would we go telling you that, lass? If you want to make it in the underworld you should learn to keep questions to yourself."

I drew back, raising my hands in an exaggerated apology. He might be acting tough but judging by the intrigued looks on their collective faces, I knew I'd stumbled onto something important to them. Whatever it was they were trying to unlock, it was worth at least as much as passage for two to The Hollow.

"If it works as well as you say," Jacob began, eyes narrowing again, "Then we would pay you good money for it. If it works."

My heart began to beat a little faster. This could work. But I had to be careful. "Enough to get me and my friend back home?"

The four smugglers turned to each other and closed ranks, whispering quietly amongst themselves for a long moment. It was Paddy who spoke as they turned back to face me.

"You bring us a lockpick like you say you can, and aye...we'll give you passage to The Hollow for two..."

I nodded, hope bursting upward and I fought to

keep the triumph off my face. "It's a deal then. I don't have the supplies, and it will take me a couple of days to make." Smitty was kind enough, but he'd make me work for my space in his forge. "I'd like to get started as soon as possible. How quickly do you think we would be able to melt down and offload the pocket watch?"

Could I have melted it down for them at Smitty's place? Sure, but that was more time I'd have to trade for. Besides, the quicker I got it off my hands, the better. Whisper made...could be tracked possibly, and better that they had it than me.

Paddy waved my concerns off, not even glancing at the others. "Give the girl an advance. The sooner she can get the project done, the better. Things are getting hot around here. We can't risk waiting any longer..."

Scotty scowled, but waved me closer with a grunt, even as he reached for the watch on the pool table. He scooped it up. "We'll get rid of it. I'd say it's worth..." He paused, turning to Jacob, who whispered something in his ear. "Fifty marks."

I gritted my teeth the moment he said it, as I would have no matter what number he gave me. Bartering... you never took the first offer, even though fifty marks would have been plenty to get what I needed. "Geez... It's going to be tough to do it for so little. I have a lot of stuff to buy for this to work right."

He narrowed his eyes at me, then grunted. "Seventy-five. And don't even think about running off with the money. I know I said we weren't debt collectors, but this deal here is different. You're on *our* turf. No matter where you go, our people will find you. There's nowhere here in Little Alabaster out of the O'Donnellys' reach."

I held out my hand, and his engulfed mine. "Deal." Seventy-five *was* a good deal, and with no other way of getting back home, I would see this through.

Paddy flashed me a final wink before striding off and disappearing through a side door with the young, quiet one in tow.

I left the tavern a few minutes later, seventy-five marks richer, and let out a long breath. The path ahead was finally clear. If all went well, Moll and I would have our ticket home within a few days' time. We just had to make it through those few days.

My mood was the highest it had been all week as I bustled down the alley…right up until I smacked face-first into a wall of muscle. Strong hands caught me as I staggered back to see Prince Duncan Westerly's piercing gray eyes looking back at me.

"Hell…Ella? Are you okay?"

"I'm fine!" Every muscle in my body seemed to tense up at once, going into full fight-or-flight mode. I held it back as much as I could, taking a quick account of the situation. Had he tracked his watch to me?

Fucking hell.

Despite the rush of anxiety, I wasn't doing anything overtly wrong. For all he knew, I was just a servant visiting a shop in The Smudge on my time off. Nothing weird or incriminating, except my reaction. I steadied my voice as much as I could manage, continuing, "What are you doing here?"

A cart rolled up behind Duncan and I craned my neck sideways to see Sir Crispin Locke hobbling up beside him.

Duncan reached into the cart and pulled out a basket full of food. Bread, fruit, some wrapped up items I couldn't identify. "There was some leftover food from the palace meal after the amphitheater event, and we decided to bring some down here."

A sexy prince who also fed those less fortunate? Damn. It was getting harder and harder to dislike the man.

"I'm happy to see you up and walking around, Sir Crispin," I said, turning away from the prince and dipping my head in greeting to the guard. "You… didn't deserve what happened out there, in the ring."

I wanted to bite my tongue off. Who said something like that about the king…in front of his brother, no less?

But Crispin just shrugged. "We don't always get what we deserve, do we? If only we did."

Prince Duncan turned and smiled. "Anyway, it was nice to see you…Ella. But we've got to go. My time-piece seems to have disappeared, as if into thin air. I'm headed to the shops to replace it."

His eyes drilled into mine and I cleared my throat, determined not to let my guilt show.

"What a shame. Those things have a habit of turning up in the strangest places, so who knows?"

He cocked his head, dark brows furrowed but his eyes never left mine. "I have a gut feeling it won't, but you're right, who can say?"

Okay, so he wasn't above yanking my chain over his suspicion that I'd taken his watch, which meant he wasn't all angel. But how much of him was devil? Then again, he wasn't having me clapped in irons, so there was that. Maybe a bit more angel than devil.

My mind shot back to our near kiss on the dance floor and my pulse skittered like I'd touched a storm bug. Duncan's keen eyes seemed to miss nothing as his gaze trailed to that very spot in my neck that danced with my heartbeat and his tongue touched his upper lip.

"Anyway," I chirped, cringing at the shrill tone of my voice. "I'd better be off, but I'm sure I'll see you... around." I flapped my hand in their direction like the chicken I was before scurrying off.

Once back through the shroud between The Smudge and Little Alabaster, I veered away from the porcelain white pathway, and headed toward the palace grounds, deep in thought. Having the prince on my side had been a boon so far, but there were a lot of potential pitfalls. Would he recognize me eventually, if he hadn't already? Would I slip and say or do something to give myself away? But the most dangerous of all...

If we were ever somewhere alone…truly alone… and he made good on the gleaming promise in his eyes, would I have the strength to turn him away? Something deep inside me already knew the answer, and I didn't like it one bit.

I was still thinking about it as I was ushered through the gates, and made my way to the hut…only to find it empty except for Fetch.

He gave a clack of his beak, and my stomach flopped like a dying fish.

"Moll?"

A peal of familiar laughter sounded from behind the house, and I rushed to the back door and yanked it open. There she was, sitting in the grass across from a young girl, both legs crossed in front of her as if she hadn't a care in the world.

"Hey, Ella!" Moll smiled up at me. Speaking.

Speaking in front of someone other than me.

CHAPTER 12

"What the fuck were you thinking?" I demanded, glaring at Moll so hard it was a wonder I didn't burst a blood vessel in my eye. I'd sent the little girl home a few minutes before and all but dragged Molly inside, but so far, she hadn't said a word in her own defense.

Even now, she wouldn't meet my gaze as she made a big show of wiping some non-existent crumbs off the kitchen counter.

"I don't know what you expect," she finally mumbled. "I'm locked in the house like a prisoner all day. I tried to stay busy by cleaning and making the place look nice—not that you noticed—but sometimes my thoughts start to swirl, and I just needed to —he's just so close, and I—" she broke off and stopped fussing at the kitchen counter, shoulders slumping.

I knew what she was thinking, but didn't want to say out loud.

As someone who struggled with my own dark thoughts, I couldn't blame her for letting hers spiral. She'd been through something terrifying, and I'd left her alone—again—a few hundred yards or so away from where her attacker lived.

The anger left me in one fell swoop, leaving behind a deep well of sadness for my friend.

"I get it Moll, I do. At least tell me you didn't talk to her the whole time she was here? Cause we can just say that it was me talking when I got back, and the kid was mistaken, or that you had one slip-up or something."

She turned to face me, and by the mulish tilt of her chin I knew...

"Oh, Molly," I whispered, a wave of nausea rolling through my belly. This was bad, so fucking bad.

"It wasn't on purpose." She jerked a thumb at a bowl of purple berries sitting on the table. "I didn't think I'd run into anybody, I saw the bushes out back and thought I could surprise you with a pie. When I went out there, the little girl came up behind me and heard me humming. She asked what song it was, and the words came out before I could stop them. But don't worry," she said, holding up her hands before I could respond, "It's going to be fine. I told her that I was under the spell of an evil Whisper who had made it so that only special children could hear my voice when I spoke, but if those special children told anyone, the spell would turn me into a frog like that story you told me one time. She totally bought it, and she likes me a lot. She definitely doesn't want me to turn into a frog." She smiled, as if she'd really done something great, and didn't just potentially fuck us both over.

I folded my arms over my chest and squinted at her. "So basically, worst case, she tells someone and we bring suspicion down on us both. And best case, you told a six-year-old girl that you were cursed and if she never sees you again—scratch that—*when* she never sees you again, she'll think you got turned into a frog because of her?"

She stared at me blankly in silence.

I ran my hands over my hair. "What were you thinking, Moll? We're already in a terrible position, so why not drag some local children down with us while we're at it?" I dropped down into the nearest chair at the kitchen table and leaned forward to rest my head in my hands.

Her eyes flashed with rare fury. "You know what, *Ella*? You knew what you were getting when you decided that you wanted to be my best friend," Moll said, suddenly indignant, raising her hands like she was on a stage. "I hate being alone. I need people, and they need me. I'm like a star, beaming golden light all over everything around me. It's a beacon people are drawn to. I can't help it. I'm doing my best here to stay quiet, but it's *hard*."

I stared at her. She was indeed my best friend, but

that didn't mean she wasn't flawed. "You know what else is hard, Moll? The edge of the axe that will separate our head from our necks if we get caught." I slapped my hand on the table, and she jumped.

Damn it. I pressed my fingers to my eyes and took a slow breath. She wasn't wrong about the way she drew people to her—it was the Gods' honest truth. But a darker truth?

We were on borrowed time. If I didn't get us out of here, Molly was going to get us both killed.

I scrubbed at my tired eyes and nodded. "Just… promise me it won't happen again. If the little girl comes around, send her away. We need to buy ourselves a couple more days." I stared at my friend, her eyes were wide and maybe a bit fearful, and I felt bad for that with everything she'd been through. But better for her to be afraid than dead. "I'll explain it all when I get home later, but I think I found our way out of here. I've got to go and meet with Bertrand. You stay here and work on your pie. Do *not* leave the hut… Pinky swear?"

Molly nodded, looking relieved to be off the hook. "Pinky swear."

We went through the motions, and then I made my way toward the front door, hesitant to leave even for a moment, because I knew her. I knew her penchant for drawing too much attention. But I had no choice.

Between my run-in with Duncan and my meeting with the O'Donnellys, I'd already been through the mental ringer. Seeing Moll outside with that little girl had put me perilously close to losing my mind.

I took my time heading to the falcon's mew, where Bertrand would be waiting for me. By the time I reached the large stone enclosure, I'd managed to calm my racing heart and mind down—at least a little. It was important that the old falconer saw me as capable and trustworthy, not freaking out on my first day with him.

He stood just outside the open door as I made my way toward him, up the beaten walkway.

"Good morning, Bertrand," I called with a wave. His bushy brows furrowed, and he glanced up at the sun. "Good to see you again and finally meet you formally."

"Hardly morning now," he said, glancing up at the sun, "but apparently only some of us are required to work a full day."

Not a great start.

I cleared my throat as I closed the distance between us. "Prince Duncan was kind enough to allow me a bit of time to get my affairs in order and all our stuff stowed away at the hut, but I'm yours for the rest of the day, so feel free to hand off all the dirty work."

I gave him my most charming smile, which clearly didn't register because he turned his back on me and headed inside the mew without a word. I followed and tried not to take his obvious disdain to heart. If someone was trying to take my job, I probably wouldn't be too thrilled either.

"This is the mew," Bertrand said, waving a hand around the open space.

I let out a low whistle as I took in my surroundings. It was massive, bigger than any house I'd ever seen in The Hollow, with various nests and birdhouses dotting the space, tucked among the rafters. There were bowls full of meat, as well as posts for the falcons to sharpen their beaks on. What was notably missing, though, were the birds themselves. Not a single falcon roosted in the mew.

Fetch pecked at my hair, and I almost wondered if he was asking me the same question I was about to pose to Bertrand myself.

"This place is great. But where are all the birds?"

Bertrand rubbed at his nose and then let out a sigh. "Working right now. Everybody's got to earn their keep," he added pointedly. "I'll call them in shortly for you to meet them."

"What sort of work are they doing? Hunting?" It seemed strange to call it work if it was indeed a hunt.

Bertrand gave a low grunt. "Let's just call it communications and leave it at that."

I frowned, wondering how I was expected to learn about falconry within the palace if he was unwilling to share things with me. I forced a smile and tried to keep my tone light.

"Interesting. Are they carrying messages?"

"That, among other things," Bertrand acknowledged, clearly put out at my pressuring him. He made his way over to a roughly hewn oak desk tucked in the corner. There was a large leather-bound book square in the center, along with a jar of ink and a feather quill pen.

He tapped the book with a dirty thumbnail.

"If anything should ever happen to me, this has all the information you need. The names of the birds, the commands they respond to, what they prefer to eat, any illnesses they've suffered, and some notes about their disposition as well. It's also a record of all the correspondence I've sent and received through the falcons."

I raised my brows in surprise and true interest. "Wow, that's amazing."

"It *is* quite a feat." He looked like he didn't want to say more, but I could tell by the note of pride in his voice that there was a part of him that wanted to share his accomplishments. "You might as well take a look. You're going to have to see if you can read my chicken scratch eventually anyway," he mumbled as he tugged the cover of the book open and flipped to a random page.

He tapped a finger at the top line. "So here you can see that Shira was sent out in the morning to do a recon mission to see if there were any flying mantises within a certain distance of Alabaster since the recent attack. She would've come back with warning cries if she spotted any."

"But how would you know where they were?" I said, blinking in confusion.

"Of course you know that the sorcerer is a Whisper?"

I nodded.

"He has the ability to communicate with animals in some sense, among other things."

My heart skidded to a stop as I stared at him open mouthed. "Relyk can talk to animals?"

I'd seen plenty of Whispers before, even in the palace the night of the ball, but someone with that magnitude of power at their disposal was the stuff of children's stories or centuries long past. He could heal wounds as grave as the king's, *and* speak to animals? It seemed unfair that he would have so many abilities.

Bertrand grimaced. "I'd say 'Talk to animals' is overstating it. He can…exert his control over them in some way, and sense what they're thinking and feeling. I myself have a strong affinity with the falcons. Do you not have that with yours?"

"Sometimes I think we can read each other's minds," I said with a nod, relieved that Relyk didn't have some pack of talking bird spies out on the hunt for Moll. I was already worried about her interaction with the neighbor girl. If we had to be on guard even amongst the bees and the birds, I'd be a nervous wreck from sunup to sundown.

Fetch scuttled along my shoulder to poke at my hair again.

"Go ahead, scope the place out," I said, following the words with a short, sharp whistle. He launched off his perch on my shoulder, and flew straight up into the rafters, circling the massive space around us, getting the lay of the land before parking it on a thirty-foot-tall pole with fake branches made to look like a tree.

I did a slow turn, taking it all in. "I gotta be honest, this is nicer than most people's houses."

Bertrand agreed with a low hum. "They're a good lot though, my birds, and they earn their keep. Come on, I'd say it's time you meet them," he said.

He made his way towards the door, and I followed behind. He let out a series of whistles in varying tones and then one longer cadence whistle that sounded more like a part of a song. I cocked my head and studied him.

"What was that last one? Is it special?" I asked.

His cheeks went ruddy and he cleared his throat. "Aye, that one's for Bonnie. She's a Gyrfalcon with a bit of an attitude problem. If I just call to her like the others, she'll play coy. I have to sing a sweet song to her like some young buck courting." He let out a *harumph* and then wiggled a pinky in one ear. "It's a bit ridiculous if you ask me. But again, she earns her keep, so I work with her."

We stood in silence for over a minute and I was about to start babbling when the familiar sound of wings flapping reached my ears. I looked up to see one, two, three then four birds coming from all directions.

The first to reach Bertrand's extended arm was a peregrine falcon, similarly colored as Fetch. Creamy belly flecked with spots, with a bright yellow beak and legs. She landed on Bertrand's arm lightly, a graceful and deft flier. "This one here is Shira. She's one of two peregrines, but she's the one with a scar on her beak. Eamon is also a peregrine, but a bit plumper. They did the exhibition." As if he'd heard his name called, a similarly speckled falcon landed beside Shira, landing much more clumsily, bumping her to the side to her squawk of dismay.

He introduced me to the others as they came, one landing on his left shoulder, one landing on his right. There were four so far, but none were named Bonnie. I asked him about it and he let out a snort.

"She'll take her sweet time, that one. I'll probably have to call her again."

Part of me liked her already, maybe because she reminded me of Moll.

"Let's bring them in and introduce them to Fetch. We'll come back and try again for Bonnie in a few," he said. He walked into the mew and the falcons instantly sensed Fetch's presence as they looked up almost in unison.

"Go on then," Bertrand said, lifting his arms and encouraging them to meet their new friend. The birds flew around the space and Fetch joined in. The easy camaraderie between them made me feel guilty for a moment that I'd never managed to find Fetch a partner in crime. Then again, like everything else, falcons were in short supply in The Hollow. As far as I knew, I was the only person who had one.

Bertrand stuck his head out the door of the mew and repeated Bonnie's song, only this time she didn't delay.

A big, beautiful, snow-white falcon came soaring towards us, and her beauty took my breath away. She was making a beeline for Bertrand, but then seemed to slow in mid-flight as she caught sight of me, and, just before she reached his extended forearm, she veered right and landed directly on my shoulder.

I craned my neck to look up at her, and got lost in her keen, onyx eyes. For a long moment, the bird and I just stared at one another until Bertrand's grunt broke that spell.

"Fickle fowl," he muttered under his breath before stalking back into the mew.

Apparently Bertrand knew how to hold a grudge, because his attitude didn't change over the next few hours. Of course, it probably didn't help that Bonnie barely left my shoulder, except to flit off and get her share of some entrails he'd laid out for the birds, then for a scant moment to meet Fetch.

I was glad to see that Fetch didn't seem to harbor any feelings of jealousy towards her, because it would have been a very long day having to deal with *two* grumpy old men.

As it stood, my back was sore from cleaning every

hidden nook and cranny of the mew that I was pretty sure hadn't been cleaned at any point in Bertrand's lifetime. By the time the sun started to set, I'd spent the vast majority of my first training day scrubbing bird shit with Bonnie heavy on one of my shoulders. I only hoped she would get over her crush soon.

I'd probably wind up scrubbing Bertrand's toilets if she didn't.

"Apprentice. I'm done for the day. You can finish up there and head out too," the old falconer said, the most he'd spoken to me in hours.

"Thanks," I set down my scrub brush and met his gaze. "Bertrand, I'm sure Bonnie is just trying to make you jealous or is curious about the new kid in town. By tomorrow, she'll be over me, like most people I meet," I tried my wide smile one more time.

"Probably." He glanced down at his watch. "I need to go. I've got to give my wife her medicine."

I blinked and wondered if maybe his shortness with me had nothing to do with Bonnie, and more to do with worry over his wife. "Is she…ill?"

He raked a hand through his sparse white hair and shook his head. "Chronic back pain, something between the bones. There's not much even the healers can do, but young Prince Duncan sends a salve that helps. We can only put it on once a day, but it eases Marjorie's pain. The rest of the time, though…" he trailed off and then snapped his mouth shut as if he caught himself saying more than he'd meant to.

Moved by his clear concern for his wife, I instinctively reached out and took his hand. My father had suffered at the end, and it had been…the worst thing in my life up till then to see that happen to the person I loved best. "I'm so very sorry she's suffering, Bertrand. That must be terrible to watch."

He lifted his head and eyed me before nodding. "I actually believe you mean that. See you tomorrow bright and early this time. Make sure you latch the door behind you when you leave."

He reached for his coat and hat and waddled out of the mew. I finished up the corner I'd been scrubbing as instructed, and then turned to look up at Bonnie, still perched on my shoulder and staring at me intently.

"Well, Miss Bonnie, it's time for us both to get some rest. But it was very nice meeting you."

She leaned in and touched her snow-white beak to my nose. If I didn't know better, I would think it was a kiss.

"Oh, you're a charmer, aren't you?" I whispered.

She didn't reply, but she did fly off into the rafters as if she'd understood everything I'd said. Bonnie was as smart as she was beautiful.

As soon as she vacated my shoulder, Fetch fluttered down to take her place, far lighter, which was greatly appreciated. "Hey there, buddy. Did you have a fun day with your new friends?" He wobbled his head back and forth and made a low chortle deep in his throat. "Good. Me too. Or, at least it ended better than it started."

Once I was sure all the birds were inside, I closed the door of the mew and latched it as Bertrand had told me to do. Sudden footsteps behind me had me wheeling around in surprise.

Had he forgotten something?

When I looked up, it was to find a young servant girl from the palace standing there. "Oh, hello there. Bertrand is gone for the night."

"Good evening," she said with a pleasant smile. "The king will be going on a hunt in the Northwest Forest tomorrow, and I'm to tell you that you're to accompany him."

My scalp tingled, and my face went hot. The last thing I needed was more time near the king. Alone was even worse.

"Me? Are you certain?" I stammered. "I'm brand new and don't even know the grounds yet. I don't think I'd be much help to him on a hunt."

She shrugged and held out a note. "Sorcerer Relyk said King Heinrich requested your presence by name, it is written here. Ella the Falconer Apprentice." I glanced down at my scrawled name as she frowned and cocked her head. "Is that a problem?"

Fuck me.

"Just the *two* of us? Is that the norm?"

Understanding dawned on her young face and she shook her head. "No, no! The king doesn't hunt alone and especially won't be doing it, or anything else, without guards, given the recent attempt on his life.

Prince Duncan will be there with Sir Crispin, along with Bertrand, and Sorcerer Relyk, of course."

Of course.

I held back the full body sigh of relief and managed a wobbly smile. "Alright, then. What time?"

"They will meet you here at dawn."

As I made my way back toward the hut a short while later, the nausea that rose with the possibility of going on a hunt alone in the woods with Prince Heinrich faded, but quick on its heels came a whole other sort of nervousness.

Why had he requested my presence at all? How did he even remember my name? He wasn't supposed to notice my existence, never mind invite me personally along to an event of any sort. I was trying to lay low, but it clearly wasn't working. Not to mention, I would also have to manage Prince Duncan and the attraction between us.

The attraction wasn't the worst part though, not really. Every time I was around him, two thoughts had me in a constant state of suspended fear.

Why had he kept my secret so far?

And what if he decided to stop?

CHAPTER 13

By the time my head hit the down pillow that night, I was so exhausted I could barely see. Worrying really took it out of a girl, and I'd been in a constant state of anxiety-laced fear for days now. Still, it was hard to stop the chatter in my brain, and it was long past midnight by the time I was finally able to drift off…

I found myself in total darkness, with only the sounds of insects and forest creatures in the distance to ground me.

"There's no place like home."

Somehow I knew I was dreaming and that the voice had come from inside my own head, but that didn't stop me from arguing the sentiment as I let out a snort and squinted my eyes in an effort to see something…anything…in the inky darkness.

"I'm with you. We do need to get back to The Hollow," I agreed with myself out loud, because it was a dream so who

really cared? "But not because it's so amazing. It's a shithole, and I'm sure there are plenty of places like it, but it's my shithole."

"Home is not The Hollow, child. You come from a land far, far away...and you must get back soon. Your people need you. You must prepare yourself."

I froze, realizing with a start that the voice wasn't mine at all. It belonged to a woman much older than me, but familiar. If I could just place it—

"Gayelette?" I asked, searching the dark in earnest for the strange street vendor now as my heart skipped a beat. There was lush grass beneath my bare feet, which gave me some small comfort, but still... "Where am I? And where are you? I can't see anything at all."

As if lifted and hung by an unseen hand, a fat, yellow moon appeared in the corner of the sky, like a glowing piece of fruit. I reached my hand up to pluck it when a second voice called my name.

"Harmony?"

A shiver rolled through me at the rumbling, male voice. This one was also somehow familiar, yet somehow not...

"Duncan?" I called hesitantly, scanning the meadow for any sign of him.

The cold laugh that followed held no humor as a hulking figure appeared in front of me, blocking out the moon. "Ah, little witch. That will leave a mark for sure."

I swallowed hard as I looked up into the face of the man I'd seen in my dreams before. Easily a dozen times over the *years. He'd been more like a shadow at first. His face hidden, a silent observer. But recently...*

I lifted my hand to my throat in an effort to hide the pulse fluttering there, like a butterfly trying to escape the webs of a spider.

He stepped closer, until the tips of his boots touched my bare toes, and the scent of the ocean spray and the bite of sweet rum rolled over me. He cupped my chin in his hand and tilted my head back until our gazes locked. The gleam in the endless black of those eyes...the flex of his jaw as he stared at my lips with unchecked desire. Slowly, he bent lower, and lower still until our mouths were a mere breath apart. Then, he paused for an eternity. I was about to put an end to the torture and crush my mouth to his when he nipped my bottom lip, hard.

It should've hurt. Fuck, it did *hurt. But it hurt so good, and I wanted more.*

"Please," I whispered, drowning in the sensations, in the touch and smell and desire.

"Ask me one more time, nice like that, and you'll forget this Duncan ever lived."

I sat up with a gasp and pressed a hand to my thumping heart.

"Leave me alone!" I whispered under my breath, sparing a glance at a sleeping Molly across the room in her own bed.

The remainder of the night was full of sleep but

only in fits and starts. I woke just ahead of the morning sun, crying out after a nightmare about a witch with green skin who reached for me and Fetch.

Now, an hour later, seated across from Bertrand on the carriage ride to the forest, I couldn't stop yawning as he spouted falcon facts.

"Yes, they are majestic creatures indeed." He tossed a treat to Eamon, who eagerly snapped it up, throwing his head back to swallow. "Does Fetch have a lot of tracking experience?" Bertrand said, glancing over the top of his glasses at me.

"We've hunted together countless times," I said, "but not with this many people. We usually go out alone, so we'll see how he does. What is it that we're going to be hunting, by the way?"

Bertrand frowned—something that he seemed to do a great deal. "We don't like to put the royals in danger, you see, so rabbits and pheasant, for the most part. But the king tends to get a bit… carried away on hunts."

My anger with Heinrich thrummed back to life at his mention. "Does he go often?"

"Before he left on his travels, he enjoyed the hunt very much, yes. The royals have had an annual outing before the Abundance Feast."

I nodded as if I knew that, Bertrand went on. "The king wanted to make sure his people know he's out and doing things as usual after the…incident. We will likely get a kill or two and then head home. It's more ceremonial than anything today. Many more hunters will be out here tomorrow, including a contingent of guards, who will harvest an array of wild game for the palace Abundance Feast."

Talking about Heinrich and his love of the hunt only made me think of Moll, and all the other women he'd put through similar or worse. How could the people of Alabaster stand behind a man like that? How could—

"Are you listening? I'm starting to wonder if you don't really want this job after all," Bertrand cut in.

I held back a deep sigh. No point in pissing him off early in the day.

"I'm sorry, Bertrand. I'm worried I won't do well out there today." It wasn't entirely a lie, of course. The situation with Moll was difficult but being in forced proximity with a man I'd tried to pry a shoe out of a few days earlier wasn't exactly helping my nerves. I was sure he was dead at the time, but who knew? Maybe there had still been some spark of life in him... and that gave him a tiny niggling sense that he knew me from somewhere?

What if that was why he'd even called on me for such an occasion? Bertrand could certainly have run the hunt on his own, and had done in the past for years...

I pushed the thought aside, reassuring myself for the dozenth time that day that the guard would have been there with chains and handcuffs rather than an invitation if they had even the faintest suspicion of who I was and what part I'd played in the 'incident.' The more likely explanation was that they wanted their new falconer to get some hunting experience, and to see if I was up to snuff.

Gods above let that be all there was to it.

The carriage slowed to a halt, and I sucked in a final, strengthening breath before stepping out of the doors. I slid to the muddy ground below, and Bertrand scowled at me as I offered an arm to help him down.

Okay, then.

Another carriage halted next to ours, and Duncan was the first to emerge. He raised a hand in greeting, turning as Sir Crispin and the sorcerer Relyk stepped out from behind him. My heart skipped a beat as one of the strange guards filed out next, leaping down with unnatural agility considering the bulk of his black armor.

He hit the ground, turning as the cloth shifted once more on the carriage behind, and he offered a hand to Heinrich as he appeared.

My blood chilled as the king's eyes fixed on me for the briefest moment, but they didn't linger. He ignored the guard's outstretched hand, stepping out of the carriage and onto the ground below.

Bertrand strode forward, dipping his head in greeting to the royals, and I dropped down to do the same on instinct. "Where should we head first, Your Majesty?"

"Hmm." The king looked upward for a moment, pensive, but it was Duncan who was the first to speak.

He nudged his friend. "Sir Crispin said that they spotted several fox dens just a mile to the east on yesterday's patrol. I'm sure there's a healthy population of rabbits in the area."

Heinrich shrugged. "So be it. It's as good a place to start as any." His nose wrinkled, and his attention shifted to the hulking guard in black armor to his left. "Do keep your distance, you stink."

The guard took two paces to the side without a word, his head never moving to look at the king or acknowledge the order other than to do as he was told. Something about the guards bothered me deeply.

I squinted. The flies were still there, weaving in and around the black armor.

A chill rolled through me.

Very strange.

Were they even…human? Their movements and reactions were somehow otherworldly as if they were pretending. And the fact that they never seemed to remove so much as their helmets only added to the effect. If I got a chance to look under that faceplate, what would I see?

Did I even want to know?

I could almost hear my stepmother's voice in my head. *"Enough with the fantastical thinking, Harmony. They're going to put you in a padded cell one of these days."*

I shook off the sense of unrest and stepped a little closer to Bertrand.

We set off on foot in the direction Duncan indicated, with Heinrich leading the way.

The King sucked in a deep breath of the cool morning air and nodded, his color far better than it had been the other night. "We'll take a full circle of the hunting grounds this year."

Bertrand gave the softest huff that I barely heard. I glanced at him, and he shook his head ever so slightly.

It was a lovely day—crisp and not too cold—but I didn't relish the prospect of being out here any longer than was necessary. A full circle sounded like an all-day thing to me. Not to mention, if we went really far, we might wind up running right into the shack Moll and I had holed up in the night of the jubilee. I wasn't sure what those creepy, fly-covered fuckers were capable of, but what if they were able to catch my scent there or something?

I swallowed hard and tried not to let myself fall down that rabbit-hole of worry.

"If I remember, you did have some success at the lake in the far back last time you both came home to visit," the sorcerer walked just behind Heinrich and his unnerving guard.

Duncan nodded in agreement, and Heinrich's lips curled into a frown as he turned back toward the rest of the party. "You got that boar there, did you not,

Duncan? The one we ate at the Abundance Feast that year?"

"Still thinking about that?" Duncan asked, a bite to his words.

The king scowled and waved him off. "Let's make it a contest this year, too. The one who catches more rabbits wins."

There was a clear tension between them, but the rivalry seemed largely one-sided. Duncan didn't seem concerned with his brother's jabs or challenges, but Heinrich had some serious insecurities.

Small penis syndrome if you asked me. My lips twitched at the thought, but I wisely kept my mouth shut.

As the deep winter evergreen forest grew dense around us, there was only a smattering of orange and yellow trees left from the fall. Beautiful, and far bigger than any place I'd ever hunted.

Bertrand let out a low whistle, and Eamon took to the skies. He made a strange clicking sound with his mouth, and the falcon shot into action, shooting even higher into the sky, eyes fixed on the ground below.

"Should I do the same?" I kept my voice low. Had the king heard me speak the night of the Jubilee as I'd stood over his seemingly dead body? I did my best to dismiss the thought yet again.

Bertrand shrugged. "Better two sets of eyes than one."

I whistled once and jabbed my finger into the air.

Fetch hurtled upward, climbing rapidly until he was a bit higher than Eamon. I rolled my eyes, hoping that competitive spirit wouldn't drive him to overperform *too* much. The last thing I needed was more attention.

The sorcerer smiled as I looked back to the path ahead. "You really do have him well-trained, and with no access to the systems or years of trial and error we've had at the palace. It's quite impressive."

"Fetch has served me well, but I believe he was trained before he came to me," I agreed.

"How did you afford him?" The sorcerer asked.

My heart skipped a beat as I moved into my well-practiced story about our first meeting—all lies. "I found him wounded in the woods when I was just a girl. By the time I nursed him back to health, we'd grown close. He wouldn't go, even when I tried to make him. He's been with me ever since."

The truth was, I couldn't remember a time when I didn't have him. When my adoptive father had found me, Fetch had already been by my side, as if my true parents had left the bird to watch over me. It was a silly fantasy, but one I refused to rationalize. Maybe they had been too poor to feed me, or maybe they just hadn't loved me enough to keep me. But at least they'd tried to ensure I would be safe...

A loud, screaming sound split the air overhead, and I looked to see Fetch dropping into a dive. We shifted directions as he hurtled toward the ground below, but before we could reach him, he was flying back to us with a whole rabbit in his beak. As he dove to me, he angled back upward so he could drop the rabbit right into my chest before soaring back into the skies.

The king spared a quick glance at me, eyeing me with those cold, piercing eyes. "Not bad. But make sure the birds don't hog all the game, now that we know we're in a good area for hunting." He turned away. "My bow, Jackal." He reached toward the black-armored guard, who pulled the longbow from his back and handed it to the king, who was already equipped with a quiver.

I inched closer to Bertrand, "Why'd he call him Jackal?"

"It's what the king calls them in private," he murmured. "They're the Empire's most elite soldiers—Relyk trained them himself and imbued their armor with magic. Even their identities are kept secret."

I nodded, looking the Jackal up and down one more time. Their strange, preternaturally fast movements would be a marvel to see in real combat, and I found myself feeling grateful there hadn't been one stealthily watching over the King the night of the Jubilee.

Probably, Heinrich liked to do his raping in private.

My fingernails dug half-moons into my palms as I tried not to let that thought take hold. I just had to get through the day. This was not the day to think about rebellions or taking down a king.

The minutes turned to hours, and it was shaping up to be quite the successful day of hunting as it drew close to noon. The large sack Crispin carried was halfway filled by the time we took our first break.

Bertrand's falcon, Eamon, had caught two rabbits, the same amount as Fetch, and the two royal brothers were neck and neck as well, going rabbit for rabbit.

"We must have nearly a dozen, that should be enough," the king said, glancing at the sack that one of his guards carried.

"Bang on, here, we've the same Your Majesty," Crispin said, looking up from the bag.

Relyk sucked in a loud ragged breath, drawing everyone's eyes as he leaned against a sturdy oak tree. "The lake isn't far now, but I grow weary. We should turn back."

He looked pale and haggard and had been fading fast over the past half hour. I studied him as he turned to the king. How old was he, even? Something about his face made it hard to say. Perhaps that was the magic of a Whisper—a slowing of aging?

The king grunted. "Locke, you stay behind, light a fire for Relyk. Warm yourselves and rest while we continue our hunt." He glanced at his brother. "Our wager doesn't seem to be going anywhere, and it hardly seems a satisfying end if one of us wins this coming out a rabbit or two ahead. Why don't we settle this with some larger game?"

Relyk seemed to pale further. "Your Majesty, I—"

Heinrich grinned at his own suggestion. "We can each take a falconer as our spotter, and whoever comes back with the biggest game by noon will be declared the winner."

The wind gusted once again, blowing off my cape hood for the umpteenth time, and I let out an annoyed breath. Having had about enough of it, I yanked it down and with it came my hair, falling in a mass of loose, inky waves around my shoulders. As I looked up, though, the king's eyes were fixed on me. A shiver ran through me as his eyes dilated and he licked his lips.

Fuck. Fuck. Fuck.

"We'd better get a move on, then." Duncan stepped smoothly between us, breaking his brother's view of me.

The king inched to the side, coming back into view. Heinrich cocked his head and studied his brother before his lips split into a cool smile. "Whoever gets the biggest kill wins."

Relyk nodded even as he slumped to a fallen log, seating himself. "We'll weigh them when we return to the palace, if there's any dispute."

The king strode toward me. "Well, I guess we should get moving. To me, falconer."

Duncan held up an arm, preempting the king's move to grab my arm. "We should flip a coin to see who gets which falconer. It's only fair and we don't want the win to be tainted, as I know that Bertrand has more experience..."

Heinrich's eyes flashed with annoyance for a moment, but he nodded. "Fine. Hurry up, then."

Duncan tugged a coin from his pocket, perched it on his thumbnail, and then flipped it up into the air. Fetch strained at my side, likely more out of his instinct to snatch the coin than out of any awareness of my inner turmoil. Going alone with the king into the forest was about the worst possible outcome for the day.

The king leered once again, tongue brushing against his lip as he opened his mouth to make his call. "Heads, of course."

I went still as a statue as the coin hurtled toward the ground, and the two brothers stepped up to get a look at it. The second or so before it landed stretched on, as if time had slowed. My heart froze as the coin thudded into the grass, and I studied Heinrich's expression, searching for any sign of the result.

His face scrunched in anger, and the passage of time seemed to return to normal speed. "Fucking tails."

Duncan reached down, pocketing it. "Hmmm…I suppose I'll take the girl, then. No doubt you have an edge, brother."

The king sucked in a breath, his hands balling into fists, but the sorcerer called out before he could reply.

"Better to have the one with experience in any case. Anything I can do for you before you go off, Your Majesty?"

Heinrich ignored the question and kept his gaze locked on Duncan. "No, I'm fine. I'll take the old man, and Duncan can take the pretty wench. I'll still beat him." There was a venom to his tone that made my blood run cold.

The Jackal followed close behind the king as he started off toward the north edge of the forest. Heinrich held up a hand and spun around with a snarl on his face. "*This* thing is coming with me, too? As if the old man doesn't stink enough."

"Security is crucial in times like these, Your Majesty," Relyk answered.

The king reached out and smacked his palm into the guard's armored chest, though the guard didn't so much as flinch. "Ten feet away, minimum."

"Yes, Your Majesty."

My heart skipped a beat as the voice sliced through the autumn air like a knife. Cold, raspy, and low, like it was half growl and half whisper. But there was no anger in it, despite the rough treatment, and he let Heinrich create a bit of distance before following him deeper into the woods.

A heavy hand dropped to my shoulder, pulling me out of the moment. "Come on, then."

I followed Duncan, adrenaline still coursing through me from the near miss.

"Really is a beautiful day out, for mid-winter," Duncan said, a hint of a smile on his face as he met my gaze.

"Gambling with the lives of servants comes easy to you, does it?" Regret set in instantly, and I tensed. What was so damned hard about keeping my mouth shut and laying low around this man? Why couldn't I just agree, and make small talk about the fucking weather?

My muscles went taut as his hand went to his pocket. Was I about to get stabbed for my insolence? But no…he pulled out the same coin he'd flipped a short while before. "It's rigged. Both tails," he said, flashing me the two identical sides of the coin.

I blinked, already seeing the flaw. "He's the one who called it. What if he chose tails?"

"Hasn't done it once since we were kids. Some things never change." He pulled a second coin from his tunic, tossing it to me. "If it's something small, I let him win, if it's something I care about, I win."

I let out a breath, unable to shake the lingering discomfort despite the explanation. The thought of being in the forest alone with that monster had my guts in a turmoil…

One of us wouldn't have walked out, of that I was sure.

It didn't matter now, though; Duncan had saved the day. For now. The king had called me a pretty wench, and technically I was in his employ. He could call me to the castle at any time.

Again, all the fucks in the world were not enough for this situation.

Duncan stopped abruptly at my side, hand dropping gently to my shoulder. "If, for whatever reason, he chose tails, I'd have come up with some other excuse. I would *never* have let him take you alone. I promise you that."

And this time, I couldn't help what I did next. After taking care of myself alone for so long, it was nice to have someone else do it for a change. I leaned into his touch for a moment rather than pulling away. He was a royal, born and raised in a palace, but I was beginning to trust him, just a little.

I glanced up to find him staring down at me. Electricity seemed to pulse between us as his hand slid up my neck, his palm cupping my cheek. A tingle shot up my back as his other hand fell to my hip, and my breath caught in anticipation as he leaned down. I could feel his sweet, warm breath feathering my lips when a piercing screech split the air. A second later, I caught a wing in the mouth as Fetch landed heavily back onto his favorite perch. He clacked his beak, threatening the prince.

Duncan stepped back, a grin tugging at his mouth. "He's a jealous one, huh?"

Fetch's interruption gave me a chance to check my emotions and remind myself of all the stupid things, kissing Duncan was probably the stupidest. I let out an exasperated breath as I turned to the falcon, tapping him gently on the forehead. "Doesn't mind other birds, but definitely jealous when it comes to people. Barely tolerates my cousin, even."

The tension between us was broken, and that was a good thing. I needed to focus on the hunt and nothing else. With a series of whistles, I sent Fetch back into the air, renewing the command to spot for game. We hunted in companionable silence for a time, and the sun was nearing its zenith by the time we made our next stop with no trace of any animal larger than a squirrel since leaving the clearing.

But did I even *want* us to find big game? Winning would only draw more attention to me and likely enrage the king further.

Duncan stopped abruptly, crouching down. "Looks pretty fresh."

I strode over to him and knelt next to the pile of half-dried deer pellets. "Which way did it go?"

He circled for a long moment, then jabbed his finger toward the ground. And, sure enough, a cluster of small impressions in the ground led away from the pile, barely visible between the fallen orange leaves.

A whistle brought Fetch surging back to my shoulder, and I was struck with a brief flash of guilt as I sent him back into the air, but in the wrong direction. Spoiling Duncan's hunt was a small price to pay for avoiding Heinrich's ire.

Duncan gestured wordlessly for me to follow, heading toward a more overgrown section. Brambles and shrubs intertwined with one another, and I winced as I noticed the narrow pathway that cut through them. Our quarry had been through that way, no doubt about it. Worse, we were now moving in the exact direction I'd sent Fetch. The falcon screeched overhead, as if on cue, and my eyes flitted upward. He turned sharply, gliding through the air just a few dozen yards ahead of us.

Duncan dashed through the rest of the bramble, somehow managing to keep his footsteps silent despite his speed. I cursed under my breath, debating whether to fake a sneeze and scare the deer off, but before I could even make a decision, a second cry split the air—panic lacing it.

Fetch.

Something was wrong, the cry was off, I'd never heard him like this. I broke into a sprint as I frantically searched the sky above.

Where the hell—

The falcon came into view, hurtling toward the ground in a mass of flailing wings and flexing talons like he'd been shot out of the sky. My heartbeat thumped heavily in my ears, nearly drowning out my voice even as I screamed.

"Fetch!"

My eyes never left him even as I tripped, smacking into the ground with a force that knocked the air from my lungs. He was going to crash, and I'd be lying here helpless as I watched it. But the falcon let out another screech just as a warbling growl sounded behind me, rumbling through my bones as only a predator could do.

I turned in slow motion horror to find a bear the size of the carriage charging right at me. Fetch shot past me and swiped at the animal with beak, wing, and claw, but the bear was oblivious to the attack, its soulless black eyes locked on me.

"Back, Fetch!" I scrambled to my feet, praying he'd listen even as I knew he wouldn't.

Fetch surged toward his eyes instead, and time seemed to slow as the bear grunted, lashing out to swipe with a paw larger than my head. The falcon crashed sideways in a mess of feathers, smacking into the ground as I screamed.

"No! Fetch!" I lunged to go to him, but the bear cut between us. It's cold, black eyes didn't so much as blink as it reared up on its hind legs, a low rumble escaping its throat before it let out a monstrous roar that rattled through my chest. Cold mud splattered across my cheek and time seemed to slow as the animal landed on all fours again, lunging forward, jaws snapping. I could count its teeth as its maw opened wider yet, coming straight for me. I scrambled back, fighting the urge to turn and sprint away with everything I had. I wasn't beating a bear in a foot race. What *was* I beating a bear in?

The fugue of terror and fury faded in a rush, leaving behind a single, terrible realization.

I'm going to die here.

"Run!"

Duncan's bellow was almost as terrifying as the bear's, and I scuttled backward, time speeding back up. He threw himself in front of me, fists raised as if he intended to fight the massive beast with his bare hands.

What the fuck was he even thinking?

A moment later, I found out as he made the first move, launching himself at the beast with a guttural roar. Even the bear seemed surprised as the two found themselves locked in what could only be called a deadly embrace. The bear towered over Duncan.

"Duncan, don't!" I found my voice, but he didn't listen.

The bear held him off with one claw and slashed with the other, but even as blood poured from his shredded bicep, the prince held fast, whipping out one booted foot and planting it into the animal's belly. The move sent the bear reeling backward with a force that I didn't understand. Duncan didn't waste time. He lunged again, this time with a closed fist into the animal's sensitive snout. Blood poured from its nostrils, and it stumbled down to its knees.

Duncan stood between me and the bear still. "Go on, now! You leave us alone; we leave you alone!"

The bear shook its massive head, blood spraying, and huffed out a breath as if considering the prince's proposal. It shook its head again, maybe still stunned from the blow to its nose. Then, with one last look at Duncan, it loped off, crashing through the woods and out of sight.

As if it had never been here.

"What the hell just h-happened?" Shock, I was in

shock, I could feel the cold of it snapping through me as I dropped to the ground.

Duncan turned and knelt beside me. "Ella…Are you alright?"

I nodded, sucking in another gasping breath. "I will be," I managed, meeting his gaze as I sat up. My breath caught at the silver eyes and diamond-shaped pupils that stared back at me—those were not the gray I remembered. I blinked as he turned away, pulling a waterskin from his belt.

"Your arm?"

"It's fine." He pointed at the bicep that I'd been *so* sure I'd seen ripped by the bear's claws. The shirt was shredded but the skin…the skin was not.

"Once you're ready," he said, handing it to me with one hand as the other went to my forehead, exploring it gently. "Did you hit your head when you fell?"

"I don't think so." I glanced up at him and realized with a start that his eyes were back to smoky gray.

Maybe I *had* hit my head when I'd fallen backward? Or maybe the change in his eyes was some hallucination triggered by shock? The sound of fluttering wings pulled my attention away, and my heart soared as Fetch flitted into view, a little unsteady as he landed on my shoulder.

I lifted a hand and laid it on his back, looking him up and down. "You okay, buddy?"

He ruffled his feathers, as if shaking off the whole

situation, then he pressed his cheek against mine, as affectionate a gesture as a falcon could manage.

"I think he's alright." I ran my other hand over his downy legs, checking for any injuries. But Fetch did not have his attention on me. No, he'd turned to Duncan. The two met eyes for a long moment, and Fetch clicked his beak and dipped his head.

I gave a wobbly smile. "He says thank you for saving me. At least, that's what I think he said, at any rate."

"He's a brave bird. I might not have done what he did if I were as small as him," Duncan said as he reached down to help me to my feet.

The humble words seemed sincere, but something deep inside me told me that wasn't true. Duncan Westerly had secrets, of that I was now sure. Yet he'd proven over and over that he was what Moll had been searching for in vain her whole life...Something I'd been convinced didn't even exist.

A Prince Charming in the flesh.

Wasn't that some fairytale shit?

CHAPTER 14

"You can take the rest of the day off," Bertrand said a couple hours later as he waved me out of the mew. "A bear attack is enough to rattle anyone, least of all a little thing like you."

I couldn't even be offended by his assessment. Not when I still felt the tremors of shock, could still see the bear's teeth as its open maw shot toward me. "Thanks, Bertrand."

Our journey back had gone quickly, with Duncan rebuffing his older brother's attempts to prolong the trip. Even when Heinrich chalked it up to him being a sore loser in their contest rather than the fact that we'd just been attacked by a fucking bear, Duncan hadn't budged. His only concern was getting me safely away from the forest and the reach of his evil brother. My chest still warmed at the thought, despite the many times I'd reminded myself that letting him grow on me was a grave mistake I would live to regret.

"Bah. Go get warm. Be back early tomorrow." He turned his back on me, bent over his ledger. Bonnie fluttered down and landed beside him, snatching his quill pen right out of his fingers, then flew out of reach.

"Cheeky girl!" He shook a fist at her, and she dropped the quill, right at his feet. I hurried forward and scooped it up, handing it to him. He raised his bushy white eyebrows at me. "What are you still doing here?"

I smiled and backed up. "Just leaving, boss."

I could have gone back to our little hut, curled under a blanket and hid from the world. But...I had a lockpick to make. And if I went back, Moll would not want me to leave.

"What she doesn't know won't hurt her, right Fetch?"

He tipped his head this way and that. Maybe in agreement?

Trudging my way back through the shroud between Little Alabaster and The Smudge, I stopped only to grab a hot bit of food from one of the street vendors—I was starving, and it would settle the nerves. I hoped.

A hand pie full of slow-roasted meat, vegetables and...cheese? I handed over the copper pennies, then wolfed the food back, offering a bit of pastry to Fetch. "Good, right?"

From there, it was on to Smitty's, and I was hoping he might be able to help me.

I knocked on the heavy wooden door to the forge.

"Go away!" Smitty bellowed. "I'm working!"

"It's me…Ella. I was hoping we could trade again?"

I needed to save the majority of my coin for the precious metals and gears I needed for the lockpick.

The door was yanked open and Smitty stared out at me, as covered in coal soot as ever. "Why didn't you just come in?"

I smiled at the grumpy welcome. "I didn't want to interrupt."

"Bah. What do you need?" He shut the door behind me and the warmth immediately sunk into my bones. I let out a heavy sigh.

"I'm making something that is going to take a lot of gears, and maybe a gemstone."

His eyes widened. "Gemstones? You got one?"

I shook my head, regretting that I'd used all mine.

"No, not yet. Nothing precious, just something that will refract light."

He grunted. "Maybe you want the jeweler, Jinkens, down the street? He's got all that piddly ass small shit."

I bit the inside of my cheek to keep from smiling. "Maybe? But I think the actual…" I paused, not wanting to get him in trouble if I got caught, "the thing holding all of it, I need to make out of iron, so it's good and strong."

Another grunt. "Show me."

He handed me a piece of chalk from his apron pocket and pointed to the floor. I bent and sketched out the design of the lockpick. How I thought the gears should go, and where the gemstone would sit so it would pull light into the keyhole making it easy to see the tumblers.

The design was such that it folded to look nothing like a lockpick and would fit flat in my pocket. And, if I got myself into a situation where I had to pull it out… "See, then it would just look like a woman's vanity, packing along a reflecting mirror to…" I shrugged, "I don't know, see if her makeup is smeared?"

Smitty crouched beside me. "I'm not going to ask why you need a lockpick like this. If you can make it, it should unlock…anything that I've ever seen."

I swallowed hard. "It's a commission piece."

"For the O'Donnellys?"

I shrugged, anxiety spiking. I wanted to trust him, but I was no fool. "I… Maybe."

He huffed a laugh. "Well, the metal you need, most of it'll be in the scrap bin. But I'd go to Jinkens first, see if he has the gears and a cheap gem. If I were you, that is."

Which is how I ended up dickering over four gears and a rough piece of ice rock crystal that I'd still need to shape to get the light.

"A hundred pieces." Jinkens pulled his wire jeweler's loupe away from his eye so he could look down his nose better at me.

I laughed and turned my back. "Not a chance. That ice crystal is rough. It might, *might* be worth forty pieces shaped! And the gears are used, look at the teeth on them! Half worn!"

Jinkens sniffed and put his loupe back over his eyes as he picked up the ice crystal. "The weight—"

"Is too much for what I asked for." I tapped my fingers on the glass case. "I asked for half that size, no more than an inch square chunk, which would be worth twenty pieces, and that's if I'm being generous."

Back and forth we went until he agreed to cut the crystal in half and sell me the bigger of the two chunks for thirty-five gold pieces. The gears I got for four pieces each. The bag of coins the O'Donnellys had given me was lighter, but I had what I needed.

Hopefully.

Back at the forge, Smitty watched me as I pulled out the metal I needed from the scrap heap and showed him. "How much?"

"Make me another knife." He leaned back on his stool. "I've already sold the other two."

I sighed, nodded and got to work. At least I knew exactly what he wanted, and I was able to knock the knife out faster than the first two. The hammer rose and fell in a rhythm that had me moving in a trance as my mind worked over the details of the lockpick.

Sweat rolled down my back and face, and my arms ached, but I had the third knife for Smitty in his hands before the dinner hour chimed.

Which left me only a few short hours before curfew to work on the lockpick.

I went right to it, laying out my pieces of metal, the gem and the gears. I used a tiny hammer this time, the work more intricate as I worked my way to the finished product. Tiny punches for the rivets, tiny taps to set the screws in later, tiny welds, everything was small.

The space where the cut gemstone went was next. A small slot shaped like a 'V' so the gem sat in the top and would pull light in—no matter how little—to assist the process of working through the tumblers in the lock.

I made to grab for the ice crystal, I just had to shape it, only to find that it was already done.

Smitty handed it off to me, perfectly shaped and polished so it sat deep in the 'V' looking more like a diamond than an ice crystal–it was so smooth and perfect. His already ruddy cheeks pinked further. "I was getting bored. That fit?"

"Thanks, Smitty." I swiped a hand across my brow. No doubt I was covered in coal ash, just like him. I set the gemstone in and then locked it down with a couple of thin wires woven across the top like a net.

I flipped it over, so that the gem disappeared and all that I was left with was a flat polished iron box that when I opened it, a reflective surface showed me a slightly distorted version of my face. Maybe enough to check makeup?

Molly would love it. Which was partly how I'd

come up with the idea, thinking about how best to hide a lockpick. No man would even bother to look at a woman's purse, full of bobby pins and lipstick.

"Curfew's coming, girl." Smitty took a step toward the door. "You be careful with the O'Donnellys. Assuming they're your clients. They've got trouble with the crown, you hear? And you work for the crown so…be careful."

Without another word, he shut the door behind himself and I was left with just the glowing embers of the coal fire. I flicked my hands over my newest invention, and it slid back into the shape of a perfect lockpick.

A lockpick for smugglers that had beef with Heinrich? That made it a little sweeter, I had to admit.

A lockpick I was going to bet mine and Molly's lives on.

No pressure, no pressure at all.

CHAPTER 15

The sun was hardly visible by the time I left the forge—curfew was coming as Smitty had said, and I had to hurry or be caught by the night watch. One hour. I had one hour at best to get to the O'Donnellys and back through the magic shroud.

Honestly, things had progressed far quicker than I'd even hoped.

With the lockpick ready, we were one step closer to being back in The Hollow. Once there…things would be better. We'd be safe.

Would you be safe? Moll will never be able to grow her hair out again. You'll have to keep it dyed dark…she'd hate that.

I hated that my thoughts felt like a betrayal. One step at a time. We'd get home and then…then we'd figure things out from there.

An image of the dark-haired stranger from my

dreams ran through my mind, unbidden. A fantasy would not help me now.

My bigger concern was Molly. Because this was the ticket out of Little Alabaster for the both of us, and I needed her to not be too in her feelings. I needed her to be…less like herself. I winced at the thought.

I pulled my hood up a little further as a guard strode past. The Smudge was swarming with the bastards, as if they were lurking around every corner now, unlike on my last visit.

No doubt due to my big fat mouth suggesting that they search for the king's attacker by casing the shops for similar shoes. No, not in so many words, but I might as well have said it.

"Abundance Feast is a day away, and we've yet to find the culprit, despite rounding up women to try on the shoe daily. You know how many warts I've seen?" one guard complained to another, as I strode by. Neither so much as looked at me, though they spoke loud enough that I heard them even after I passed.

"And to stab him with a shoe? Crazy, she had to be crazy to think she'd get away with it!"

I cursed inwardly, mentally replaying said stabbing for the hundredth time. Not because of Molly, but because I still just couldn't understand how Heinrich had survived.

What kind of person could take a glass heel to the heart, and then be out hunting only days later? I shivered just thinking about his leering, predatory gaze.

The thought of Heinrich remaining king made my eye twitch, but there was nothing I could do about it. The hunt had shown me just how quickly things could turn on me. Not that I didn't know, but the reminder was like a slap to the face.

I was nothing.

And Heinrich?

He was a fucking king. Untouchable. Even a blow to the heart couldn't kill him, and there wasn't a damn thing I could do about it.

Now that I could finally see a clear path out of here, there was only one downside. As much as I hated to admit it, leaving Duncan would be hard. The feeling of his hand on the small of my back, his dispersing of food to the people in The Smudge, the way he'd leapt in front of a fucking *bear* to save me...

All of it. He had shaken up everything I'd known about nobles, and it was getting increasingly hard to pretend otherwise. The way he'd insisted on bringing me back, even as Heinrich bragged and gloated about the mangled boar he and Bertrand had managed to kill, was so different than any noble I'd ever heard of. I'd written off the idea of an honorable ruler as a fantasy, no matter how many times they'd been mentioned in the fairytales. But it seemed like a stance I might have to reconsider. The system was broken, but, if any man was fit to rule, it was Duncan Westerly.

The sound of laughter pricked at my ears, and I pulled myself back to the present.

A place like The Smudge could be dangerous at the best of times, never mind after nightfall—which I was dangerously close to. But my goal was in sight.

Hurrying, I was at the big door of The Hoof and Saddle in three more strides and knocked out the pattern. Three. Two. Three. The bartender let me in with just a wrinkle of his nose this time, then stood back as I looked around the room.

Jacob was pressed against one wall, with an apple perched on his balding head, while the other three brothers stood a dozen or so feet away from him. The bartender and other patrons looked on from the far side of the bar, nervously watching their antics.

The youngest one turned and shushed me before he pulled back a dart and stared down at his *very* nervous-looking brother.

"Hold still now, Jake," Paddy laughed. "You know the kid's aim isn't great."

Jacob let out a low moan.

"One, two…" The boy's arm snapped forward in a smooth, practiced motion, and the dart hurtled through the air at tremendous speed.

He spun the moment it left his hand; he took a single, confident stride away from the throwing line, not even seeing the dart land. "Easy—"

The yelp that pierced the air silenced him, and I cringed as I saw the dart that had lodged itself two inches deep into Jacob's shoulder. Better that than an eyeball at least.

He tore it free, chucking it toward the youngest brother in an explosion of fury. "Fucking kids, you—"

"You had it coming for what happened last time, if you really think about it," Paddy said, smacking his knee in a fit of laughter.

Jacob sprang forward as if to strike the boy, and Scotty leapt in between them, holding up his arm as the youngest one snickered.

"What the hell are you guys doing?" A bubble of laughter burst from my lips as they froze in place like they'd been caught by their mom.

"It's *just* the black-haired lass, here I thought it was Auntie Lacey, come to beat us," Scotty muttered.

"*Just?*" Paddy asked, lips already tipping into a smile. "She's plenty more than just, if you're asking me."

I ignored his not-so-subtle attempt to hit on me. "Dare I ask why you are throwing darts at Jacob?"

They shared a round of looks that I didn't understand, though there were plenty of snickers and muttered expletives.

While they may have lived a hard life, by Little Alabaster standards, they'd kept their sense of humor...but how the hell they'd managed to secure their near-monopoly on smuggling in these parts was beyond me. Not one of them seemed quite sharp enough to run a group of smugglers and not get caught.

Paddy gestured to his bespectacled brother. "We had a job this morning, and Jacob was slowest when we were running from the guards. It's a penalty game…of sorts."

"Did you finish it already, then? The thing we discussed." Scotty strode over, expression growing serious as I pulled the easy lockpick from my pocket.

"I did. Do you have a lock you want me to demonstrate on?" Excitement burned in my belly. I'd tried it quickly on Smitty's lock, but that had been simple. Still, it was quicker by far than my last lockpick.

Scotty stepped uncomfortably close to my side, staring down at the invention. "Let's head to the back for a little more privacy… Andrew, grab those fancy locks."

The youngest brother—finally named—nodded, dashing down a side hall in advance of the rest of us. I sucked in a breath, doing my best to appear unfazed as I followed the brothers down the narrow hall to the backroom once more, the pool table as it had been on my first visit. As nerve-wracking as this was, it wasn't like I had much of a choice. This was it. Do or die.

I was really hoping it wasn't die.

I'd prove the value of my invention and secure our passage to the Hollow, or they'd rob me blind and chuck me back on the streets, if not worse.

Andrew came back a couple minutes later with a leather bag slung over his shoulder. He made a beeline for the large square table in the corner of the cluttered room and emptied the contents of the bag onto the dusty tabletop against the wall.

I moved to stand beside him and gazed down at the array of locks spread over the surface, taking them in one by one.

There were six in total, I let my fingers trace over them.

"Two are child's play. I don't need a fancy lockpick to open them. A pair of needles would do."

Scotty looked to Andrew, who nodded in agreement. "She's right. You don't have to bother with those two. What about this one?" he said, selecting a large, heavy lock and handing it over. This one was different, more difficult for sure.

I peered into the elaborate keyhole, taking note of the multiple dips and divots. Then, I picked it up and slid the flat, master key of the lockpick into the place. The gem caught the light, and I could see all the mechanisms clearly.

"Watch carefully," I whispered, holding the lock close to one eye and shutting the other. "Each of these tiny buttons will raise or lower the internal mechanisms inside the master blank up to a half a millimeter. Once it's filled the space, you lock it in place like so," I paused, clicking a second button, "and then you move onto the next until you've built a temporary key that lines up with the space within the lock."

I blocked everything else from my mind as I did just that.

"All it takes is a steady hand and a little practice and —" I broke off, a sense of pure satisfaction coursing through me as the lock clicked and I tugged it open. "Done!"

Paddy clapped Andrew on the shoulder. "Better be careful, boyo. She's awful fast. You might be looking for a new job."

Young Andrew gave him a playful shove back. "Well, I didn't have one of those fancy lock pickers now, did I? All right, how about this next one?" Andrew said, holding up another lock. This one featured a round hole, so there was no real way to tell what was going on inside the mechanism, but that was okay.

I motioned at it. "The good thing about my easy lockpick is that it's built to be versatile, and there aren't many locks it won't get into."

"We have two of that type," Scotty said, tipping his head in challenge as he eyeballed me. "Why don't you race Andrew here, and we'll see who can do it faster."

I was about to agree and then had a thought. "All right, but if I win, I want something from you."

"You're not exactly in a position to be negotiating, woman," Scotty snapped back.

Paddy crossed his arms over his chest, cocking his head. "What exactly are you looking for?"

"If you didn't melt that watch down already, I'd like it back," I said simply. I wasn't about to tell them that Duncan had saved my life that morning, and that the least I could do was return his watch to him. That was the *only* reason, too. I refused to examine why taking it had bothered me so much. Plenty of people had done far worse for a whole lot less. But ever since Duncan had put his life on the line to rescue me from that bear, I had this pit in my stomach at the thought of leaving him without even his damn watch. Stupid, I know.

If I got the watch back, I could leave it behind at the hut before Moll and I skipped town. At least then he'd know what he'd done to help had meant something to me...

Scotty scratched at his nose and then shrugged. "Fine, fuck it. I didn't want to have to deal with that anyway. Besides, Andrew here has been messing with those locks since he's been in diapers. You're about to lose this bet. And when you do, you'll give us whatever you got left in your bag of coins."

Well shit. I grit my teeth and give him a nod. "Fine." I still liked my chances; I just didn't want to give up the little coin I had left.

Andrew selected the lock that was twin to mine, only instead of bronze, it was colored silver. Then, he tugged a toolkit from his pocket and unzipped it. After carefully selecting a pick, he eyed me expectantly.

"Ready?"

"As I'll ever be," I said, picking up my lock and holding it close to my face.

"Ready, set, go!" Paddy called gleefully.

Again, I sucked in a deep breath and shut everything out, focusing only on the lock. I slid the flat blank key back into its slot and tugged out a cylindrical pick. Then, I slid it into the keyhole.

This time there was no looking down the barrel to see what matched—no amount of light from the gemstone would help. This one was all feel.

I turned the pick half click to the left, attuning my body to the slightest bit of tension against my fingertips. When it came, I stopped and pressed a button that filled the space.

Next section.

I spun the pick again, making a full 360, but this time there was no tension to be felt.

Strange.

I squeezed my eyes tighter, and my head started to pound. My hands went clammy.

Not this. Not now...

I pushed through the sensation and tried to picture the inside of the lock in my mind. It came to me in a flash, like a picture, as my brain created a schematic of the empty space.

Two more protrusions. One, a half click to the right —I pushed the corresponding button—and the second a quarter down from the first.

I didn't wait to hear the click as the lock disengaged. I just opened my eyes and held out my hand for the watch.

A second later, Andrew called out, "Done!" as his lock slid open and he held it up.

"Sorry, buddy," Paddy said with a chuckle. "The pretty lady got you by about half a second."

Andrew looked down to find the open lock

swinging on the end of my index finger, and he drew back like I'd slapped him right in the forehead.

"Not possible!" he said, staring at me as if I was a ghost. "I've done that one a million times. There's no way you could have used that gadget to open that lock in that amount of time after trying it once. It should have taken you an hour, maybe more."

I held out the lock pick for his inspection. "That's what I was trying to tell you. It's a great invention."

"Fuck the invention," he whispered, looking over towards his brothers. "It's her. *She* needs to do it. That's our best chance; she's got a feel for this…"

They all exchanged looks, and their silence had my stomach roiling.

"Look…guys…I've done my job. I brought you a fancy, easy lockpick. We had a deal. You get me and my friend out now."

Scotty stepped forward, taking the pick from my unresisting hand, his face closing down. I never did like him. "Deal's changed. I'll give you the watch back. I have no problem with that, but we're going to need you to do the job yourself with your…fancy easy lockpick."

"I didn't sign up to be a thief," I said, shaking my head and backing away. There was bad blood between them and the crown already in some way, that's what Smitty had said, and I trusted the old blacksmith—at least as much as I could trust anyone here.

"That's rich given the watch you stole and tried to

sell us to make this thing," Scotty said with a snort, holding up the lockpick.

I shook my head, not sure if I should try to back out or snag my lockpick first. "Those were extreme circumstances. Whether I get caught stealing here or the other side of the shroud, I'll be hanged. I'm not even supposed to be on this side of the Cradle. You guys have less to lose than I do."

"Be that as it may," Paddy said, brow wrinkled with what looked like genuine regret. "All this drama since the Jubilee has made things a lot more difficult— particularly the job we need to do. And I have a feeling you and your friend know a little something about all that trouble, don't you?"

And to think he used to be my favorite of the bunch…

I let out a hiss, knowing they had me cornered. It wasn't a threat outright, but it might as well have been. Either I agreed to steal whatever it was, or they would turn me and Moll in.

This was the risk I'd taken by trusting thieves, but I couldn't turn back the hands of time now. Gayelette had sent me here and…well, I did strangely still trust the weird old flower lady.

"Fine, you bastards. You win. Where am I breaking into?"

Jacob pushed his glasses up higher on his nose. "The palace dungeon."

"To get what?" I asked the question before I thought

it through. Of course, there was only one thing in a dungeon that would have value. A life.

Please, let me be wrong,

Paddy let out a heavy sigh. "Billy, the oldest of us, and the heartbeat of the O'Donnelly clan."

I let my eyes drift shut and tried to will away the nausea. Fucking hell. They didn't want me to steal some piece of jewelry, or a bucket of gold. They wanted me to spearhead a prison break and snatch their brother out of the palace dungeon right under Heinrich and Relyk's noses.

Lovely.

I hated being right.

CHAPTER 16

"I was thinking…maybe I can come to work with you today?"

I blinked blearily at Moll and stifled a yawn as she plopped onto the end of my bed. What time was it, even? Surely not yet time for breakfast…

"What do you mean?" She wasn't going to go away, so I propped my pillow higher to sit up.

"Like, as your assistant. I promise to keep my trap shut, and I will even do all the yucky work, no problem. I just…" Her animated face fell, and she turned away. "I haven't been sleeping well and being alone here all the time without anyone to talk to is driving me nuts, Harm."

I got that. Being alone with her thoughts after something so terrible couldn't have been easy, but we had a mission. And bringing Moll out to interact with people days after trying to murder the king when half of Little Alabaster was looking for her seemed like begging for trouble.

I let out a low sigh. "It's not a good idea, Moll." My body and head were still fatigued from the day before. I had bruises across my legs from tumbling away from the bear, and my hands were split in places from the hammer blisters. I needed this conversation like I needed a hole in the head.

She was about to launch into another plea when a knock sounded at the door.

"I'll get that," she said, holding up an index finger, "But we aren't done here." She yanked on her prosthetic and headed to the front door. A moment later, I could hear a low male voice speaking.

Bertrand? I wondered. No, it wasn't him, he wouldn't have bothered to be quiet. The voice was... soft almost.

It was early morning, and I wasn't due at work for almost another hour, so who could it be if not Bertrand? I was just about to go out and check when Moll came barging back into the room, with a box in hand. She kicked off her prosthetic, using said box as a weapon to shove me backward until my knees buckled against the featherbed and I was forced to sit.

"What the hell?" I demanded, accepting the package. She glanced out the shuttered window as if that was going to give her any information.

"It was Sir Crispin," she hissed, holding a finger to her lips, "the prince's friend who brought it. He said

Duncan sent this for you to wear tonight for the Abundance Feast at the palace. Why didn't you tell me you were invited to the castle?" she demanded.

I stared down at the shiny white box in shock.

"Seriously? I didn't even know I was going…"

Abundance Feast day was when most people spent time in their homes with their family, where they reflected on their good fortune, or prayed for better fortune. I'd heard that here in Little Alabaster, they even took the next day off work. Of course, it didn't go down like that in The Hollow, but we did make an effort to add something a bit fancy to our nighttime meal if we could, and we did a lot of praying for better things.

Relyk had mentioned the palace still planned to have its own celebration, but I hadn't realized staff would be included.

My cheeks burned as I pushed the box off my lap and onto the featherbed, as if I didn't want to look inside. "That's so strange," I said, refusing to meet Moll's gaze, doing all I could to *not* think of how Duncan's hand had felt against my cheek.

"Is it really? Your voice sounds weird, Harm." She turned and grabbed hold of the stool in the corner of the room and dragged it in front of me. She sat down, fanned her skirts, and leaned forward, her elbows on her knees. "Do you have something to tell me?" Her eyes glowed with a fierce light. "Like what happened on the hunt yesterday? You mentioned you were paired up with Duncan, Second Prince of Alabaster…Seems to me like you may have caught some big game after all…"

I let out a forced laugh and shook my head, the heat in my face increasing. "I already told you. He was very nice and tried to help Fetch and I when we ran into some trouble. Other than that, nothing happened."

Other than that, definitely something.

The almost-kiss that had haunted my dreams—leaving me with purple smudges beneath my eyes this morning—had barely left my thoughts since it had *almost* happened. And that was saying something, given all the other things my thoughts should be working on.

You know, small things, like not finding ourselves under the executioner's axe.

"Well, if you're not going to open it, I am. I can't stand it another second!"

She looked more alive than I'd seen her since before she'd left for the Jubilee, and I waved at the box with a laugh.

"By all means, have at it. It's probably just a fancy invite, you know how they are here, everything is over the top—"

She let out a squeal and dove on the box before I finished speaking, tearing into it with wild abandon. What she pulled out took my breath away, but not hers. A flash of red so deep and rich that bordered on black.

"What the fuck is this?" she stared at the item she held up, then tossed it back into the box, forehead wrinkled in disappointment. "No gown?"

"I am the newly hired palace falconer, you know," I reminded her as I reached into the box and lifted out the beautifully tailored crimson jacket. It was softer than a mare's nose and smartly trimmed in black crushed velvet.

"Pants, though?" she wrinkled her nose.

I looked down at what remained in the box to find buttery, soft black leather trousers with criss-cross stitching up the side that I knew would fit me like a glove. Tucked beneath them were a pair of red, knee-high leather boots, the same deep shade as the riding jacket. My throat ached as I stared at the clothes, and I willed myself not to tear up.

"Now that I see that color against your skin, I have to admit he did choose well, even if it isn't a gown," Moll admitted with a little sigh. "Would have been nice if he'd put something in here for me."

Her words rolled off me, water off a duck's back. I hadn't had a new pair of boots in at least a decade. I likely wouldn't wear them once we left this place. I'd be gutted on the streets of The Hollow for something so exquisite. But for tonight, I would enjoy the shit out of them. And the jacket and the pants, too.

Tonight, I would be a royal falconer down to my…boots.

I tucked the clothes reverently back into the box and closed the top.

"On that note, I've really got to go to work." I pushed myself from the featherbed and made my way towards the door, but Moll wasn't about to let me go so easily.

"Before that, though...forget me going to the mew with you. How about I come to the Abundance Feast? I am your cousin, after all..."

"You can't be serious right now." I stared at Moll, mouth agape.

She perched her hands on her hips and glared back at me, not an ounce of shame in her face. "What, because a girl has taken a vow of silence she can't like to party?" she asked, voice shrill.

I had to take a deep breath, steadying myself before I spoke. "Moll. You're the *most wanted* woman in Alabaster right now. How do you keep managing to forget that?" I put as much softness as I could manage into my tone, hoping to prevent a blowout.

She began to pace around the bedroom and let out a low laugh. "How could I forget it? You tell me like thirty times a day. I could be of some help, Harm. You yourself just said the O'Donnellys hired you to free their brother from the dungeons. You don't even know where the dungeons *are*. I'm good at hiding and listening. Not to mention I can be super charming even if I can't talk. I can scout the area for you, look around, see if I can find some hidden entrances."

I cut her off with a swipe of my hand through the air and decided on the latter. "You need to stop. I know you want to be helpful, Moll, but the best thing you can do to help is just stay out of the way and keep quiet."

She opened her mouth to continue arguing, but snapped it shut when I held up a hand.

"Enough." I bit back the tone I wanted to use, reminding myself of all she'd been through. "It's not happening. I promise I'll bring back a plate of snacks to rival even the finest royal buffet. And I'll even listen for all the gossip. We can stay up half the night and dissect who's cheating on who, and who wore the worst color for their skin tone while we stuff our faces. Okay?"

"I don't care about all that!" she shouted, tears in her eyes now. "I'm worried about you being there with… him. I want to help—"

"Help with what, Moll? Getting caught?" I pulled out my ace and used it. "You have the most stunning face of anyone I know. One look close up, even without all your red curls and Heinrich will *know you.* Tell me you understand?"

Her throat worked and she nodded as she turned away. Her voice sounded strained as she murmured a reply. "You're right, I am unforgettable. Fine. I understand."

Appealing to her vanity always worked, which was why I used the trick seldom. You should never overplay your ace, or it might not work the next time.

By the time I made my way to the mew that morning, I felt slightly less filled with doom than the day before. Granted, our situation hadn't improved much, in truth. The O'Donnellys' latest demands had only made my job of getting us out of here more difficult.

But with the invite to the palace, at least I had a path to potential success now. A way to scope out the place, find the dungeon, and hopefully figure out a way to get around back and see the drawings on the amphitheater up close.

"You might even have a friend and ally..." a small voice in my mind whispered.

I shoved it aside and forced myself to think about anything but Duncan as I completed the short walk to work.

"Oh, good morning there," Bertrand said, as I stepped inside.

"Good morning to you as well, sir. You look rested."

He nodded and shot me an uncharacteristic wink. "That's because I am. Riding high on Eamon's and my victory from yesterday. Sorry to rub it in, kid," he said. But the smile beneath his walrus-like mustache told me he wasn't that sorry, not one bit.

I wasn't mad at all. Let him have his moment of glory. When I was long gone from here, hopefully, he'd remember my short time in the mew somewhat fondly, instead of cursing my name.

"I guess we better get started. The sorcerer said I clearly need to spend time getting you up to a higher skill level and knowledge."

Which was why, for the next few hours, Bertrand regaled me with falcon facts. Most I knew, some I didn't. Regardless, the droning gave me time to work on some other problems in the back of my head. Like how to find my way down to the dungeons without getting caught.

"Something most don't know is that the falcons used to deliver messages *inside* the palace—"

"I'm sorry, what?" I cut in, not sure I heard him right, because this just might be the answer I was looking for. "Say that again? That seems…unusual."

He scratched at his chin and then nodded. "There is a network of passageways for them built right into the ceilings. Every major room has a little chute, and we even sometimes have falcons posted with a guard in the throne and war rooms, in case they need to pass a message along quickly. Or we used to. Probably use them less often than we should, though."

He reached for his leather-covered book and proceeded to launch into a discussion about book-keeping and how important it was to keep track of how many kills each falcon brought in each day so they could keep an eye on game populations in the palace hunting grounds.

I, on the other hand, continued thinking about those chutes—even better than I could have hoped. Initially I'd thought I could send Fetch through the castle, as if delivering messages, then 'go find' my missing falcon, depending on how big they were. Assuming they went all the way down to the dungeons, I could potentially pass by completely unnoticed.

At least until I got to the guards.

I winced.

"You got gut pains?"

I shook my head. "No, sorry, just thinking about..." Gods, how did I ask him about the number of guards in the dungeon without raising suspicion, "thinking about that poor stable girl, being harassed by...ten guards I heard."

Bertrand grunted and shook his head. "Poor girl indeed. Doubt she did anything at all to the king, but you didn't hear that from me." He paused long enough that I thought he wouldn't bite. "But ain't ten guards down there, no more than two or three at a time."

Perfect. And not. Bertrand went back to telling me the speeds of different falcons in flight, and my mind wandered far away from bird talk.

If the dungeons were watched by multiple guards even when they were locked, I'd have to figure out how to make the incapacitator launch a second time with a shorter recharge.

That was going to be tricky. Especially if I still wanted to control the power of the thing. As much as I needed to get Billy free if I wanted the O'Donnellys to get us out of here, I wasn't about to turn a corner from thief and accomplice to full on murderer.

After meeting Duncan and Sir Crispin, I had to believe not everyone in Little Alabaster was evil, even if they did swear fealty to a tarnished crown. If I could get away without having lives on my conscience, that would be grand. In large part because if I killed someone the hunt would be not just for Moll at that point, but for us both. And I didn't have any hair dyes that could disguise my dark curls.

The rest of the day passed in a haze as I worked side by side with Bertrand. I was a fast learner, and even when he showed me something I already knew, I kept my mouth shut and listened, or at least appeared to listen. By the end of the day, he'd stopped taking shots at me about my loss on the hunt the day before, and had even cracked a few jokes, not at my expense...

Was it possible the old man was warming to me?

"Bert, love, are you still here?" a low voice called through the door just as I was packing up to leave.

An old woman whose back made the shape of a C stood in the doorway, clearly in pain as she tried to crane her neck up high enough to see us.

Bertrand's wife. I'd seen her at the exhibition.

"Oh, hello there," she said as I instinctively stooped to put my face in her line of vision. "You must be Ella."

"I am," I replied and held up my hand, "and you must be Marjorie. Bertrand's told me so much about you."

She managed a pained smile and shook my hand gently, her skin feeling paper thin against my own. My heart ached as I stared into her lined face. Her gray eyes were sharp and inquisitive, and she had a pert nose and high cheekbones that spoke of beauty at one point in her life. But pain had stolen that from her, along with a lot of other things, I was guessing.

"There she is!" Bertrand said as he made his way

towards his bride. He bent low and pressed a kiss to her forehead, his whole demeanor changing as he interacted with her. The grumpy old man lit up, love and concern filling his face. "Why did you come all the way here?" he asked. "I told you I would be home before supper."

"I was stiff and needed to get out for a walk, but I'm afraid I may have overdone it. Walked too far to just turn around, so I came here, to take a moment."

"I'll get your chair." He scurried off faster than I've ever seen him move, and appeared a moment later, wheeling a wooden chair on wheels.

"That's amazing," I said, studying the engineering of the thing.

I'd created one similar to it for Killana, a little girl who'd been born unable to walk in The Hollow. She could still have her friends and siblings push her around and be with them outside. But this one had some bells and whistles I hadn't considered, like a parking brake and a tray that you could lift and secure in front of the person. I tucked the idea away, thinking how much Killana would love those changes, and smiled as Bertrand helped his wife into the chair.

Marjorie settled down with a sigh and a tightening of her lips. "The prince came by the house and dropped off some more salve for me. I think I'll need you to put it on when we get home. He did say that Othron blooms will be in short supply once the heavy frost sets in. They do have some dried specimens left at the palace, but he isn't sure if it will be enough." She shook her head ruefully. "I tried to give it back to him, but he wouldn't take it."

"You should accept it," I interjected, realizing too late that this conversation was between husband and wife and probably none of my business. But Marjorie didn't seem bothered. "I'm sure he wants to help," I continued.

"He does, to a fault," she said with a low chuckle. "He needs the medication for himself though—"

Bertrand cut in smoothly, "We best be getting home, dear. The young'un will be attending the Abundance Feast at the palace tonight," he said, shooting Marjorie a pointed look.

Based on Bertrand's hurried interruption, it seemed like either no one was supposed to know that Prince Duncan was giving Marjorie medication, *or* they weren't supposed to know that he was taking it himself. Was Duncan ill? He didn't look it. Another nugget I tucked away to gnaw on later.

"Won't you be attending as well?" I asked Bertrand.

"Nope. I'll stay home with the missus. Prince Duncan always sends over a basket full of treats for us to enjoy all by ourselves on Abundance Feast, and I wouldn't have it any other way."

Marjorie patted his liver-spotted hand, affectionately, and then gave it a squeeze. "You're a good man, Bertrand."

Watching them, I almost felt like Moll must all the

time…like I could believe in true love and romance. That there were happy endings.

Almost. I didn't like how my throat tightened, and I thought not of Duncan, but of a fantasy man who haunted my dreams—a man who wasn't real?

No, that way lay madness and heartbreak.

"I better get going. Enjoy the rest of your evening, and your picnic. It was really nice to meet you, Marjorie," I said, my voice a little thick with unspoken emotions.

And it had been nice to meet her, to see the change a good woman brought out in a man who loved her. She seemed like a truly lovely lady. But as I headed off across the grounds towards my hut, my thoughts were firmly on the young, enigmatic prince. I couldn't help but wonder…

How many more secrets did Prince Duncan have?

CHAPTER 17

As it turned out, the Abundance Feast was a much smaller affair than the Winter Jubilee had been, thank the heavens. I was uncomfortable enough in this crowd of eighty or so people, but it was a lot less intimidating than a crowd of a thousand where any one of them could have recognized me from a few nights before. Dressed now with my hair in a thick braid down my back and my new falconer's uniform, I highly doubted that anyone would recognize me.

Then again, I seemed to be the only "servant" in attendance that wasn't actually working.

Shit. What was going on?

Duncan's eyes landed on me as I stepped into the room, and it took all I had not to fidget. Okay, maybe one person would recognize me.

Still, it seemed as if I wouldn't have to worry about

much on that front, as he was across the table, and I was quickly wedged between the sorcerer Relyk who had the king on his other side, and a chatty, well-dressed merchant couple named the Faradays. They looked cut from the same cloth as if they were siblings instead of a married couple, with light brown hair, the same-colored clothing—a deep burnt orange —and ruddy cheeks from imbibing far too much already.

Currently, they prattled on about how much they dreaded full winter coming because it meant constant whining from the poor about the price of coal and firewood.

"'Why does the crown need to tax such items?' they ask me. I tell them straight out...there were many a monarch in centuries past who kept all the coal for himself instead of allowing the poor to purchase it at all," Mr. Faraday said, as he forked up a fat glistening sausage and held it near his gaping maw. "They just don't know how good they have it."

Mrs. Faraday nodded as she pushed a pile of carrots around her plate aimlessly, her nose wrinkled. "Entitlement. That's the thing of it, isn't it? You give them coal, and next they want furs. You give them furs, and then they'll want diamonds. It's a slippery slope, and I for one am glad we are not stepping upon it."

I nearly chewed my tongue bloody to stay silent, but that was almost too much.

What the fuck would the poor do with diamonds

other than sell them for coal or firewood? Jewels certainly wouldn't keep you warm at night.

"Our new falconer comes from humble beginnings herself, don't you, Ella? I'd love to hear your perspective on this matter of diplomacy," Relyk said, watching me down the length of his narrow nose. He looked tired again. Exhausted even, but that didn't make him any less imposing—I'd seen his power as a Whisper, and I was not so stupid as to challenge him.

What was it about him that he always made me feel like I was under a microscope? Moreover, was it just me, or was it that way with anyone new to the palace?

Then again, maybe it was my guilty conscience making me paranoid. His king had almost been murdered a few nights ago. He had the right to ask questions as he saw fit.

I spared a glance at said king, who was propped up at the head of the table, looking even worse than he had at the hunt the day before. A fly buzzed around him before landing on his cheek, but he didn't even raise a hand to wave it away. Instead, his head lolled to the side. If his bleary eyes weren't open and blinking, I might have thought he was asleep.

"Ella?" the sorcerer pressed, pulling me back to the conversation.

"I'm sorry. Y-yes..." I dabbed my upper lip with a napkin and before setting it on the table, doing my best to consider what might pass for diplomatic. "Well, I do think there's a fine line between being a benevolent king and allowing your people to walk all over you," I said, fighting not to grit my teeth the whole time. "What do you think, Your Majesty?"

I don't know what made me dare to speak to the king directly. It was part morbid curiosity about the way his head lolled, and part defiance. Relyk reached out a surreptitious hand and touched the king's ring briefly. It was only when the sorcerer turned his head that I noticed a bald spot in his otherwise thick mane of gray locks.

Strange…

"His Majesty is rather tired and—" Relyk broke off as the king cut in, suddenly pepping up.

"I think those questioning the crown's taxation policies are lucky the Faradays didn't report them for treason." Heinrich's teeth flashed in something more like the baring of teeth than a smile, his eyes swinging the full force of his ire past me. "And on that note… why *didn't* you report them, Philip?"

The clink of glasses and the low, amiable chatter directly around us came to a halt, and Philip Faraday stiffened beside me. His Adam's apple bobbed beneath his cravat, and he cleared his throat. "Well, Your Majesty, I certainly would have, had he continued, but I set him straight immediately, and he saw the error of his ways. If I had any inkling otherwise, of course I would have notified the authorities immediately."

Mrs. Faraday bobbed her head like a pigeon. "He certainly would have."

The king's eyes glittered like two chips of pale-blue ice as he studied Mr. Faraday, clearly relishing the other man's floundering in a way that sent a chill down the back of my neck. Worse? He turned those ice chips on me.

"Since we're gathering opinions around the table tonight, what does our new falconer think? If you heard someone disparaging the policies of your liege, would you keep it to yourself?" He raised his voice as he gazed around the table, and the room grew even quieter. "Are there others here who would keep such potentially damaging secrets from me? Mayhap, that's how I wound up with a hole in my chest."

My hands grew clammy as I stayed silent and still, hoping he'd forgotten that he'd asked me a question.

"We're all waiting to hear your opinion."

So much for being forgotten.

I cleared my throat and nodded—I did not want anyone losing their heads because I had brought the king into this conversation like a fool. "I think anyone who poses a credible threat to the crown should be dealt with swiftly and without mercy. As for paupers who are cold or hungry during lean times, an errant word gets spoken here or there in a moment of weakness. And I'm sure staunch supporters of the crown like the Faradays were able to recognize the difference."

The sorcerer's eyes drilled into me, but I kept my gaze trained on the king, head slightly lowered in deference. This could really go either way, and I was preparing myself for the worst, ready to be released from my position, or potentially cuffed up the side of the head, depending on Heinrich's whim.

What came, though, was far worse. His voice lowered, husky and…full of something I did not want to hear from him.

Desire.

"I find you fascinating, falconer. Relyk, switch chairs with this woman. I want to get to know her better."

Twice now, he'd shown more than a passing interest in me, and I didn't like where this was headed. But there was little I could do in the moment. Neither Relyk or I could defy the king.

I took hold of my wine glass, and pushed my chair back, then stood on shaking legs, trying not to think about Moll and the bruises that still circled her wrists. Tried not to let my fear show, because wouldn't he love that? He probably got off on the terror he inspired in women.

Relyk stood as well and stepped back. He motioned at his chair, as he took mine next to the Faradays. The chatter began again as the tension seemed to leave everybody in the room but me.

I was about to sit down in the offered chair beside King Heinrich when Duncan stood and held up his cup of wine.

"A toast," he said, looking slightly unsteady on his feet.

I'd been so busy treading water in my little corner, I hadn't noticed that he'd clearly drank more than his share of port already.

"A toast to my brother Heinrich, who has not only survived scurvy on the high seas, but also a number of wooden sword fights that could have ended very poorly for one of us as children, and of course, this most recent attack. We're so glad you survived, Brother."

He held up his glass high and glanced around the table with a bleary-eyed smile.

"Long live the king!" The others around the table also stood and raised their glasses high and I mimicked the gesture, mumbling the words under my breath.

"Long live the king." I tossed back my wine, cringing as it raced down my throat, leaving a burning path in its wake. I tried to fight my irritation at Duncan's sudden appreciation for his brother, focusing instead on thinking up some excuse to explore the castle to see if my plan to follow Fetch into the chutes might work.

I wouldn't get to Billy or the dungeons today, but I at least had to figure out where the oldest of the O'Donnelly clan was locked away if I had any hopes of completing my mission. With King Heinrich's attentions clearly turned my way, it seemed more imperative than ever to get out of Little Alabaster as soon as possible.

Everybody returned to their seats, and I was just

about to take mine when Prince Duncan sidled up beside me.

"Looks like your glass is empty, Falconer," he called, his voice overly loud in my ear. He leaned and began to pour the plum wine into my glass from a jug. Suddenly he jerked away, letting out a loud chuckle, sending a spray of magenta liquid everywhere and sending my shoulder into the king, nearly knocking us both over. As it was, I just hit the floor fully, landing on my knees, feeling the impact ripple up my body.

Fuck, banging my knees on a marble floor was going to leave some bruises.

"Gods…sorry…seems deeper in my cups than I thought. I'm so sorry, I've ruined your jacket. Please, Ella, let me find you something to replace that one," Duncan mumbled, reaching for me.

He held out a hand and I took it, allowing him to help me stand. I spared a glance at King Heinrich to see how he took me smashing into him, but he was once again sitting propped up against the chair, head lolled to one side, motionless. Was it due to some lingering effect of the wound to his heart?

I turned my attention back to Duncan and nodded. "I'd appreciate it. Excuse me, please," I added, managing a small smile for the king. "I'll return as soon as I've gotten something clean to wear."

Duncan led me out of the dining hall and deeper into the palace. Only when he pulled me off to a side room with an open door did I finally let out the breath I'd been holding and my whole body began to shake.

"Are you okay? Were you injured? You're shaking." he demanded. His overly loud, boisterous voice suddenly clear as a bell and as solemn as a sermon. "Ella, look at me. I asked if you were all right. Are you hurt?"

I blinked up at him and took a few slow, long breaths. "I'm okay. Just shaken up, that's all."

His eyes searched my face, seeking answers I didn't want to give. "I know you don't trust me, and I understand that. My ilk has shown its colors to yours one too many times, I'm sure. But I hope I've proven to you by now that I'm on *your* side. I need you to believe me when I tell you; you cannot stay here any longer. Relyk has taken an interest in you from the beginning. And now Heinrich's done the same. These men are ruthless. And in spite of the sorcerer's seeming kindness, I can promise you it's a farce."

For a long moment, I stayed silent, my heart pounding and my mind racing. What could I possibly tell him that wouldn't be putting my life, and, more importantly, Moll's life, in his hands?

"I can't keep them from you forever. At least tell me how I can help."

Gods, if only he'd made that offer a few days ago I wouldn't be in the bind I was now with the O'Donnellys. He liked me or at least desired me. But did that mean I could trust him with the truth? I looked up and stared into his gray eyes.

"If you tell me, I'll tell you," I said before I could stop myself. His strong throat muscles worked. "You have secrets too."

He looked away with a low growl, turned and began to pace the room. "You don't know what you're asking."

"I do know what I'm asking. I'm asking you to trust me first, and then I will trust you. It seems like a fair trade." I crossed my arms and waited. It was the only way I'd give him the truth...or at least some of it, at any rate.

"Except I'd be putting you in more danger by telling you," he muttered under his breath.

I was about to reply when a sudden movement just outside the window caught my attention. It took me a second to process what I was seeing—a flash of blue eyes, a glint of a wide mouth and dyed dark hair—but once I did, I nearly keeled over.

What the fuck, Moll?

"What is it?" Duncan asked, moving to follow my gaze. Panicked, I rolled up onto my toes and grabbed him by the back of the neck, turning him toward me.

"Nothing. I just want you to know that I really appreciate everything you've done for me. You saved me from hunting alone with your brother, then saved me from a bear...and now you saved me from having to sit with Heinrich tonight..." I hadn't planned on doing this now, but I needed the distraction. "I…found this outside my hut. You must've dropped it."

I tugged the gold watch from my pocket and slipped it into his hand.

"What amazing luck," he said with a low whistle as he stared down at it. "Who could've imagined?"

"Right?" We shared a smile and then I let mine slip away as I stepped back. "Duncan, I want to trust you, but I've been burned before. I need some time to think it through. But I hear your words, and I'll heed your warning." I took another step back and frowned as if a thought just occurred to me. "Can you make my excuses? I'll sneak out those doors and head home. I think it's best if I limit my time with both Heinrich and his sorcerer, like you said."

"Definitely." He tucked a stray lock of hair behind my ear, sending a shiver rolling over me. "I'll walk you back. I don't like the idea of you out alone at night."

I shook my head silently to buy myself a moment because my tongue was stuck to the roof of my mouth at the look of longing in his eyes as they drifted over my face, resting on my lips.

"It will only call more attention to me if we leave together," I pointed out.

He tipped his head in a reluctant nod. "You're right. And the more interest I show in you, the more Heinrich will pay attention. You go ahead, I'll see you tomorrow. Hopefully, we can have a proper talk then. I want to help you. You just need to tell me how, Ella."

He ran the pad of his thumb over my bottom lip and then turned on his heel and left the room.

I stood there in a stupor for another ten seconds before my brain rang another warning bell. With a quick glance around to make sure he hadn't come back into the room, I rushed to the doors that led outside and quietly tugged one open. I tiptoed across the lawn to where I'd spotted the catalyst of my panic.

There, with her body wedged in the middle of a manicured, evergreen shrubbery, right up against the exterior of the castle stood Moll. Her ear was pressed against the glass of one of the dining room windows, eyes pinched shut in concentration.

I closed my eyes and pressed my fingers to the bridge of my nose, trying to quell the rising fury so I wouldn't grab her and shake her till her teeth rattled out of her pretty, stupid head.

"Molly Miller!" I hissed. "What the fuck are you doing here?"

CHAPTER 18

pparently, I needn't have bothered being quiet, because she was so engrossed in whatever was happening inside the dining hall, she didn't even hear me.

I marched toward the shrub and flicked her—hard—on the back of the head.

"What the hell?" she gasped, wheeling around to face her attacker, eyes wide, fists raised.

"What the hell indeed," I shot back, my voice low and furious.

She blinked up at me, her shocked face lit by the moon.

"Harm? Wh-what are you doing out here?"

I dragged her away from the window and deeper into the surrounding shrubs. "What am *I* doing out here? What are *you* doing here, Molly? Because I distinctly recall telling you to stay the fuck home. And you agreed!"

She glared at me defiantly. "I came to make sure you were okay. Sort of like you did for me at the Jubilee. And thank gods you did, am I right?"

She was right. But she was also wrong. I had walked in the lion's den tonight because our lives depended on it, not because I was husband hunting or bored, with no one to talk to.

And I wasn't about to give her an inch here. This move was foolish, bordering on suicidal. "Big difference. You were trespassing on hallowed ground and in imminent danger. I am an invited guest here—"

"Exactly! Don't you think that's weird?" she asked with a shrug and a wild-eyed shake of her head. "Why were *you* invited? Was Bertrand invited?"

"Yes, he was." I gnawed on the inside of my cheek and then flinched. "No. I don't know, actually. He just said he wouldn't be attending because he and Marjorie don't like parties, and she's in pain."

"Convenient. How about any of the other servants? Not to be mean, Harm, but why you?"

She wasn't wrong, and I *had* noticed that I was the only palace employee in the room that wasn't either pouring wine or serving food.

I shook my head furiously and wagged a finger at her. "Don't try to change the subject! You and I both know I had no choice but to come, whatever their reasoning for the invite was. *You*, on the other hand, need to get the hell out of here immediately so I finish doing what I came here to do."

"I'm not leaving unless you come with me." She lifted her chin high and stared me down.

She was literally going to be the death of us.

"I can't do that. I have to figure out where the dungeons are first so I can come up with a plan to help the O'Donnellys and get us both the fuck out of here! I may not get another chance."

She plopped herself down on the ground and crossed her legs. "Go ahead. I'll wait until you get back. But in the event you don't come back for some reason, I can promise you this. I won't be sitting in that hut all alone wondering if someone hurt you…or worse."

I tossed my head back and stared at the night sky, muttering curses under my breath.

"Just let me hide here, and I won't come out. Pinky swear." She lowered her voice and reached for my hand. "Something feels off, Harm. I can sense it in my bones."

I wasn't about to tell her I'd come to the same realization with what Duncan had told me, just a few minutes before, and the observation we'd both made about my invitation only solidified it.

"Fine. But don't move a muscle. If someone sees you, just…I don't know. Hold your side and moan alot. They'll assume you came to find me because you had a belly ache."

Despite finally agreeing with her to save time and my sanity, Moll and I weren't done yet. Hard decisions had to be made, and if I was the one who had to make them, so be it.

"Appendicitis! I can fake that real good," she said with a grin.

With that less than reassuring promise, I headed back to the double doors I'd left slightly ajar and slipped inside the room. Standing at the doors that led back into the hall, I took a quick glance to the right, then the left, then turned and walked away from the dining room.

This was insane. If I was caught, our death warrant was signed. But what choice did I have? I wouldn't get a better chance to find the dungeons. At least for now, all was quiet and dark as the servants were busy hosting the whims of the guests.

The dungeons *were* down somewhere below, so I kept my eyes peeled for stairways.

I skulked down the corridor, hand trailing along the stone wall as if I could meld my body with it if I heard someone coming. I could barely hear myself think over the sound of my own heartbeat as I delved deeper into the bowels of the palace, further from the only exit I knew.

I passed an open door and paused to peer inside. A parlor decorated from floor to ceiling in dusty rose. Silk curtains worth more than my shack in The Hollow, a chaise lounge and sofa that looked like they'd never been sat on, and a massive credenza full of crystal figurines and candlesticks.

I continued on, stopping to survey each unlocked

room I passed, hoping one would lead to a set of stairs. A men's lounge with a snooker table and bar that reeked of expensive cigar smoke. A room full of decorative wrapping paper and bows... an entire space dedicated to making something beautiful, only to see it thrown away. I counted twelve useless, open rooms in all, before I finally came upon a closed door at the end of the hall.

I jiggled the knob and it didn't budge. I pressed my ear to the door and closed my eyes. Silence.

Could it possibly be the steps leading to the dungeon? Or maybe a private library that would offer up some information or a map of the palace that I could use?

Only one way to find out.

I tugged out my easy lockpick and gingerly twiddled with the door. Less than ten seconds later, the lock tumbled with a click, and I stepped inside.

By the light of the moon streaming through the many windows, I could make out dozens of canvases perched on easels scattered around the spacious room. Squat tubs of paint and brushes littered every available surface, and paint-speckled white cloths covered the floors.

An art room.

Disappointment left a bitter taste in my mouth as I hovered there for a long moment and then crept further inside. I was here now, and maybe there was a reason for the locked door that could give me even a little bit of help.

Most of the canvases were blank, and the ones that weren't seemed haphazard. Wild slashes of paint and amorphous shapes that didn't amount to anything. I could almost sense the artist's frustration, and I couldn't help but wonder who it was...

There was nothing for me here. I turned to leave and caught sight of what looked like a mound of blankets in the corner. Adrenaline had my pulse pounding as I headed that way on pure instinct, pulling me to get a better look at it.

With a shaking hand, I lifted one corner of the wool cover and peered down at the pile of canvases. As I leaned in and got a closer look at the one on top, my stomach flipped.

On the left side, a castle loomed...Alabaster palace. The skies above it were dark, and birds circled overhead. I knew in my heart they were vultures. The despair rolling off the image made my blood run cold.

Hovering just a short distance away, leaving gray skies toward blue, was a tiny hot air balloon. It wasn't until I pulled back the curtain to let a little more moonlight in that I could see the image clearly.

Inside the basket stood a man wearing a wizard's hat with yellow stars perched on his head. The woman at his side had her fist raised high in the air in triumph.

Scrawled across the bottom, in crimson letters?

There's no place like home...

"What the fuck?" If there was no place like home,

why were these two fleeing?

I quickly shuffled to the next painting in the pile and realized I'd *definitely* seen it before. Once when I was a child, and once on the exterior wall of the motherfucking amphitheater. The image of an emerald city with the monkeys flying around it. I nearly did a double-take when I realized the figure in the foreground was no longer smudged like the one on the amphitheater wall. It was very clearly a woman with a falcon on her shoulder…wearing a pair of knee-high crimson boots.

She was *me*.

Swaying in place, I traced the image to find the paint was dry. Duncan had only given me the boots today. Did that mean he was the painter? Had he been the one to draw all over the amphitheater walls as well? If so, why?

I was so engrossed in my reeling thoughts, trying to make sense of what I was looking at, I didn't hear the footsteps approaching until they were close.

Too close.

"Hello? Is someone in there?"

My skin broke out in icy chills as I froze in place. Every excuse I'd crafted to explain my presence vacated my brain en masse. I had nothing to explain my presence in a room I most certainly should not be in.

"Harmony? Is that you?"

Genevieve Salim. The palace maid that had nearly caught sight of me at the Jubilee.

I turned slowly, schooling my features as best I could.

"Oh hello, Gen!" I forced a shaky smile, but I could already feel the blood rushing to my head, no doubt giving me a guilty flush. If I had a full spell and passed out, there was zero question Genevieve would scream for help and then the whole palace would know I'd been snooping around.

So calm the fuck down, or you're as good as dead...Moll too.

Unsurprisingly, the stern mental reminder only made it worse.

The young maid cocked her head, eyes narrowed. "What are you doing in here?"

What, indeed?

"Funny story. I, um, was at the Feast, and spilled some wine on myself." I gestured to my jacket with an eye roll. "Clumsy fool. I've only been on the job a couple of days—as the palace falconer, would you believe? I wanted to impress, but I made a mess of things. Anyhow, I came to find a powder room to clean up and use the loo, and got a bit turned-around. This is a really big place. Palace. You know what I mean?"

Her eyes stayed just as narrowed and she crossed her arms over her chest. "So you walked the length of this hundred-yard corridor, found a locked door, and thought this was the powder room you were looking for?" She shot a pointed look at the blanket I was still holding. "Were you planning to shit on the blanket, or is that for wiping?"

Gen always was a quick wit. She was also pragmatic...

We stared at one another for a long, silent moment. Then, I dropped the blanket, and the farce.

"How much?"

To her credit, Gen didn't pretend to misunderstand.

"Fifty marks and I turn around and walk out. Never saw a thing."

I flinched and shook my head. "I don't have it." I'd spent most of what the O'Donnellys had given me on supplies for the lockpick.

She slipped her hands into her apron pockets and shrugged. "What *do* you have?"

"Twenty-three and change."

Gen shook her head. "Look, Harm. I've always liked you, but I'm not stupid. Now that I see you here sneaking around, plus the description of the woman who attacked King Heinrich...we both know it was either you on her behalf or Molly who did the deed." She held up a staying hand. "Don't bother denying it. He's a piece of shit who surely deserved what he got. But it's a big and dangerous secret for me to keep. If anyone ever found out I knew something and didn't come forward, I'd be as bad off as you. But because we're both from The Hollow, I'm willing to take the risk. It's got to be worth it, though. Even if you don't care about your own, surely Moll's neck is worth more than twenty-three marks?"

She had me over a barrel, and she knew it.

"I truly don't have it, but I can get you more, if you just give me a day."

She stared at me long and hard. "I live in The Smudge at Wren's Boarding House. You or your falcon bring me fifty marks by day after tomorrow, midnight, or this canary starts singing."

"I can do that," I lied, knowing I'd either be dead or long gone by then.

"And I'll take the twenty-three now."

I was disgusted on one hand, but another part of me understood. It was hard to get ahead, being poor sucked. I fished the coins from my pocket and crossed the room to hand them over. Apparently, I didn't hide my disdain, because she let out a low snort.

"This isn't to buy some cashmere scarf, Harmony. I have my own problems. My gran is seventy. Her hands are so gnarled she can't sew anymore. I send what I can, but she skips supper most nights. Fifty marks will buy her supplies to start a little candle-making business instead." The corner of her thin mouth kicked up as she continued. "Besides, it's not like your conscience is exactly clean. There are three innocent women locked in the dungeon downstairs right now because of you and your previously redheaded friend. But that doesn't bother you one bit, I guess?"

Bile rose up to burn the back of my throat. "Th-three?"

She pursed her lips. "Aye. The stable girl and her

mother, and then another they picked up in town this morning who fit the glass slipper and couldn't come up with an alibi."

Fucking hell. But maybe Gen could help me, whether she realized it or not.

"And the dungeon...where is it located?"

Gen shot a glance over her shoulder and shifted restlessly from foot to foot. "The southwestern corner. You won't be able to get in from inside the palace. There are too many people roaming around, not to mention the guards."

Time to push for more, to make this worth it. "So how do I get in from the outside?"

"I've already said too much." Gen blew out a sigh and started backing out of the room. "I would talk to the old falconer. He would know better than anyone from what I've heard. I've got to go, and you should too. The sorcerer comes here at night to paint when he gets restless, and if he finds you here..."

I blinked at her in surprise, the not-so-veiled threat barely registering. "Relyk? Is this his room alone, or do others use it?"

"Only him, why?"

I shook my head as I processed her answer. Relyk had known it was me in that drawing he'd worked so hard to erase. Meaning he didn't want anyone else to know. Was that why he'd taken such an interest in me, and even offered me a job? To keep me close until he figured out what those pictures—and my presence in them—meant?

They were clearly important if he'd taken the time to recreate them privately.

"Stay if you want, but don't say I didn't warn you. These halls won't stay empty much longer."

With that, Gen wheeled around and was out the door in a flash. The sound of her footsteps disappeared down the hallway.

She was right, and there would be plenty of time for me to try and connect the dots later. I quickly straightened the pile of paintings and settled the blanket as it had been. Then, I headed out, making sure to lock the door behind me.

I snuck back outside the same way I'd come without further issue and was giddy with relief a few minutes later when I caught sight of Moll hunkered down, deep in the shrubbery.

"Harm!" she whispered, face shining as I stepped into view. "You're back."

"I am. But we've got to get out of here. I've definitely overstayed my welcome."

More than ever, I wished I could get around back and see if any new drawings could be found on the amphitheater walls, but I knew I'd pushed my luck as far as it could go without breaking.

We made our way across the palace grounds on silent feet, but as we came to a fork on the path, I halted Moll's progress with a hand on her forearm.

"We're not going home yet. We're going this way," I

said, gesturing toward town.

"Why would we do that?"

"I have to go talk to the O'Donnellys."

"It's cold and dark out…and the curfew! What if we get caught? Can't it wait until morning?"

"It can't. It's a risk we'll have to take." I tugged her along with me just as Fetch came soaring down to glide along beside us.

She frowned but shrugged. "Okay, whatever you say. How did it go in there? Did you figure out where the dungeon is?"

"Once we're off palace grounds, I'll tell you all about it."

I needed a minute to decide what to share. In the end I opted for everything except the part about the three women locked away for crimes we'd committed. There was no point in burdening her with that knowledge when there was nothing she could do about it at the moment. I filled her in on the rest as we headed off the palace grounds toward town. I was a little worried as we passed through the wall, but there were no guards in sight, and we managed to slip past the scattered patrols that roamed the streets of The Smudge once we got inside.

Moll peppered me with whispered questions as we walked, ducking and dodging up and down alleys to avoid being seen.

"So, wait…there was a painting of you? In those boots? I don't get it."

"Me either." But I had every intention of picking Duncan's brain on the subject next time I saw him.

"And Gen said she thinks Bertrand can help you?"

"That's what she said, although I'm not sure I'm comfortable testing that theory by asking him. My plan is to distract him or something so I can really paw through the desk at the mew myself. I'm sure he has the schematics of those falcon chutes—surely they sent messages to the dungeon, right? The man is a record-keeping savant."

"You know, I've been thinking…what are we going to do when we get back home, anyway? Just because we manage to escape Alabaster doesn't mean we're in the clear. They'll come looking for us eventually, won't they?"

Damn, well, she'd come to the same conclusion I had—that even the Hollow would be a temporary stop.

"Undoubtedly. Which is why you and I won't be staying long. We're going to gather up everything of importance, sell what we can, and secure passage out of there."

We'd go far enough where even Heinrich and his creepy sorcerer couldn't find us. The nearest of the other two kingdoms was days away on horseback, and that was assuming you didn't get picked off by a mantis. The faster way was by hot air balloon, but those came along with the cost of hiring someone to fly it plus at least three lookouts to safeguard any passengers from mantis attacks.

In short, balloons were for the wealthy, and we surely were not that.

I had to hope we'd be able to hitch a ride with one of the rare trading caravans that were bold enough to risk life and limb to brave the wilds.

"I've always wanted us to travel together," Moll said, turning a smile on me that made me look away with a stab of guilt. "Maybe we can even go as far as Bryn-garde...they say the animals there are unlike anything you've ever seen. They have these little blue monkeys that try to steal the buttons off your shirts, and tortoises that never die. They're like a thousand years old! And there is so much food there, you can live off the fruit trees alone."

"Sounds amazing."

"If not there, we could try Valencourt. Supposedly, that was the last place The Speaker visited for supplies before disappearing altogether."

The Speaker. About as mythical as a unicorn as far as I was concerned. The most powerful Whisper...gone for decades. I let her talk as I checked the next street to make sure we were clear.

"Oh yeah? Where did you hear that?"

"When I was spying behind that bush. I told you, I'm a good listener. I hear all kinds of stuff. The nobles were kissing up to Heinrich and Duncan, talking about how their father, King Rudolph, had driven The Speaker into hiding and vanquished the revolution for good."

"Well, The Speaker isn't real. Or, if he was, he's long dead."

Impoverished people loved a good hero or deity to cling to. I was guilty of it myself, wishing someone would come and save me and the people I cared about from The Hollow. It took me until my early twenties to realize no one was coming. We had to find a way to better our circumstances or die trying.

Moll opened her mouth to argue, and I held a finger to my lips. "Gotta be quiet now, we're almost there."

She stayed mum after that until we got to the door of The Hoof and Saddle. I rapped out the secret knock and waited, the slick of nausea in my belly spreading.

"Look, Moll...I need to tell you something, and you aren't going to like it."

The peep slot slid open and a familiar brown eye stared back at me.

"Come on, then, before the nightwatch catches ya," he grumbled.

The door swung open a moment later, and the door guard waved us inside. "They're in the back."

The pub wasn't nearly as empty as I'd seen it, and I made sure to keep my gaze on the floor as we shuffled our way through the thin crowd into the back room.

Paddy, Scotty, and Jacob were seated at a table, heads bent close as they talked in low tones. Andrew, the youngest, was nowhere to be seen.

"Gentlemen," I called by way of greeting.

They all looked up and Paddy grinned even as Jacob

scowled.

"What are you doing back so soon?"

"I need to alter our agreement…just a little," I added as Jacob let out a snort.

"A deal is a deal. If you're saying you can't get Billy out now—"

I held up my hands, stalling him. "Nope, that's not what I'm saying at all. I'm in a really good spot with that, actually. I have a plan in place I think might actually work. All that's left is the doing of it. But in order to get it done, I need you to get my friend back to The Hollow."

"We already told you, do the job and we'll get you's both back."

I shrugged. "Things have changed. She needs to go tonight. Now. Or we walk out, and Billy rots in the dungeon. If my falcon brings me word that Moll has gotten home safe by tomorrow afternoon, I'll make my move. Billy will be on the outside of the palace walls by midnight. Those are my terms, take it or leave it."

"What are you talking about?" Molly demanded, vow of silence forgotten as she perched her hands on her hips. "Not going to happen."

"Don't," I croaked, my throat sticking on the words. "Please don't argue. You're leaving. I'm staying. That's final."

"No." She shook her head furiously. "No way. Harm, you can't do that. You—"

"Nothing you say is going to change my mind."

"I won't leave you in this place alone, Harm. We're peas and mash, remember? Ham and eggs…" Her voice was thready with panic as she lurched toward me, and I pulled away.

There was only one way to get her to go, and that was to *make* her go.

I lifted my chin and leveled her with a killing glare. "You're a liability. You've been tottling around outside making friends with the local kiddos, sneaking around in the bushes, generally determined to make a mess of things. Is that the goal, Molly? Because it seems like it. Are you looking to get us both killed?"

She looked like I'd kicked her in the gut, and I hated myself for it.

"No…of course not. I just want to help you."

"Exactly," I snapped. "And every time you 'help' things just get worse. The best thing you can do is get the fuck out of the way, so I have even a slight chance of following after you in one piece. Can you do that for me?"

Tears streamed down her cheeks as she stared at me in silence, but I didn't take a word of it back. Even the three O'Donnelly brothers present shot me judgy glares.

She must've sensed it too, because she turned and shot a beseeching look at Paddy.

"Can you help? Can you…take us both?"

He shook his head. "Sorry, love. We need her services something fierce, and she's got the upper hand right now. You've got to do as she says and come with us."

Molly backed away and folded her arms over her chest. "I won't."

His dimple flashed as he gave her a soft smile. "I like your spunk, but that's not going to be how it goes. Either we take you the easy way, or we gag you and bag you…" He laid a hand on his hip to rest just above the hilt of his knife, and Molly paled. Then, she turned to me, her eyes like twin chips of blue diamond.

"You're just a fucking asshole. A foolish, bossy asshole and you're going to get yourself killed. But if that's how you want it, fine."

Anger and hurt snapped through me. I had a lot of flaws but what she was saying didn't fit. "You looking in the mirror again, Moll?"

If I thought she was pale before, it was nothing to the drain of color—she was white as fresh snow in The Hollow. "You bitch." She wheeled around and headed for the door without looking back.

All my anger fled, and only sorrow remained. I tapped Fetch gently on the beak, jerking my head in Molly's direction.

"Go ahead with Moll."

He chortled and then flew after her.

"I don't have to tell you again, if you cross us—"

I cut off Jacob before he was done. "Yeah, yeah, I know. Save your breath." Because whatever he had planned to say couldn't make me feel any worse than I did right now.

As the O'Donnellys followed Molly out into the main tavern, I hung back, trying not to cry. I'd done something to Molly that I hadn't in our twenty-five years of friendship. I'd hurt her.

On purpose.

And only the gods knew whether I'd ever have a chance to make it up to her...

CHAPTER 19

I stared out the window into the dark and winced at the reflection staring back at me. It had been eight hours since I'd dropped Moll off at The Hoof and Saddle and made my way back to the hut. Morning would come soon enough, and I hadn't slept a wink. My cheeks were pale and the purple smudges beneath my eyes were visible even in the wavy panes of glass.

"Serves you right," I muttered to myself as I settled deeper into my chair and pulled the woolen blanket closer around my shoulders. Anybody who could talk to a friend that way *should* have insomnia.

Part of me wondered if she was sleeping herself. She hadn't exactly been kind either…

I pinched my lids closed as the memory of her cornflower blue eyes staring back at me came rushing in. So hurt and filled with accusation. I knew it had to be done but it didn't make it any easier.

There was a low tapping at the door, and the blanket fell from my shoulders as I leapt to my feet.

I opened the door to find Fetch on the stoop. "Hey buddy, I'm so glad you made it back! Is Moll okay?"

I bent low and the old bird climbed onto my hand and lifted one talon to reveal a rolled-up sheet of yellowing parchment.

A note…from Moll?

I rushed into the kitchen and lit a lantern before setting Fetch on the back of a chair. Then with shaking hands, I unrolled the little square of paper and spread it onto the table to read.

I'm not dead.

But also, fuck you.

My head spun as I blinked and then blinked again. The hastily written words blurred before my eyes, and semi-hysterical laughter bubbled from my mouth.

"Oh, Moll…you never change, do you?"

The laughter quickly turned to tears, and I slumped over the table pressing my head against the cool wood, not bothering to stop the flow. Whatever happened now, at least I knew she was safe—even if our friendship had died in the heat of those words, she would live. And if I had to make the choice again, I'd do it exactly the same way because a life without Molly in it wasn't worth living.

I gently pet Fetch's head, and he leaned into the

caress. "You're such a good boy. Thank you for watching out for her."

I blew out a long breath and made a circle around the kitchen. My appetite was non-existent, but I knew I should eat something. I hadn't slept and there was much to be done later, despite the holiday off work. I'd need as much energy as I could muster.

I broke off the heel of a loaf of black bread that Moll had made the day before, not bothering with butter or jam. I just tore off a hunk and popped it into my mouth. It was dry and dense and lacked salt, but in the moment, it was just what I needed. A taste of Molly's terrible cooking.

We'd be together again soon. I was going to make sure of it. Then we could both apologize for the things we said.

I had just finished sharing my meager meal with Fetch and was trying to decide whether I should try to get an hour or two of sleep or to give it up when a low knock sounded at my door.

I tensed instantly and rushed to open it. If Molly had found a way to sneak back here after I had worked so hard to get her out, I was going to kill her…

I swung the door open to find Duncan Westerly, Prince of Alabaster standing there. Hair unkempt, gritty eyes looking as bleary as mine. I wrapped my arms around my waist, glad I hadn't taken the time to change into my night clothes.

"Good morning, Your Highness…" I looked into the

still-dark sky, and realized with a start that the sun hadn't even begun to rise yet. "Or should I say good... night? Is something wrong?" I asked, gripping the doorknob more tightly.

"Yes." He shook his head and raked a hand over his stubbled jaw. "No. I mean, I was just having trouble sleeping and went for a ride. I saw your lantern lit as I passed by. There's something I'd like to show you. Will you come with me?"

It was a terrible idea. Still, there would be no sleep for me for the remainder of this night, and the thought of sitting in this hut all by myself, picturing Molly's betrayed and angry face made me sick. Besides, I had some questions to ask him about the images I'd seen earlier.

"Absolutely. Just let me get my jacket."

"I've got a blanket on the back of my horse. I'll keep you warm." Our eyes met, and I barely suppressed a shiver. "Should you let your cousin know you're leaving?"

I shook my head and looked away. "No. She...is away the next few days visiting our aunt in The Smudge."

He didn't ask questions, and I didn't elaborate further. I just called for Fetch and followed Duncan to a beautiful, chestnut stallion who tossed his head as we approached.

"Atticus, this is Ella. Ella, meet my stallion Atticus."

I reached out slowly to pet the horse's soft muzzle. Fetch eyed him as he leaned into my touch.

"That's a surprise," Duncan said. "He's a good boy, but he's not usually so affectionate."

With that, Duncan held out his hands to create a makeshift stirrup for me to climb onto the horse. I sent Fetch to the skies before swinging one leg over with a grunt. A wave of heat rolled through me as Duncan leapt up behind me with ease, his body pressed up against my back.

"Where are we going?" I asked, doing my best to ignore the tension as he nudged the horse into motion.

"You'll see soon enough," he replied, his breath warm in my hair.

I could have pressed him harder, could have argued and told him I wasn't going to go unless he told me where we were headed. Instead, the stress and exhaustion of the day hit me all at once and the adrenaline that had kept me going drained away in a *whoosh*. I leaned back and let my eyes drift shut as he tightened one arm around my waist and held the reins with the other.

And for the first time since I left The Hollow, what seemed like a million years ago, I felt safe. Like I could finally let down my guard.

I don't know if I fell asleep at the easy rock and roll of the horse's gait or from the warmth of Duncan's arms. But the next time I opened my eyes, we were at the top of a hill looking down. Little Alabaster was laid out before us on one side, and parts of The Hollow were visible on the other. The first blush of dawn lit the sky in a riot of pinks and oranges.

"This is amazing," I whispered, loath to break the spell Mother Nature was weaving.

"Isn't it?" he asked.

For a minute, we just sat and enjoyed the view. Then he swung one leg over the stallion's rump and landed lightly on his feet.

"I brought us a picnic," he said. "It's not much because I didn't expect company when I left the castle, but I'm happy to share." He reached out, his hands tightening over my hips as he lifted me out of the saddle. Like I weighed no more than a feather. Atticus moved at the last minute, nudging me closer to his master until I slid down the front of Duncan's body. I gasped as I brushed against every inch of lean muscle, my whole body tingling from the contact.

"Ah, Ella...I don't know who you really are or why you showed up in my life now, but I'm glad of it," he murmured.

My breath was suspended in my chest as I stared up into his beautiful gray eyes and tried desperately not to get lost in them.

I don't know who started it, but a moment later, I was on my tiptoes and his head was bent and our mouths were fused. I had wound my arms around Duncan's neck. Atticus let out a snort and began to stomp his feet.

Duncan let out a chuckle as he pulled away. "We have a routine," he said, patting his horse's neck gently before reaching into his pocket and pulling out an apple. The stallion took it carefully between his teeth and crunched down hard. "He carries me without complaining and I give him apples."

"Seems like a fair trade," I said, glad to find that my voice didn't sound husky or strained even though I could barely catch my breath. I knew what Moll would say—

"I'd give him a ride, no apple required."

Duncan took my hand and led me towards the very crest of the hill. Then he spread out the blanket he'd brought. It was massive, big enough for the both of us to sit and then for him to wrap it around us like we were ensconced in one fluffy hot cross bun. I let out a happy sigh as we watched the sun climb up over the horizon.

"This is it right here," Duncan said, pointing to something in the distance. "In just a moment you'll see what I wanted to show you. There!"

I squinted and The Cradle between Little Alabaster and The Hollow seemed to shimmer and disappear. It was just a trick of the light as the sun came over the horizon at the exact moment, but in that instant, the land looked like it was one with nothing to divide it. The sight gave me a twinge in my heart. A dream of something not possible.

"I wish it could be like that." As soon as the words

left my lips I froze, realizing that I basically just all but blasphemed in front of the Crown Prince. But he only pulled me tighter against him.

"I wish it could be like that, too." There was a sudden tension in him as he continued, his voice low and urgent. "And if all goes to plan, it will be soon."

I stiffened and craned my neck to study his face.

"What do you mean?"

His jaw clenched and his nostrils flared. "I want to change the way we live—the way we all live. We shouldn't be divided by walls that keep one group of people hungry and the other blind to the truth. There is enough for everyone to live in comfort. We have to tear down these walls that separate us and figure out how to work together to make things more equitable."

"But...it can't happen. There's no way those in power would ever give it up."

His eyes blazed with passion and steely determination. "So we *take* it."

I drew back, stunned. "Duncan...what are you saying?"

"I'm going to stage a coup. And I'm trusting you, Ella with this. In the hopes that you will trust me, too."

CHAPTER 20

I stared at him, mouth agape, unable to speak as his words set in.

A coup.

Duncan was going to unseat his brother? Not that I hadn't considered rebellion myself once I'd seen Heinrich up close and decidedly not dead. But it was one thing to think it, to threaten it in your mind, another to say it out loud and…mean it.

A dozen moments from the past few days replayed in my mind, given new meaning by this revelation. It all made so much sense.

Duncan didn't turn from me. "I wanted to tell you sooner, but I needed to be sure. It's not only my life that is at stake in all this."

"Crispin?" I flashed back to that brief shoulder grab that'd stopped Duncan from pursuing Heinrich in the amphitheater. It had been more of a "not yet" than a "don't do it."

He frowned, going silent for a long moment. "And others. I can't go into specifics, but I have a strong group of supporters who are willing to go to battle for me if it comes to it. I'm hoping it won't. When Heinrich was injured, I thought we wouldn't have to fight, that we'd had a boon from the gods. But…"

"But he pulled through," I whispered.

"Very much thanks to Relyk. I still don't know how he did it. I was there, Ella. I saw the wound, and…I would have sworn my brother was dead."

I nodded, shifting my gaze to the wall below. He wanted to tear. It. Down.

Was such a thing even possible?

"I've shared my biggest secret with you." he caught my chin and turned my face to him, his eyes drilling into mine. "Now it's your turn…Who are you, really? There is something about you, I cannot explain it, but I've known it since we first met."

My throat went tight as I met his earnest gaze again, and Gayelette's cryptic words floated to the forefront of my mind…

"Open your eyes and you will see who to trust."

"My name is Harmony Fallowell. I live in The Hollow. I came to Alabaster the night of the Jubilee, as I'm sure you already know. I got stuck here after…" I trailed off, unsure of what to say next.

There was truth, and there was *truth*. Could I really tell the brother of the king what happened that night?

What if my instincts were wrong? What if this was all some elaborate trap to get me to confess?

"You can tell me anything, Harmony. I will never betray you. I've been under your spell since the second I laid eyes on you." He touched a gentle finger to my chin, reestablishing eye contact before he continued. "Your cousin was the one who stabbed Heinrich, isn't she?"

It was more of a statement than a question, and I couldn't muster the strength to deny it. "How long have you known?"

His eyes narrowed in thought. "At first, I knew only that you had snuck into the Jubilee, but that isn't the first time someone has done that. It was more a gut feeling...a sense I got whenever you looked at Heinrich. I could feel your disgust and hatred. Also not new. Plenty of people despise him, with good reason. The final piece of the puzzle slid into place when I saw how protective you were with Molly and got a closer look at her prosthetic. Smart," he added with a grin.

"People like you don't usually look at people like us...not really. It was a gamble," I admitted with a wry smile.

"And it worked...on a lot of people. Though I wonder if Relyk suspects anything."

I pulled the blanket a little tighter around my shoulder. "He definitely suspects me of something. Duncan...did you see that picture on the amphitheater when it first appeared? The one of the city made of emeralds?"

He squinted in thought. "Vaguely, but I admit, there was a lot going on. I figured some Whispers had vandalized the place, but the murals weren't offensive or dangerous, so I didn't pay them much mind. Why?"

"Well, the one thing he managed to scrub away with magic was…me. Originally, I was in that picture, with Fetch on my shoulder, and wearing the boots you gave me days *after* the picture appeared."

Duncan stared at me. "I didn't even know I was going to give those to you. I chose them the night before. How could *he* have known?"

"There's more," I admitted softly.

We'd reached the crossroads. How much to tell him here? It was time to tread carefully. If I told him of my plans, it could ruin everything…for both of us. He'd want to help. And if we got caught, not only would I have failed Moll, I would've taken Duncan and his dream with me. Not an option. Because whatever feelings I'd harbored about nobles in the past, Duncan had proven one thing for sure.

Prince Charming *did* exist, and he was beside me right now, in the flesh.

I couldn't torpedo the start of a much-needed revolution to save my own skin. I needed to do this alone—I would finish the O'Donnellys' job and get back to Moll. Then we'd leave the Hollow for good. There would be no guilt about leaving Heinrich in power, because Duncan would take his place.

In the meantime, maybe he had some information that *could* help…

"When I was at the party last night, I didn't go right home. I went snooping to see if I could find anything that might help us escape," I hedged, settling on a lie of omission. "And I ended up in some room down a long hallway. It was full of canvases and a bunch of paintings. There were replicas of the drawings on the amphitheater. Relyk had created them. He knew I was coming. Somehow, through whatever dark magic he wields, it was foretold."

His brows knit together. "Then why not kill you on the spot when he saw you in The Smudge?"

"The only thing I can think of is that he still needs me. For what, I don't know. Maybe to help him figure out what the pictures mean or who created them. What do you think?"

He shook his head, blowing out a breath of frustration. "Hard to tell with him, he keeps his secrets close to his chest. I desperately want to help you figure it all out, but with our plan already in motion, I have to be careful the next few days. I'll keep you safe in the meantime, and make sure that he and my brother are too dead to do whatever it was they were planning in the first place. I wish I could do more right now, but it will only raise suspicions if you suddenly disappear."

"You've done so much already," I whispered, the

guilt nearly splitting me in two. "Especially that first day by telling the guard that Heinrich would never be interested in women like us. If they checked us thoroughly…"

I winced at the thought.

"Molly's hair color didn't really suit her face, so my guess is that she was the redhead Heinrich lured into the gardens that night. He got violent, her shoe came off in the struggle, and you arrived in the nick of time to extricate her."

Pretty close, and I wasn't about to correct him over semantics. It was one thing to trust him with my secrets. It was another to trust him with Moll's.

"I don't blame you. I'd have done the same for someone I loved," he said.

Electricity sparked between us as his fingers interlaced with mine. It felt natural…right.

I let out a sigh and laid my head onto his shoulder, wishing things could've been different.

"I know it must've been scary. If I could've gotten you out of Alabaster before now, I would have."

Call me a fool, but I believed him.

"Soon, though…Harmony."

Sooner than he knew. I shoved the thought away. "What's your plan to take the throne? The sorcerer seems like he'd be a powerful enemy if he's as strong of a Whisper as he seems."

"Moreso, even. He hides his strength because if people knew, they would be terrified. He tries to pretend he's the voice of reason, but he's as malicious and crafty as they come. I think you may have created the perfect window for us to strike, though."

"*Me?*"

"I know it sounds crazy, but…I'm sure my brother died when Molly stabbed him. I saw him with my own eyes; His body was already cold by the time Relyk got to him. And he still isn't alive, even now. Not truly."

The man running the kingdom was little more than a walking corpse. Or was it Relyk running the kingdom then? "So what're you going to do?"

"I'm sure you've already noticed as much, but Relyk is growing weaker and having a hard time keeping up appearances as the days pass. My brother's condition is deteriorating, and Relyk won't be able to keep him in one piece forever. He's likely already scrambling to bring in some distant cousin to replace him rather than me, so this is our shot."

"Why not you? You're next in line."

Duncan's lips twisted into a bitter smile. "It would never happen. The sorcerer likes his kings weak-willed and easily manipulated. I'm quite certain the only reason he hasn't tried to have me killed is because it's too close to the attempt on Heinrich's life. He doesn't want people asking questions. He wants fat, happy, silent sheep. But I've finally got some of the sheep bleating. And, based on how quickly the strain of keeping Heinrich alive is draining his strength, I think he should be weak enough for us to strike in a couple days' time."

I burrowed my face tightly against his shoulder, letting his warm, woodsy scent close over me like a second blanket.

"Even if he's weakened, do you think you'll be able to win?"

"I can't know for sure. He's always been so diligent about hiding his strength. But I can't wait until he's decided on a successor. Then we would have a war on two fronts. This is the best chance we're going to get."

"And what happens if you succeed in overthrowing them? Will you be our next King?"

"For a time. I have…" his expression darkened, and he looked away. "Let's just say I have my own issues that wouldn't make me the best option, either. My long-term goals involve getting rid of the monarchy entirely, but someone will have to oversee things until new laws are created. That would be me and a team of elected advisers. The dream is an Alabaster with no walls and no king."

I had so many questions and was trying to navigate how to ask them when suddenly, Duncan's hand shot out in front of us in a blur.

He lifted one finger to his lips as he slowly rose to his feet. My stomach lurched as he unclenched his fist to reveal a dead, bloated fly.

Jackal.

He dropped it and reached for his sword as I rolled to my feet, heartbeat pounding in my ears.

"Get down!" he yelled, nearly in unison with Fetch's warning screech from a nearby tree.

I feinted left as an arrow whizzed through the air where I'd stood a moment earlier. I yelped, skittering a few feet away before turning to get a better look at what was going on.

Atticus drummed his front feet, slamming his hooves into the ground, and let out a series of agitated snorts as he paced, but he didn't run off.

"Stay close and keep your eyes peeled for more," Duncan said, eyes glued to the dark clad figure closing in on him. Its hood was not fully on, and for a moment its face was partially exposed.

Flies burst into the air as the black hood slipped back. Crimson lines bisected gaunt cheeks in a twisted, otherworldly approximation of a man's face.

I bit at my inner lip, cursing. Duncan was huge, towering over me by a solid foot, but the Jackal gave him a run for his money. It was going to be a brutal fight.

Duncan was the first to act. He lunged forward, his great sword tearing through the air in a massive, two-handed swing.

The Jackal leapt just inches out of range, then charged in a blur the moment the danger had passed. His blade was lighter and thinner, and, contrary to what

I would've expected based on his appearance, he was *fast*. He parried a follow-up attack, his blade snaking toward Duncan's shoulder in a single, fluid motion.

The prince ducked at the last second. He raised his sword, readying himself for a counter, but there was no time. The Jackal let the momentum carry him through, tossing his blade from one hand to the other as he spun all the way around, throwing himself right into the next attack.

Faster than any fighter I'd seen.

That thin blade snaked out for swing after swing, never failing to get within inches of Duncan's head or chest. If this continued, it could only end one way.

The clatter of clashing swords split the air as Duncan batted down a thrust, and he charged forward, throwing caution to the wind as he unleashed an attack of his own.

The Jackal jolted sideways, seeming to disappear from view as it rolled under the swing, smashing its arm into Duncan's leg. The prince grunted, his foot shooting out in a kick, but the Jackal had already risen, his blade flashing toward his throat.

I fumbled wildly through my bag, unable to take my eyes off of the horrible scene in front of me. If I didn't do something, Duncan, the one person capable of saving Alabaster and The Hollow, was going to die.

He leapt back, the Jackal's sword landing a glancing blow across his shoulder. Blood soaked his shirt instantly, but he didn't waver, as if he didn't even feel the bite of the blade.

The prince's massive sword whistled through the air as it hurtled toward his opponent, and my heart skipped a beat as he followed it up with a left-handed punch.

How the hell could he wield that thing with one hand?

The crack of bones sent a chill down my spine as the Jackal strode *into* the blow, unfazed.

Duncan parried a series of attacks, still obviously on the back foot as I tore the incapacitator from my bag. If there was a time to use it, this was it.

I inched sideways, watching the creature's movements and searching for the perfect moment. If I could just find a way to get at his back while he was preoccupied with Duncan…

The monster whirled, completely ignoring Duncan as he leapt toward me in a blur. I grasped wildly for the trigger on my weapon, but the speed difference was too much. He appeared just a few feet away, flies pouring from his mouth by the hundreds as his sword slashed at my neck.

I stumbled back, heart still thundering in my chest as I held the device up, steeling myself for the inevitable.

Duncan's broad shoulders blocked my vision just as the Jackal was about to strike.

"Stay back." The prince's voice was deadly calm as he parried another attack.

Fetch fell to my shoulder as I scrambled away, watching in horror as the monster moved into another one of its impossibly fast flurries. His blade whipped through the air at a speed I couldn't imagine any human being able to compete with. But Duncan advanced on the beast, his speed nearly matching the monsters, bashing the smaller blade out of the way and sending it rolling to the ground below.

The Jackal let out a terrible screech, dropping for his weapon. Duncan shot forward simultaneously, sword whirling for the monster's arm.

My breath caught in my throat as the Jackal changed course entirely, lurching to a stop then leaping in the opposite direction, hand stretched toward Duncan's chest.

An undulating wave of inky black burst out of its palm, completely blotting out the space between them in black mist. Duncan rolled sideways, grunting in pain as the mist consumed the upper part of his left shoulder. A section of the tree behind him withered and died upon contact, as if it had aged a hundred years in an instant.

Duncan caught himself on the hilt of his sword, the tip pressing into the ground as he recovered his balance.

My blood ran cold as the Jackal let out a guttural, horrifying mockery of a laugh. I squeezed my invention tight in clammy hands, dashing forward as the creature lunged toward an injured Duncan.

The prince's blade whipped up from his side in a heartbeat, and not just for a regular attack. Duncan *hurled* the blade at the Jackal, roaring as he charged forward to meet the creature head-on.

The Jackal batted the weapon aside, a look of terror consuming its face for the first time as it moved to block the follow-up punch. And it was right to be scared, because a moment later, Duncan's massive fist smashed into its jaw with a sickening crunch. He yanked the monster back as it turned to run, throwing it to the ground and leaping on top of it.

Dozens of brutal, bone-crunching blows landed in a row, sending out spurts of green, putrid blood that coated the ground below. The creature had been still for half a minute by the time Duncan rose, making his way over to his fallen sword.

He hefted it with a ragged breath, then brought it down on the creature's neck in a lumberjack's swing— bone and green blood splattering to my feet.

A wave of nausea washed over me, but I didn't turn my head as the Jackal's head rolled away. A cloud of flies burst out through the neck hole filling the air around the body.

"Holy shit."

"Didn't want to take any chances that it wasn't dead," Duncan said, panting.

I hazarded a glance his way, keeping my eyes off of

the mangled body at his feet. "I don't blame you. I've never seen anything fight like that."

He looked up at me, clenching his fist. "I've always wondered if I could take one. I guess we found out."

"Your eyes. They looked different," I said, jabbing my finger toward him. "The same as the day of the hunting trip."

His lean jaw worked as he glanced down at the body. "I'm a Whisper. My power gives me unholy strength in times of need...but it comes with a price." His tone was clipped as he continued. "We have more immediate concerns, though. This assassination attempt is a big escalation for Relyk. In hindsight, I have to assume it isn't the first, either."

My mind whirred and then it hit me. "The bear attack?" I gasped.

"With him already using energy to keep Heinrich on his feet, controlling the bear, even for a short time, must've drained him."

"Which must have been why he looked so sick when we got back."

"That's my guess. Up until recently, we've danced around one another, playing nice. I'd hoped it would stay that way until we were ready to make our move, but either he got wind of our plan, or he knows that Heinrich isn't long for this world and needed to clear the way for his successor. I've got to get rid of the body, meet up with Crispin and figure out where to go from here."

I nodded, hands trembling as I stuffed the incapacitator back into my pouch. "I understand. Is your shoulder okay?"

The cloth of his tunic looked totally normal, but a dark, bruise-like patch was visible just above it. He rolled it around a few times, then shrugged. "It's been better. But the stuff barely caught me, I should be fine. The other is healed already. A perk to my abilities—quick healing."

Duncan dragged the Jackal's corpse to the edge of the cliff and tossed him over while I worked to calm Atticus. It took a few minutes to soothe the spooked chestnut enough for him to let us mount, but then we were on our way, far faster than our leisurely trip to the outlook.

"So what now?" I asked, eyes darting around in search of another rogue fly.

"I'm trying to figure that out, but I need to start by going back to the palace."

I craned my neck to stare behind me. "You *what?*"

Duncan nudged the horse into a trot and let out a sigh. "My people need me. If the sorcerer is onto me, who knows who else he's onto? Lord Willoughby is waiting for me to gather the other lords to my side. And I can't give up now and run away when we're this close. I have to pretend his Jackal never caught up to me and hope by the time he discovers the truth, it will be too late."

"Won't he just try to kill you again?"

"It'd be a big risk on his part, as long as I don't let him catch me alone, and I stay close to the castle. People would start to ask questions, and he doesn't want that. He'll pull back and regroup before trying again. I'm confident of that. It should give us enough time to make our move."

I didn't like it, but I could hardly argue. I was planning something equally dangerous and at least as foolish. Almost like he knew, he continued on.

"In the meantime, I'm going to need you to go somewhere safe in case this blows up. I'll have a way easier time focusing on what I need to do if I know you're safe and far from the fighting."

Where had I heard those words before? Ah, yes. I'd said them to Moll just before I basically told her she was a burden and sent her packing.

His arms tightened carefully around me. "There's a hunting shack deep in the Northwest Forest. I'd like to take you there now. I doubt anyone even remembers it's there."

He described it in detail, but he didn't need to have bothered. I remembered the place all too well. Moll and I had spent our first night in Little Alabaster there. The shack would be as good a place as any to prepare for tonight's mission. And Duncan was right. He'd do better not to be worried about me right now when he had bigger fish to fry.

I made a mental note...once I was safe, I'd send

Fetch with a message. It wasn't much, but it was something.

"I'll go, if that's what you want."

"I do. I'll send Crispin with supplies later this morning, and as soon as I can, I'll come get you."

Guilt rolled through me as I nodded, but this was the only way.

"If I'm not there in three days' time, you need to sneak off into The Smudge and hide as best you can," he said. "It'll mean…that things didn't go as planned."

"I will," I said, furthering my lie.

We made the ride to the shack in near silence after that, both of us tense and on high alert. It wasn't until we closed the door behind us that I felt like I could breathe.

"I'm worried about you. They could be waiting for you back at the castle," I said, pacing the worn floorboards as he headed to the fireplace and let out a growl.

"Hold that thought."

I held that thought and a thousand others as I continued to pace, waiting for him to return. Ten minutes later, he stepped through the door with an armload of deadwood and kindling.

"I'll not have you freeze here if Crispin can't make it back before dark." With that terse explanation, he dropped to a squat and made short work of starting a fire.

"What about the smoke?"

"These woods are dense. If you keep it small,

neither Relyk nor any of his people will notice. They've got enough to worry about…like trying to split one life force into two bodies without dying, and whether I'm going to come back and cut their heads off."

He stood and swiped his hands on the thighs of his pants before turning to face me. The look in his eyes was one I could only describe as…love? Surely not… we'd only just met. But I knew it as sure as I knew my own name. And I'd seen it so rarely in my life that it nearly brought me low.

"Harmony, I—"

"What if we just go?" I nearly blurted, the fear gripping my chest suddenly too much to bear as I closed the distance between us to lay my hands on his shoulders. *"What if you forget the whole coup thing, we just go and get Molly and run away to…I don't know where. Someplace far, far away. One of the other kingdoms."*

But I didn't say any of that.

"Can't someone else stage the coup?" I tried weakly.

"There *is* no one else. You know that."

"Then at least stay with me now. Just for a little while, before…"

Before what? We both died? Before I left and he stayed, and we never saw each other again?

"Please." The word stuck in my throat, but he was already shaking his head, his expression a bittersweet blend of resignation, grief, and promise as he rested his hands on my hips.

"You have no idea how much I wish I could. But I

have to get back before everyone rises. There's no telling what today might bring, and I can't let those who've supported me face those dangers alone." He cupped my face, and I pressed my cheek into his hand. "You have my word on this, though. I will cut down anyone who tries to stop me from getting back to you."

He studied my face once more as if trying to memorize every line before crushing his lips to mine for the briefest of instants. Then, he was gone.

I pressed my fingers to my mouth as I closed the door behind him, wishing we had a little more time. Wishing that I'd been able to say goodbye for real. Because fool or no, I believed he would come back for me.

Would that love turn to hate when he found out I was gone, and that I'd lied right to his face?

CHAPTER 21

After Duncan left, that day passed as slow as molasses deep in winter. Every time I looked outside, it seemed like the sun was still fighting its way through the gray skies. But when night finally fell, it seemed too soon for what I had to do…

As I stepped out of the tiny hunting shack, Fetch seated upon my shoulder, I wondered if the full moon I was looking at would be the last I'd ever see.

What would Moll say if she were here?

A smile tugged at my lips as the words came to mind in her lilting voice.

Stop being such a negative Nelly. You've got this!

I closed the door behind me and shivered in the icy night air. There was a fair chance I would get as far as the palace grounds and wind up with an arrow sticking out of my chest for the trouble.

Had Duncan managed to enter back into the fold as

if nothing happened? Or had the sorcerer figured out that his Jackal goon had attempted and failed to complete his assassination mission?

There was only one way to find out. I picked my way through the forest, keeping my ears strained for any sound that shouldn't be there as I went. By the time I reached the edge of the woods, I was marginally less terrified.

No flies in the air, which was a good thing. This time of year, in the mid-winter, they could only mean one thing.

It was well into supper time for most, but still, I was pleasantly surprised to find that I hadn't run into a single soul as I made my way onto the palace grounds, besides the lone guard posted at the gate.

I'd seen him before, and he let me pass with a distracted wave.

"You belong here," I reminded myself in a whisper as I tossed my shoulders back and marched on toward the mew. "Just keep moving and don't stop."

But a part of me wondered why the place wasn't teeming with soldiers if Relyk had caught onto Duncan's plans.

The thought had barely crossed my mind when, in the distance, I saw a cadre of guards marching toward the house of a nearby noble. I slowed my steps but didn't stop as I craned my neck to see. They rapped quickly on the door but didn't wait until it opened, kicking it open themselves instead.

"Lord Willoughby, we have some questions to ask you and your wife," one of the guards said, his voice ringing through the night. My upper lip broke out in sweat, and I hastened my stride. Lord Willoughby. Wasn't that who Duncan said was working with him?

Shitfuckdamn.

Had they already caught Duncan? Or were these preliminary questions? I hated not knowing, but I had to keep going. By the time I got to the mew, my clothes were damp with sweat despite the frigid weather, and it took every ounce of my energy to control my breathing. I wouldn't be able to help anyone else if I didn't save myself

The only way to do that was to escape Little Alabaster and get to the other side of the wall. Then I could try to figure out how to help Duncan and his cause. The mew was silent as I approached and I unlatched the door, taking a quick look over my shoulder before slipping inside.

The birds must have sensed my presence or maybe Fetch's, because there was a ruffle of feathers even in the darkness. I lit the stubby candle I'd secreted away in the bag secured around my waist. "Hello, my pretties," I whispered as the falcons flew down, one at a time, from their perches.

Bonnie landed first, taking the shoulder opposite Fetch's perch. "Good evening, beautiful girl," I murmured, taking a long moment to scratch at her neck. She cooed, clearly enjoying the attention. "I wish

I could stay and visit, but I've got some work to do." She nipped lightly at my nose, hard enough to sting but not hard enough to draw blood, then flew off. Bertrand was right. She was a brat, but that only made me like her more.

I couldn't help but wish there was some world where I could have had this life, surrounded by falcons and a mentor like Bertrand. A life where I could go home and eat until my belly was full and laugh about my day with Molly, and maybe even spend my nights with Duncan…

Or a man with black hair and eyes like midnight? No, that was a fantasy. Duncan at least, was real.

Despite my foolish musings, what I really needed was to get the fuck out of this place as soon as possible.

I padded over to Bertrand's desk and began to methodically go through the contents. For nearly an hour, I pawed through journal entries and piles of paper, but I couldn't find any blueprints of the falcon chutes at the palace, and I was starting to panic. I was about to close the final drawer when I caught sight of a sheet of paper at the very bottom of the last pile that looked different from the rest, thinner but large and folded into quarters.

I plucked it from the drawer and unfolded it. Gasping as the ink revealed itself, I'd found it.

A blueprint.

My throat went tight, and I blinked back tears. This was it. A blueprint of all the falcon chutes in the palace.

I tucked it into the bag at my waist with a trembling hand, and then I slowly closed the drawer. Part of me had thought I was going to have to go into the chutes blind, just opening a random chute and praying I found my way. But now, with the information in hand, an ember of hope bloomed in my belly. This might actually work.

I spared a quick glance up into the rafters, catching sight of Bonnie's white downy feathers one last time, and gave her a wave. "Take good care, pretty girl. It was my honor to meet you."

I backed out of the mew and latched the door behind me. I stood there, frozen in place for a long moment. There was surely a chance that Relyk would come if things began to unravel, requiring one of the falcons to deliver a message. If that happened, I might just get caught while I was inside the chutes. But the only alternative was one I couldn't even allow myself to consider. So I closed the door and latched it, leaving it up to fate.

"Are they dead, then?"

My stomach bottomed out as I wheeled around to find Bertrand standing a few feet behind me, his rheumy eyes searching my face in the moonlight.

"My birds…did you kill them?"

"I—Of course not."

He nodded slowly. "I didn't think you would. But I had to ask. Did you get what you came for?"

I wet my lips, unsure of how much to tell him.

"Bertrand, it's safer if you don't know. Please just let me walk away."

He cocked his head and assessed me for a long moment. "Show me." He waved one hand, gesturing at the bag around my waist.

I blew out a sigh and unzipped the pouch to pull out the map I'd secreted inside, then held it out to him.

He pursed his lips and then shook his head. "Nope. These are obsolete. They were redrawn after they put an addition on the palace about five years ago. That's the problem with keeping every single piece of paper," he acknowledged with a half-smile. "Come on, I'll get you what you need."

I stared at him in disbelief, unsure I'd heard him right. "Why are you helping me?"

He unlatched the door and led the way back into the mew, then closed it behind us before answering. "The prince is taking a stand and you're a part of it. I might be old, but I'm not stupid. I realized something was amiss the day we went on the hunt. Then I over-heard something that made me sure of it."

"What was that?"

"After the hunt, King Heinrich asked the sorcerer if he could..." The old man's wrinkly throat worked as he swallowed hard, "*have* you. The sorcerer explained that wouldn't be possible. He said he had to stabilize the realm before he could search for answers, but that he knew you somehow played a part in its future."

I gaped at him, more confused than ever. "What does that mean?"

Bertrand shrugged. "That I don't know. What I do know is that you need to do whatever it is that you've got to and then get out of here. I'll do whatever I can to help you out of loyalty to the prince. He's a good man. The best of them, really."

Guilt swamped me, and I nearly confessed then and there that Duncan had nothing to do with this. It was only an image of Moll's face floating through my mind that stopped me. That and the fact that, while this particular mission wasn't related to the coup, I was a supporter of Duncan's too…

"I appreciate that," I said, reaching out to squeeze his shoulder. "But I have to warn you…involving yourself in this could put you and Marjorie in grave danger."

He let out a chuckle and reached into the top drawer of his desk. "Me and Marjorie have come to an understanding. She's getting worse, and the prince needs his medication for himself. It wasn't a cure for her. It just bought us some good hours with less pain. But those moments are fewer and further between each day. We've lived good, long lives together, and neither one of us is afraid to die. So if my last act is one of defiance against the powers that be, I'm okay with that. Let them come."

There was no rifling around or searching. Bertrand leafed through some pages, landing exactly where he needed to from a secret compartment that I'd not seen, then pulled out another folded sheet.

"Here are the most recent schematics. They're about a year and a half old. Where you headed in the palace, precisely? I might have some idea of where you need to start."

Truth time. "The dungeon… There are some people down there that I need to free."

"Ah." He laid the paper out on his desk and poked at an area with his index finger. "You're going to want to start here, then, and follow this path," he said, tracing a trail. "There's a section here. There are areas that get tight, so it might not be easy going the whole time."

He grabbed a quill and dipped it in ink before tracing that same trail so I could follow it later. Then he folded up the map and handed it over.

"I'll stay here for the next two hours and make sure that none of the falcons leave. If they're called, I'll do my best to create a delay, at the very least. The quicker you go, the better. Things have been tense around here today, and I suspect something big is coming soon. The sorcerer doesn't look well, but it's only a matter of time before he regains his strength, and you don't want to be here when that happens."

"And what of Prince Duncan?" I asked, unable to help myself. "Do you know if he's all right?"

He nodded. "I saw him a little bit ago, right before supper with Sir Crispin in the courtyard. Unless some-thing's happened in the interim, I think he's all right."

He opened his mouth as if he was going to ask me another question, but then he closed it. "Good luck."

With that, he gave Fetch a light pat on the head and then waved me off. As I stepped back out into the night air, a million questions buzzed in my mind like a swarm of bees.

Relyk had clearly known I was coming to Little Alabaster. Had he read it in tea leaves to foretell the future, or only when he saw the drawings on the amphitheater? Did he think I was the key to figuring out the mystery of those drawings? Or did he somehow know I was connected to the attempted murder of the king?

And the most terrifying question of all...

What if this was all a trap...Would he be there, guarding the chutes, waiting for me?

There was only one way to find out.

CHAPTER 22

a chill arced up my spine as I inched forward another step along the roof parapet, trying not to look at the forty-foot drop waiting for me if I slipped. Even Fetch seemed concerned, his talons applying subtle pressure through my leather shoulder pad as he stood stock-still.

One foot in front of the other. Just keep moving, don't look down.

A group of nobles made idle conversation in the courtyard below, completely unaware of the intruder currently traversing the palace's tiled roof. I halted for a second, wiping a clammy hand across my shirt as the grate of the falcon chute came into view. There was a hole in the middle for the falcons to dive through, but there was also a latch for someone to crawl in to fix things as needed.

I dropped into a crouch, maneuvering my way

under the final window at a snail's pace. A tinge of anticipation interrupted the waves of anxiety that'd been rolling through me since I'd first climbed up onto the roof.

My time spent in The Hollow earning coin as everything from tinker to chimney sweep had excised any fear of tight spaces, so the impending switch from slippery roof-stalking to shimmying was a welcome one.

I strode the rest of the way across, leaning forward to grab the edges of the grate as soon as it came into reach.

Safe.

Getting in was an easy enough task, and I was pleasantly surprised by the amount of space. I'd expected to have to crawl the whole way through.

I pulled one of the candles from my pouch, lit it, then began inching forward. Falcons had excellent night vision, and the wisps of torchlight filtering through the narrow slits below were far from adequate for my very human eyes.

I frowned, pushing past a wave of revulsion as the candle sparked to life, illuminating the space. Streaks of brown-and-white spattered the floor and walls, and the smell grew stronger with every step. I didn't have time to worry about it much, though. At least it was dry, seeing as the chutes weren't used much. My heart skipped a beat as soft footsteps echoed up from below, and I poked my head through the nearest chute to get a better look. A small patrol of guards marched down the hall, their quiet chatter barely audible at this height.

My stomach growled, and I slowed my pace even more as I continued scuttling down the chute in a low crouch. The fact that I could hear them at all was concerning, because that meant, if the room was quiet enough, they could hear me moving around up here, too...

The footsteps disappeared before long, and, luckily, it wasn't a trend. I made it to the first major bend without incident, then took a right after a quick consult with Bertrand's map.

Dozens of tunnels led out of this main one, with each of them no doubt leading to even more off-shoot channels. A message could be sent directly to almost any room in the building within minutes, and I couldn't shake the grudging respect I felt for the architects of the place. The shafts were hardly even noticeable from the floor below, and it was only now that I was up here that I could fully appreciate the effort that would've gone into creating such an intricate network.

A sudden squeak shook me from my thoughts, and I turned to find a massive rat staring up at me, his beady red eyes glowing in the candlelight. Apparently, even the rodents were well-fed in Little Alabaster because the bastard was two feet long. I'd seen more than my share of rats in The Hollow, but had any of them looked muscular?

It's just because you're so close to it. Calm down and breathe...

My fingers dug into my palm, and I forced my body completely still even as every fiber of my being was urging me to wave my arms and holler until it fucked off. Even Fetch seemed wary, not budging from his perch on my shoulder, though he eyed the rodent as if he'd like to take a shot at it.

He's as afraid of you as you are of him, I reminded myself. I waved a silent hand in the rat's direction, but he apparently took it as a slight, because he let out another squeak and launched himself straight at me. I scuttled back and my boots crossed, sending me tumbling ass over tea kettle. Pain shot up my arm as my elbow clanged against the shaft's iron wall. I bit down hard on my lower lip, resisting the urge to cry out.

Okay, maybe not quite *as afraid as I was.*

Fetch clicked his beak and flapped his wings as the cat-sized rat scurried past, disappearing into the inky blackness beyond. I waited a long moment, straining to hear any sounds below but was met with only silence.

"What kind of falcon are you?" I whispered, holding in a hysterical, adrenaline-fueled giggle.

Fetch was as brave as they came—hell, he'd taken on a bear for me—but apparently even he had his limits. Facing off against a ten-pound rat was that limit, and I had to respect it.

We wove our way through the next few turns with

hardly a peep from the palace below. Bertrand had chosen our path well. When the passage began to slope steadily downward, I knew we were approaching the lower levels of the palace. I kept a guiding hand against the wall as we proceeded. Only a couple turns more, and, according to the map, we were about to arrive at the next one.

I glanced down the chute as we arrived, my stomach twisting with anxiety as the sound of voices pricked at my ears, coming from the room below that sub-shaft. To make matters worse, this one sloped downward more sharply, leading underground where the dungeon was. For a falcon, no problem with a bit of a dive. For me? This was going to be interesting.

I turned, shimmying butt-first down the shaft. I wedged myself against the wall of the chute with my boot and then glanced down to consult the map. I was on the ceiling of the kitchen area, apparently. And the voices below confirmed that with a half-audible discussion about the palace's grain stores and something about making rye loaves instead of wheat.

Just a bit further.

I slid down, landing lightly on the next chute. Crouched, I worked my way around the next bend—a crossroads of four directions—and stopped short. I needed to go straight, but directly ahead of me was a gaping hole in what had been the metal of a grate. It was as if it had been chewed through by rats. Only the other side of the hole was...nothing. Rather than revealing any part of the palace below, the hole led only to an inky, endless void.

A knot formed in my belly as I stared into the all-too-familiar rift.

The darkness that had eaten away at the box the glass shoes had come in, what felt like a lifetime ago. The day of the Jubilee, where it all started.

I suppressed a wave of nausea, not daring to move another inch. What would happen if I stepped past it?

I held my candle out with a shaky hand and inserted the bottom inch into the hole. An icy chill shot through my hand, and I snapped backward, withdrawing it. My heart hammered against my ribcage as I stared at the shortened stump of wax in shock. It was still cold to the touch, but, more alarmingly, the bottom chunk had been sliced clean off, consumed by the nothing.

Moll's voice rang in my ears. *"Don't think about it. Don't you dare even think about it, Harmony Marie Fallowell. You just have to push through right now. Just not that way."*

She was right. If I let myself fall down this rabbit hole into a full-blown panic, I was never getting out of here. Whatever the black holes were, I had nothing to do with them, right?

Right.

Sweat pooled at my brow, and Fetch shifted restlessly on my shoulder as I squirmed backward, reaching for my map. I stared down at it, doing my best to remain calm. There was a half-dozen more chutes, but all required me to climb back up that steep incline to get back to the main shaft.

I crawled back, nibbling at my inner lip as I stared up. It would be damn-near impossible to get back up at all, never mind doing it quietly. So what the hell *did* I do? I could use the map to forge a different path, but according to Bertrand, some channels were too narrow for me to fit, and I had no way of knowing which until I got there…

My head started to thump as I stared down the maze of the map, and my lungs tightened.

Think.

No! a little voice inside my head chimed in. *Stop thinking. Open your mind to the possibilities of the gifts you possess.*

I let my eyes drift shut, pushing the blueprint from my mind completely. Then, I tried to imagine the maze of chutes as the interior of a lock, with channels and divots and dips and turns. My head felt like it was about to split open, but just as I was going to open my eyes, an image blinked to life in my head…

And I *saw.*

I *knew.*

There was no second-guessing as I took the chute to my left and made a series of turns. It was a less direct route, but I made good progress. By the time I slid silently down the final shaft toward the chute that opened to the dungeon entrance, I was shaky with adrenaline.

Thank you, Gayelette. It was her voice, her direction that had given me the courage to reach for something…more.

I wanted to weep with relief, but there was no time for theatrics. I tugged out the incapacitator and extended it all the way, my hands sticky with sweat. The guard was just around the corner. I had to move quickly and confidently, there would be no second chances if I lost the element of surprise…

One… two—

I sucked in a final, strengthening breath, then lunged forward, jabbing my incapacitator at him.

The guard spun toward me, fumbling for his sword as I squeezed down on the trigger for dear life. He stumbled backward as sparks arced from the tip, and my heartbeat thrummed in my ears as I waited.

Please work, please work.

The stick vibrated to life in my hands, and I winced as the electricity inside surged out at him, consuming him in a blinding spray of sparks and light. I released it, muttering a quick apology as he slumped to the floor below.

I strode forward, grabbing his sword with one hand and putting my other to his neck.

Thump, thump, thump.

I breathed out in relief as I strapped the blade and scabbard to my belt.

Not dead.

And, really, I should've killed him, if all I cared about was getting Billy O'Donnelly and escaping to The Hollow to meet up with Moll.

But that *wasn't* all I cared about.

I refused to become like them, even in my quest for justice. I'd kill if someone attacked me, and I'd have stabbed the king himself in Moll's defense with zero regrets, but this was different. This man was doing his job and following orders like so many under the rule of a tyrant. That didn't make him blameless, but the system at large was the real problem. I'd show mercy when I could.

I folded up my incapacitator and stuffed it into my bag, pulling out my lockpick in the same motion. The lock on the main door to the dungeon looked complicated, but I had yet to meet my match and today was *not* going to be the day. Not with my easy lockpick.

I knelt, jamming the front of the pick into the keyhole and pressing the button. As expected, no luck. I fiddled a bit longer, forcing my eyes closed and focusing on it with everything I had. A mental map of the lock's innards floated to the forefront of my mind. I drew back on the pick a hair and adjusted my fingers to set everything in place. Then, I held my breath and pressed down.

The metal lock clicked open, and I forced down my anxiety as I gently pushed the door open. I waited a few beats, but no other guards emerged. I spared a glance for the one on the ground, wrinkling my nose as a foul odor wafted over to me.

Jackal?!

My eyes shot up, scanning the room I'd just come from, then settled back on the guard as realization struck. The guy had shit himself from being hit with the incapacitator.

Better than a Jackal for sure.

I nudged the door open further with my leg and grabbed hold of the guard's shoulders, heaving with everything I had as I dragged him into the dungeon with me. I tossed him into the open cell to the right and locked him inside. He'd still be able to call out once he woke up, but at least this way he couldn't run for help or come after me.

I opened my mouth to tell Fetch to scout ahead, but he glided off before I could. What I'd done before had been special, and I doubted that I could replicate it at will, but something had clearly changed. I could almost *sense* his eagerness as he streaked through the gray, stone dungeon, his eyes and ears open for danger. If I managed to stay alive, I'd have plenty of time to think about all that. I rounded the first corner, my confusion deepening with each cell I passed. Not a single prisoner so far.

The map I'd gotten from Bertrand didn't have much detail about non-vented areas like the dungeons, but there did appear to be a whole other wing to the place, and it didn't look very far.

I cursed under my breath, squeezing the hilt of my stolen sword. It'd be a good fifteen minutes before my incapacitator was ready for another use, and I didn't like my odds in a sword fight against a well-trained soldier.

So did that mean I should wait? If I did, how long would it take before another guard came by and noticed the first one's absence?

"Who the hell are you?"

I jumped, my gaze snapping forward as the voice cut through the otherwise silent dungeon. A woman's apple-cheeked face appeared three cells down, pressed tight against the iron bars.

I breathed out in relief, striding toward the cell. "Are you the only one in this whole wing? I'm looking for a man."

Her tawny curls shook as she pulled a shrug. "I can be a man if you want me to be," she said with a broad wink. "Just let me out."

I pulled out my lockpick, bent low, and got to work, hoping my kind deed would net me some information. "Look, I'll let you out, regardless. But I'm hoping you can help me. Have you heard any guards or other prisoners talking about a guy named Billy?" If he was anywhere near as strange as his brothers, he'd be pretty hard to forget.

She let out a sigh, her brilliant, sky-blue eyes threatening to roll into the back of her head. "*I'm* Billy. I take it that my dum dum brothers didn't tell you I'm a woman."

I rocked back on my heels and let out a relieved breath as I continued to work. "They didn't mention it, no."

The telltale click had me tugging hard at the iron lock and, a second later, the cell door swung open. Billy strode through, her cupid's bow lips curling into an impish grin as she wiggled her fingers in greeting. "So how many heads do we gotta crack to get out of here?"

"Haven't seen a guard since the one at the entrance," I said, gesturing for her to follow as I took a final glance at my map. The fastest way out was through, if we could just make it to the next falcon shaft. It was the one I would've entered through if not for the dead-end.

Turning back was hardly an option now, anyway. The shaft I'd entered through was nigh-inaccessible at that height, and there was no way of knowing whether a patrol had noticed the missing guard. I'd just have to hope I could use the map and whatever skill I had inside my head to find us an alternate path back through the chutes and out of this fucking place.

She frowned slightly, taking long strides to keep pace with me. She was *tiny*. A full head shorter than me —hardly what I'd expected from the boss of the O'Donnelly brothers—but I couldn't deny that she had…moxie as her brother's would no doubt say.

"The place is usually crawling with the fuckers; how'd you get it so empty?"

"Something big is going on in Little Alabaster right now, the guards have been occupied with other things," I said.

She groaned. "Fookin' hell…please tell me that my idiot brothers don't have anything to do with the 'big' something…"

"They do not." We passed another dozen or so empty cells, and I chewed at my inner lip.

Still no sign of Amelia or her mother.

"This is the womens' wing, I take it?"

"More like a *woman*'s wing. Only the guards are left to keep me company now. Been trying to lure one of them with the promise of a little sucky sucky, but he won't take the bait. Guess he's a tad smarter than he looks." She nudged me, waiting for me to look over before snapping her teeth down pointedly.

"What about before these past couple days? No one else here?" I asked, ignoring her wordless admission that she had no qualms about biting a man's dick off. "I'm looking for a girl named Amelia and her mother, though I'm not sure they ended up here."

Billy's face scrunched. "Yeesh. Those two…Hope they weren't your kinfolk. Those rat-bastard guards brought them in. They were only here for a few hours before that creepy fucker Relyk had them brought to his interrogation room for questioning by him and the king." She pursed her lips and shook her head. "Never saw them again."

I closed my eyes, trying my best to suppress the tide

of horror and guilt that threatened to consume me. However you sliced it, their blood was on my hands. If I'd stood up and confessed what had really happened, they'd both be alive.

But Moll would be dead, a little voice reasoned. *It's not your fault that Relyk and the king are evil bastards.*

I shook off the guilt and tried to focus. There would be time for reflection and regrets later. For now, it was going to take everything I had to get Billy and I out of here alive.

Fetch's talons tightened suddenly on my shoulder as a soft thumping broke the silence.

Fuck.

I put a hand out, stopping Billy behind me. My other hand strayed toward my pouch on instinct as the door began to shake, but the incapacitator still needed some time to recharge before it'd be of much use. That left me two options: beat whoever it was in a sword fight or run back the way we came and hope we found an escape route before they caught us or sounded the alarm.

None of those options were great.

I rested my hand on the hilt of my sword as I stepped closer, and the door rumbled open. Then I tugged it free as the guard stepped through.

Apparently, Billy had something else in mind, and she pushed past me. "Hey there, handsome," she called, hauling up the hem of her shirt and baring her substantial breasts.

The guard stood stock still, eyes pinned to the woman's tits as his Adam's apple bobbed in his throat.

"Uhh...I...you—"

But Billy didn't wait for him to get his thoughts together as she leapt forward in a blur, her leg darting out to roundhouse kick him in the face, then dropping to a knee and punching him straight in the twig and berries. He let out a choked gurgle and went to his own knees. Billy jabbed two fingers directly into his eye, as if the previous blows hadn't been enough. His howl of pain was cut short as she angled her hand and chopped him in the side of the neck. He dropped like a rock and smacked his head on the floor.

Billy yanked his sword from its scabbard, righted her shirt, and shot me a questioning look.

"What's next?"

CHAPTER 23

"This way, into the chute." I helped Billy up first, and then she reached back for me. Fetch flew in and landed lightly on my shoulder.

"We keep quiet, light feet, no talking unless absolutely necessary. Got it?" I looked at Billy and she grinned, giving me two thumbs up.

I took the lead, holding the map and using it and… whatever was going on inside my head to get us out of here.

If I'd thought I was sweating before, it was nothing to the liquid pouring off me now.

Almost. We were almost there. Another glance at the map, tracing the lines with one finger. I motioned for Billy and gave her a nod.

I broke into a jog as we rounded the final bend. One more quick scuttle through the last falcon shaft and we'd end up in the outside world, assuming no more dead-end situations arose.

We were going to make it. I still couldn't believe it, but we were actually going to make it...

I peered down at the ground below, beckoning Billy to step up beside me. Our trip through the chutes had been a smooth one, and I prayed our good fortune would continue. The exit chute I'd chosen was a dozen or so feet above the ground, and my knees smarted as I stuck the landing. Still it was a hell of a lot better than the hour-long rooftop stealth mission I'd gone through to get in.

Billy grunted as she hit the grass behind me, glancing around expectantly. "Where are the boys?"

"They're waiting for us in The Smudge."

She let out a sharp *tsk*. "Leaving a lady to do all their dirty work. Sounds about right, lazy chumps."

I allowed myself a chuckle as I turned toward the large flag hanging from the inside of the walls that surrounded the palace. I'd scoped the place out as a good escape route earlier. A cluster of well-manicured trees provided some cover, and the guard patrols were usually focused on the front and back of the palace grounds.

"We're gonna have to go over," I said, glancing at the smaller woman.

She gawked. "You expect me to climb that?"

"Of course not. I have a way up if we can just get to the base of it." I fished the grappling hook from my pouch, briefly noting that I'd come full circle. In by grappling hook what felt a lifetime ago, and out the same way.

I gestured for Billy to stay low as I took my first step into the courtyard. Guards patrolled the grounds by torchlight, but, as expected, there were far fewer than usual, and I could see their fires flickering in the distance.

I let out a breath as my thoughts shifted to Duncan. Surely, if something had happened to him, the palace would be in a state of pandemonium? Unless Relyk had done it in secret and no one knew about it yet...

What if we left and I never knew what happened to him? How would I sleep at night, wondering if he was convicted of treason and sentenced to the dungeon I'd just left?

...Or worse?

In that moment, I made a decision—a crazy, stupid decision. I would get Billy to her brothers to ensure Molly's safety and see my friend one last time. Then, I would double back to join Duncan and offer my help. If there was a revolution afoot, I would be a part of it, whatever the risk.

We scurried across the palace grounds, and I took careful aim as we got to the base of the wall. The grappling hook flew upward as I pulled the trigger, and I winced as it clinked against the hard white stone of the wall.

I held my breath, scanning for threats on either

side, but saw nothing. After a few hard tugs on the rope, I beckoned Billy closer, grabbing her around the waist.

Her blue eyes sparkled as she leaned back, grinning up at me. "You could at least take me for dinner first, you cheeky slut."

That got a ghost of a smile out of me, and I tightened my grip. "Hold on."

She did, and, after a final pull on the line, I flipped the switch that would send us skyward. We ate through the distance in seconds, grabbing hold of the spiked barrier that marked the top of the wall and scrambled over the top.

The patrols seemed more numerous from this height, tiny red-orange blots inching along in the otherwise inky dark, and I whistled softly, sending Fetch into the air. "Keep watch and make sure we're not walking into any of those guard patrols."

"How am I supposed to do th—" Billy broke off and gaped at me. "Wait, are you talking to the damn falcon?"

"Yep. He's… different than other birds. We have an understanding."

She narrowed her eyes and nodded. "What's your name, anyway?"

"Harmony," I said, seeing no point in lying now. "Harmony Fallowell."

She studied me and let out a sniff. "Well, something

tells me you're different than other birds yourself, Harmony Fallowell. You should consider getting into smuggling. I could line up work for you like you wouldn't believe."

"You can consider this my first and last foray."

We maneuvered over the wall, then using the hook again, rappelled down to the cobblestone street. Noble's homes glowed softly with light, but there was more than enough cover to avoid the patrols and see their bright torches coming as we continued on.

"How'd those lunks get you involved in this?" Billy asked as the illusory wall of the Smudge came into view.

"It's a long story, but I need to get out of Little Alabaster and back into The Hollow. At first, I was just going to build that easy lockpick for them, but they had me in a tight spot."

Her hand went to my shoulder, and I turned, surprised to see the somber expression on her face. "They really are decent lads at heart. I'm sure they've been running around like chickens with their heads cut off since I've been gone, and they're jumping on the first opportunity they saw to get me out."

"Chickens with their heads cut off sounds about right," I said, putting my finger to my lips as another guard's torch came into view.

We scurried by when they turned the corner, jogging the final length to the Smudge's wall.

Another patrol rounded the corner just before we got there, and my heart pounded as we dashed past, Fetch flying beside my head, ignoring their frenzied shouts. Billy sprinted ahead of me, the false wall shimmering with magic as she ran right through it.

"Up this way," she hissed, halting in front of a small cluster of crates. She climbed to the highest one like they were stairs, then leapt to the roof top a few feet away.

She held out a hand as I did the same, hefting me the last few inches until I was there, too. I turned back to see the guards just making their way through the wall.

"Don't worry, they don't know The Smudge like I do."

And, just like that, we gave them the slip, but we took a circuitous route to get to The Hoof and Saddle just to be sure.

I was first to leap to the ground below, and my heart skipped a beat as a large, shadowed figure stepped out to greet me. Scotty stared down at me, expression shifting from surprised to angry in a heartbeat.

"Where is she?"

The door creaked open behind him, and Paddy stepped out, his other two brothers in tow, at exactly the same moment that Billy smacked down onto the street behind me.

"I heard you were giving this lovely lady a hard

time." Her hands went to her hips, and she narrowed her eyes at them, but the facade broke within seconds as the brothers swarmed her.

Even the normally difficult Scotty had tears in his eyes, and Billy had to bodily shove them off of her, one by one. "We still have a job to do, and we owe this girl a swift resolution after what she just put herself through to get me out, with no backup from you lugs!"

Paddy clapped me on the shoulder, nodding to his sister. "Agreed. We should get her to the tunnel straightaway and sort this all out."

"Where is it? I have this grappling hook we can use if—" I stumbled back as Billy reached out, flicking me on the forehead, hard.

"You done good. Now, leave the rest to the professionals, lass." Her face hardened, and her voice took on a deep, commanding tone as she began barking orders.

She jabbed her finger at the roof of a nearby house. "Jacob, Andrew, you two take the high route. Use the usual signal if you see anything we should be worried about. Scotty, you're our point man. Make sure you don't walk us right into a damn patrol like you did last time."

"That was—" The oaf of a man cut off as she shushed him, settling for a discouraged nod of his head.

"Paddy, you watch the rear." She strode over, clapping me on the back. "And you're with me. We'll have you back in The Hollow before you can say O'Donnellys."

Resisting the urge to parrot the name back to her, I jumped into action with the rest of them. And, despite the impression I'd had of them before this, I couldn't help but soften toward them some. They clearly loved each other very much.

We scurried through The Smudge quickly and quietly. Jacob and Andrew hooted from above in an imitation of owls so perfect that even Fetch seemed to buy it, stirring anxiously on my shoulder. With them giving us warnings, we managed to skirt around each and every patrol even though the place was swarming with them. I had yet to see a single guard by the time we were halfway to The Smudge's edge, which only made it more surprising when a hunched figure emerged from the nearest hut.

Paddy's steadying hand fell to my shoulder as I staggered back in surprise.

"Don't worry, lass, it's just—"

"Gayelette," I chimed in, a chill rolling through me.

As the flower cart pulled to a stop, I was surprised to see the sign on the outside had new hours posted.

OPEN Friday 9-MIDNIGHT. I blinked and then turned to the older woman, who looked me up and down. "You're finally starting to see."

I opened my mouth to respond, but she silenced me with a hand.

"Don't waste time now that you're on the right path,

child. You must go now; the next chapter awaits! But beware of the holes in the pages. Darkness that way lies."

I stared at her long and hard, remembering how her words had come to my aid in the chutes, nearly too late. "Can you tell me why the pictures from my book keep showing up? What does it mean?"

She pursed her lips and shook her head slowly.

"Please! If you really want to help me, stop being so mysterious. Just tell me what to do next and I'll do it."

Her smile was gentle. "The answers to our questions don't matter half as much as the journey we take to find them. *That* is where we grow, child. Now hurry! Before it's too late."

I nodded silently, still reeling with confusion at her words as we rushed off.

"Shite on a shingle…that was creepy. Have you spoken with her before?" Paddy whispered, sidling up beside me.

"I have."

Billy slowed her pace to let me catch up. "We see her once in a while, and then not for years before she comes 'round again like she never left. No idea where she goes in between. I wouldn't pay her too much mind, though, she's a bit touched in the head."

I didn't argue, but I knew she was wrong. Gayelette's cryptic advice the first time we met had been key to the success of my mission saving Billy. Knowing she felt like I was on the right path when everything was so fucked up right now gave me some small amount of comfort.

Billy let out a hiss as she looked over her shoulder. "Oy, Paddy, that isn't quite what I had in mind when I told you to 'watch the rear'. Keep your eyes on the road and off of our client's backside, if you please."

I shot him a look and he threw up his hands as if he was shocked at the accusation.

"I'm sure I've no idea what you're talking about, sister," he said, his tone far from convincing.

A pair of loud hoots sounded from overhead, and the teasing ceased instantly.

"Patrol behind us," Billy muttered.

Scotty broke into a full-on run as he led us down the nearest side road. My knees ached as we ran, still sore from the steep drop off the palace wall, but I wasn't about to be the caboose of this train.

"Not far now," Billy said as the dense city gave way to an open field.

The Cradle that separated The Hollow from Little Alabaster loomed. Soon, I'd be back with Molly. At least for a little while.

If only you could've taken Duncan with you.

But his destiny was bigger than mine, and, if the stars aligned, I'd see him again once I'd gotten Moll sorted and on the road to safety.

I scanned the moonlit field, looking past the rows of crops and trees and wondering where the hell a tunnel could possibly be hidden that would lead all the way back to The Hollow. The O'Donnellys hadn't led me astray yet, so I put my trust in them now.

Our feet sunk into muddy ground as we dashed through a field dotted with evergreens. We wove our way to the right of the field, emerging next to a grassy hill, and Scotty slowed to a stop.

He was panting heavily as he looked up. "Should we wait for the others? I'm sure we gave the guards the slip by now."

"Jacob and Andrew are quick. We'll keep moving for now, they'll catch up."

A dilapidated wooden house came into view, and we approached via the eastern side of the hill. By the time we reached the metal doors to the cellar, pounding footsteps sounded behind us. We all waited; breath suspended as Paddy disappeared for a moment.

"Nothing to worry about. It's just the lads," he called softly, stepping back into view

Billy nodded. "Keep watch for now, I'll call you when we're about to get into the tunnel."

Andrew let out a low laugh as he and his bespectacled older brother approached. "Holy shit that was close. Did you guys really not see that pack of guards? They were on your tails almost until you got up to the farm."

"I've never seen this many out at once," Jacob added.

Billy nodded. "The palace was left largely unguarded, so there's definitely something going on that has nothing to do with us."

Scotty eyed me, still panting from our run through The Smudge. "You know anything about that?"

I shrugged. "Hard to say exactly, but things have been tense for days now." I was skirting the question, but any information about Duncan's coup wasn't mine to share.

Billy made her way to Andrew, slapping him on the back with one hand and gesturing toward the cellar doors with the other. "Get 'er open."

I moved to offer my lockpick, but it clicked open before I could. He turned, shooting me a triumphant smile as Scotty hefted open the double doors.

Billy leaned in, yanking the torch from the wall, then lit a match. "The tunnel is a mile or so long. We'll see you through to the other side."

A musty smell wafted upward as Scotty took a creaking step onto the wooden staircase leading into it. The rest of us moved to follow, but Paddy sprinted up behind us before we could enter.

"What's the matter?" Billy demanded.

"Jackals on their way!" Paddy glanced over his shoulder, and my ears rang as Duncan and Crispin came sprinting up behind him. His gaze collided with mine, but where I'd expected to find anger and accusations, all I saw was relief.

He'd come.

For me.

I blinked hard, blowing out a breath that had been trapped in my chest since I'd last seen him.

No time for that nonsense, birdbrain. Focus!

"Are you sure it's Jackals?" I managed, the memory of Duncan's brutal fight with one still fresh in my mind.

"Positive!" He gestured wildly for us to continue moving. "Three of the fuckers. We need to go, right now!"

CHAPTER 24

"What are you doing here?" I hissed as the group of us rushed down the stairs, two at a time, following Scotty's lead.

"Relyk got wind of the coup," Duncan said, one hand on the small of my back as we ran through the narrow tunnel. "He started interrogating the nobles. I sent Crispin to the shack, and you weren't there. Nearly gave me a heart attack."

"Duncan, I-"

"It's alright," he cut in. "I get it. You had to do what you had to do. By the time I went to the dungeons to look for you, there were already half a dozen of my supporters strung up in the town square. It was only a matter of time before Relyk got the information he needed about who was leading the charge. We'll have to regroup and attack them later, from the outside in."

I couldn't deny he was a sight for sore eyes, and

seeing him alive was a relief I couldn't even process yet. But…

"You could've gotten out another way. We're just going to slow you down."

"I wouldn't leave, not knowing if you were still back there and in danger?" He let out a low growl. "A dozen Jackals couldn't have kept me from finding you."

My battered heart thumped hard. "How did you even know I'd be in the dungeon?"

The realization hit me at the same time as he spoke.

"Bertrand. He waited a long while but started to get nervous when Relyk called for a falcon to act as a spotter for one of the nobles who tried to run. They started bolting once they realized what was happening."

The puzzle pieces fit together. "Bertrand was afraid the sorcerer would send the falcon into the chutes and find me," I finished for him. "God, poor Bertrand. I didn't mean to put him in that position."

"I'm glad you did. I'm here with you now." His fingers closed on my waist more tightly, and I wished to hell I could hug him.

"When the two of you love birds are done flirting, maybe we can focus on a plan of what the fuck we're going to do on the other side if we manage to shake these ghouls, yeah?"

"Sorry, Billy," I said, my breath coming short from the exertion. My legs burned, but I didn't stop. Getting decapitated by a Jackal would hurt a whole lot worse than sore knees and muscles.

My legs churned faster as I tried to think logically despite the fear.

"Once we reach the end, we get out, shut the doors and gather whatever we can to pile on top. Paddy, where exactly does the tunnel open up?"

"Right under that mostly burned down barn near the pond, a short distance from the town proper."

"Perfect." There were loads of rocks surrounding the pond. Most too large for me to lift, but Duncan would surely be able to heft them while we gathered some of the smaller ones. I could run to the Petway's shack less than a hundred yards from there and borrow some weapons if need be. They were a good family and would help if they knew my plight.

The sound of footsteps echoed behind us and my stomach turned.

"They're getting close, we've got to move! The exit is just up ahead. I just have to put the ladder up and open the doors," Jacob called.

"Get it done." Crispin turned to Duncan for approval. "We'll hold them off."

Duncan hefted his sword, and his friend did the same.

"We'll all help while he works on the ladder," I said, but Duncan grabbed my arm as I reached for my pouch. The incapacitator was charged by now, I could help too.

"The tunnel is too narrow, Harmony. We'll buy the time we need."

I opened my mouth to argue, but he was right. Only two could stand comfortably abreast, and, while it was possible to support them from behind, it would also serve to block their retreat.

"Leave it to the professionals, lass," Crispin agreed, flashing a calm smile before turning toward the sound of oncoming feet.

The pair charged down the tunnel in unison, and I resisted the urge to cover my ears as they rounded the corner. Duncan's battle cry split the air, followed by a blood curdling shriek.

My breath caught in my throat as blades began to clash. At this point, all I could do was hope.

Another roar shook the cavern, and Fetch shook out his wings as dirt rained down on us from the ceiling of the tunnel.

I couldn't see anything, but a ghoulish howl told me a blade had found its mark in a Jackal. Frantic footsteps were audible a moment before Crispin and Duncan reappeared around the corner, a cloud of black creeping up behind them.

"How's that exit coming along, brother mine?" Billy asked, an edge to her voice that was part warning, part fear.

"The doors are twisted at the hinges, but I've almost got them. One minute."

"That big one is even stronger than the others," Crispin gasped as he strode up to us, chest heaving.

"They seem to be waiting for that black mist to clear," Duncan added, sparing a glance back. His biceps were slick with sweat from the brief exchange, and his sword was wet with green Jackal blood.

My heart pounded in my ears as I turned from Jacob to the shrinking cloud of mist behind us. They'd blocked off their own progress with the stuff, but it was dissipating far too quickly.

Even if we managed to get the doors open, there would be no time to figure out how to keep them closed if those monsters wanted out. They were just too strong...

Duncan's eyes were liquid silver as he gripped my shoulder, holding my gaze in the dim light. As if he were thinking the same thing.

"Forgive me," he whispered. "And don't give up, keep fighting."

I grabbed his arm to demand an explanation as he shot a grim look at Crispin, who nodded.

"Billy, you get Harmony and your family out. Crispin and I make a final stand here and hold them off until you seal the entrance." He stared at Billy with those preternatural eyes. "Do not let her turn back. Is that understood?"

Horror rolled through me, and I shook him roughly, sending Fetch off my shoulder. "No! No, I'm not going to just lock you in with those creatures to die!"

"They tried to kill me once. How did that turn out?" he whispered. But we both knew it was bullshit. One wasn't three, and these Jackals were the cream of the crop.

"Ladder's up, let's move!"

The snarling and the pounding of incoming boots was almost upon us as Paddy hitched his hands under my arms and hoisted me onto the rickety ladder.

"Lead the way and climb or everyone behind you dies, and it's on your head!" he shouted. That got me moving, as he must've known it would.

The sudden clash of swords was faint over the pounding in my head as I put one foot in front of the other, barely able to see the rungs with the tears running from my eyes.

I reached the open doors just behind Fetch and stepped off the ladder, turning back to help Paddy, who was directly behind me.

Maybe if they hurried, there was still a chance for all of us to get out. Maybe if…

But my thoughts were derailed by the sound of a familiar voice over my shoulder. "Get your scrawny ass out of the way so I can blow this fucker to smithereens, would you?"

Moll stood a few yards away, wearing a yellow dress with a corset, no less, without even a coat. Her slippered foot rested on a neat little pile of familiar looking red sticks with strings trailing off them. My bang 'em ups!

"Hello again, love," Paddy said as he leapt onto the floor of the barn. "Excellent timing."

O'Donnellys continued scuttling up the ladder and through the open doors as Moll and I stared at each other. Her eyes were as wet as mine, and her bottom lip trembled despite the tough guy act. I wanted to hug her, but knew it would be impossible to keep it together for both of us if I did...

"What the hell are you wearing?" I deadpanned.

"What...heroes can't be sexy?" she shot back with a hint of a smile.

A howl of pain rang out from below, and I winced. It hadn't sounded like Duncan, but I couldn't be sure.

Billy stepped off the ladder and she and Jacob both reached down to grab Scotty by the forearms and hoist him the rest of the way.

"We've got backup, boys!" Billy called down to Duncan and Crispin. "Lay them low and get up here so we can finish the job."

Paddy stuck his head through the doors and into the tunnel, watching upside down. "We ain't closing these doors without you."

The responding snarl was most definitely Duncan, and he wasn't happy, but I didn't care. This had to work...it would work.

"One final push, Cris. Give it everything you've got!"

A guttural war cry echoed from the tunnel below,

and my head pounded with adrenaline and fear. If only I could see what was happening—

"They got 'em!" Paddy howled. "The Jackals are flat on their backs!"

Crispin came barreling up through the open doors, Duncan hot on his heels.

"Now!" Billy called to Moll, who lit the fuse on the crimson sticks and tossed them into the tunnel.

All of them.

I'd never had use for more than two at a time, I had no idea what kind of damage five would do.

Like a well-oiled machine, the rest of us got on either side of the doors and yanked them shut with a clang.

"Run!"

We all just made it outside when a series of back-to-back booms rocked the ground beneath us. The charred, skeletal remains of the barn shook, and for a second, I thought it might collapse altogether. Then, it and the trembling earth settled.

All was still and silent but for our labored breathing, leaving white puffs in the night sky.

Crispin moved first, striding toward the rusty doors. Smoke rose from them in whisps as he cocked his head to listen.

"I don't hear any movement at all, and the doors are red-hot. I can't imagine anything survived that explosion." He straightened and offered a weary smile. "I think we're in the clear. For now."

I closed my eyes and said a silent prayer of thanks before opening them to find Duncan standing right by my side. A trail of blood ran down his arm as he reached for my hand, but we would deal with that later.

Moll was safe, and we had all made it through that tunnel in one piece. Right now, that was all that mattered.

A SHORT WHILE LATER, we all stood in the center of The Hollow. It was nearly morning, and the last dregs of adrenaline driving me had faded during the run from the barn. I couldn't remember when I'd last slept, and my legs trembled with exhaustion. I wasn't sure I could make it another step.

I spared a glance at the rest of our bedraggled crew. They weren't in much better shape than I was. We needed to eat and rest for a spell, or we'd be useless.

"We've got to keep moving," Paddy said, bending at the waist to catch his breath. "The palace guards will be swarming this place for Billy soon enough."

Duncan let out a low laugh as he cocked his hands on his hips. "The palace guards don't give a rip about your sister anymore, O'Donnelly. They have a rogue prince and his treasonous knight to find. Haven't you heard? Those two were planning a coup."

Billy's eyes narrowed as she assessed the two men. "Pardon me saying so, but that's a pretty pathetic coup.

What, you thought the two of you would be able to take down the whole lot of them? That fucking sorcerer included?" She let out a snort. "Not likely."

I pressed two fingers to my pounding temple and shook my head. "It wasn't supposed to happen last night. They had rallied a group of supporters."

Duncan nodded. "Things...changed when I found out Harmony wasn't where I left her."

Understanding dawned in her shrewd, blue eyes and her lips twisted into a smile. "Loverboy couldn't bring himself to let you handle it on your own. Had to be Prince Charming, did he?"

I couldn't think about that right now, or how the truth in her words made me feel. Instead, I focused on what I was good at.

Planning, and execution of said plan.

I held up both my hands, drawing everyone's attention. "I know I'm not in charge here, but we need to reevaluate. Our place is a couple miles from here, and we aren't far off from sunrise. We don't want to be out walking about if we hope to lay low. I'm dressed for a party, two of you are covered in blood, Billy's spent a week in a dungeon and looks like something you'd dig out of a crypt—no offense—and Duncan is the fucking prince of the realm. We don't exactly blend in."

Paddy's dimple flashed. "She's right, you know. Me and her are pretty as ever, but the rest of you are pretty shite right now."

I blew out a long breath, dreading what I was about

to say, but knowing I had to say it. "Look...there's a place we can hide out for a bit and rest, big enough for everyone. Clean water, clothes, some food. It's right around the corner..."

"Tell me you're not serious," Molly hissed, reaching out to pinch my arm. "We're in the middle of a shit sandwich, and you want to add your step-monster to the mix? You're out of your mind."

I rubbed at the stinging spot and moved away so she couldn't do it again. "I don't see that we have a choice."

"Well, you might not, but me and mine do," Billy said, eyeing her brothers before moving to stand close to me. "We're too conspicuous together. Besides, the O'Donnellys work best on our own. I appreciate what you've done for us, but it's time we take our leave."

Scotty let out a sigh of relief. "About time. All this chatter is giving me fits."

Duncan reached into his pocket to pull out a pouch full of coins and held it out to Billy. "To help you find a place to hide, or passage out of here. A caravan leaves for Bryngarde in two days."

She accepted the coins with a nod of thanks and then backed away.

"Then it's back to the motherland, I guess. Ta, all. Maybe we'll see you in another lifetime."

With that, she broke into a jog and her brothers followed behind. A twinge of sadness crept over me as

I watched them go. They'd been in my life for only a few days, but I knew I would never forget them.

The sky was turning from black to purple as I started walking in the direction of my stepmother's house, dread building with each heavy step.

"I guess we're off to meet your family, then?" Duncan asked.

Molly gagged and Duncan sent her an incredulous look.

"We just battled three Jackals and lived to tell the tale. It can't be worse than that..." He laughed, but I did not laugh with him.

Molly, though, let out a snort. "You haven't met Druzilla, Pain, and Suffering. At least you know those fly-covered fuckers will just try and kill you. These three? These three will just make you wish for death."

She couldn't have been more right, and as we headed to my stepmother's house, I found myself wishing for Jackals...

CHAPTER 25

"And you're certain that she's not going to sound the alarm the second she sees us and realizes what's going on?" Molly asked for the third time as we walked up the short rundown path.

Almost there.

"Certain is a strong word," I hedged. "But I do think she'll be bowled over with Duncan's presence and she'll err on the side of being a suck-up. At least for a little while." I shrugged and rapped on the door three times hard. "But I guess we'll find out in a second."

Sometimes, when the shitstorm came, you had to take cover where you found it. And while Druzilla and my stepbrothers weren't exactly the stuff of dreams, they were the only family I had. Fetch bobbed and weaved on my shoulder, as if contemplating whether to take his chances elsewhere, eventually settling in, loyal bird that he was.

The door opened much more quickly than I would have expected at this time of morning and by the one person who never opened the door. My stepmother appeared before us in her fluffy dark brown robe with her hair wrapped in a night bonnet.

"Harmony, what on earth are you doing here at this time of night?" Her eyes flitted away from mine as she glared at Fetch and fidgeted with the belt at her waist. "The turkey meat is gone. I did as you told me and sent some to Xavier and that little Petway scamp, but when you never came back for the rest, we ate it. It would've turned by now if we didn't put it in the smoker in any case, and I've told you before, we don't work for you."

It took a second, but I could tell the moment she noticed the three people behind me, because she instantly raised a hand to her bonnet with a gasp. "You brought guests," she demanded, her thin brows instantly caving into a frown. "You could have at least warned me, you know. I'll not be hosting a bunch of your hooligan friends or wasting my good tea leaves on the likes of—" She broke off and her eyes went wide as she stared into Duncan's face and recognition dawned.

How the hell she recognized him, I will never know. Maybe she saw something of his father in his face— she'd attended balls back before she'd married Paw.

"Oh, my. Is that—Are you—?" She lifted a fluttering hand over her heart and took a step back, clearly in shock. "Your Highness," she whispered as she dipped into a deep curtsy. "I-I had no idea. Please forgive me for my rudeness." She moved to one side of the door and waved him in like he was…royalty. "Spalding!" she hollered over her shoulder and then screamed even louder. "Spalding. Get up this instant!"

As the rest of us stepped past her, she almost knocked Molly over to get closer to Duncan.

"Please forgive my daughter's rudeness. I'm Druzilla Fallowell, Harmony's mother."

"Step," I interjected in a low voice.

"Fine, you ungrateful wretch. *Step*mother." She fixed a beatific smile on her face as she turned back towards Duncan. "I've always felt that blood ties were over-rated. It's the person that raises you and nourishes you and takes care of you when you're afraid that truly makes a mother. Don't you think, Prince Duncan?"

"I wouldn't know," he said with a thin smile. "Mine was a prostitute who handed me over to my father in exchange for enough gold to leave Alabaster."

Moll met my gaze with wide eyes, and I shrugged. The official word was that Duncan's mother had been married to the king in a secret ceremony and then died in childbirth before their marriage could be announced. Apparently, the prince had decided there was no longer a need to keep up appearances now that he planned to dismantle the monarchy.

Maybe it was the absurdity of it all, or maybe I was just punch-drunk and exhausted, but a giggle bubbled from my lips as Druzilla's mouth opened and closed like a landed carp. I had to clap my hand over my lips to keep it from spilling out in peals of hysterical, unstoppable laughter.

"Yes. Well...that doesn't sound very nice, does it?" She cleared her throat and waved to the modest parlor with a sweeping hand. "Please. Sit. Put your feet up if you like."

"What are you caterwauling about, Mother?" Spalding grumbled as he entered the room scratching his balls, wearing only sleeping pants, his thin chest bare.

"Look who's come to visit, dear!" she said, scurrying his way and shooting him an urgent look. "It's Prince Duncan."

"And this is Sir Crispin Locke," Duncan said, waving a hand toward his guard.

"Pleasure." She barely spared the man a look before beaming at the prince once again. "Spalding is my oldest son. His brother Wayne is working the night shift at the mill. He should be home in a couple of hours." She turned to a still groggy Spalding. "Put some proper clothes on, then get the kettle on to boil and take out those lovely biscuits that we scrimped for to enjoy on Abundance Day, hmm?"

He trudged off, steps slow and heavy.

"So...to what do I owe this honor?" she asked, gesturing again for us to sit as she lowered herself onto the love seat.

Duncan rose his brows at me in question, and I shook my head. I needed to cherry-pick what I told her and how I said it, or she would absolutely lose her mind.

"Look, Druzilla," I began as I moved to sit across from her. "We need—"

"Actually, you know what? Maybe you'd rather stand, Harmony…you're covered in filth." She wrinkled her nose as she looked me up and down.

I stared at her, used to her rules.

Molly on the other hand… "What the hell is wrong with y—"

"Good point!" Duncan cut off Molly's incoming tirade, turning the full wattage of his smile Druzilla's way. "We're *all* filthy, and there's no reason to muddy up your lovely furniture. Maybe we could make use of your bath while you fix us something to eat and drink?"

Her eyes locked on that devilish dimple for so long, I wondered if she might be in a trance, but then she blinked. "Oh. Yes, alright. Three of you are in need of a good soaking, but I only have one bathtub, and once we fill it, it will take hours for the well to refill so it can be used again… Your Highness, I insist you take the bath. Harmony and your knight can use the wash basins."

"Harmony shall take the bath; Crispin and I can manage fine with the basin." Duncan continued to smile.

"I beg your pardon, Your Highness, but my daughter needs nothing special—"

"Step," Molly growled. This was one of the many reasons I loved her. She wasn't perfect, but there was no one more loyal.

"My *step*daughter didn't need a hot, fancy bath when she lived under my roof, and she doesn't need one now." She let out an indignant sniff. "That's how children become *spoiled*."

I saw the anger flash in Duncan's eyes despite the smile, and I held up a hand, hoping to nip this impending argument in the bud. "It's no problem at all. She's right, a good scrub and some clean clothes will do the trick. Go on, Duncan. I'll show Crispin to the basin."

"Tell you what," Duncan said, tugging a gold coin from his pocket. "We'll flip for the tub. The three of us." He eyed Crispin and wiggled his fingers. "Heads or tails?"

He flipped the coin in the air and Crispin called it, his lips twitching as he did.

"Tails."

"Ooh, bad luck, my friend. It's heads." Duncan faced me, a glint in his eye. "Here we go, Harm. I'll call it this time…Tails!"

As he caught the coin and slapped it to the back of his hand, I already knew what would be there, and a warm rush of affection flowed through me even as my eyes stung.

How could he come from that place and still be so fucking good?

Druzilla stared at the coin clearly showing heads. She tried to splutter but Duncan was already speaking.

"Fair is fair, Mrs. Fallowell. Now how about you show me those basins and then head into the kitchen with Spalding to work on that meal while the rest of us make ourselves presentable. Then we can chat about the reason for our visit."

Druzilla nodded, looking slightly dazed as she led the men from the room.

Half an hour later, things were looking up despite the chilly reception I'd received—not that it was a surprise. The hot water soaked some of my soreness away, and I didn't smell like a sewer or falcon shit anymore. Druzilla even let me borrow a fitted jacket that was too small for her—my crimson one was ripped in several places. By the time I scrubbed the mud and gunk off my boots, I was feeling better. The men seemed refreshed as well, even if their clothes were bloodstained.

The five of us wound up seated around the kitchen table sharing a meal of buttermilk biscuits, rich gravy, and steaming mugs of strong, hot coffee instead of tea. I was almost feeling human again when I spoke.

"Did you clean your wounds well?" I asked both Duncan and Crispin.

"All is well," Crispin said. "Couple of bleeders but mostly superficial. My internal organs feel like they've been pureed though after a few of those blows landed." He and Duncan both chuckled and I let out a sigh of relief. Laughing about it was good. I hoped that meant neither were critically injured.

Duncan dipped his head toward my stepmother. "Thank you for your hospitality, Druzilla. We're happy to answer your questions now."

"Actually, Your Highness, would you permit me to speak to my...husband's daughter alone for a moment, please?"

My face must've registered my shock and discomfort, because Duncan was already shaking his head. "No need for that. We can all talk—"

"It's okay, Duncan." I gave him a reassuring smile as I moved Fetch from my shoulder to perch on the back of the chair. "It's better this way."

Druzilla patted the corners of her mouth with her napkin as she stood, and I followed suit.

"Call me if anyone needs a horse-kick to the spleen," Molly murmured as I passed by her chair.

"Will do."

By the time we got to Druzilla's bedroom and she closed the door, I was ready. Mentally armored up and loaded for bear if she came at me—hell, it couldn't be worse than facing a real bear.

I almost changed my mind on that sentiment when she stepped closer and pulled me in for the world's most awkward hug.

Fear of the unknown coursed through me and I froze, stiff as a board.

"Wh-what the fuck are you doing?"

"I'm embracing you, Harmony. What does it feel like?"

It *felt* like I was wrestling with a bag of coat hangers, but I kept that thought to myself as she pulled away and ran a hand over her hair as if she were making sure there wasn't a strand out of place.

"I think I've pieced some of it together once I got over the shock of your arrival. We got a special delivery of flyers a few days ago about the attack on the king. They mentioned a redhead, but I didn't really think anything of it. Then when I saw Molly's hair earlier, cut short and dyed that horrific color..." She touched her bonnet absently before continuing. "That's why you left here so quickly, isn't it? She snuck into the Jubilee, and you were worried for her after the gossip Wayne shared."

I nodded. No point in denying it now. "Yes."

"But you were too late. Did he..." she trailed off and pressed a shaking hand to her mouth. Part of me wanted to comfort her, but I held back.

"No. It was a close thing but we stopped him. She stopped him."

"Good. That's good." She let her eyes drift shut as her shoulders drooped. "It's a terrible thing, that. The powerlessness of it. It's hard to forget, and sometimes it rears its head when you least expect it—years can go by and...it comes back in a rush, attacking you like the first time."

Words escaped me as the truth settled over me, sure

as could be. Druzilla knew what it meant to be violated firsthand. No matter our years of differences and the pain she caused me, my chest ached for her and tears pricked at my eyes.

"I'm sorry, Druzilla." It was all I had to offer her, yet she didn't seem to hear me.

She lifted her head and glanced over at a framed picture of my father that sat on her maple dresser. "You know, I chose him because I needed someone to marry quickly, and my options were limited due to my... condition. Imagine my surprise when your father not only raised a son that wasn't his but also helped me heal with his gentle love and adoration."

I blinked at her, stunned. Druzilla hadn't married my dad because of his charm. She married him because her rapist had left her pregnant.

How terrifying that must've been.

In the next moment, my thoughts shifted to my father...I opened my mouth, but she beat me to it.

"He knew from the start. I hadn't planned to tell him, but he knew and asked me outright. I told him the truth and he never once made me regret it. Never once even mentioned it again. He just...loved me unconditionally and always. I'm embarrassed to say that I took it for granted after a time. I could've been a better wife. I should've been a better...stepmother. But regrets are a bit like your brothers. They hurt to think about and accomplish nothing." She let out a tiny laugh at her own joke, and I managed a smile of my own.

"They're plenty old enough to move out, you know."

"They are. But then I'd be alone with far too much time to wallow in all those regrets and the memories I can't escape." She shrugged her narrow shoulders. "So here we are. Now it's your turn to fill in some of the blanks for me. How did you wind up with a prince and his guard in tow?"

I gave her the short version of events, ending on Duncan's now-botched plan for a revolution.

"When we left Little Alabaster, they were hanging nobles who were for the cause. Right now, our goal is to get out of The Hollow and somewhere safe so we can regroup. Duncan's hope is to put together an army of his own and take down the monarchy. I'm...I'm going to go with him and help him in whatever way I can."

Saying it out loud made me realize just how ridiculous it all sounded, but it was the truth, and I wasn't taking it back.

"What do you need from me?"

It was a question she'd literally never asked, so it took a second to process. "Honestly, two things. One, we'll take anything you have in the way of weapons. Duncan has gold and some things we can trade, but we only have a couple of swords and a few other items to help us through. If the sorcerer and his guards catch us en route before we reach a safe place, we're...well, we're sitting ducks."

She gave a crisp nod. "The boys have some weapons

you can take, a bow and arrow, and some axes. What else?"

Relyk would track me, I was sure of it. "I need you to leave here and hide for a time. Duncan will give you some coins. Go stay with your cousin, Ilsa. I'm just not sure if they know my real name now, or if they might come looking for my family."

She pursed her lips and nodded. "Not that we've been much of that to you. But again, I won't waste time on regrets. You've got to get out of here. I wish…I wish I'd had a friend like you when I was a girl, Harmony. Molly is lucky to have you."

Shock on shock, I felt like I was in a dream. But true to her word, Druzilla gave me all the help I asked for.

By the time we headed out the door a short time later, we were much better situated than when we'd arrived. Druzilla had given us a pack filled with what food they had on hand as well as some spare clothing, and weapons. She had even argued with Duncan— albeit briefly—when he handed her a pile of coins that paid for her kindness ten times over. I'd taken the opportunity to make sure the coins I'd promised to Gen for her silence, got to her grandmother in The Hollow, who would then let Gen know she got the coins. Druzilla agreed, even though it left her with less.

What I left with was priceless—a final understanding, truths revealed, and a past made a little better.

None of it was my fault…Even she knew she'd been wrong. Hurt people hurt people. I didn't have to forget what she'd done, but I would forgive it, as much for myself as for her and my father.

"I still think she's a piece of shit," Molly said as we walked toward main street, eyes peeled for black flies, ears pricked for the sound of men on horseback. The morning sun was up, though, and it was unseasonably mild, which made it all the more strange when flashes of white fluttered down from the sky, whispering to the ground in front of us.

Not snow, I realized with a start.

Flyers.

Typically, the palace had them sent in the dead of night so we would awaken to them scattered in the streets. Propaganda bullshit about how teamwork made the dream work, touting the virtues of nationalism.

Today, though, there was a good chance at least a couple of our faces would be plastered dead center of said flyers.

We all stood, faces upturned, waiting for the first of them to reach us. Fetch shifted on my shoulder, but Duncan was able to snatch one out of the air before he could fly up, and we all huddled around to see.

"Well?" I demanded, not close enough to read the writing.

His eyes narrowed as he scanned the page and then looked up, bewildered.

"Bertrand." He held the paper out for the rest of us to read.

To all those in The Hollow,

My falcons deliver one last missive, and it will be of my own mind, not the drivel sorcerer Relyk wishes you to read. Today, I take a stand, and I ask you to join me. We can no longer allow ourselves to be oppressed. To a man...to a woman, we must fight the powers that be and demand a change. To be treated with dignity, and kindness. No person should work their fingers to the bone and still go to bed hungry. No person should go without medicine they need because they don't have coin to pay for it and are too old to work. We must tear down the wall that divides us. We need a change in regime, to a man who sees us all! That man is Prince Duncan.

All Hail, King Duncan!

Bertrand, The Falconer

"Bloody hell," Crispin hissed, raking a hand through his hair.

My arms broke out in gooseflesh, and I rocked back on my heels as the others exchanged stunned looks.

This message was a death sentence. Surely, Bertrand knew that when he signed his name in big, bold letters. As I thought back on my last conversation with him, I realized I'd missed so much of what wasn't said. He'd spoken of Marjorie's pain. Of how she chose to stay alive for him because she didn't want him to be alone. Of how he'd lived a good, full life, and was ready to move onto the next...

And he'd opted to go out with a bang, supporting Duncan as best he could.

"He asked me for extra laudanum to help Marjorie sleep," Duncan whispered, closing his eyes for a long moment and blowing out a heavy sigh. "Now, I have to assume it was for both of them…"

The thought gave me some comfort. At least they would die peacefully in each other's arms.

I couldn't help but think of Bonnie, Eamon and the others. Surely, Bertrand had made sure the falcons were safe before— "Ah yes!" A scratchy voice cut through the grief and worry. "Word from the palace at last! It seems our esteemed leaders have more wisdom to share. Gobble it up, Hollowers. And ask yourself, what can you do for your country today? What can *you* do to serve your liege, who has served you so well?"

"Fucking Pete," Molly muttered under her breath as she turned to glare at the strange, old preacher who had dragged up his makeshift pulpit. "He just doesn't quit, does he? No one wants to hear it!" Molly hollered, flipping him the bird from across the street.

"We have to get a move on," Duncan said, tucking the flyer into his pocket. "Relyk has surely raised the whole army by now and is on the march. Assuming even those who oppose him got in line once he started killing, he should be coming through here to find me any time now. All he has to do is follow the dead Jackals, he'll know I am here."

"Come closer, countrymen," Pete called, beckoning us closer. "Come…let me tell you about the brave King Hein–"

He broke off with a gasp, his wild eyes locking on my boots, of all things. A strange sense of deja vu passed through me, and I shivered as his face lit up with joy.

"It's you…I had no idea! Thank the gods!"

I opened my mouth to reply, but no words came as the ground shifted beneath me, opened like a gaping mouth, and swallowed me whole.

CHAPTER 26

I sat up with a start and winced as a dull ache reverberated through my skull. What the hell had happened? One second, I was on the street listening to Pete, the next, I was plummeting through a sinkhole, landing like a bag of rocks on the ground below. As if I weren't already bruised enough.

I spit out a bit of dirt and wiped the back of my hand over my mouth. The space was dark, dry and dusty.

"Hello, Harmony!"

Pulse hammering, I looked around the dark room and tried to find the speaker, to no avail. Warm light suddenly flooded the space and I squinted, shielding my eyes.

"Pete? Is that you?"

The old preacher stepped into view holding a flickering lantern aloft.

"It is."

His smile stretched from ear to ear, the light giving his skin a reddish hue that made him look maniacal and I found myself scuttling backward until my shoulder blades hit a wall.

"Look, I'm not sure what's going on here, but if I could just get back with my friends..."

I'd always thought of the old man as harmless. His claims about the crown were so ludicrous, he rarely found a friendly ear for them, and he hadn't ever hurt anyone...that I knew of, anyway. But as I took a frantic look around the tiny room, I had to wonder if maybe I'd misjudged him. A man who created a trap door to kidnap women and lock them in a dark room likely wasn't up to something good.

Only one question remained.

Was he planning to keep me alive or kill me?

"I'm so sorry about the hard landing there. I made this little underground room nearly twenty years ago, and I haven't exactly been good about maintenance. There was supposed to be a cushy feather bed for you to land on, but it seems to have rotted."

He stepped closer and I pawed for the dagger Druzilla had given me, brandishing it in front of me.

"If you're doing this on Relyk's behalf, you need to know some things. Even now, he's killing nobles in Alabaster, hanging them in public for all to see. He's gone mad with power, and—"

"Nothing's changed on that front, my child," Pete

said with a chuckle. "The sorcerer's quest for power is insatiable. He's a monster and always has been."

I stared at him, baffled by his words. "You're always on about how great he is, and how the king is basically a deity on earth..."

"Oh, that." He tossed off a wave and began to pace the room in a figure eight. "I needed to wait in The Hollow until the right time, undisturbed. What better way to stay out of the crosshairs of the crown than to praise the ever-living tar out of them?"

"So you didn't mean any of it? All these years?" I demanded, forgetting to cower and letting my dagger fall to my side.

"Heavens, no."

"You've been preaching the virtues of the monarchy forever. I remember seeing you in town on that pulpit even when I was a child."

He paused in his pacing. "I've been here waiting. For *you*," he said with a shrug. "Honestly, I can't believe you've been here all along, *right* under my nose. You sure took your time getting those damned boots, eh?"

I still wasn't sure what the significance of the boots was, but I did my best to answer him. "I couldn't afford boots like this, now or then. The only reason I have them is because they were a gift."

He pursed his lips and then nodded. "Of course, of course, it's always about timing when it comes to things of this nature. I can only assume one of us wasn't quite ready for the challenge ahead until *now*.

On that note, I think it's time I introduced myself properly." He moved closer and held out a hand. "You know me by Pete, but I'm known far and wide as *The Speaker*. Perhaps you've heard of me?"

The breath left me in one fell swoop as I stared at him in stunned silence. If someone had come and slapped me with a brick, I wouldn't have been more shocked.

"You?" I shook my head slowly as I looked him up and down. "*You're* The Speaker?"

That couldn't be right. The Speaker hadn't been seen or heard from in decades. In fact, I'd been pretty sure he was nothing more than a legend.

He shot me a sad smile. "When Relyk and King Rudolph went on a tear to rid The Hollow of Whispers with any real power without a noble bloodline, *my* father left to create a safe haven for those who were persecuted for the crime of having magic while being poor, and any non-Whisper who opposed the crown."

He began to pace again, his expression dreamy, lost in thought.

"There were fifty of us to start, but over the years we grew and gained power. Once he passed, I took the mantle and would return to The Hollow to bring more Whispers and their allies into the fold. We lived as nomads and traveled in the dark of night, avoiding the mantises and Relyk alike. For a long time, we remained undetected. But as our numbers grew, it became too hard to hide. We had to settle somewhere, far enough away from Alabaster that Relyk wouldn't even think to come find us. To the coldest, darkest place the world has ever known."

"The Shadow Abyss," I murmured softly as I shook my head. "But how? Surely the cold—"

"In due course, Harmony," he said before launching back into his tale. "Once we were able to plant roots, create a true community, and hone our powers, we grew strong. I was sure our time was coming. That we would be able to take on the sorcerer and overthrow the monarchy. But when I went back with a contingent of my strongest Whispers to recruit more believers, one last time, we were met by a small group of soldiers dressed in armor, black as night. Relyk stood behind them and despite us outnumbering them ten to one...he was smiling."

I swallowed hard, knowing what was coming next...seeing the scene unfold in my mind.

His throat worked as he continued. "They were unreal. Unnatural in their speed and strength. While I had Whispers that could match them, Relyk himself was at their side. We couldn't prevail. We battled for a time, and I think there were moments that surprised him, but when it looked like we had a chance, he flattened ten of my people with the wave of his hand. It was then I knew I'd been a fool. I was nowhere close to being able to defeat him—I was young still. He was toying with me like a cat playing with its food."

If I'd any doubt about his story, that alone made me

believe his story. I'd seen Relyk's power, and I did not doubt it.

"There were only four of us left," Pete continued, "and I was prepared to die. But my best friend, the strongest Whisper in our collective aside from myself, wouldn't let me. She grabbed me by the shirt, told me our people needed me, and then she hurled me into the night sky. I softened my landing with my magic, and found myself half a mile away, just yards from our hot air balloon. Relyk must have been too weakened from expending so much power to give chase, so I was able to escape and return to my people. The others with me died that day. Relyk touted his victory, told everyone in the land that he and King Rudolph had vanquished The Speaker, and that wasn't far from the truth. I remained in hiding, mourning our losses with my people, until the prophecy. Twenty-five years ago, it came to us, and my path was clear. Victory would be ours, but it would take time and patience. So I came back to The Hollow disguised as Preacher Pete and waited for the future to unfold, for the signs to be revealed. Harmony, I waited for *you*."

I shook my head slowly, still trying to digest it all.

"How, though? How do you know it's me?"

"Listen to the words, the prophecy tells me so." He cleared his throat and spoke again, his voice booming this time. "Fair of face, with boots of red, her name is peace, a wizard's dread. I've been watching Serenity, the cabinet-maker's daughter, all this time. Thank the gods I didn't kidnap *her*, eh?" He laughed. "She's a bit of a horse face, but her name means peace and calm. We all call you Harm…about the opposite to peace as you could be! But I never thought much about your full name."

I gnawed on my lower lip, letting that sink in. Relyk's painting had also depicted me in my new boots, like some sort of prophecy. But still that didn't mean it was me.

Right?

The thing was, so much had happened in such a short time, and if I looked at it clearly, I was in the center of all of it.

And still…

"That's what you've got? Is that really enough to bank a whole revolution on?"

He held up a single finger and shook it at the ceiling. "Nope. There's so much more, but time is ticking. We must go before it's too late. Come with me, you and your friends, and it will all become clear." He paused and stared at me; his expression solemn. "Will you? Come with me, and fulfill your destiny? There is more to you than I think any of us realize, Harmony, you just have to…open yourself to the possibilities."

Something inside me sparked to life as he spoke, like my mind *had* opened up to the possibility of a whole new reality. It made me think of Gayelette. Her words came rushing back to me, as if she stood and whispered them in my ear.

Open your eyes and you will see who to trust.

Open your mind to the possibilities of the gifts you possess.

Open your ears and you will hear those who speak.

My heart beat faster at the realization that everything Pete had said might be true and right.

His smile faded as he watched me intently. "So will you come with me, Harmony?"

I was trapped in a cellar with a man I'd only known to be a raving loon, and a mouthpiece for the crown to boot. But maybe I was the mad one here, because I found myself nodding.

"I don't know for sure if I'm the person in your prophecy, but I'm willing to come and find out."

"Ah, lovely!" The Speaker grinned and sat down his lantern to applaud in giddy delight. "Come, come. We must go."

I stood and tucked my dagger away before falling into step beside him.

"Are my friends still in the street?" I'd lost at least a quarter of an hour here talking to Pete, and I was worried they were out there, refusing to leave without me but exposed to Relyk and his men.

"No. They got dropped into a tunnel just outside the door. I imagine they're trying to get in this room to rescue you as we speak."

He lifted a hand to the bolt on a massive, iron door and then yanked it open. The second the door swung wide, I could hear Molly and Duncan calling my name.

"Oh thank heavens," Molly rushed toward me. Her pupils were dilated and unfocused in the dark and she blinked like an owl. "What the hell, Pete?" she demanded, she gave The Speaker a hard shove to the chest even as Duncan grabbed him by the throat.

"Okay, let's all calm down here," I said, tugging at Duncan's arm. "Everything is fine. We just needed to talk. Let him go, Duncan."

His muscles trembled beneath my hand, and I knew he didn't want to.

"Please. He's not...he's not who you think he is."

He released The Speaker and turned to face me. "What the hell just happened? Did he hurt you?"

I laced my fingers with his and was about to explain when The Speaker let out an excited squeak.

"Perfect. Do you see it? Just perfect!" He cleared his throat again, and boomed out what I could only assume was more of the prophecy. "'Then prince and pauper, hand and hand. To finish the job, to heal the land.'" He clapped his hands together. "The pieces are all coming together indeed!"

Duncan shot me a questioning look and I let out a long breath as Fetch landed on one shoulder.

"Speaker, meet my friends. Everyone, this is The Speaker. And has he got a story to tell..."

CHAPTER 27

"Why do they call you that... 'The Speaker'?" I asked a while later as we walked along, using the tunnels Pete had built over the years, preparing for this exact moment so we could escape undetected.

His lips twisted into a wry smile. "A bit of a joke between my father and I when I was a boy. He was more powerful then, you see, but I was cocky and brash. I told him that, if he was a Whisper, when I grew up, I would become a shout. It's an homage to him and his influence that I erred on the side of humility and went with something in between."

By the time we emerged from the tunnel exit a short while later, everyone was up to speed, and just as shocked as I was that we'd stumbled upon the legend that was The Speaker...a Whisper who, if legend was right, might be as strong as Relyk. We walked the last couple of miles in silence, and I imagined everyone was doing the same as me... trying to get their heads around all that had changed in the blink of an eye.

"I missed this so much. Fresh air, no stupid flyers spreading lies..." The Speaker raised his hands to either side and let out a sigh. Endless hills rolled toward the horizon, flanked by clusters of imposing mountains whose snowy peaks stretched into the clouds. Trees larger than any I'd ever seen peppered the ground in bunches, billowing in the cool wind.

There was just so much...space. Moll's hand found my arm as I slowed to a halt, dumfounded.

"Incredible," I murmured, sucking in a deep breath that tasted like...freedom.

The Speaker gestured all around, but his eyes stayed fixed on me. "Behold, child of prophecy. This is what Relyk has denied you. What he has tried to deny all those in The Hollow, The Smudge, and even Little Alabaster."

I nodded, still taking in the landscape. Fetch took to the sky, unbidden, flipping through the air in a series of flamboyant maneuvers.

"Will he be alright with the flying mantises?" Wards kept our skies at least somewhat safe, but out here...

"He's far faster than any mantis. Let him get a taste of true freedom as well!" The Speaker said.

"How far is your balloon from here?" Duncan asked, considerably less enthused than Moll and I were. Maybe because he still didn't trust that the man before us was who he said he was. Or maybe because traveling was old hat to him and he wasn't impressed.

But for us, just being on the other side of the Great Wall was both scary and electrifying.

"Not far. Just a moment." The Speaker strode over to a nearby rock, lifting up his shirt as he sat.

I leaned closer, curious as a small, metallic disk at the center of his chest came into view. He gripped the edges between his thumb and forefinger and yanked on it, hard. Blood dripped down to his belly as he pulled it free, revealing the thin, three-inch spike that'd been buried in his flesh.

His body spasmed for a moment, and he waved off Crispin as he moved closer to help. The Speaker let out a long sigh before carefully setting the pin into his bag. "Much better."

"What the hell was that?" Moll said, giving voice to my thoughts.

"Relyk has a ward over The Hollow that alerts him to any hint of strong magic in the city. I've been suppressing mine all these years." His face lit up as he said it, and he reopened his pouch. "Which reminds me…"

He unfolded an indigo hat, peppered with bright yellow stars, and gave it a few shakes before setting it on his head. The tip flopped to one side as he rose, raising a fist. "And, just like that, The Speaker returns!"

"Is it magic?" I asked, suddenly dizzy. I'd seen that

hat, stars and all, on the old man in one of Relyk's paintings.

Pete turned his back, and I saw the moment the painting had encapsulated right then. The only thing missing was me standing directly beside him, fist held high.

Holiest of shits, that was wild. It was also exhilarating. Instead of questioning my sanity yet again, it confirmed what Gayelette had told me. I was on the right path. Thank the gods!

"Nah. It's just an old wizard's hat."

"Relyk had a painting of this. Or, at least, of the two of us, at any rate. We were in a hot air balloon together leaving Alabaster." My chest ached as I stared at him, stricken with a sudden, horrible realization. "Bertrand, my friend, overheard Relyk saying that he needed me alive and now I know why. He wanted me to lead him to you. And I did it. You came out of hiding because of me."

He patted my back gently. "I was only in hiding waiting for you, Harmony. Waiting for *us* to fulfill our destinies. Don't despair. Things are exactly as they are meant to be." He turned to look out at the endless expanse of hills as he began muttering to himself. "Now let me see... Was it that one? No, maybe..."

He settled on one of the hills after a long moment, jabbing his finger toward it. "My balloon is just behind that hill. I think. Most likely. Should only be a couple hours' walk. Maybe half a day? Hard to say this far away."

Moll and I exchanged nervous glances. Was this truly the heroic revolutionary of legend that could lead an army to defeat the sorcerer? Was it possible that whatever magic and skill he'd had twenty-five years ago was gone? He'd been more serious down in the tunnel room, but now he seemed out of touch and almost childlike. And where was all the magic? He hadn't shown us a spit of it yet…

My lack of sleep caught up with me as we marched, and I was running on fumes by the time we reached the hill's base. I turned back toward the city for the hundredth time, squinting as I searched the sky for other balloons.

"Still no one following us."

"They've got to check all of Alabaster before they venture over The Great Wall," The Speaker said. "Even if Relyk knows we planned to leave in a balloon, he doesn't know we've got one already. Which means we've got a head start."

"And what of the mantises once we're in the air?" Crispin asked. "The falcons are faster, but we won't be. It usually takes three guards on deck just to hold them off during flight."

"My balloon Libby is a heck of a lot different than your Imperial balloons. She's made for speed. Plus, your guards aren't me." He grinned, wiggling his fingers as he said it. "They don't have magic."

I was beginning to wonder if he did either, but I left that unsaid as I rubbed the grit from my burning eyes. "How much further?"

His face scrunched up for a moment, as if considering. "An hour at most."

I let out a breath, forcing myself to keep trudging along. *Just a bit further and you can sleep,* I reminded myself, praying The Speaker's balloon was large and steady enough to make that a reality. It had been in hiding for as long as him. For all we knew, it could be destroyed by now.

Duncan moved to my side, his hand dropping lightly to my shoulder. "Do you need to take a break? It's not like they're right on our tails, it should be fine to—"

"Sir," Crispin called from behind, and I turned to see him pointing to something in the sky.

I squinted, heart thumping. "Balloon?"

He didn't bother answering as two flying mantises emerged from a cloud in the distance.

"Fucking hell," Moll swore, her fingers digging into my palm as three more filed out behind them.

"Maybe they haven't spotted us yet." My blood froze as the first of their screeches split the air, and I could almost feel the bloodlust rolling off them as they changed course, heading straight our way. The man at the amphitheater had been right; these were no simple predators, they were mindless killing machines. They jostled and crashed into one another as they hurtled toward us, but their eyes never strayed from their prey.

Us.

Duncan leapt in front of me, drawing his sword. "You and Molly stay behind Crispin and me, and see if you can find a chance to make a break for it. I assume you're best at long range, Speaker?"

A wave of anger washed away my panic, and I grabbed Duncan's uninjured shoulder. "I won't let you pull that hero shit again this time. I'm going to fight by your side, or you're going to have to fight *me* before you take on those fuckers." I pulled the incapacitator from my pouch, sliding the extender to max length. It gave me a good four feet.

Duncan scowled, cursing as he pulled a dagger from his belt. "Let me and Crispin fight. You look for opportunities to stun one of them while they're distracted. And take this just in case one of them gets by us."

I glanced over as Crispin handed his own dagger to Moll. She pulled it close to her chest, turning to shoot me a nod. A shiver rolled through me as I glanced back to the sky. The closer they got, the bigger they looked. It was five on five, in a way, but three on one had looked like a barely even match in the amphitheater, and those had all been trained guards.

Were we really going to die at the claws of these mindless beasts, after all we'd been through?

Our fate seemed to be in The Speaker's hands, and I

winced at the thought. He was more like someone's harmless, addled uncle than a hero.

I inched closer to Moll, heart slowing to a near standstill as the mantises closed in.

Fifty feet. Thirty. Twenty.

Duncan roared, he and Crispin leaping forward in unison as the first three mantises slammed into the ground. The clanging of steel split the air, but my attention was fixed on the other mantis, which was hurtling directly at us.

I leapt between it and Moll as it landed. "Fetch, go!"

I sent him to the skies as I pulled the trigger on my incapacitator. A rush of adrenaline surged through me as it lit up, blasting the monster with a surge of energy that left it stunned.

I dashed in with my dagger to finish the job while it flopped, but there was no time.

The final mantis streaked into my field of vision as Fetch screeched in warning.

Behind!

Moll whirled, holding out her shorter incapacitator toward the diving beast, and time slowed to a near-halt. Fuck fuck fuck. The largest of the bunch by a country mile, the mantis would lop her head off before she even got in range. So what do I do?

I broke into a full-on sprint, screaming as loudly as I could and holding my dagger out toward its chest. If I could just get it to focus on me, then maybe she could—

My eardrums screamed with pain as a thunderclap dropped me to my knees, but my eyes never wavered as a bolt of purple lightning streaked out from behind me. It slammed into the giant mantis in a flash of light, leaving nothing but a mist of green guts where its torso should've been.

Moll's incapacitator went off then, blasting uselessly into the air, but it didn't matter. She was alive.

The Speaker whooped from behind, the sound barely audible through the ringing in my ears, and I couldn't blame him. Hope welled up in my chest as I rose, charging toward the still-immobilized smaller mantis. It flailed, as if desperately trying to control its unresponsive body, but I was too fast, burying my dagger to the hilt, right into the center of his forehead.

A wave of sick washed over me as I tore the blade free, but I pushed past it, stabbing the mantis again for good measure.

Now it was time to help Duncan.

I spun, moving to do so, only to find him staring back at me. His eyes were narrowed, blazing silver, and a single mantis lay behind him, hacked into four pieces. The other two were already a hundred yards away, flying into the distance, fleeing us. Maybe fleeing the purple lightning.

A wide-eyed Crispin jabbed his finger toward the large mantis that The Speaker had vaporized. "What the hell happened there?"

The Speaker shrugged, his wizard's hat flopping as

he cracked and flexed his knuckles. "I may have put a bit too much power into it. I'm a little rusty."

"If you have magic like that at your fingertips, we might have a chance," Duncan said, pulling me close. I leaned in, not even bothered by the green blood splattered all over his shirt.

"It will take more than just me. The true extent of Relyk's magic hasn't been seen in decades." The Speaker's tone had lost its whimsical, song-like lilt. "As much as I hate to admit it, his powers eclipse mine ten-fold."

Ten-fold?

That was…so many fold…

I sucked in a breath, turning toward the obliterated corpse he'd left behind just a few minutes earlier. "Then how could we even hope to win?"

His eyes shimmered, and his lips tipped into a grin. "Because, child of the prophecy…we have you! You're the key, Harmony. And now that I've used my magic this close to the city, we're marked." He seemed almost giddy at the thought rather than terrified.

"You think he's already sensed it, then? Your magic?"

"Not just yet, but his wards will alert him that we were here, and once we get to the balloon, I'll need to use magic to move quickly. It will leave a trail behind us. The die has been cast." He swiped the tip of his wizard hat out of his face and whirled, throwing his arm to the side in a flash of light. A gout of flame surged from his fingertips, scorching a patch of grass a dozen feet away.

"What are you—?"

"Taking the fight to *our* people. To *our* village. Let him come. When he does, we'll be ready to face him, and it'll be the last thing he ever does."

The fire in his eyes now went far beyond the fervor for the crown he'd faked as Preacher Pete. And, as crazy as it was?

I was actually starting to believe him.

CHAPTER 28

"*H*arm?"

A low voice called my name, luring me from a dream world.

"Harmony?"

I yawned, opening my eyes to see Moll leaning over me, her eyes wide. "You've been asleep all morning. I was starting to get worried you wouldn't wake up."

I rose, glancing over to see Fetch on a makeshift perch a few yards away. "Has anything happened since I passed out?"

"The Speaker has been waiting for you to wake up, I think he has something to show you."

By the time we got to The Speaker's balloon, exhaustion had me weaving on my feet, despite Duncan's offer to carry me. To my surprise, old Libby had been intact despite my worries, and our long journey aboard her passed in a haze as I drifted in and out of much-needed sleep. Last thing I remembered was landing somewhere in the dark, being in Duncan's arms as he carried me from the balloon and set me down on a comfy feather bed before kissing my forehead and disappearing.

This comfy featherbed, in fact.

I rubbed at my temples, sucking the last bit of moisture out of my tongue. "Is there any water in here?"

Moll strode across the room, filling the glass from a bucket. "I actually made some lunch a while back, if you're game for leftovers."

We still hadn't really spoken about what had happened between us, but that was alright by me for now. We needed to focus on surviving.

"Can't believe you didn't wake up from the cold on the way here," Moll said, carrying over a plate for me. "It was brutal."

"Worse than it is right now?" I asked, a slight shiver rolling through me. Legend had it that the closer you got to the edge of the world and the Shadow Abyss, the colder it got.

"Way worse," she said, eyes bulging as she set the plate in front of me. "I was starting to wonder how we were going to manage once we got here. And then suddenly, once we reached the village, it was pretty much like back home. Cold, but bearable."

We emerged from the tent a short while later,

sending a nearby cluster of villagers into a flurry of nervous glances and pointed fingers.

"Where are we heading?" I asked, suppressing a wave of nausea as I suddenly became aware of the altitude.

Unlike The Hollow, this village was built high in the trees. Snow-dusted trees loomed in all directions, though most of their height lay beneath us. Branches mingled with sturdy, rustic homes on the broad, tree-top platform we stood upon. I ground my teeth as my eyes fixed on the shoddy, wooden bridge Moll was leading us toward.

"The Speaker lives in the Sky Tree."

I hadn't heard the name, but I knew what tree she meant immediately as I took in the enormous oak that towered above everything else in the area, her highest branches stretching all the way to the clouds. Stranger yet, it was the only tree that wasn't bare for winter. Its leaves were a deep green, and twice the size of those of a normal oak.

"Great, straight across the bridge of death?"

Her smile was a flash. "Yeah, I thought you'd like it."

I rubbed at my bleary eyes, taking in the sheer scale of what they had going on here. The Speaker wasn't just running a little gang of upstarts, like the stories claimed. This was a full-fledged village in the trees, with hundreds of residents. How many of them were Whispers?

Moll took the lead as we neared the bridge, waving at a group of children as they stepped off it.

"Wanna play hide-and-seek again, Molly?" the girl at the front asked, coming to a stop. The upturned acorn cap she wore as a hat wobbled as she rubbed at her cold-reddened nose. She glanced at her hand, her face scrunching up in disgust as she wiped the snot directly onto her pants.

Moll winced, chuckling as she pulled a handkerchief from her pocket and handed it to the girl before gently stroking the hat-covered hair. Probably the only spot that there wasn't snot. "I can't right now. We have important business with The Speaker."

"Woah," the girl said, eyes widening.

"Make sure you stay warm," Moll said, patting her gently, her smile wistful. The children were all decked out in furs, but their reddened ears and noses made it clear that they had spent a lot of time outside.

"We are!" The girl gestured toward a chubby boy in the middle of her troupe. "Do it, Keegan!"

He looked down nervously as the other children all turned their attention on him, but nodded. "Sure, alright."

I held in a gasp as tendrils of flame spurted from his upturned palms. The other children cheered with glee, leaning their heads toward it, just close enough to warm themselves.

"Did you see that?" I asked, turning to Moll.

"And that doesn't even scratch the surface of it,"

Moll said as we continued walking. "Almost everyone seems to be a Whisper of some sort."

It fit with what The Speaker had told us about Relyk's persecution, but there was still something strange about actually seeing how commonplace magic was here. A blacksmith hummed a tune while reshaping suits of armor with a wave of his hand as we passed, and a Whisper botanist seemed to pull a whole new branch out of the heart of her tree, all just to hang a shirt out to dry in the winter wind.

The Speaker was outside when we arrived at the Sky Tree a short while later. He waved, dismissing the cluster of villagers he'd been speaking with as he headed our way. "Feeling rested, Harmony?"

"Much better, thank you." I strode the rest of the way toward him, my stomach finally settling now that we were done crossing those damned wobbling bridges.

"I'll leave you to it," Moll said. "I've offered to help give some of the mamas a break to sleep while I rock a few wee ones."

Before I could say so much as goodbye, she turned and was gone.

I tossed a wave off to Moll's retreating back and followed The Speaker as he marched past one of the houses and right up to the trunk.

"So warm," I commented, cocking my head at him. What Molly had said came back to me in a rush. The air here was nothing like the brisk winter bite at the edge of the village. I hadn't paid attention as we walked, but, standing this close to him, it was extremely noticeable. "Your magic...is it giving off heat?"

"Not my magic. Hers," he said, gesturing toward the tree. "It would be too cold to live this close to The Shadow Abyss if not for the Sky Tree. It was my father's greatest triumph."

"He planted it?"

"Not quite. When he arrived here with the first group of Whispers, it was here, just visible beneath the ice and snow. In spite of it all, the sapling had managed to beat the odds and survive. They imbued it with their magic, shaping it into what it is today. Enough for us to experience seasons, and grow crops. Best of all, it's kept us safe from Relyk's gaze. Until now, the scope of his search has been limited to the areas he considered to be habitable."

"Amazing," I whispered, reaching out a tentative hand. It was only then that I noticed a bit of writing that had been etched into the bark, barely visible in the heavy shadow of the tree's massive canopy.

I squinted and walked around the tree until the rest of the scrawling text was visible.

The prophecy...

THE DAY WILL COME, *so don't be late*
She's in The Hollow, to fulfill her fate

Fair of face, with boots of red
Her name is peace, A wizard's dread
Daughter, tinker, smuggler, spy
A falcon's heart, a jeweler's eye
She's the one who holds the key
To unlock the ring and set you free
Shine a light and steal the dark
Help her see, ignite the spark
She alone cannot succeed
She needs you all to complete the deed
Then prince and pauper, hand and hand
To finish the job, to heal the land
Only then can she hope to turn the page
Daughter, tinker, pirate, mage.

IT WAS as if I was under water…the words blurred before my eyes, my ears felt full, my lungs heavy. How could this be?

I opened and closed my mouth, but no words came out.

The Speaker's voice was uncharacteristically solemn as he spoke. "It appeared on the tree overnight more than two decades ago. No one knows how. Many even thought I had gone mad when I went to The Hollow." He flashed a half-smile as he added, "Guess I proved them wrong."

The day will come, don't be late…

"You wasted more than two decades of your life waiting for me. That's—"

"Crazy. I know it must seem that way. And there were times I nearly faltered."

I shook my head slowly, still reeling. "I'm trying to process it all, but it's a lot." While some of it made perfect sense, other bits eluded me. *Daughter, tinker, pirate, mage? Daughter and tinker, yes, but...* "And what do you think the part about igniting the spark means?"

"I'll get to that in a moment," he said, jabbing his finger toward a spot a few inches below the bottom. "But also to note, there's something else strange about this tree."

I leaned closer, craning my neck to see around him. My blood froze. A pulsing, all-too-familiar hole had been chewed into the bark below the prophecy. Blacker than black, it was a colorless, two-dimensional void, as if a hole had been torn into the fabric of reality itself. A wave of revulsion washed over me, as it had the previous times I'd seen it. There was something twisted and dark about it, almost profane.

"There was a hole like that in the shoebox that held the glass slippers. And then I saw one in the palace as well, when I went to save Billy."

The Speaker locked eyes with me, his furrowed brow and downturned lips contrasting sharply with his ridiculous hat. "Do you know anything about what causes it?"

I shook my head. "I just know that to step through it would mean death. Of that I'm certain. At first I thought it was Relyk's doing, but now I'm not so sure..."

"Agree. This isn't Relyk's work. The magic feels different. Perhaps just as dark, but somehow not of this world." The Speaker frowned. "It reminds me of the Shadow Abyss, as if some dark force has pricked holes through our world, letting in the darkness beyond."

I nodded slowly, suppressing a shiver. "Terrible."

"Finding a way to fight back against it will be our next battle, once Relyk is defeated." He shook his head as if to clear it of such thoughts. "These strange holes in our world will have to remain a mystery for now, because we need to focus on getting you ready to step fully into your destiny." He waved toward the house we'd passed a moment earlier. "Come inside, and I'll tell you everything I know."

The Speaker opened the door, and I was thrown by how similar it looked to the one I'd slept in. "Is this your home?"

"It is. Though I haven't been here in so long it hardly feels that way." He strode over to the large rocking chair in the corner of the room, groaning as he dropped into it. "Feel free to sit wherever you like."

I made my way over to a box made of wood with a down-filled cushion laid across the top of it and sat, wishing I had something to do with my hands.

The Speaker pulled a small, wooden box from his pocket, holding it out into the light of his table lamp.

"It took us years to track it down, but we believe this is the item the prophecy is referring to."

He pulled open the box, revealing a tiny, innocuous looking jeweler's loupe with a tiny light attached at the top. I stared down at it, hoping my skepticism didn't show on my face. It was finely polished, but looked no different from the dozens I'd seen in my time as a tinkerer.

"What does it do?"

"I wish I knew." He slid it across the table. "That's for you to figure out. The prophecy calls you a jeweler, and I'm supposed to provide the light to illuminate the dark. I can *feel* the magic in it, but nothing we've tried has made it work."

I lifted it from the box, and then held it to one eye, depressing the tiny button to light the bulb. Then, I held my breath and stared down at the veins in my hand. They looked no different than they would've if I'd used any old loupe...

I lifted my head with a frown. "I know the prophecy suggests that I can unlock its power, but I've got to be honest. I don't know the first thing about magic."

The Speaker squinted, his eyes fixing on Fetch for a long moment. "Then why do I sense it, even now. That bird... you have a special connection with him, yes?"

"I've had him since I was a girl, we—"

He shook a dismissive hand, silencing me. "You're very powerful, Harmony. Surely there had to have been signs. Perhaps you've been blocked somehow?"

"A Whisper?"

He frowned. "Yes...but not. Your magic is like nothing I've sensed before."

I let his words set in, wanting to deny them, but I couldn't. "There have been some moments, recently..." I trailed off as a series of memories replayed in my mind. With Fetch, with the locks at The Hoof and Saddle, in the falcon channels, even in the creation of the easy lockpick. It should have been obvious. And maybe if I hadn't been constantly waiting to get discovered and hanged it would've been. Some part of me had surely known, and had chosen not to think it through or put a name to it. Had I known that one more thing would've pushed me over the edge and rendered me useless...

I looked back up, meeting The Speaker's eyes.

"Okay. I accept that *possibly* I'm a Whisper of some sort. I still don't see how that solves our issue with the loupe. How could I expect to succeed where you have failed?"

My breath caught as he lurched forward in his chair, the veins in his forehead bulging.

"You, falcon, come to me!" he commanded, raising his forearm as if giving Fetch a place to perch. I glanced to my shoulder and Fetch stirred slightly, cocking his head at me as he clicked his beak. But he didn't make a move.

The Speaker leaned back in his chair, his normal, kind expression returning to his face. "That's how,

Harmony. Because my power may eclipse that of any Whisper alive, but that doesn't mean that I can do anything they can do. I gave it everything I had to use my magic and call him to me, but your connection was simply too strong. Most Whispers are highly specialized, and their talents are honed over a lifetime. But mine is different. In certain things I excel, and in others I have but a taste of what the best Whispers are capable of. Perhaps if I studied these last twenty-five years, and took the time necessary to learn, I could have reached some semblance of the same mastery, but, alas, our time in this world is limited…and I chose to wait for you instead. The prophecy calls you a jeweler, and a tinker, among other things." He pulled the emerald ring from his pinky, tossing it roughly onto the wooden table between us. "The loupe isn't for inspecting hands, Harmony…it's for this."

"That's it? That's the ring that will set us free?" I murmured in a hushed voice. The gemstone was raised, like half an egg, and the second I touched it, I knew it held magic. It fairly vibrated with energy.

I reopened the loupe, turning on the light and flicking one of the higher magnification lenses into place as I inspected the ring. I tilted it from side to side, searching for anything unusual.

"Well?" The Speaker asked, breaking my concentration. I held up a finger, reliving that moment in the Falcon chute. If I could just capture the essence of that moment…that perfect moment where everything clicked into place and I could see the path I needed to take, then maybe…

I squinted, tensing all of the muscles in my body in an attempt to draw on my latent magic, and still, nothing.

"The ring was passed down from my ancestors. It is said that the draught locked inside will give the drinker a power unlike any other. It won't last long, but I am confident unlocking it is the key to winning our battle against Relyk."

No pressure.

If only it really were locked. I was good at locks, but this was more of a puzzle…

I inspected it again, tilting the ring from side to side and watching the minuscule bubbles shift. "You've tried cracking it open, I'm sure."

"Many times. Look at the metal. Not a scratch on it, right?"

It was just as he said. Vague fingerprints were visible in the lustrous gold, but it was as if it had been freshly forged, rather than having been passed through generations to get to this point.

"We will still make our stand without the draught…" said The Speaker. "There's no better place or time to fight Relyk than now—he's at his weakest with having kept the king alive for so long."

I leaned across the table, pushing the ring back toward him, but he cocked an eyebrow, rather than moving to grab it.

"What do you want me to do with it? You're the one who at least has a chance of unlocking it. Keep it with you. Hopefully you'll come up with something before…"

Before Relyk and his army came and mowed us all down like weeds.

I nodded, withdrawing the ring and stuffing it into my pocket. It was the only ace up our sleeve. I needed to figure out how to play it or we were all dead.

The Speaker let out an exaggerated groan as he stood from his chair, his hand going to his lower back. "Let's check with our lookout. Last we spoke he was trying to get a bead on Relyk's position to see how much longer we have to prepare."

He strode out from his humble cabin, and I followed, making our way to the other side of The Sky Tree's platform. Fetch flinched as The Speaker let loose an unexpected whistle. There was a rustling overhead, and an older man appeared, deftly sliding down a thick vine from the highest branches of the mountain-sized tree.

My eyes strayed to the horizon as I watched, and my breath caught in my throat, the sight seeming just as shocking as the first time I'd seen it. On one side lay an expanse of bare winter forest, and to the other, toward the east there was nothing but a strange, inky blackness, as beautiful as it was horrifying. I glanced up, a chill shooting up my spine as I caught sight of the straight line where it made contact with the cloudy blue sky.

We were actually at the edge of the world.

The Shadow Abyss.

I was drawn to it, the sudden urge to throw myself off the edge catching me off guard.

"Speaker," the older man said, but just like all of the other villagers, he did not bow.

"How long are we thinking?" The Speaker asked, adjusting his wizard's hat to sit more squarely on his head.

"He travels fast, maybe a day and a half away." He turned, craning his neck as if trying to find a good angle through the branches, then waved The Speaker over. "Take a look." The scout bent his hand into a circle, as if holding a looking glass, and pressed it to The Speaker's eye.

A human telescope. Amazing.

The Speaker was grinning by the time he pulled away, and rubbing his hands together. "He is moving fast, as you said. We'll have our work cut out for us," he said. "This will be a rebellion for the ages."

"Can I look?" I stepped over to the scout and he nodded, holding his hand out for me.

Balloons by the dozen flew over a seemingly endless horde of guards and foot soldiers. A single man sat in back, pulled along in some kind of chariot. I squinted, and the Whisper pulled his hand even tighter, leaving only a narrow slit for me to look through.

There he was.

The sorcerer Relyk, looking as fresh as the day I'd first met him, as if he'd never been weakened at all. His long, gray hair was full and back to its former glory, with no missing spots that I could see. Gone were his sorcerer's garb, replaced by a courtly outfit. But most concerning of all?

The golden crown that sat perched on his head.

Relyk was *king*.

CHAPTER 29

I hurled the ring across the room with a muttered curse, stomping toward our cabin's door.

Five *fucking* hours, and still no dice. I hadn't managed to bring out even a flicker of magic for all my time spent on it, never mind getting any ideas about how to actually open the ring. There were no hints, not a single clue how it worked.

I clenched my hand around the hard wood of the loupe, suppressing the urge to toss it as well. The Speaker had been adamant about me focusing on the ring while all the others prepared for the upcoming battle, setting traps and talking strategy, but at this point I felt like I was bashing my head against a wall.

The cool winter air washed over me as I pushed open the door, taking a step outside. I heard distant voices from the other platforms, and even from the forest floor below, but I ignored all of them, moving instead toward the platform's western edge.

The words of the prophecy had clearly seemed to speak of me, but right now, I felt like the furthest thing from some supposed hero. I fiddled with the loupe in my pocket absentmindedly as I stepped up to the platform's wooden fence. A mix of fear and awe swirled inside me as I stared off at the edge of our world, just the straight edge of land until it fell away, as if cut with a knife, and then a wash of whirling, writhing black. I'd known the edge had existed, but I'd never thought I'd see it myself. Despite the terror of the unknown, there was a part of me that wondered…what else was out there in the great beyond? What would happen if I stepped into that swirling blackness?

Fetch spun back down onto my shoulder, pushing his cheek up against mine in his strange gesture of falcon affection as if to comfort me.

"You're a real peach, my friend. I don't know what I'd do without you."

In hindsight, it was sort of ridiculous that I hadn't realized sooner that I was at least some sort of a Whisper. Fetch and I had always been able to communicate in a way that no normal falconer and falcon could manage. In some cases, better than any two *humans* could manage. But magic had been such a small part of our world in The Hollow. A stray Whisper or two lurked around, healing minor wounds or selling potions, but they were a rarity. Nothing like in Little

Alabaster, and not even *close* to here. What would my life have been like if I had grown up in a place such as this? If I'd been encouraged to build my skills?

Relyk's suppression of magic had succeeded in keeping him in power all these years. Did we even stand a chance without the potion? He'd clearly given up even the ruse of a king being in power, if the crown was any indication. Any weakness he'd suffered by trying to keep Heinrich alive had clearly passed. And we were outnumbered to boot. How would the village's Whispers fare against well-trained soldiers?

The sound of boots on wood turned me around and I sucked in a breath as Duncan placed himself next to me. He put his hands over the fence as well, staring off into the blackness.

"No one will blame you if you can't open the ring," Duncan started.

"It's not about blame. It's about responsibility. Everyone has been waiting for me this whole time because of that prophecy. If we lose here…it will be my fault."

"That's a lot of pressure." His hand strayed to mine as he continued. "Even if you can't do it, we can still win. My coup didn't have nearly this many fighters, and you should see how powerful some of the Whispers here are, Harm. Relyk has bitten off more than he can chew. There's a chance…I know there is, with or without the ring."

"The way The Speaker looks when he talks about it

tells a different story, and he's faced him head-on," I said.

He squeezed my hand tightly, tugging my chin in his direction with the other. "No matter what happens, I want you to know that I believe in you. You're the most amazing woman I've ever met, and when this is all over, I hope you'll let me prove it to you. Don't," he said, cutting off my response with a fingertip to my lips. "You don't have to respond or make promises you can't keep. I just needed to tell you in case…"

In case I fucking blew it and we all wound up being worm food.

Heavy footsteps plodded behind us, and I turned to see The Speaker walking our way with Moll in tow. She raised an eyebrow at me, a smile playing at her lips, but it was The Speaker who spoke.

"Come, come. We've accomplished much in the way of preparation. Now is the time to talk, laugh, live, love! This is the night to revel in all the beauty our world holds, to remember everything we fight for!"

Duncan and I fell in behind them, and we arrived at the treetop tavern in the center of the village a few minutes later. Villagers danced and gambled and chatted in various groups all around. Even Crispin had found his way to a corner and was belting out a tone-deaf verse with a buxom frost Whisper, who had frozen the dance floor beneath their feet and left them skating together side by side. I hadn't planned to drink, but the atmosphere was infectious, and, when The

Speaker pushed a pint into my chest, I found myself taking a healthy swig. It was sweet and nutty and went down far smoother than the alcohol I knew back in The Hollow.

"The good thing about the acorn honey mead is… no hangovers."

I let out a huzzah and took another swig.

"Hungry?" Duncan asked, handing over a plate full of roast boar, mushrooms, and squash. A fresh sourdough roll sat on the edge, steaming butter melting into the center of it.

I thanked him, and dug in, determined to live like it was my last night…

Our last night.

"A dance, Prince Duncan?" a pretty older woman with black hair asked as she held out a hand.

"Just Duncan, Bethea, but yes. I'd love to."

The two took to the non-frozen side of the dance floor, and I smiled as I watched them launch into a joyous reel.

"You better eat before it gets cold," Moll said, sidling up beside me. Her eyes were a bit bleary, and I chuckled.

"And you better lay off the mead, or you're going to start getting weepy and telling me how I'm your best friend, and how you feel bad for being a dick back in Little Alabaster…"

She playfully punched my arm and let out a hiccup. "Seriously, though, you so are, and I am…I just…I just couldn't forget what he'd done to me, and it made me scared, and I couldn't seem to make a good decision. And then I'd get more scared and then angry, and at myself too, I was trying so hard to get us out, that I never thought I'd be raped, Harm. I just…"

I dropped my plate to the table and caught her gently by the arms, horror washing over me. "Molly. You said he didn't…"

"I lied," she whispered. "I lied because you were already trying so hard to get us out, to get me out and I didn't want you to worry more than you already were. That's why I had such a hard time alone in the hut. I just couldn't escape my thoughts…the memory…"

I pulled her into my arms, hugging her as tightly as I could as she sobbed, and my tears trickled off my chin and into her hair. "It's not your fault, Molly. It's not your fault. I'm sorry I was hard on you too. I'm so sorry."

We cried together, and I didn't care that anyone and everyone could see us. For all they knew, we were just saying tearful potential goodbyes. They had no idea what we'd been through. What Molly had been through.

I don't know how long we clung to each other, a lot of minutes before Molly pulled back, sniffling and wiping tears from her face, then mine. "Don't cry, Harm. We're supposed to celebrate tonight."

I wiped tears from her cheeks. "Okay, but…"

"No buts." She gave me a wobbly smile. "Let's eat, drink and be merry. Okay?"

I nodded. There would be a time when we could talk more, when I could let her tell me whatever she needed to, or nothing at all, it would be up to her. But I would give her that time, whenever she wanted it.

Moll shoved my plate back into my hands as she took a piece for herself. A moan slid out of her. "This is good."

I popped a morsel of boar into my mouth and closed my eyes while I chewed, relishing the gamey, salty flavor. Not starving was a privilege I would never take for granted. I focused on that.

"Did you try the acorn mash? It's delicious." The light in her eyes dulled as she swayed in her seat. "Also, do you wonder how The Hollow might've been if we had been allowed magic? Look at this place." She waved a hand around her. "Even the uses of acorn. They make cups out of them, and food, and drinks…all because of this one guy who's an arbor Whisper. Relyk fucked us. He fucked us all."

She let out another hiccup and I held up my cup and clinked it against hers.

"To the demise of Relyk, who fucked us all! May he rot for his crimes for all eternity!"

"Cheers to that!" she crowed, shooting a fist in the air.

Cheers rang all around us as others joined in. "And may the crows pluck out his eyes for his lies!" the frost

Whisper who had been skating along with Crispin added.

Another roar rang through the room and more curses followed, getting sillier each time.

My stomach hurt from laughter by the time The Speaker found his way to the center of us all, adjusting his wizard's hat with every other step. He raised his glass into the air, and his expression grew somber immediately.

"Down with Relyk, indeed. But more important than that, I need you to know…no matter what awaits us, I am so proud to call each and every one of you my friends and brothers and sisters in battle. My grandfather always said that a revolution is never truly lost, as long as there is at least one who still believes, but it is only now that I truly understand. Whether we seize the day or not, tales of our bravery will spread far and wide, and we will become the kindling for another revolution, just as those before us lit the fire for ours.

Tyranny *cannot* last forever, and I ask all of you to consider our place within this larger picture. Tomorrow's fight is not only for us, it's for all those who will come after. For the beggars and miners, for the farmers and widows, for the children who are written off from birth because they were born on the wrong side of a wall.

We must never forget what it is that we fight for. As powerful as he is, even Relyk is just a symbol: a symbol of the oppression and evil that we seek to destroy. We stand alongside the great revolutionaries of old in this fight, and our triumph is inevitable, regardless of tomorrow's outcome. When all is said and done, magic, and authority *will* be returned to where it rightly belongs: the hands of the people. All the people."

The crowd erupted in a roar of applause and shouts as he brought the pint to his lips, gulping it down in a single swig. In that moment—wizard hat and spilled beer be damned—he looked downright heroic.

And I could almost believe we had a chance.

CHAPTER 30

ears pricked at my eyes as I stared into the green depths of the jewel for the hundredth time since before the sunrise. I knew this ring like the back of my own hand by now…every facet, every curve, and yet that knowledge hadn't make a lick of difference.

Worse? Our spotter had lost track of Relyk and his men in the middle of the night, and, based on their trajectory and previous speed, war would be upon us in hours—maybe less—and I'd made zero progress.

I took a steadying breath, fighting not to let frustration consume me.

"Harm?" A voice came from the door, pulling me out of my self-pity.

"Yes Moll?" I asked, my gaze still pinned on the ring.

"I know you're busy, but can you take a quick second to come look at some of the traps we made."

I scowled harder at the ring, resisting the urge to take my irritation out on her. "Moll, I need to keep going on this, there's not much time—" I broke off and rolled my shoulders to ease the tension pooling there. Maybe a change of scenery was exactly what I needed. "Okay, sure. Show me."

Moll grinned as I stood, her mood lighter today since her confession last night. "We'll have to take the ladder, but it's not far after that." She paused and cocked her head at me. "You just gonna leave that thing on?" she asked, jerking her chin toward my face.

"What?" I lifted a hand to see what she meant and realized I still had the loupe over one eye. "Oh!"

I'd gotten sick of holding it and had mounted it to a strip of leather so I could fasten it on like a miner's headlamp. I lifted it to rest high on my forehead and followed her out.

Wooden and rope ladders snaked down from every platform, giving residents an easy way to access the forest floor below. I followed her, a wave of nerves rolling over me as we got to the sketchy ladder. A kid arrived before us, and he gave us a wave before leaping into action. He hopped off over the side of the platform, his hand on the first rung for only a second before he began his rapid descent like a spider monkey, seeming to barely connect with the wood slats.

I swallowed my worry, glancing down as I hitched one foot onto the first rung.

"He's almost halfway to the ground already," Moll marveled.

The people here had thoroughly adapted to life in the trees, and it seemed normal to them in a way I could hardly imagine. My clammy hands had dried from the rope by the time we reached the bottom, and I let out a relieved breath as my feet touched down on solid, familiar ground.

The Speaker's people were spread all around, focused on their tasks, working on various traps and preparations. I had to admit, I was impressed. This wasn't just a band of malcontents, it was a respectable army. Relyk's contingent of guards outnumbered us, but our fighters were magic users almost to a man, and I knew that the sorcerer could not say the same. Was he really *so* powerful that his magic could offset *this* many Whispers? Especially those with righteous fury on their side? Those who fought for their children and their homes?

"How awesome is that?"

I followed Moll's pointed finger to the literal edge of our world. I'd seen it several times in the past couple of days, but it never failed to make me feel small and never failed to call me to it. My first up-close look from the ground was even more impressive than the view from above. It was as if our world had been sliced off from a larger world, with a perfectly flat edge. Just gazing down even from yards away, my head started to spin, and I took a few more steps back.

"It's incredible."

Moll knelt, grabbing a small stone from the ground nearby. "It really is. That's what gave me this idea for my trap. Watch." She tossed the stone over the edge, and it hurtled into the abyss below where it arced out, then fell. "See? Still has the same rules as we do." She gestured toward a boulder that sat just near the edge of the Shadow Abyss. "Duncan helped me move it."

I followed her gaze, seeing the rope that led from the rock into the forest behind us. "Ooh, that *is* a good idea!"

I could see it already; when triggered, the rope would snag its target by the ankle and send them hurtling off the edge of the earth. Only there was a problem...

I pointed. "It's too close to all the ladders. What if one of the children comes down in the midst of the fighting, despite being told not to, and gets hurled off the face of the earth?" The reminder of all the kids here made my stomach lurch and my head pound. "In fact, you should go, too. Forget the traps. Just head deeper into the southern forest and take all the kids with you—"

"Stop. Harm, stop and take a breath, okay?" She tugged a lock of my hair until I met her cornflower gaze. "It's too late for any of that. He'll find anyone who tries to escape. At least if they all stay here, they have every adult in the village on the ground protecting them up in the trees. And fighting harder yet for their babies. I know I would."

"They should've evacuated. They should've—"

"They wouldn't. They didn't. Because they believe in *you*."

My ears rang and my vision went hazy. I was about to slap myself hard in the face, Druzilla-style, when it came to me in a rush.

Open your mind to the possibilities.

Pressure makes diamonds.

"I...I just thought of something, I've got to go." I mumbled, "Move that trap farther away to be safe, okay?"

I ran back to the ladder we'd climbed down. I'd barely gotten a foot on the bottom rung when a horn blared in the distance, the sound vibrating through my chest, making the hair on my arms stand at attention.

He was here. Relyk and his army had arrived.

Villagers poured out of every hut, and I scurried up the ladder as the sound of pounding horse hooves grew in the distance.

I raced up the ladder, and to my sleeping space. The ring sat on the table, light glinting off it. I snatched it up and gripped it tight.

"Fetch, come on!" I called to him as I spun and raced back to the ladder for the second time that day.

Fetch landed on my shoulder, and I slid The Speaker's ring on my finger. Arrows sailed from our line of archers at the platform's edge, and I could only pray that I'd made it in time as the first sounds of clashing swords rang out from below.

A jolt of pain shot through my knees as I leapt down the last few rungs and scanned the battlefield, taking stock of the situation as quickly as possible.

There were two clear sides, with rows of Relyk's troops battering at our less-coordinated ranks. As expected, though, magic made up for our lack of coordination. Fire, wind, and ice flared all around, pushing Relyk's armored soldiers back.

I scanned the battlefield, doing my best to ignore the sounds of death echoing through the forest all around me. I'd have plenty of time to help later, but, right now, getting the ring to The Speaker was my only priority.

"They believe in you."

Please let me be right.

The frost Whisper that Crispin had danced with the night before stood on one side, leading a cluster of villagers, but I looked past her, fixing my gaze on Duncan. He cleaved a guard of Relyk's in half, his broadsword slicing through the man's armor as if it was made of paper. Bile rose to burn my throat, but I forced it down as I charged toward his squad.

"Duncan!"

"You need to get inside, Harm, you—" He whirled back toward the battle, smashing right through a man's helmet with a gauntleted fist.

"I need to get to The Speaker. I...I have the answer!"

Crispin nudged him aside, taking his place at the center of the pack. "Go! This is what we've been waiting for. I'll hold things down," he grunted as an arrow bounced off his shield.

Duncan cursed, sparing a final glance for his friend. "You'd better not die."

He sprinted my way, coming to a halt as he fixed his eyes on me. "The Speaker was over this way, last I saw. Give me the ring and I'll take it to him."

His eyes were narrow and liquid silver, like they always were when he fought, and when—

"You know it has to be me, Duncan. I can't explain it, but if I can get to The Speaker, I think I can do it."

He clenched a fist, smashing it into a nearby tree with another curse, then let out a breath. "Stay behind me."

We charged in the direction he'd indicated, and it didn't take long to figure out where The Speaker was. A cluster of villagers were being pushed back by a half-dozen soldiers when as many vines snaked from the nearest tree, and yanked Relyk's men into the air. They screamed, struggling to escape, but it did little to help them as the vines squeezed in on them, crushing armor and chest alike.

The wood squished right through the first man with a sickening, cracking sound that was audible even though we were dozens of feet away, and the others weren't far behind. Pieces of their bodies dropped from the tree like fruit, smacking into the ground below.

When I looked up, The Speaker stood ten yards away, hand extended toward the enemy, face twisted with rage.

So far, it seemed like Relyk's side had taken more casualties. Perhaps The Speaker had underestimated his own power? He blasted through another soldier with a lightning bolt, incinerating him like he had with the Mantis. He was a one-man wrecking crew.

Duncan gestured, changing directions. "We'll circle around and come up behind him, so we don't get cut off."

A thundering boom split the air, followed by a scorching gust with enough force to bring me to my knees. I scuttled backward to look up and saw that the band of Whispers The Speaker had just saved were completely gone, reduced to nothing but a pile of smoldering ash.

"No!"

Duncan threw his body in front of mine and held out his sword as Relyk made a beeline for The Speaker, six Jackals behind him.

"Nice hat," Relyk called with a cruel laugh.

I pushed against Duncan, inching my way closer, and he moved with me.

The Speaker's face was a mask of despair as he looked up from the remains of his fallen comrades. He gestured toward Relyk's golden crown, his lips twisting into a smirk. "At least I came by mine honestly."

The sorcerer waved for his Jackals to advance, his

hand going to his shimmering crown. "This? I've always been in charge, hat or no. The nobles get uncomfortable if you show them how truly powerless they are, so I've ruled from the shadows. But the time for that is over now. Keeping the nobles fat and happy was easy, but starving and in chains is just as g—"

A fireball zipped from The Speaker's hands, cutting off Relyk's monologue. The sorcerer batted it aside with a hand, mouth curling in disgust. "A commoner being born with so much magic is an abomination. Jackals, kill them all."

"We've got to make a move." I surged forward, trying to cover the last bit of distance as the black-plated warriors made first contact with the Whispers that moved to protect The Speaker, forming a human wall in front of him.

Duncan yanked me to a stop as a dark figure streaked toward us. Then, he launched us both five feet in the air as a war hammer smashed into the ground where I'd stood a moment earlier.

Jackal. And a massive one at that.

"The one from the tunnel..." Duncan muttered, already dropping low into a fighting stance.

The creature twirled the massive weapon around in his hand like it was hollow wood rather than solid steel, leaping toward us for another strike.

Duncan grunted, blocking the blow with his great sword.

"Keep moving, Harm—" The Jackal's leg snaked out,

connecting with Duncan's ribs with a *crack*, cutting him short.

The prince lunged forward, his blade passing just inches from the monster's face as it dodged. My heart skipped a beat as it held out its hand, a dark fog forming at its fingertips.

No.

My head hummed and throbbed even as my breath went short, but this time I didn't fight it. A half a dozen possibilities flashed through my mind at once.

That one would work.

I fumbled through my pouch, breaking into a full-on sprint. If I could just—

My hand settled on my grappling hook, and I whipped it out, smashing down on the trigger. The fog shot toward Duncan as the hook sprang forward, smacking directly into the Jackal's faceplate.

The monster staggered back, releasing the spell. Duncan didn't hesitate. Even as the war hammer came slinging down once again, he leapt forward rather than back. He roared as the shaft slammed into his shoulder, but mere pain was not enough to stop him. Not when he was like this. His hand snapped forward, taking the Jackal by the neck and hurling it to the ground. The cracked steel of its face plate splintered as Duncan rained blow after blow upon it.

But as the last of the black armor protecting the Jackal's face fell away, he stopped and drew back in shock.

"Wh—"

I followed Duncan's gaze, a wave of horror rolling over me as I took in the creature's desiccated, rotten skin and bare muscle fibers wrapped tight around high cheekbones that spoke of royalty, the vague shape of the eye sockets and nose, and a telltale tuft of blond hair.

"Heinrich...?" Duncan muttered, stunned.

"Miss me, brother?" Heinrich asked, his voice even colder and harsher than it had been in life. He leapt to his feet in a single, jerky motion.

Duncan lunged forward, letting loose a flurry of slashes that had Heinrich on the back foot, but not for long. A second later, he was the one on the attack, swinging wildly with a preternatural howl.

I dashed toward them, yanking out my incapacitator and pressing it right against Heinrich's chest. His arm shot toward me, but it was too late. His body twisted and writhed as I blasted him with energy, my other hand snaking toward my dagger.

A voice called my name just as pain shot up my arm and my blade stopped abruptly, mid-air, as if striking an invisible wall. I staggered back, eyes flitting upward, but it was already clear what was happening. Relyk, strongest magic user in all the land, had fixed his attention on me.

Duncan grunted as he flew back, propelled by Relyk's magic, and a thin smile played at the sorcerer's lips as dark energy gathered in his hand. "This is the end, little falconer. With your death, my rule is assured."

I had failed.

I gritted my teeth, waiting for death as the purple ball of magic shot toward us. But it didn't come. I blinked my eyes open a moment later, a jolt of shock running through me at what I saw.

Crispin Locke and his squad stood between Relyk and I, alight with bluish energy. *The Speaker's,* I realized with a start, not even knowing how I knew. It…felt like The Speaker's energy. Crispin dropped to his knees, panting as the last of the sorcerer's magic dissipated against his shield.

I winced, rolling back, as movement flashed to my left. Heinrich sprang upward, raising a single gauntlet toward me. I fumbled wildly for my knife, unable to tear my gaze free of his narrow, murderous eyes. The blade thudded to the ground, and I scrambled back just as another figure came into view.

Duncan?

No, it wasn't the hulking prince. It was Moll. Soft, sweet Moll, mouth twisted into a snarl as she screamed like a banshee, dagger clenched tight in both hands. My heart soared as she found her mark, the entire length of the blade sinking into the center of his forehead just as he was turning to stop her.

Moll let loose a triumphant roar, tears streaming down her cheeks, tearing the blade free as he fell back, then descended upon him for an entirely unnecessary series of follow up stabs on the already-dead Jackal. Flies burst out of him with each stab from her blade, and her shirt was soaked with his sticky, near-black blood by the time she fell back, panting. "Never again you bastard! You will never hurt another woman again!"

There was so much I wanted to say, but it was hardly the time, so I settled for, "Good job."

A heavy hand fell to my shoulder. I spun to see Duncan behind me, clutching his chest. "We need to keep moving. We can get to The Speaker while Relyk's attention is fixed on Crispin."

He pulled away, his gaze shifting to Moll. "You did well. Leave the rest to us."

And, for once, she didn't argue. "Done."

"See you when this is all over," I said, pleased to see her hobbling back into the forest as I followed Duncan's lead. She'd done what she had to do, and I could only hope it would help her heal.

Enhanced with The Speaker's power, Crispin and his squad were a beacon of hope amidst the chaotic battlefield. Guards fell in droves and the villagers began to rally around them, holding the line against Relyk and his forces.

The Speaker himself was standing just behind those lines, barely moving as he forced every bit of his energy into Crispin and the other Whispers. Volleys of arrows rained down from the trees above, forcing Relyk to waste time shielding himself rather than focusing purely on offense.

And, for a moment, I allowed myself to hope. We were a few dozen feet away, and things seemed to have shifted in our favor. If I could just get a little further…

I was halfway through my next step when Relyk's piercing voice cut through the air. "Kneel."

My legs buckled beneath me as his magic rushed into me, accompanied by a wave of nausea. I sucked in a breath, glancing around. The fighting had ceased, with villagers and soldiers alike dropping to their knees at his command. I gritted my teeth, calling on every ounce of willpower I could muster.

I *had* to make it to The Speaker.

My head pounded with the struggle, and I let out a groan as I forced myself back up onto two legs, wobbling like a newborn colt. Jolts of agony arced up my legs as I forced one foot in front of the other, hobbling toward The Speaker as quickly as I could manage. Relyk had turned away, and I couldn't imagine getting a better chance than this.

"Jackals, to me!"

The remaining undead soldiers jerked into the air, hurtling toward the now-hovering sorcerer. A nauseous ball formed in my stomach as they stopped abruptly, dangling an arm's reach away from him as if hanging from puppet strings.

Agonized screams tore from their lips as dark energy began surging from every crack in their armor and moved toward Relyk. They seized and shook, fighting against their master as their life force flooded directly into him, illuminating his skin with unholy light. Pieces of armor dropped one by one as the Jackals fell. Clouds of flies swarmed from their mouths as their green, rotting flesh bubbled and writhed, giving way to the raw, red skin beneath. And, for a brief moment, they looked almost human.

"Ahh." Black fire bloomed in Relyk's hand. "Perhaps this was the way, all along."

Duncan grunted, and I turned to see him struggling to his feet, eyes pinned on one of the Jackals in particular.

"Father?"

CHAPTER 31

I reeled, recognition blossoming as I crept toward The Speaker, my eyes fixed on King Rudolph…or what was left of him.

The Jackals were more than just a troupe of monstrous guards. They were former kings that Relyk had decided to replace. That was how he kept himself strong. By consuming the souls of those he had claimed to serve…

Rudolph's eyes fixed on Duncan, and his jaw worked, as if trying to force out a word as he quivered and shrank. Life energy flooded out of him in waves, his face contorting with fear as skin pulled away from his cheeks in strips. He wasn't a good man, but it was impossible to find any pleasure in what was happening to him now.

The sorcerer met Duncan's eyes, a cruel smile on his lips as dark energy coalesced around him. "Just because they've served their purpose during their reign doesn't mean they're useless. Kings hold inherent power, and now it's at my fingertips."

Duncan roared, nocking an arrow as he forced himself to his feet, then took aim at his suffering father. I winced as it shot through the air, catching the former king in the throat. He pitched forward with a gurgle.

My heart froze as Relyk's gaze shifted to Duncan. It was now or never.

Jolts of pain pounded through my skull, as I fought against his magic, the throbbing growing worse with each passing second. I fixed my gaze on the green ring on my finger, calling on my magic with everything I had. I didn't really know what I was doing, everything was on instinct.

But instinct had saved my ass more than once.

I yanked the loupe down over my right eye, and prayed I'd been right…

A blinding wave of light surged forth, consuming everything in sight except the ring. My finger tingled with energy as I tapped the top of the stone, and it seemed to expand a dozen times over, filling my entire field of vision. A primal scream built in my chest and, instead of swallowing it or letting it scare me, I let it out…and all the magic came with it.

Every nook and cranny of the ring became familiar. From the setting at the base of the gem to the viscosity of the liquid inside, it was all laid bare. I twisted the top twice, then pushed it forward with a satisfying click.

Not open, but unlocked. And I knew, as surely as I knew anything, that it could be cracked open with the slightest tug.

I fell back to my senses in an instant, the thrumming pain fading as quickly as it had arrived. I blinked, staring down in awe. The green ring had turned bright white...like a diamond.

"Speaker!" I shouted, my voice cracked and hoarse as I limped another step toward him.

Movement flashed at my right, and I covered my head, rolling forward as I caught sight of the dark fireball hurtling toward me. The Speaker cried out, roaring as he dropped a shimmering wall of magic in front of it.

They warred against each other for a long moment, and The Speaker fell to the ground, panting raggedly as both spells dissipated.

Relyk cackled as I hobbled forward another step, another ball of fire forming in his fingertips. "All these years to prepare, and this is the best you can manage?" His icy voice seemed to cut through to my very soul as he repeated, "*Kneel.*"

I stumbled, terror spiking through me as I dropped to my knees, completely unable to resist him. I had my ace up my sleeve still. My connection to Fetch was like nothing else. Even the Speaker couldn't command him, and I trusted, with all my heart, that Relyk couldn't either.

My teeth ached as they ground against each other,

and it took everything I had just to lift my arm, tossing the ring a few feet into the air.

"Catch!"

Fetch shot off my shoulder, toward The Speaker like an arrow, snapping the ring up with his talons without slowing. I gasped, falling still, and each heartbeat felt like minutes as the bird hurtled toward The Speaker. *Please, Fetch, you can do it. Take it to him. You can do—*

My breath caught in my throat as the ring tore free of his talons, pulled by an unseen force. I fixed my gaze on Relyk, preparing for the worst, but it shot the other direction instead, and I turned my head in time to see The Speaker's hand reach up to grab it.

His eyes fixed on me as he cracked open the ring, gulping down the draught in a swig. Relyk released another fireball at the same time, aiming it directly at The Speaker as his wizard hat flopped to the ground at his side, his hair surging upward, every strand standing on end as ethereal life poured out of him. He winked at me. "Never doubted you for a second."

The sorcerer's black flame flickered out of existence at a wave of The Speaker's hand, and he let out a humorless laugh.

"You said that kings have inherent power, Relyk. And it's true, but you're missing something crucial. *All* people possess power. Your mistake was thinking it was your right to take it from them."

Blue lightning shot from the sky, and Relyk's eyes

lit up with terror as it slammed into him with a booming crack. His magical hold on the battlefield faded in a heartbeat, and I stumbled to my feet in unison with hundreds of others.

My fingers dug into my palms as Relyk rose, healing from the attack in an instant. An inky cloud jetted from his hand as he charged right toward The Speaker. "You're nothing but an insect like the rest of them. No matter what you do, you will *never* defeat me."

The black fog rolled out, consuming everything it touched. I looked on in horror as soldiers and villagers alike stumbled and dropped to the ground, dead. Fetch smacked back into my shoulder as I dashed sideways, keeping my eyes fixed on the two spellcasters even as I ran.

The Speaker ignored the wave of death and decay, pure magical energy flooded out of him and formed a massive wall of magic as he charged at his sworn enemy. A thunderous crack split the battlefield as it smashed into Relyk, sending a final puff of fog spurting into the sky as his back collided with a tree so hard that it rocked the canopy overhead. He gritted his teeth, pushing to his feet only to catch another wall of energy right to the chest.

A glimmer of hope resurfaced, only to be dashed right down as The Speaker let out a wracking cough, dropping to the ground. Blood dripped from his mouth as he struggled to stand.

"Done already?" Relyk called, mocking, but he was clearly suffering just as much. Blood had soaked right through his shirt, and he was walking normally now, rather than levitating. If only we had more time...

"Are you kidding? I've been waiting my whole life for a chance like this." Another burst of blood flew from his lips, and his mouth split into a grin. Whispers rallied around him as if to join the fight against Relyk, but he used magic to drive them skittering back as he stood and moved toward the sorcerer.

That's when the realization hit me like a hammer. He didn't want their protection any longer...

Because he'd never planned to make it out of this fight alive in the first place.

Tears pricked at my eyes as he raised his hand, a full-body tremor rolling through him as he gathered his power to him. He looked over his shoulder, his eyes finding mine.

"Go, Harmony! And don't look back. Your next chapter awaits, past the edge!"

The winds whipped and whistled as a strange sound seemed to call me from the ends of the earth, drawing me to it. As if someone else was controlling me, I flicked the lens of the loupe to see in the distance. There, in the farthest corner visible...what was it? A tiny triangle with a number just below it.

Like a book...It was just like a dog-eared corner of the page from a book!

You can't finish the story unless you turn the page...

A male voice rang out in my mind, a warm baritone, with a subtle accent I couldn't place. I remembered it from my dreams, so long ago.

Molly slid beside me even as Duncan rushed over, brandishing his sword. "I'll cover you!"

And he did, cutting down the soldiers who tried to pursue us as if they were nothing. The village Whispers did their part, too, forming a wall behind us until we reached the edge of the earth.

"I'm-I'm supposed to jump," I said, barely able to catch my breath as my mind and my heart raced. "Do you see it? Right there…The edge of the page?"

"No," Duncan said softly. "But *you* see it, and that's all that matters."

"I can't. This isn't right to leave you to this fight alone!"

Even now…I was pulled in two directions—toward the unknown, and toward the battle behind me. Fetch swooped close and landed lightly on my shoulder.

Time to go, kid.

I blinked at him, not sure I was hearing what I thought I was hearing, but there was no more from him.

Duncan put his hand on my lower back. "It's your destiny, Harm. And you'd better fulfill it because something is happening to our world. And it seems like it is up to you to save us."

He turned me ever so slightly. To the left of us was a black hole, growing by the second. Out of the hole swarmed a mass of black worms, gnawing their way toward that dog-eared corner. I didn't know what they were, or why they were here, but I knew they had the power to ruin everything.

Worlds.

Lives.

Destinies.

With the same instinct that had pushed me to open the ring, I knew that time was up. They were all right, I had to go.

I yanked the loupe off and looked up at Duncan, heart in my mouth. "I…we…"

"That's your destiny, and this is mine. My people need me now." His molten silver eyes were filled with sorrow as he drove his fingers into my hair and tugged me close for one last kiss before pulling away. "Our paths will cross again someday, Harmony Fallowell. And next time? I won't let go."

If I spent one more second looking into those eyes, I wasn't sure I'd be able to leave at all. So I steeled myself and turned to Moll. "And you…I understand if you don't want to—"

"Nice try. You're not dumping me again! We're ham and eggs, you and me." She grabbed my hand and laced her fingers with mine, her eyes watery but shining. "Where you go, I go. You ready?"

"No, but let's do this." I slid the loupe back over one eye, flipping the highest magnification lens into place as I spared a final glance over my shoulder despite The Speaker's request to not look back.

A burst of blue light split the sky as his fist smashed into Relyk's face. He lunged forward for one more strike, but stepped back as the sorcerer began to burst at the seams, exploding into a mist of inky black, flies swarming up around him. The Speaker's booming laugh echoed through the forest despite the distance, and he knelt to grab his wizard hat even as blood streamed from his mouth. He plopped it on his head, and, for the briefest of moments, he looked back at me, a smile crossing his face. Then, in a flash, he was gone, winking from existence like a shooting star that had reached its end.

He did it. *We* did it.

Tears stung my eyes, but if I let myself feel now, I'd split clean open and crumple in a mess of grief. I turned away and knelt down, gripping the dog-eared page with one hand. Then, I squeezed Moll's hand tight.

"Set...go!"

Together, we leapt off the side of the world, dragging the page with us. Time and space wavered and shifted as the last gasps of the waning battle faded, leaving behind only the sound of whipping wind and the beat of my heart. We were weightless and floating for a blissful few moments, enveloped in a swirling vortex of color. I turned from side to side, my senses overwhelmed by the endless prism of light. Distorted letters and fractions of words began to appear, hazy and blurred at first, then bold and clear, yet still somehow unreadable.

A force yanked us back abruptly, hard enough to make my teeth clack, and the wild colors and strange letters faded in the blink of an eye, giving way to a dimly lit sky.

A cool breeze washed against my cheek, and I blinked repeatedly, pure terror spiking through me as I looked all around, trying desperately to get a bearing on where I was. And then, a new voice rang in my head, clear as a bell.

You got away this time but make no mistake. Soon enough I'll get you my pretty, and your little bird, too!

Then, we plummeted like stones, falling down, down…

We screamed in tandem, flapping our free arms as if we might be able to stay in the sky if we tried hard enough. Even Fetch joined in, digging his talons deeper into my shoulder pad even as his wings extended, as if he planned on pulling me out of the fall.

Thank the gods we weren't above solid ground.

When we hit the water, it sucked us under, clutching us in an icy embrace.

Moll's hand was wrenched from mine as salt water shot up my nose and into my mouth. Kicking hard, I made a push upward, gasping and swiping at my stinging eyes as I broke the surface.

"Moll! Fetch!"

A wracking cough came from behind me, and I turned to Moll, bedraggled and...her red hair was back! The salt water poured off her face, stained brown with dye. I let out a sigh of relief as I caught sight of Fetch circling above me, silhouetted by moonlight, and he let out a cry of acknowledgment.

We were alive.

"What the fuck is that?" Molly rasped as she paddled up beside me, her gaze pinned on something over my left shoulder.

I turned to see a massive galleon gliding across the water toward us. It didn't take a Whisper to know that the black sails emblazoned with a skull and crossbones weren't a good sign...And the words that rang through the darkness a moment later weren't any better.

"Enemy spotted off the starboard deck! Ready the cannons and shoot to kill!"

Inked in Onyx is coming faster than you can load a cannon!

Join my newsletter for updates on upcoming books, behind the scenes info, and exclusive content.

* 9 7 8 1 9 9 8 6 7 6 0 5 7 *